Praise for *Jungian Archetypes*

"A patient once asked me 'What are all those science magazines doing in your waiting room?' Real Jungian analysts, she believed, read only *Parabola*, *Shaman's Drum*, or *Modern Wicca*. It's a safe bet that she's not likely to read this book. Too bad. If she did she'd learn things about Jung that would pleasantly surprise her.

Jung was a scientist. Analysts are as well, although some don't realize it. Others, strangely enough, seem to want to deny it. But many of us love science, consider ourselves to be squarely in the scientific tradition, and stand in awe of its methods and discoveries. Robin Robertson writes for this latter group. He particularly enjoys mathematics, which, as the language of science, has its own paradoxes, contradictions, and metaphors.

In *Jungian Archetypes: Jung, Gödel, and the History of Archetypes*, he traces the history of science as expressed through mathematics . . . . Robertson's book is a dialogue between the history of science and Jungian theory . . . . His outline of the history of science is excellent . . . . His review of Jung is equally adept. He writes clearly, simply, and completely . . . he is very good at simplifying the complex."

—John R. Van Eenwyk
Pacific Northwest Society of Jungian Analysts
Excerpted from *The Journal of Analytical Psychology*, January, 1997

"*Jungian Archetypes* is the most recent summation of [Robertson's] pioneering work in drawing together the scattered strings of historical thought on the possibilities and limitations of human consciousness . . . . Step by step Robertson softly invites us to review once again the eternal questions of meaning and value that awakened our consciousness in youth and lead us on the numinous quests that hopefully continue to stir our endeavors in maturity. He makes the profoundly complex issues of Cantor's Set Theory of Transfinite Numbers and Gödel's Proof of the limitations of mathematical logic—surely esoterica for most ordinary mortals—open and available to the literate reader. More, he convinces us of their relevance for our personal growth and the sense of meaning we seek in depth psychology. In this broadly appealing book, Robertson is doing something vastly more than simply explicating Jungian psychology: He is involved in sketching a plausible technical foundation for archetypal psychology in the coming millennium."

— Ernest L. Rossi, Ph.D.
Psychological Perspectives, Issue 33, 1996

"Robertson meticulously and effectively exposes the parallels between Jung the psychologist and Gödel the mathematician. His documentation of illustrated historical contributors to both fields is interesting and informing. In a direct style of writing, he has woven the development of abstract concepts and scientific research into a cohesive whole, showing that, at their root, psychology, philosophy, and science are different languages for the same understandings. For those who are skeptical and feel that science and psychology are antithetical to each other, *Jungian Archetypes* will provide proof to the contrary."

— John Maerz
Starchild Books, Port Charlotte, FL
New Age Retailer, October, 1996

"Robin Robertson focuses on the quest for understanding the nature of hidden reality and especially on the roles that mathematics and psychology have played in that quest. It begins with a review of the foundations of both disciplines with their culmination in the works of Gödel and Jung. It ends with an appraisal of the limits to knowledge and with an expression of the need for a holistic union of mind with the unknowable aspects of the universe. These are invoked for the good of the individual, the intellectual enterprise, and humanity. I will claim that it also has relevance in posing a challenge to our discipline of dynamics and complexity. The book is exceptionally well crafted and clearly written."

— Fred Abraham
The Blueberry Brain Institute
Society for Chaos Theory in Psychology and Life Sciences Newsletter
January–March, 1996, Vol. 3, No. 3

JUNGIAN ARCHETYPES

On The Hudson

Jung

BOOK SERIES

The Jung on the Hudson Book Series was instituted by the New York Center for Jungian Studies in 1997. This ongoing series is designed to present books that will be of interest to individuals of all fields, as well as mental health professionals, who are interested in exploring the relevance of the psychology and ideas of C. G. Jung to their personal lives and professional activities.

For more information about this series and the New York Center for Jungian Studies contact: Aryeh Maidenbaum, Ph.D., New York Center for Jungian Studies, 41 Park Avenue, Suite 1D, New York, NY 10016, telephone (212) 689-8238, fax (212) 889-7634.

For more information about becoming part of this series contact: Betty Lundsted, Nicolas-Hays, P. O. Box 2039, York Beach, ME 03910-2039, telephone (207) 363-4393 ext. 12, email: nhi@weiserbooks.com.

JUNGIAN ARCHETYPES

Jung, Gödel, and the History of Archetypes

Robin Robertson

NICOLAS-HAYS
York Beach, Maine

First published in 1995 by
Nicolas-Hays, Inc.
P. O. Box 612
York Beach, ME 03910-0612

Distributed to the trade by
Samuel Weiser, Inc.
P. O. Box 612
York Beach, ME 03910-0612

Library of Congress Cataloging-in-Publication Data
Robertson, Robin
    Jungian archetypes : Jung, Gödel, and the history of archetypes /
    p.   cm.
    Includes bibliographical references and index.
    1. Archetype (Psychology)   2. Subconsciousness.   3. Psychology—
History.   4. Gödel's theorem.   5. Jung, C. G. (Carl Gustav),
1875–1961.   I. Title
BF175.5.A72R64   1995
155.2´64—dc20   95–19454
                                                                CIP
    ISBN 0–89254–029–X
    EB

Cover art copyright © 1995 Rob Shouten
Used by kind permission of the artist.

Typeset in 11 point Bembo

Printed in the United States of America

01 00
10 9 8 7 6 5 4 3 2

TABLE OF CONTENTS

ILLUSTRATIONS

To Lore Zeller, who has been so kind
to so many of us in Jungian psychology.

And to my late friend Gail Duke,
who always asked me to write more about mathematics.

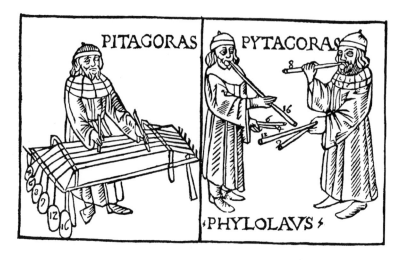

PYTHAGORAS

Preface

Most of what is greatest in man is called forth in response to the thwarting of his hopes by immutable natural obstacles; by the pretence of omnipotence, he becomes trivial and a little absurd.[1]

Twenty-five hundred years ago, the nearly mythical Greek mathematician Pythagoras [570–500 B.C.] founded a school of philosophy and mysticism on the premise that "all is number,"[2] i.e., all reality is based on manifestations of the simple counting numbers. This doctrine was shaken by the discovery that the square root of 2 could not be expressed as a simple ratio of counting numbers. This discovery was so terrifying to the followers of Pythagoras that it could only be revealed to adepts who had already passed deeply into the mysteries of reality.

A century-and-a-half later, the Greek mathematician and philosopher Plato [428–348 B.C.] argued that behind the appearances of outer reality lies a deeper, truer world: the world of *ideas* (or *ideals* as they have been termed since the 18th century) of which physical reality is but a poor copy. We are like people living in a cave, unaware of the wide world without. We live our lives always facing the rear of the cave, content to watch shadows cast on the wall, discussing them as if they were solid and real. In actuality, the real world—the world of ideas—lies behind us. All that we think real are merely shadows created as those ideas pass back and

---

[1] Bertrand Russell, *Our Knowledge of the External World* (New York: Mentor Books, 1956), p. 31.

[2] Carl B. Boyer, *A History of Mathematics* (Princeton: Princeton University Press, 1968), p. 54.

forth before the eternal fire that lies still further away from human perception.

A combination of these ideas grew and developed in the academy founded by Plato in Athens in 385 B.C., culminating in the

PLATO

philosophies of both St. Augustine [354–430] and the great Neoplatonists: Plotinus [205–270], Porphyry [232–304], Iamblicus [270–330], and Proclus [410–485]. After the Christian emperor Justin closed the academy (which he consider irreligious) in A.D. 529, these ideas went underground during the thousand years of the Middle Ages, from the fifth to the 15th century. Though their history during this period is more problematic, these ideas never fully died, and continued to crop up throughout both the Eastern and Western

worlds during the Middle Ages. For example, the ideas of Plato and Pythagoras were kept alive in the Eastern world by the esoteric Moslem traditions of the Sufis. In the West, the ideas were largely submerged, though Franciscan monks preserved St. Augustine's philosophy. Philosophical idealism began to peek its head out again in the West late in the Middle Ages, due both to contact with Moslems during the years of bitter fighting of the Crusades, and through the inter-mixing of Moslem, Jewish and Christian scholars in Spain. One person affected by this doctrine who will appear later in this book is the 16th century physician and metaphysician, Paracelsus.

In this book, we will pick up the story during the Renaissance, a critical point in the history of human thought, when we first began to look out at the world and carefully observe and record what we saw. With this new emphasis on the practical details of the physical world, one couldn't ask for a more opposite approach to reality from that of Pythagoras and Plato. Yet sometimes it pays to take a new direction before we return to our roots. This first half of the book will trace how this new Renaissance ideal slowly evolved and transformed, going so far in this new direction that it came around the corner and arrived back where it had left Pythagoras and Plato.

The second part of the book will explore how the ideas of Plato and Pythagoras reappeared in the archetypal hypothesis of psychologist C. G. Jung, and the mirroring mathematical ideas of Kurt Gödel. With Jung and Gödel we enter a new phase of the evolution of the archetypal hypothesis. Coming at the tail end of a rationalist/materialist tradition, their new versions of the ideas of Pythagoras and Plato have a resonance beyond those of their far-seeing predecessors. Yet Jung and Gödel are once again espousing the Platonic philosophy that beyond both the outer physical world and the inner world of the psyche lies a world of ideals (which Jung calls *archetypes*). And, strangely enough, both Jung and Gödel argue that the primary archetypes which determine the order and struc-ture of reality are the simple counting numbers so beloved of Pythagoras.

ACKNOWLEDGMENTS

I'm grateful for the many discussions I've had over the years with David A. Moonitz regarding the mathematical issues presented in this book. Many thanks to my friends in the Society for Chaos Theory in Psychology and the Life Sciences; our discussions about the relationship between brain, mind, and world have brought many of the issues in this book into better focus; and finally, deep appreciation to my editor and publisher Betty Lundsted, who did a wonderful job working with very difficult material; her editorial suggestions made a marked improvement in this book.

CHAPTER 1

THE RENAISSANCE IDEAL

The eminent historian of science Alexandre Koyré liked to emphasize the difficulties in conception and philosophy that accompanied the revolutionary shift in thinking required of the Renaissance thinkers. Their transition in advancing from the closed world of Aristotle's universe to the infinite world of the post-Copernican era was in many respects a painful and traumatic one, but profound in its implications for the subsequent history of Western thought.[1]

LOOKING OUT AT THE WORLD

Though the growth of Christianity had been the greatest unifying force in the history of the Western World, it effectively brought an end to speculative thought about nature. During the thousand years of the Middle Ages, between the fifth and the 15th centuries, God's word was considered a better guide than human experience or reason. Scholastic philosophers were satisfied to perfect the dialectic and analytic methods of Aristotle. Since scholastic philosophy proceeded from religious dogma, not from observed fact, the beginnings of science were set back many centuries.

Advances in knowledge start with questions: where do we come from? Where are we going? What is the nature of the world?

---

[1] Joseph Warren Dauben, *Georg Cantor: His Mathematics and Philosophy of the Infinite* (Princeton: Princeton University Press, 1979), p. 4.

What is our nature? What is the relationship between our nature and the nature of the world? Great changes in worldview involve not only new answers to these eternal questions, but perhaps more importantly, new ways of asking the same questions. During the thousand years of the Middle Ages (the fifth to the 15th century), the Western world largely accepted that God created the world and so asked: What is the nature of God? What is the relationship between God and humanity? Most medieval thinkers started from the presumption of a static world over which they had little or no control. Their curiosity centered around God, not the world. According to medieval historian Etienne Gilson, there were two kinds of medieval thinkers: those who believed that "since God has spoken to us it is no longer necessary for us to think," and those who believed that "the divine law required man to seek God by the rational methods of philosophy."[2] Both types proceeded from fixed premises; the idea that thinkers should repeatedly check both premise and conclusion against experience was alien to the main stream of Medieval thought.

During the 14th, 15th, and 16th centuries, Renaissance thinkers suddenly awoke, looked at the world with new eyes, and asked a different question: What is the nature of the world? That question caused them to turn their eyes outward toward the world and to begin to describe what they saw there. When that description led to new questions, they proposed solutions, then turned once more to the world to check the validity of their conclusions. The Renaissance ideal was aptly expressed in statements by Leonardo DaVinci [1452–1519], such as "Experience never errs; it is only your judgements that err by promising themselves such as are not caused by your experiments," or "all our knowledge has its origin in our perceptions."[3]

DaVinci was able to combine this belief in the power of experience with a belief in God because of a changing view of God.

---

[2]Anne Fremantle, ed., *The Age of Belief: The Medieval Philosophers* (New York: Mentor Books, Houghton Mifflin, 1954), p. xii.
[3]Jean Paul Richter, *The Notebooks of Leonardo DaVinci*, 2 vols (New York: Dover Publications, 1970), p. 288.

Da Vinci addressed his God with "O admirable impartiality of Thine, Thou first Mover; Thou hast not permitted that any force should fail of the order or quality of its necessary results."[4] In other words, God had done his job by creating an ordered world; now it was up to us to use our reason to discover the rules that governed that world. Da Vinci said that: "the senses are of the earth; Reason stands apart in contemplation."[5] Once that step had been taken, it was inevitable that we would eventually turn reason upon itself, and try to describe the nature of the mind. However, that wasn't to occur until long after the intoxicating first flush of discovery of the physical world had passed.

This new combination of freedom and responsibility produced a flourishing of genius that was unprecedented in European history. Da Vinci, Michelangelo, Erasmus, Luther, and Copernicus were all born within the fifty-year-period between 1450 and 1500.[6] Erasmus and Luther each fought the intellectual domination of the "Holy Mother the Church" in his own characteristic way. Erasmus, a man of the mind, tried to pursue truth to its logical conclusions regardless of church dogma. Luther, "that most unphilosophical of characters,"[7] broke the domination of the Church and created the Protestant movement. Each was attempting to give humanity a central place in the scheme of things, yet each was deeply religious.

Michelangelo [1475–1564] and Da Vinci for the first time made humanity the central subject of art. Medieval art dealt with humanity only in generalities; its real subject was God. Michelangelo created art that pictured not only a particular man or woman, but more than that, a heroic man or woman. Michelangelo's art cried that we could all be as the gods. Da Vinci, the quintessential Renaissance artist, created art that captured ordinary reality so extraordinarily that the viewer began to realize what a mystery lay

---

[4]Jean Paul Richter, *The Notebooks of Leonardo Da Vinci*, p. 285.
[5]Jean Paul Richter, *The Notebooks of Leonardo Da Vinci*, p. 287.
[6]As well as Paracelsus, whom we will discuss later.
[7]Giorgio De Santillana, ed., *The Age of Adventure: The Renaissance Philosophers* (New York: Mentor Books/Houghton Mifflin, 1956), p. 143.

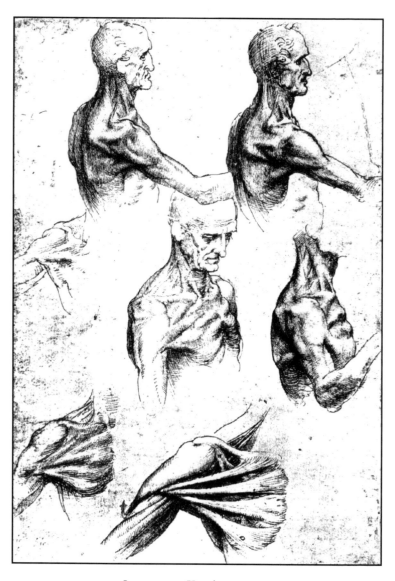

LEONARDO DA VINCI'S DRAWINGS.

within each person, each object. Both were, in their characteristic styles, bringing God down from the heavens, and placing divinity in the world.

There were limits, however, to this new Renaissance ideal. Just as Medieval thinkers failed to question their premises and check them against reality, Renaissance thinkers didn't think to question the validity of the act of observation itself. They assumed that their observations were of necessity accurate representations of the world. During the Middle Ages, the world was accepted as God's creation and, therefore, eternal and immutable. During the Renaissance, the world became a mystery to be examined and explained, but the mind doing the examining and explaining remained unquestioned. There was an implicit belief that "the human mind is, in effect, a mirror that reflects without distortion the indwelling structure of the external world."[8]

This new Renaissance view regarded human beings primarily as observers and the physical world as the proper object of their observation. This separation of observer from observed led to a new stage of consciousness, in which eventually all humanity became aware of its individuality. Without that separation, it would have been impossible for art and science to develop. Without it, there would have been no mass democracy, no social or religious reform. Yet, despite the necessity for humanity to take this step, the fact remains that it is essentially based on a false assumption, for there is no inherent separation of observer from that which is observed. The assumption that there is would create not only wondrous new discoveries, but also a deep and troubling sickness of the soul. This new view of reality would develop into the rationalist/materialist position that separated mind and body, and alienated human beings first from the world, then from each other, and finally from their own inner experience. Eventually we would reach the point at which we are now, a point where the rift has to be healed if we are to advance further.

---

[8]Henry D. Aiken, ed., *The Age of Ideology: The 19th Century Philosophers* (New York: Mentor Books/Houghton Mifflin, 1956), p. 31.

MATHEMATICS AND SCIENCE

> The originality of mathematics consists in the fact that in
> mathematical science connections between things are ex-
> hibited which, apart from the agency of human reason,
> are extremely unobvious.[9]

Mathematics has been used as a tool from humanity's earliest times.
No human community has been identified which does not use at
least the smaller integers. Nomadic cultures, constantly on the
move, needed mathematical tools to calculate direction and distance. Later, agricultural societies needed more advanced mathematical tools to count the population, draw property lines, to
record accurately the progress of the seasons on which their crops
depended, to construct a calendar, for sales and bartering, to calculate inheritance: in short, tools of counting and measurement.
From its inception, mathematics developed along two frequently
intertwined paths: arithmetic (the study of number),[10] and geometry (the study of space). Much of our story in the pages to come re-
volves around the relationship between these two paths, their
progressive differentiation from each other, and the eventual realization that they represented two different approaches to reality.

Both conceptual approaches are so old that it is impossible to
formally identify their beginnings. Arithmetic deals with the separate, the discrete, the individual; geometry with the continuous,
the connected, the whole. Arithmetic began with the individuality
of the small counting numbers and advanced by studying the many
and varied relationships between those numbers. Geometry began
with the space that surrounds us, and modeled that reality with
ideal points and lines, figures and solids. The combination of the
two approaches provided ways to use measured quantities to calcu-

---

[9] Alfred North Whitehead, *Science and the Modern World* (New York: Mentor Books/New
American Library, 1948), p. 20.

[10] In general, mathematicians use the word arithmetic to mean not only the operations of addition and subtraction, multiplication and division, which we learn in grade school, but the
more abstract operations of algebra as well. Throughout this book, arithmetic will be used in
that sense as a shorthand for the mathematical study of numbers.

late the lengths of sides and the sizes of angles which had never actually been measured.

> Mathematics as a science commenced when first someone, probably a Greek, proved propositions about *any* things or about *some* things, without specification of definite particular things. These propositions were first enunciated by the Greeks for geometry; and, accordingly, geometry was the great Greek mathematical science.[11]

By 600 B.C., Greek mathematician Thales had already taken geometry out of the stage where it was merely a collection of individual tricks, and begun geometry as a deductive science. Within the next century, the wonderful theorem that goes by Pythagoras' name was formalized—i.e., the square of the hypotenuse of a right triangle equals the sum of the squares of the two legs. By about 300 B.C., in his *Elements*, Greek mathematician Euclid had systematically col-

EUCLID

lected all known geometric knowledge, and presented it as a deductive science complete with a formal manner of proof.

Arithmetic also had its early triumphs, which were recorded in mathematical textbooks, including the *Arithmetica* of Greek mathematician Diophantus in the third century A.D., and Arabic mathematician al-Khowârizmî's *Algebra* in the ninth century A.D.[12] However, both were closer to useful collections of mathematical

---

[11] Alfred North Whitehead, *An Introduction to Mathematics*, revised edition (New York: Galaxy Book/Oxford University Press, 1911/1958), p. 7.

[12] From which arithmetic and algebra took their names.

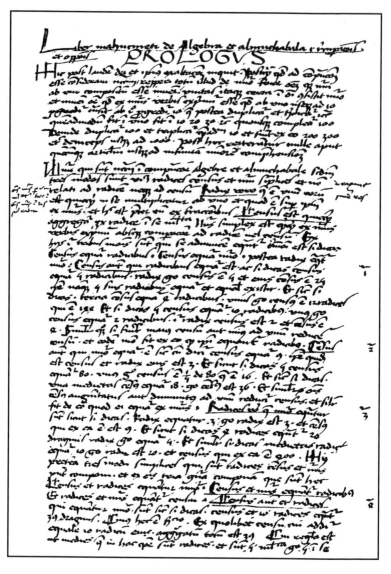

FIRST PAGE AL-KHOWÂRIZIMÎ'S ALGEBRA.

tricks than to systematic formal systems of thought. Euclid's geometry was the first, and for nearly two thousand years, the only known complete and self-consistent scientific system.

Let no one enter who does not know geometry.[13]

Euclid's geometry defined the elementary objects with which it would deal; i.e., *points, lines, figures,* and *angles.* It defined the mathematical operations that it would perform on those elementary objects. Finally, it stated certain *axioms;* i.e., assumptions which were assumed to be self-evident.[14] From those spare tools—elementary objects, operations, and axioms—a logically consistent set of proofs could be derived. Nothing derived from those axioms conflicted with anything else derived from those axioms. Thus the system was consistent. Further, anything that could be truly asserted about points and lines and figures and angles could be derived from those axioms. Thus the system was complete.[15] Euclid's geometry provided a model on which other formal systems could pattern themselves. However, it was to prove a model difficult to emulate.

Though geometry deals with mathematical abstractions called points and lines and angles, those abstract entities were derived from the points and lines and angles encountered in the physical world. Numbers—the royalty of the kingdom of arithmetic—are more abstract. There is no such thing as a number existing in physical reality—our sense of numbers is relational. The thing common between my "two" eyes and my "two" ears and my "two" arms and my "two" legs is that there are "two" of each. A relationship doesn't exist as a "thing"—it is a statement about the connections between "things." Arithmetic provides a system for formally dealing with numbers and the relationship between numbers, hence the relationships between relationships.

---

[13]Inscription on Plato's door.

[14]It is important to realize that the axioms asserted nothing about the nature of the physical world; they were merely assumptions that would be used within this mathematical system. Until the 19th century, even mathematicians didn't fully realize this. It was common to point to physical reality for proof of the self-evident truth of Euclid's axioms.

[15]It awaited the 19th century to question whether geometry was truly complete and consistent.

Now, the first noticeable fact about arithmetic is that it applies to everything, to tastes and to sounds, to apples and to angels, to the ideas of the mind and to the bones of the body. The nature of the things is perfectly indifferent, of all things it is true that two and two makes four.[16]

Throughout the Middle Ages, mathematics lay quietly waiting. When the Renaissance brought with it the observational method, it would combine with mathematics to produce science. Though science would not develop fully until the 17th century, one man combined observation with mathematics to give it a push during the Renaissance.

COPERNICUS AND THE OBSERVATIONAL METHOD

. . . as soon as certain people learn that in these books of mine which I have written about the revolution of the spheres of the world, I attribute certain motions to the terrestrial globe, they will immediately shout to have me and my opinion hooted off the stage.[17]

At much the same time that Da Vinci and Michelangelo brought divinity down to Earth, Nicholas Copernicus [1473–1543] gazed upward at the heavens. Before Copernicus, Earth was assumed to be the central object in the universe, eternally fixed and unmoving. Ptolemy (second century A.D.) had speculated that a series of clear, perfectly formed, nesting spheres surrounded Earth. The Sun, the planets, and the stars rested on those spheres. Since astronomical observations are critical for agriculture, a great deal was already known about the actual positions and movements of the heavenly bodies. But observations had to fit theory, not theory to observations. Since calculations based on Ptolemy's perfect spheres did not fit those observations, more and more complex rationalizations had

---

[16]Alfred North Whitehead, *An Introduction to Mathematics*, p. 2.
[17]Preface to Nicolas Copernicus, *Concerning the Revolution of the Heavenly Bodies* (1543). In Giorgio de Santillana, *The Age of Adventure: The Renaissance Philosophers*, (1956), pp. 160–161.

to be made in order to preserve Earth's central position.[18]

Copernicus had the brilliant realization that perhaps movement was, in part, the perception of the viewer. Perhaps Earth was moving around the Sun. His view seemed sacrilegious to 16th-century churchmen, who were convinced that God had created the world and everything in it in six days. From that time on, the world was static and unchanging, with a few known exceptions, such as the Flood, which were recorded in the Bible. For churchmen and for most educated Europeans, Ptolemy's views were merely a scientific explication of what they already knew from the Bible. Knowledge of the world didn't need to come from observation; that knowledge was already contained in the Bible.

COPERNICUS

Copernicus' theory was the first intimation that perhaps the nature of reality depended on the position of the observer, a view that, in the 20th century, Einstein was to make so central in his theory of relativity. In a Copernican world, observations and conclusions became central, because in a world of flux and movement, everything depended on the observer.[19] This emphasis on the central position of normal human beings, and the importance of their observations, was the great break between Renaissance and Medieval thought. As we have already stressed, the Scholastic thought of the Middle Ages dealt only with the consequences of a priori principles; it never found it necessary to compare its conclusions with observations in the outer world.

---

[18] His immutable spheres multiplied into hierarchies of ever tinier spheres within spheres.

[19] Giorgio De Santillana, *The Age of Adventure*, p. 143. Interestingly, some modern physicists have taken this concept to its natural conclusions; i.e., they assume that the world only exists if it is observed. This view was anticipated by the 18th-century philosopher Bishop Berkeley. Later in this book, we will discuss why Berkeley proposed such a startling view, and how it was answered by Immanuel Kant.

The Renaissance brought a new vision of humanity at the center of the world, observing all that went on about us. This separation of observer and observed was a necessary step to advance beyond Medieval thought patterns, but it inevitably also led to alienation from the world. And with alienation came an increased tendency to view not only the things of the world, but human beings themselves, as just more objects to be observed. Leonardo da Vinci exclaimed that "instrumental or mechanical science is of all the noblest and the most useful."[20] There was a power in this vision that is too often either accepted without question by materialists, or dismissed as dehumanizing by idealists. European humanity had been static for nearly thirteen hundred years, from the end of the early days of Christianity to the beginning of the Renaissance. The separation of observer and observed led ineluctably to the four steps that became the scientific method:

(1) observe dispassionately;

(2) record those observations accurately, *including quantitative measurement*;

(3) propose hypotheses to explain them;

(4) design *quantitatively measurable* experiments to test their validity;

and repeat those four steps as often as necessary. Without either the careful observation or the quantitative measurement, there is no scientific method.

The mastery that we began to acquire over our environment was intoxicating. But hidden within the scientific method lay the problem of how to reconcile the world without (i.e., the physical world) with the world within (i.e., the world of the mind). That would, of course, ineluctably lead to the development of psychology, though only after centuries. But first came the triumphs of science, and a new mathematics to match.

---

[20]Quotation in Jean Paul Richter, *The Notebooks of Leonardo Da Vinci*, p. 289.

CHAPTER 2

THE BIRTH OF SCIENCE

The history of the 17th-century science reads as though it were some vivid dream of Plato or Pythagoras. In this characteristic the 17th century was only the forerunner of its successors.[1]

ANALYTIC GEOMETRY

The first great advance in mathematical abstraction beyond Euclid was made by 17th-century mathematician/philosopher René Descartes [1596–1650], when he subsumed geometry within arithmetic. As a philosopher, Descartes' famous assertion: "Cogito, ergo sum" (I think, therefore I am) was the first clear expression of the Renaissance ideal. As a statement about the whole person, Descartes' assertion is ridiculous. For millennia before men and women had any conscious awareness—which is clearly what Descartes means by "think"—they existed as sensing, feeling animals. But as a statement that a new level of consciousness had come into existence, Descartes' assertion is a bold proclamation.[2]

[Descartes'] *Géométrie* (1637) brought the whole field of classical geometry within the scope of the algebraists. The book was originally published as an appendix to the

---

[1] Alfred North Whitehead, *Science and the Modern World* (New York: Mentor Books/New American Library, 1925/1948), p. 34.
[2] It was far too early to realize that self-referential statements—in this case, the human mind discussing itself—are fraught with difficulty. Later in this book, we will discuss how one mathematician, Kurt Gödel, gave explicit mathematical expression to this difficulty.

RENÉ DESCARTES

Discours de la Méthode, the discourse on reason, in which the author explained his rationalistic approach to the study of nature.[3]

Descartes' great advance in mathematics was of a piece with his advance in philosophy. He realized that it was possible to express geometry in terms of numbers and relationships between numbers rather than in terms of "things" like points and lines.[4] By our time, his basic idea has penetrated even into the way we identify locations in a city. As an example, consider an imaginary city where numbered blocks run north/south and avenues run east/west. From some central spot in the city, these numbered streets proceed out in each direction beginning with 1st Street, 2nd Street, etc. To distinguish which direction, we'll refer to 1st Street East or 1st Street West. Similarly the avenues proceed outward: 1st Avenue North (or South), 2nd Avenue North, etc. If we want to uniquely identify a house, we give it a street number. For example, 512 East 8th Street. We know that this house is located 8 blocks to the East of our central location, and a little over 5 blocks to the north on 8th Street.[5]

Descartes did exactly the same thing with the number plane. Again just imagine a flat plane stretching out endlessly in all directions. Pick a spot in the middle, which we'll call the *origin*, then imagine counting off in fixed intervals in all four directions: 1, 2, 3, ... Those to the right of the origin, and those above the origin will be positive: +1, +2, +3, ... Those to the left of the origin, or below the origin will be negative: −1, −2, −3, ... In practice, the + sign is dropped from the positive numbers, since unless the number is negative, we can presume it is positive. Any point on the graph

---

[3] Dirk J. Struik, *A Concise History of Mathematics,* 4th rev. ed. (New York: Dover Publications, 1948/1987), p. 96.

[4] We will have more to say about relationship throughout this book, but for now it is enough to realize that relationship is a mental concept: it can only take place within the mind. Hence, by reducing geometry (which was an abstraction of physical reality), to numbers and the relationships between numbers, Descartes was taking the first great step toward subjugating physical reality to the dictates of the mind.

[5] I am indebted to famed mathematical biographer Eric Temple Bell for this example. See his *Men of Mathematics* (New York: Simon and Schuster, 1937/1965), pp. 57–58.

can be identified uniquely by only two numbers, called *coordinates*, which tell where the point is horizontally and vertically. For example, the origin is (0,0). By convention, the first number given is the horizontal position (called the x direction), and the second the vertical (called the y). So (+5, −2) would indicate a point 5 units to the right of the origin and 2 units down from the origin. Fractional points can be referred to just as easily. For example, (+2½, −3) would be a point halfway between the 2nd and 3rd units to the right, and 3 units down. (See figure 2.1 below for examples of coordinates.)

Now imagine a straight line that passes through the origin at a 45 degree angle. If we wrote down all the coordinates for this line—e.g., (−2,−2), (−1,−1), (0,0), (1,1), . . .—we would find that its horizontal position equals its vertical position. In algebra, we would say $y = x$ (see figure 2.2). Or take a circle, which has a radius of 2, centered on the origin. Then we once more examine the coordinates of the points to see if there is a relationship between the horizontal and vertical points. This time it's not so obvious, but the relationship turns out to be $x^2 + y^2 = 4$. (See figure 2.3.)

Any regular geometric figure could be expressed with Descartes' system of coordinates. Mathematicians could then use

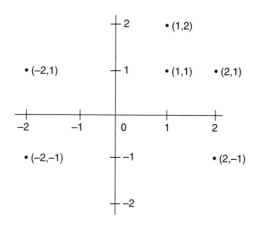

FIGURE 2.1.   COORDINATES ON THE PLANE.

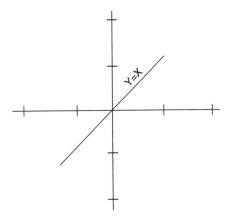

FIGURE 2.2. A STRAIGHT LINE ON THE PLANE.

algebraic techniques to develop relationships that were not readily apparent in the geometric figures. Because this provided a way of analyzing geometric problems, Descartes' discovery was termed *analytic geometry*.[6] Of this discovery, 18th-century philosopher John Stuart Mill was later to say that:

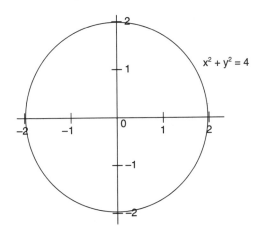

FIGURE 2.3. A CIRCLE ON THE PLANE.

---

[6] First published in his *Discours de la Méthode* of 1637. See selection in *Descartes: Philosophical Writings* (New York: Modern Library, 1958), pp. 90–144.

ouale ie fais des cercles du centre H , dont les rayons
font efgaux aux lignes R 6, R 8, & femblables, qui coup-
pent les autres cercles aux poins marqués 4.

On pourroit encore trouuer vne infinité d'autres
moyens pour defcrire ces mefmes ouales. comme par
exemple, on peut tracer la premiere A V, lorfqu'on fup-
pofe les lignes F A & A G eftre efgales, fi on diuife la
toute F G au point L, en forte que F L foit a L G, com-

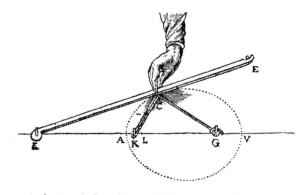

me A 5 à A 6. c'eft à dire qu'elles ayent la proportion,
qui mefure les refractions. Puis ayant diuifé A L en deux
parties efgales au point K, qu'on face tourner vne reigle,
comme F E, autour du point F, en preffant du doigt C,
la chorde E C, qui eftant attachée au bout de cete reigle
vers E, fe replie de C vers K, puis de K derechef vers C,
& de C vers G, ou fon autre bout foit attaché, en forte
que la longeur de cete chorde foit compofée de celle
des lignes G A plus A L plus F E moins A F. & ce fera
le mouuement du point C, qui defcrira cete ouale, a
l'imitation de ce qui a efté dit en la Dioptriq; de l'Ellipfe,
&

> . . . [analytic geometry] far more than any of his meta-physical speculations, immortalized the name of Descartes, and constitutes the greatest single step ever made in the progress of the exact sciences.[7]

However, despite Mill's claim, there was a mathematical tool that far exceeded analytic geometry in the impact it had on "the exact sciences." That tool was the calculus, which was developed at much the same time but independently by Sir Isaac Newton and Baron Gottfried Wilhelm von Leibniz. However, before we can talk about calculus, we need to know something about Newton and his profound impact on the world.

ISAAC NEWTON

> Nature and Nature's laws lay hid in night;
> God said, Let Newton be! and all was light.[8]

When Isaac Newton [1642–1727] was born, science as we know it was just coming into existence. It was still a small thing, exciting to those who could see its possibilities, but little known otherwise. When Newton died in 1727, science was the dominant force in human thought, and Newton was the primary cause for that change in status. The 17th century was a time in some ways like our own, an "interesting time," a time of change and unpredictability, when many contradictory ideas fought for supremacy. With the end of the absolute dominance that religion and the "ancients"[9] had previously had over Western thought, a vacuum was left, waiting to be filled by some new, comprehensive explanation of reality. Newton, with his *Optiks* and *Principia*, seemed to his contemporaries to have explained all of nature. Not even religion or the ancients had ever

---

[7] Eric Temple Bell, *Men of Mathematics*, p. 35.
[8] Alexander Pope, "Intended for Sir Isaac Newton," in Lewis Kroneberger, ed., *Alexander Pope: Selected Works* (New York: The Modern Library, 1951), p. 330.
[9] The Middle Ages' most characteristic term for the great Greek thinkers.

ISAAC NEWTON

subsumed so much of reality under a single umbrella. Before Newton, there were speculations; after Newton there were Laws!

Newton conceived most of the ideas he would develop over the rest of his life during a single eighteen month period. He was 23, and had just received his B.A. "without particular distinction." The plague was roaring through Europe and Newton retired to his parents' home until the University reopened. During that period, he discovered differential and integral calculus, his theory of colors, and the concept of gravity as a force that held the universe together. These were to form the core of his life's work in science.[10]

Newton's Laws explained motion, force, and light in straightforward ways that lent themselves to practical application. Newton's Laws concerned material particles, their motion and their interaction. He even regarded light as composed of particles and resisted to his death the idea that light was a wave phenomenon. Newton's world was a world of absolutes: absolute space and time, and perfect, indivisible particles moving in that absolute space and time. In Newton's words from the *Principia*:

> Absolute space, in its own nature, without relation to anything external remains always similar and immovable. Absolute, true, and mathematical time, in itself, and from its own nature, flows equally without relation to anything external.[11]

---

[10] George Gamow, *The Great Physicists from Galileo to Einstein* (New York: Dover Publications, 1961), pp. 52–53.

[11] George Gamow, *The Great Physicists from Galileo to Einstein*, p. 174.

It should be obvious that such a world is a construct of thought. Neither Newton nor any one of us has ever experienced absolute space or absolute time. All human experiences of space and time are of a particular space and time. Absolute space and time are concepts that Newton used in order to develop general theories of nature. Those general theories could then be applied to particular cases. The power of Newton's concept of absolute space and time is less in its possible truth than in its broad utility. In short, it was a "scientific" theory in the best sense of the term.

CALCULUS

The next great advance in mathematics, following Descartes' discovery of analytic geometry, was the simultaneous development of calculus by Newton and Leibniz.[12] Though Newton changed the world as no one else has before or since, Baron Gottfried Wilhelm von Leibniz [1646–1716] did not need to take second place to anyone, even Newton, when it came to intellectual achievement. He has often been called the last universal man because of the extreme breadth of his knowledge. In the next chapter, we will discuss his developments in logic, which started a domino effect that led first to Immanuel Kant's categories of judgment, and eventually to Kurt Gödel's proof of the limits of logic. Both Newton and Leibniz transcended the seeming dichotomy between pure and applied mathematicians presented in the introduction. Both tried to advance not only human thought, but also the applications of human thought to the physical world.

The great weakness that analytic geometry had in dealing with physical reality was that reality was in continuous flux, and analytic geometry had no way of expressing continuous change. Arithmetic can express any quantifiable physical relationship be-

---

[12] As we will see with other such major discoveries, the idea was just beneath the surface, an archetype waiting to find symbolic expression. In some ways, French mathematician Pierre Fermat (whom E. T. Bell tellingly terms "the Prince of Amateurs") anticipated both Newton and Leibniz. Fermat, however, failed to fully develop the concept.

I.

NOVA METHODUS PRO MAXIMIS ET MINIMIS, ITEMQUE TANGENTIBUS, QUAE NEC FRACTAS NEC IRRATIONALES QUANTITATES MORATUR, ET SINGULARE PRO ILLIS CALCULI GENUS *).

Sit (fig. 111) axis AX, et curvae plures, ut VV, WW, YY, ZZ, quarum ordinatae ad axem normales, VX, WX, YX, ZX, quae vocentur respective v, w, y, x, et ipsa AX, abscissa ab axe, vocetur x. Tangentes sint VB, WC, YD, ZE, axi occurrentes respective in punctis B, C, D, E. Jam recta aliqua pro arbitrio assumta vocetur dx, et recta, quae sit ad dx, ut v (vel w, vel y, vel z) est ad XB (vel XC, vel XD, vel XE) vocetur dv (vel dw, vel dy, vel dz) sive differentia ipsarum v (vel ipsarum w, vel y, vel z). His positis, calculi regulae erunt tales.

Sit a quantitas data constans, erit da aequalis 0, et $\overline{dax}$ erit aequalis adx. Si sit y aequ. v (seu ordinata quaevis curvae YY aequalis cuivis ordinatae respondenti curvae VV) erit dy aequ. dv. Jam *Additio et Subtractio*: si sit z — y + w + x aequ. v, erit dz — y + w + x seu dv aequ. dz — dy + dw + dx. *Multiplicatio*: $\overline{dxv}$ aequ. xdv + vdx, seu posito y aequ. xv, fiet dy aequ. xdv + vdx. In arbitrio enim est vel formulam, ut xv, vel compendio pro ea literam, ut y, adhibere. Notandum, et x et dx eodem modo in hoc calculo tractari, ut y et dy, vel aliam literam indeterminatam cum sua differentiali. Notandum etiam, non dari semper regressum a differentiali Aequatione, nisi cum quadam cautione, de quo alibi.

Porro *Divisio*: $d\frac{v}{y}$ vel (posito z aequ. $\frac{v}{y}$) dz aequ. $\frac{\pm vdy \mp ydv}{yy}$.

Quoad *Signa* hoc probe notandum, cum in calculo pro litera substituitur simpliciter ejus differentialis, servari quidem eadem signa, et pro + z scribi + dz, pro — z scribi — dz, ut ex addi-

---

*) Act. Erud. Lips. an. 1684.

OPENING OF LEIBNIZ'S FIRST PAPER ON CALCULUS.

tween objects, but it has no way of deriving changes in its own expressions. It can't lift itself up by its own bootstraps, so to speak. A new mathematical tool was needed: calculus.

Imagine an irregular closed figure drawn on a piece of paper; purely as an example, picture something like a lumpy circle (figure 2.4.A). How can we find the area occupied by that shape? We can start by drawing a rectangle that is as small as possible yet fully contains the figure (figure 2.4.B). Most of us learned in school that the area of a rectangle is the product of its length times its height; so we can easily determine the rectangle's area. In mathematical terms, we can call the area of the rectangle an *upper limit* on the area of the figure; that is, by using the area of the rectangle as an approximation to the area of the lumpy circle, we can insure that the true area must be smaller than our estimate.

If, like our lumpy circle, the figure is quite asymmetric, we can improve our estimate by drawing two rectangles of different sizes next to each other, which together cover the whole figure (figure 2.4.C). By calculating the area of each rectangle and adding the two, the upper limit will be smaller than before, closer to the actual area of the figure. If we increase the number of rectangles, our estimate will get better and better (figure 2.4.D). The limit will get smaller and smaller, and approach the actual area more and more closely. With a thousand rectangles, the limit would be so close to the actual area that for all practical purposes, we could consider it to be identical. However, it's important to realize that it would still not be exact.

Now try and make a leap in thought. Imagine that we extend the number of rectangles endlessly. If we had some way of calculating the limit of this process by adding up an infinite number of such areas, the limit would no longer be merely an approximation to the

FIGURE 2.4. STAGES OF A LIMIT.

area of the figure; it would be exactly the area of the figure! That is just what calculus does.[13]

> The word *function* (or its Latin equivalent) seems to have been introduced into mathematics by Leibniz in 1694; the concept now dominates much of mathematics and is indispensable in science.[14]

> The mathematical use of the term *function* has been adopted also in common life. For example, "his temper is a function of his digestion," uses this term exactly in this mathematical sense. It means that a rule can be assigned which will tell you what his temper will be when you know how his digestion is working.[15]

Descartes' analytic geometry provided a way of describing any geometric figure in terms of numeric coordinates, and then converting those coordinates to an algebraic *function*. A function is nothing more than a shorthand symbolic way of presenting a sequence of numbers that follow a pattern. For example, the equation $Y = 2X$ is a shorthand way to say that for any number X, Y is twice that value. If $X = 1$, $Y = 2$; if $X = 1/3$, $Y = 2/3$, and so on. Mathematicians would say that Y is a function of X, which they would indicate in mathematical notation by $Y = f(x)$; in this simple case, $f(x) = 2X$. X would be considered a *variable*, because its value can vary over a wide range. The key thing to remember is that the function is defined clearly no matter what particular value X takes on. Hence a function is a very compact way to express a great amount of information.

Take a slightly more complicated equation: $Y = 3X^2 + 5$. If $X = 0$, we would get Y by squaring 0 (i.e., still 0), multiplying that by 3 (still 0), then adding 5, to give a final result of 5. If $X = 1/2$, squaring it would give 1/4; multiplying by 3 would give 3/4;

---

[13] See chapter 4 for more on this concept of limits.
[14] Eric Temple Bell, *Men of Mathematics*, p. 98.
[15] Alfred North Whitehead, *An Introduction to Mathematics* (New York: Galaxy Book/Oxford University Press), p. 107.

adding 5 would give a final value for *Y* of 5-3/4. In each of the above cases, *Y* is said to be a function of *X*; i.e., when *X* changes, so does *Y* in a known way.

Leibniz and Newton independently developed a method for calculating (hence calculus) the area contained within any figure describable as a mathematical function. However, their discovery could be used for far more than the calculation of areas. In effect, calculus provided a technique for breaking anything into an infinite number of pieces and summing the infinitely small sizes of each piece; therefore, change could be quantified. For example, assume someone tells us that a rocket ship is accelerating at such-and-such a rate, a rate that can only be expressed as a complex algebraic formula. We could use calculus to derive what the velocity would be after any interval of time.

From the velocity we could further use calculus to derive the distance the rocket ship had moved. Or, proceeding in the opposite direction, calculus could just as easily be used to derive the acceleration from the velocity as the velocity from the acceleration. As long as something is changing continuously across time or space, and that something can be expressed in an algebraic formula, calculus can calculate the change.

Calculus provided physical science, especially physics and astronomy, with a tool of incredible versatility. Bishop Berkeley, of whose philosophy we will have much to say, claimed that:

> The method of Fluxions [Newton's term for calculus] is the general key by help whereof the modern mathematicians unlock the secrets of Geometry, and consequently of Nature.[16]

Prior to the 20th century, even the most complex problems in physics and astronomy required no mathematical tool beyond calculus or extensions of calculus such as differential equations or tensor mechanics. Thus calculus marked the high water mark for mathematics as a directing force for science.

---

[16]Berkeley, *The Analyst*, 1734, in David Eugene Smith, *A Source Book in Mathematics*. Reprint of 1929 edition. (New York: Dover, 1959), p. 628. Brackets mine.

GREAT THEORIES

In transitional times theorists express new visions of reality, trying to replace the old ineffectual visions. The mark of great theorists is the extent to which their vision captures the imagination of others. The fact that so many can respond to the new description of reality implies that it was in the air, but the great minds are there first. They see the vision in both broader perspective and finer detail than the others around them. Frequently their vision will be too far ahead of its time, and rejected. But the visions of the greatest theorists eventually triumph.

A great theory, whether in science or the arts, has to express the main outlines of a total picture of reality. There is little room in it for caveats and exceptions. A great theory necessarily explains both what the previous theory already dealt with, and the problems that caused the original theory to be called into doubt. However, as time passes, and lesser men apply the theory, little problems are found. Since the theory explains so much of reality so well, these exceptions are either ignored or explained away with sophistry. Labyrinthine corollaries are added to the theory; overly subtle definitions are applied to show why a straightforward understanding of a concept is inadequate. It is only when the exceptions can no longer be ignored that still another new theory emerges. It in turn is likely to be absolute and total because it reflects a new vision. This is the cycle of creativity. Such great new theories are rare. The discovery and formulation of calculus and Newton's Laws marked the shift from the religious view to the scientific view of the cosmos.

Great new theories reflect the *Zeitgeist*.[17] Most often, a great new theory develops because there is a need for such a theory. If the need is not great enough, the energy to produce such a massive rethinking of reality is just not present. Newton's vision of indivisible particles, of absolute space and time, was not only Newton's vision, but the vision of his time. Medieval thinkers were stuck in a world where everything was meant to serve God's purpose, where everything was joined in a static whole. In contrast,

---

[17] I.e., spirit of the times.

Renaissance thinkers desperately wanted change and separation. They wanted to be free to pursue their own visions unhampered by religious limits. This is not to say that they were irreligious, far from it. But they wanted to separate their thoughts from their spiritual needs, to pursue their thoughts wherever they would take them. That was the *Zeitgeist* that Newton expressed.[18]

Even Newton, with his profound impact on the later course of the world, was more a representative of his time than its creator. The development of the scientific method and its application to astronomy, physics, and philosophy can arguably be attributed to Galileo, who died the year Newton was born. A full half century before Newton, Descartes' contemporary Thomas Hobbes [1588–1679] reduced the mind even more than Locke did later; Hobbes saw no need for anything mental that couldn't be reduced directly to sense perceptions.[19] But the world was not yet fully ready for the materialist position on which science depended. It is only when the time and the thinker appear together that we have a true paradigm shift. The 17th century was such a time, and Newton was the right thinker for the time. As we will see in the next chapter, the 18th century was too early for another paradigm shift. Even the great Immanuel Kant was unable to make a dent in the new worldview which Newton had brought.

---

[18] See Thomas S. Kuhn, *The Structure of Scientific Revolutions* (Chicago: University of Chicago Press, 1970) for more on the nature of scientific revolutions.
[19] Stuart Hampshire, ed., *The Age of Reason: The 17th Century Philosophers* (New York: Mentor Books/Houghton Mifflin, 1956), pp. 34–58.

CHAPTER 3

WHAT DO WE KNOW, AND
HOW DO WE KNOW IT?

The most incomprehensible thing about the world is that it is comprehensible.[1]

I have the result, but I do not yet know how to get it.[2]

LOCKE AND LEIBNIZ

Influenced by his contemporary, Isaac Newton, 17th century philosopher John Locke [1632–1704] first voiced the empiricist's creed, a philosophy still espoused by many scientists. He described the human mind as a sort of empty vessel containing separate and distinct particles called ideas. All ideas were either simple or complex. The simple ideas came directly from experience; the complex from the mind operating on simple ideas. All ideas thus came directly or indirectly from experience; experience could be either external sensory experience or internal experience of the mind's own states. Though full of difficulties, Locke's views are representative of the mainstream of thought prior to the 20th century. As we will see, however, these seemingly straightforward assumptions would lead to some very puzzling results when taken to their logical conclusions in the 18th century by Bishop George Berkeley and David Hume.[3]

---

[1] Albert Einstein, quoted in Isaac Asimov and Jason A. Shulman, eds., *Isaac Asimov's Book of Science and Nature Quotations* (New York: Weidenfeld & Nicholson, 1988), p. 211.

[2] Mathematician Karl Friedrich Gauss, quoted in *Isaac Asimov's Book of Science and Nature Quotations*, p. 115.

[3] See Sir Isaiah Berlin, ed., *The Age of Enlightenment: The 18th Century Philosophers* (New York: Mentor Books/Houghton Mifflin, 1956), pp. 30–112 for material on Locke.

> Leibniz was perhaps the most universal genius of the modern world, comparable in insight with Newton, wider in range and lesser only in ultimate achievement. . . . Even now the whole of his work has not been published. He was the last man who could hope to master the whole range of modern knowledge, and to be an encyclopedia in himself.[4]

In the previous chapter we discussed Leibniz as the joint discoverer with Newton of the calculus. But Leibniz had even higher aims. While still a young man, Leibniz already had the goal of developing:

GOTTFRIED WILHELM LEIBNIZ

> . . . a general method in which all truths of reason would be reduced to a kind of calculation. At the same time this would be a sort of universal language or scripts, but infinitely different from those projected hitherto; for the symbols and even the words in it would direct the reason; and errors, except for those of fact, would be mere mistakes in calculation.[5]

While not able to achieve this mighty goal—which Kurt Gödel would later prove to be impossible—Leibniz did make the first advance in logic since the time of Aristotle. He separated judgments

[4]Stuart Hampshire, *The Age of Reason*, p. 143.

[5]From *De Arte Combinatoria*, 1666. Quotation in Frederick David Abraham, Ralph H. Abraham, and Christopher D. Shaw, *A Visual Introduction to Dynamical Systems Theory for Psychology* (Santa Cruz: Aerial Press, 1990), pp. iii–21.

systematically into two categories: *analytic* and *synthetic*, also called *a priori* and *a posteriori*. Analytic, or a priori, judgments are those in which the conclusion is known prior to experience, such as "all wives are women." The conclusion is already contained in the definition of the subject, since a wife is a married woman. All mathematical logic is analytic—though not mathematics itself, which Gödel proved transcended logic. An example of a synthetic, or a posteriori, judgment would be: most women over the age of 21 are wives. In order to determine if this is true, the world has to be observed. That observation might prove that most such women were, in fact, not married.[6]

> The strength of analytic judgments lies in their necessity, and the weakness of such judgments in that they tell us nothing new. The strength of synthetic judgments lies in their ability to tell us something new; and the weakness of such judgments, in their having no necessity. If we could have judgments providing us with both information and necessity, we should have the best of both worlds.[7]

BERKELEY AND HUME

As the 18th century dawned, the combination of Locke's empiricism and Leibniz' categories of judgment awaited a genius who would put them to proper use. That genius was to be Immanuel Kant. But before Kant came a pair of philosophers, each of whom would influence Kant: Bishop George Berkeley [1685–1753] and David Hume [1711–1776]. Berkeley was the exact counterpoint to the empiricism of John Locke. He voiced what later came to be called *philosophical idealism*. Briefly, his position was that ideas are all that can ever be experienced.

---

[6] See Stuart Hampshire, *The Age of Reason*, pp. 142-182, for material on Leibniz.
[7] W. L. Reese, *Dictionary of Philosophy and Religion: Eastern and Western Thought* (Atlantic Highlands, NJ: Humanities Press, 1980), p. 277.

Locke asserted that all our ideas are directly or indirectly derived from sensory experience. Berkeley agreed, but further argued that it was nonsense to speak of a physical world separate from our perceptions of it. In the 17th century, Descartes claimed that "I think, therefore I am." Berkeley took that a step further and concluded that all we can ever experience are our thoughts. As far as any of us are concerned, there is no world unless we think of it. Now Berkeley was deeply religious, so he got himself out of this dilemma by arguing that the world does exist, even if we can't prove it from our own experience, since it exists in God's mind. The latter argument didn't have much impact on other philosophers, who did not know how to deal with Berkeley's initial argument that we can never prove the existence of an outer world.[8]

While Bishop Berkeley denied the existence of the material world, David Hume denied causality. Hume stressed the importance that the assumption of causality plays in normal life. If we see (A) a billiard ball strike a second ball, and then we see (B) the second ball move, we say that the first event (A) caused the second event (B). It is the assumption of such necessary causality that forms the core of all of Newton's Laws, of all science. Hume drew attention to what is actually experienced in a so-called cause-and-effect relationship. Hume pointed out that all that is really known is that two events (A) and (B) are contiguous in space, and that (A) preceded (B) in time. In order for (A) to cause (B), there also needs to be some necessary connection between the two events. Hume insisted that there is no such necessary connection that can be logically demonstrated.

> The sole criterion of necessary truth, according to Hume, is the law of non-contradiction. If a proposition cannot be denied without contradiction, it is necessarily true.[9]

---

[8]See Sir Isaiah Berlin, *The Age of Enlightenment*, pp. 115–161, for material on Bishop Berkeley.

[9]Henry D. Aiken, *The Age of Ideology: The 19th Century Philosophers* (New York: Mentor Books/Houghton Mifflin, 1956), p. 32.

In other words, the "sole criterion of necessary truth" is what Leibniz called analytic judgment, where the conclusion is contained in the subject. But the conclusion that (B) follows (A) is only a synthetic judgment; i.e., an observation about the outer world. As Leibniz pointed out, these are separate types of judgment. A synthetic judgment can never have the necessity of an a priori, analytic judgment. All that can be known of the world is a posteriori, derived from experience.

In considering the collision of the two billiard balls, many alternate, though improbable, assumptions could be made without logical contradictions. It could be assumed that the second ball was alive and jumped for joy, or that a flying saucer shot a ray gun at the ball and that's why it jumped. Neither of these assumptions may seem very likely, but there is no *logical contradiction* in asserting them. It is only experience that causes us to conclude that (A) caused (B). We conclude that because we have seen objects strike other objects, and the second object moves.

All cause-and-effect is the same. What actually happens is that if two events are observed to be contiguous in time and space often enough, a necessary connection is assumed to exist between them and we say that one event caused the other. Hume's argument seemed unassailable. If there could be no logical necessity in any judgment about the outer world, anything could happen at any time. Hume's argument had to be answered by philosophers, or philosophy was at a dead end. And, of course, it is the assumption of such necessary causality that forms all of Newton's Laws, all of science prior to the 20th century.[10]

KANT'S CATEGORIES OF THE MIND

Kant staged what he himself called a Copernican revolution in the field. For instead of trying, as Hume had done, to explain concepts in terms of experience, Kant set out to explain experience in terms of concepts.[11]

---

[10] See Sir Isaiah Berlin, *The Age of Enlightenment*, pp. 162–260, for material on David Hume.
[11] Bertrand Russell, *Wisdom of the West* (New York: Fawcett World Library, 1959), p. 311.

Immanuel Kant [1724–1804] inaugurated modern philosophy in 1781 with his *Critique of Pure Reason*. Kant agreed that analytic truth and synthetic truth are indeed separate and distinct. However, since it is within the human mind that both are experienced, Kant argued that there also existed a third category of judgments which were neither analytic nor synthetic. These were synthetic a priori judgments, such as $2 + 2 = 4$, or a straight line is the shortest distance between two points, or every event has a cause. Berkeley asserted that the outer world can never be experienced, only the inner world of thoughts and feelings; Kant agreed. Hume said there can be no logical necessity in any conclusions about the world; Kant agreed. But Kant saw deeper than Berkeley or Hume. Kant argued that synthetic judgments were not really about the world around us, but rather about the world as filtered through the human mind.

For example, he argued that we never experience raw sensory data; all our experiences are in a certain time and place. He said that time and space are examples of inherent categories, contained in all humans, through which we experience reality. Kant said that judgment consisted of taking sensory data in through these inherent structures, and applying logic to reach a conclusion. In Kant's words, "thoughts without content are empty, and intuitions without concepts are blind."[12]

Benjamin Whorf and other linguists have discovered that Kant was wrong in his assumption that everyone experiences time and space in the same way. Whorf found that the Hopi Indians, among others, have a very different sense of time and space than the normal Westerner. To quote Whorf:

> . . . the Hopi thought world has no imaginary space; . . . it may not locate thought dealing with real space anywhere but in real space, nor insulate space from the effects of thought.[13]

> Many of Kant's particular analyses are no longer acceptable to analytical philosophers; nor is his general scheme, with

---

[12] W. L. Reese, *Dictionary of Philosophy and Religion*, pp. 276–280.
[13] Quotation in Edward T. Hall, *The Silent Language* (Greenwich, CT: Fawcett Publications, 1959), p. 92.

its profoundly dualist conception of human nature, its unknowable thing-in-itself. . . . But Kant still represents the
ideal of what the philosophical mind at its best can be.[14]

Why, then, if the particulars of Kant's ideas are no longer accepted,
is Kant so important? Kant saw the profound truth that there are
inherent structures in the human mind (regardless of whether he
was correct in describing those structures), and that those structures
mediated between the physical world outside us, and the psychic
world of our thoughts. He realized that those inherent structures
were something more than groupings of sensory experience, as
Locke had tried to insist. While fully accepting Berkeley's argument
that only ideas can be experienced, Kant refused to accept the
solipsistic conclusion that therefore there is no physical world. Kant
insisted that both inner and outer worlds existed and that they con-
joined in these inherent structures.

There is an actual world out there that we observe, but we can
only see it through the lens of our own mental perceptions. In effect, Kant was arguing that psychology should be the most important of all the sciences, since our innate psychological makeup
inherently colors all observation of nature, and all logical conclusions we make about those observations. We might never be able to
experience *das ding an sich*,[15] but our minds are themselves structured much as the world is structured, and contain necessarily true
categories with which we perceive the world. This was an argument that would have been unthinkable before the Renaissance,
and even before the birth of the science. Kant's argument changed
the direction of philosophy to a degree comparable only to that of
Plato over two millennia earlier. Unfortunately, it had little or no
impact on science, then or now.

With the Renaissance, humanity was once more free to
think what they would. But there was no examination of what
thought itself was. When Descartes established that, for himself,
he knew he existed because he thought, he was expressing the
Zeitgeist of a time intoxicated with its power to think. Newton

---

[14] Henry D. Aiken, *The Age of Ideology*, p. 273.
[15] The thing in itself.

turned his immense intellect to the world and saw a world that was convenient for thought: composed of separate and distinct particles in some absolute, unchanging space and time. Locke was the first to examine the nature of thought itself. Under the sway of Newton's ideas, he asserted that thought consisted of separate and distinct sensory experiences that correspond one-to-one with the physical world. Berkeley and Hume found that materialism, taken to its logical conclusion, produced idealism; i.e., we know no world except the world of our thoughts, and there is no logical necessity in any assertions about the world outside our thoughts.

Finally, Kant saw that humans inherently organize reality; thoughts are not just atoms of sensory experience or closed logical chains. He argued that physical reality is experienced only through inner structures which organize the "world of a thousand things."[16] The fact that human beings are able to structure physical reality sufficiently to process sensory perceptions at all argues strongly that there are inborn, identical psychic structures in all of us.

Of course, like all highly original ideas, Kant's categories present a more straightforward picture than we find in reality. Current research shows that our sense organs themselves organize reality. Further organization goes on as sensory data is presented to the brain. But the full chain of operations is far from understood at this point in time. Regardless of this complexity, the point remains that if Kant was right, then an understanding of the nature of the human mind was critical in determining truth. The study of the human mind—psychology—needed to become a field in itself, and not just an adjunct to other fields. However, the time was not yet ripe, and modern psychology wasn't to begin until the second half of the 19th century, when the twin poles of experimental and clinical psychology came into existence. Kant had the most profound effect of any philosopher since Plato, but the world of the late 18th century was not yet ready to accept the full impact of his teachings.

---

[16]A Chinese phrase for the multiplicity of details the world contains, which they then contrast with the oneness inside, which is much like Kant's organizing principle.

~~~~~

CHAPTER 4

PRAGMATIC RESPONSES

[Newton's] Principia *had been published only five years when Dr. Bentley, the famous classical scholar and tyrant of Trinity, asked and got Newton's consent to lecture on the laws of gravitation as the final example of God's design. The result was that what had been a living discovery hardened quickly into a rigid prison of system. To 18th century thinkers, at least in England, the universe was settled, once and for all.*[1]

SCIENTISTS IGNORE PHILOSOPHICAL PROBLEMS

Instead of grappling with the philosophical problems presented by Berkeley, Hume, and Kant, and the mathematical problems which underlay calculus, 18th-century scientists took a pragmatic attitude toward them. Newton's Laws seemed an effective counter-argument to Berkeley and Hume by their very existence. Though Berkeley and Hume denied that we could ever speak with necessity about the physical world, Newton seemed to have done just that. Within the framework of Newton's Laws, it was sufficient for scientists to propose provisional theories about the world. As evidence came along that the theories didn't answer, well then, modify the theories.

Like their fellow scientists, mathematicians took the same laissez faire attitude toward the questions raised by the use of infinite processes in calculus. Since calculus provided correct answers to mathematical and scientific problems that had previously been im-

---

[1]Jacob Bronowski, *The Common Sense of Science* (New York: Modern Library/Random House, 1953), p. 47.

possible to answer, just be happy to use the results. This was a wonderfully pragmatic way to deal with reality. And since it was so inordinately successful, who was to argue?

DEVELOPMENT AND EXTENSION OF CALCULUS

Mathematicians were almost totally involved developing and extending calculus in the 18th century. Inexplicably, the center for this mathematical effort was neither in the England of Newton nor the Germany of Leibniz, but in Switzerland.[2] The Swiss contingent was led in numbers by the amazing Bernoulli family. First came brothers Jacob [1654–1705] and Johann [1667–1748]; then in the next generation Nikolaus and Daniel; then two other mathematical Johann's and one further Jacob in the generation after that (as well as some scattered lesser mathematicians and scientists). This single family extended and developed analytic geometry, differential and integral calculus, differential equations, the calculus of variations, and probability theory.[3]

Of even more significance was the most productive mathematician of all time, Leonhard Euler [1707–1783]. A contemporary said that Euler could calculate "just as men breathe, as eagles sustain themselves in the air."[4] He was renowned among contemporary mathematicians for his ability to intuitively jump to solutions of problems that had puzzled lesser mathematicians for years (in several instances, even the Bernoullis). In Bell's words:

> . . . an algorist is a mathematician to whom such ingenious tricks come naturally. There is no uniform mode of procedure—algorists, like facile rhymesters, are born, not made. . . . As an algorist, Euler has never been surpassed.[5]

---

[2] From whence nearly two centuries later C. G. Jung would also emerge.

[3] French mathematician/philosopher Blaise Pascal first developed a theory of probability in the 17th century. Though of immense importance in the history of mathematics, we have had to forego discussing probability theory, as it lay outside the history of mathematics which led up to Kurt Gödel's discoveries in the 20th century.

[4] Quote attributed to French academician Francois Agago, in Carl B. Boyer, *A History of Mathematics* (Princeton: Princeton University Press, 1968), p. 482.

[5] Eric Temple Bell, *Men of Mathematics* (New York: Simon & Schuster, 1937/1961), p. 140.

Happily, Euler did more than just jump like a mathematical grasshopper from one pretty problem to another: he also systematically collected and recorded both his results, and the related prior work of others, in volumes of a thoroughness and completeness unknown before. As if this wasn't enough, beyond his extreme productivity, his algorithmic ability, and his thoroughness of presentation, was an uncanny ability to capture these new mathematical ideas in symbolic ways that have largely survived to this day. In *A Concise History of Mathematics*, Dirk Struik says that:

LEONHARD EULER

> Euler made signal contributions in every field of mathematics which existed in his day. He published his results not only in articles of various length, but also in an impressive number of large textbooks which ordered and codified the material assembled during the ages. In several fields, Euler's presentation has been almost final.[6]

Of equal interest for our history are Euler's weaknesses, since they reflect the weaknesses of science and mathematics in general at that early stage of their development. Science and modern mathematics were still so new that they gloried in new discovery, not formality. Little did they know that deep problems can lie hidden beneath the surface. The key insight that made calculus possible was the realization that infinity was not just an abstraction; infinity could be

---

[6]Dirk J. Struik, *A Concise History of Mathematics* (New York: Dover, 1948/1987), p.120.

quantified. However, no mathematician of the time understood the implications of quantifying infinity.

> Leibniz held that, mysterious as it may sound, there were actually existing such things as infinitely small quantities, and of course infinitely small numbers corresponding to them.[7]

> Infinite processes were still carelessly handled in the 18th century and much of the work of the leading mathematicians of that period impresses us as wildly enthusiastic experimentation. . . . The whole question of the foundation of the calculus remained a subject of debate, and so did all the questions relating to infinite processes.[8]

Newton and Leibniz were never clear just what they meant when they considered the infinite processes that calculus depended on. In the previous chapter, we quoted Berkeley on the power of Newton's "fluxions" (i.e., calculus). But Berkeley was equally critical of the philosophical basis of calculus. In the same volume in which he praised Newton, a 1734 philosophical tract called *The Analyst*, he asks with much justification:

> . . . And what are these fluxions? The velocities of evanescent increments. And what are these same evanescent increments? They are neither finite quantities, nor quantities infinitely small, nor yet nothing. May we not call them ghosts of departed quantities? . . . He who can digest a second or third fluxion, a second or their difference, need not, methinks, be squeamish about any point in divinity.[9]

---

[7]Alfred North Whitehead, *An Introduction to Mathematics* (New York: Galaxy Book/Oxford University Press, 1911/1958), p. 169. Leibniz was hardly alone in this; Newton was equally confused.

[8]Dirk J. Struik, *A Concise History of Mathematics*, pp.124–125.

[9]David Eugene Smith, *A Source Book in Mathematics*. Reprint of 1929 edition (New York: Dover Publications, 1959), pp. 633, 629–630.

The word that later increasingly came to be used for fluxions was *infinitesimals*; by which mathematicians meant some strange numbers which were "greater than zero, yet less than any positive number."[10] The Bernoullis and Euler did little to demystify calculus. Much like John Locke with his philosophical extension of Newton's science, they were more interested in applying Newton's and Leibniz' mathematics than they were in questioning its

JEAN LE ROND D'ALEMBERT

validity. France's leading mathematician in the 18th century, Jean Le Rond d'Alembert [1717–1783], did provide a partial solution to the problem, with his concept of a limit. In his words, "the theory of limits is the true metaphysics of the differential calculus."[11] While of extreme significance, the concept of limits did not have an instant impact on mathematics, in part because of the awkwardness of d'Alembert's presentation. However, d'Alembert's crude concept of mathematical limits would at least plug the hole in the dike for the moment.

> In fact, the subject was right, though the explanations were wrong. It is this possibility of being right, albeit with entirely wrong explanations of what is being done, that so often makes external criticism—that is so far as it is meant to stop the pursuit of a method—singularly barren and futile in the progress of science.[12]

---

[10] This definition of infinitesimals was given me in a private conversation by mathematician David Moonitz in 1994. No rigorous, self-consistent theory of infinitesimals was developed until Abraham Robinson's *Non-Standard Analysis* (Amsterdam: North-Holland Publishing Company, 1966).

[11] Eric Temple Bell, *Men of Mathematics*, p. 267.

[12] Alfred North Whitehead, *An Introduction to Mathematics*, p. 169.

Consider the example given previously, where we calculated a progressively better approximation to the area of an irregular figure by covering it with rectangles and calculating their areas. We referred to the sum of their areas as an upper limit on the area of the figure. As the number of rectangles gets larger and larger, the limit shrinks and the approximation gets better. No matter how close we want the approximation to be, say within a millionth of an inch, we can use a sufficient number of rectangles such that the difference will be less.

As we watch those successive upper limits shrink, they will eventually approach some absolute limit. There can only be one such limit—this was the key idea which d'Alembert had a difficult time describing. For example, let's assume there is a second such limit. Measure the difference between the two limits—let's call it d. Then use a sufficient number of rectangles so that the approximation to the true area is less than $d/2$. Since the distance between the two limits is d, and since we can make the difference between the actual area and the approximation less than $d/2$, only one of the two limits can satisfy that condition. Whichever of the two it is, it must be the true limit. Thus, if a limit can be approached, the limit is unique.

Readers who have been able to follow the above description of a limit should congratulate themselves. This is one of the most profound discoveries of mathematics, which is frequently a stumbling block for beginning calculus students, as it was for Newton, Leibniz, the Bernoullis and Euler. Far too frequently it is just learned by rote, without any understanding of the profundity underlying its mechanics. What is significant is that we are able to talk about an infinite limit without bringing in anything but finite numbers. With only slight alterations, this description of a limit can be made mathematically rigorous, as was finally done by German mathematician Karl Weierstrass in the second half of the 19th century. His method obviated the need to discuss infinity or infinitesimals, because it defined limits entirely in terms of finite quantities.[13]

---

[13]See chapter 7.

It is important, however, not to overvalue the importance of rigor; after all Newton and Leibniz were able to develop a workable model of calculus that was used successfully for a hundred and fifty years, before such a mathematically precise explanation was available. Though rigor is important, mathematical intuition is still more important.

ASSOCIATIONISM

The 18th century was full of parallel ideas interacting in complex patterns. Though the center for development of Newton's mathematical ideas shifted to Switzerland, the future United Kingdom became the center of the philosophical debate. While Irishman Berkeley and Scotsman Hume were presenting their challenges to Locke and Newton, David Hartley (in Britain) and Thomas Reid (in Scotland) were defending and extending Locke's philosophy, in much the same way Euler was developing Newton's mathematical ideas.

Thomas Reid [1710–1796] formed a school of philosophy, called appropriately the Scottish School. Reid and his followers, advocating "common sense" and "instinct," threw out the whole argument presented by Berkeley and Hume. If Berkeley and Hume denied the existence of physical reality, then their arguments weren't worth considering. However, a quote attributed to Dr. Thomas Brown, one of Reid's followers, shows that Reid's and Hume's views were more similar than Reid would have liked to believe.

> Yes, Reid bawled out we must believe in an outward world; but added in a whisper, we can give no reason for our belief. Hume cries out we can give no reason for such a notion; and whispers, I own we cannot get rid of it.[14]

---

[14] Quotation in Edna Heidbreder, *Seven Psychologies* (New York: Appleton-Century-Crofts, 1933), p. 52.

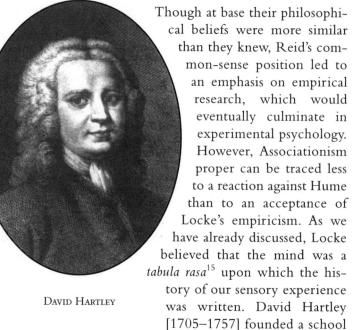

David Hartley

Though at base their philosophical beliefs were more similar than they knew, Reid's common-sense position led to an emphasis on empirical research, which would eventually culminate in experimental psychology. However, Associationism proper can be traced less to a reaction against Hume than to an acceptance of Locke's empiricism. As we have already discussed, Locke believed that the mind was a *tabula rasa*[15] upon which the history of our sensory experience was written. David Hartley [1705–1757] founded a school of thought based on Locke's ideas.

> The general law of association is that if sensations have often been experienced together, the corresponding ideas will tend to occur together. . . . association may be either successive or simultaneous. The former determines the course of thought in time; the latter accounts for the formation of complex ideas. These few principles form the basis of associationism.[16]

Implicit in associationism is the idea that the physical and psychic worlds are separate but parallel, and that somehow there is no contradiction in such a separation. This idea of *parallelism* was first explicitly discussed a century earlier by prescient 17th-century philosopher, Baruch Spinoza [1632–1677], who argued that René

---

[15]A blank slate.
[16]Quotation in Edna Heidbreder, *Seven Psychologies*, p. 54.

Descartes' separation of mind and matter was misguided. Spinoza argued that:

> . . . thought and the system of things in space are only two aspects of a single reality, and are at every point inseparable.[17]

For Spinoza, mind and matter were parallel only because they were particular manifestations of a single reality. As we will see later in this book, in their later days, both Jung and Gödel believed in a single underlying reality, of which both the physical world and the mental world are manifestations. Jung termed this reality the *unus mundus*,[18] and argued that each of us possesses an inborn unifying structure,[19] through which we can experience that underlying reality. In contrast, Spinoza's unitary reality, which he called interchangeably God or Nature, was a cold mechanical realm, much like the clock-like universe that later developed out of Newton's ideas. For Spinoza, as later for Kant, human beings and nature were eternally separate. Still, Spinoza was remarkably farsighted in seeing the problems inherent in parallelism at such an early period in time.[20]

Without the assumptions of such a single reality, parallelism has deep philosophical problems. If mind and matter are separate and distinct substances, then there can be no connection between events in one and events in the other. Yet it is just this parallelism that is implicit in associationism. Since associationism led to much of modern experimental psychology, this is a critical problem for psychology. As the 18th century gave way to the 19th, such problems began to find expression in both the philosophy of the mind, and in mathematics.

---

[17]Stuart Hampshire, ed., *The Age of Reason: The 17th Century Philosophers* (Boston: Mentor Books/Houghton Mifflin, 1956), p. 101.

[18]Unitary world; see C. G. Jung, *Collected Works, Vol. 14: Mysterium Coniunctionis*, Bollingen Series XX (Princeton: Princeton University Press, 1963), pp. 759–775.

[19]The transcendent function or *Self*. See chapter 15.

[20]See Stuart Hampshire, *The Age of Reason*, pp. 99–141, for material on Spinoza.

CHEMISTRY LEADS TO
JOHN STUART MILL'S CREATIVE SYNTHESIS

> . . . the pure associationist's account of our mental life is al-
> most as bewildering as that of the pure spiritualist. This
> multitude of ideas, existing absolutely, yet clinging to-
> gether, and weaving an endless carpet of themselves, like
> dominoes in ceaseless change, or the bits of glass in a kalei-
> doscope—whence do they get their fantastic laws of cling-
> ing, and why do they cling in just the shapes they do?[21]

Associationism was based on an extremely simple set of ideas. Dr.
Thomas Brown summarized the few laws of associationism as "the
laws of recency, frequency, and intensity—that much-used trio."[22]
Though these laws are clear and simple to understand, difficulties
developed in trying to describe exactly how association worked. It
is one thing to believe that complex ideas all derive ultimately from
simple, sensory perceptions. It is quite another to show how this
actually operates in even the simplest situation. This is much the
same dilemma 20th century behaviorists experienced in trying to
reduce the complexity of the human mind to a simple reflex-arc,
but that is getting ahead of our story.

The empiricist/associationist tradition was still firmly in place
in the first half of the 19th century, and associationism held sway.
James Mill's *Analysis of the Phenomena of the Human Mind* (1829) was
representative of the thought of his time.

> James Mill believed that the mind has no creative function
> because he felt that association was a purely passive process.
> In other words, sensations that have occurred together in a
> certain order are mechanically reproduced as ideas, and
> these resulting ideas occur in the same order as their corre-
> sponding sensations. Association was thus treated in very

---

[21] William James, *The Principles of Psychology*, 2 vols., 1890 (New York: Dover Publications, reprint, 1950), vol. I, p. 3.
[22] Quotation in Edna Heidbreder, *Seven Psychologies*, p. 55.

mechanistic terms, with the resulting ideas being merely the accumulation or sum of the individual elements.[23]

Philosophy is the mother of the sciences—each was initially merely an area of interest for philosophy. Each in turn grew independent enough to call itself a separate field: first mathematics, then physics, later chemistry and biology. The branch of philosophy which was later to become psychology turned to each of the sciences in turn in an attempt to describe the workings of the mind. For example, as we have already seen, in the 18th century and early 19th century, associationism drew on Newtonian physics for its unspoken philosophy. But this view was to be supplanted in turn, when the new science of chemistry emerged. And, as we will see later, when psychology actually appeared as a new field, biology was the science at the cutting edge, so it would in turn provide a philosophical model for the mind.

Chemistry developed as a separate field of study in the second half of the 18th century and the early days of the 19th century. Antoine Lavoisier conducted methodical experiments in combustion, which led among other things to the first version of the law of conservation of matter. Daniel Rutherford and Henry Cavendish discovered nitrogen, Karl Wilhelm Scheele and Joseph Priestly, oxygen. It was an exciting era when discoveries came tumbling out one after another, and chemistry began to take shape as a separate, fully quantitative science. By the time James Mill's son, philosopher John Stuart Mill [1806–1873], developed his view of the mind in the mid-19th century, chemistry was firmly in place as not only a theoretical, but a practical science.

Chemistry, an art whereby sensible bodies contained in vessels . . . are so changed, by means of certain instruments, and principally fire, that their several powers and virtues are thereby discovered, with a view to philosophy or medicine.[24]

---

[23] Duane Schultz, *A History of Modern Psychology* (New York: Academic Press, 1969), p. 27.

[24] Quotation from Samuel Johnson, in Isaac Asimov and Jason A. Shulman, eds. *Isaac Asimov's Book of Science and Nature Quotations* (New York: Weidenfeld & Nicholson, 1988), p. 44.

Mill was convinced that there was more to the mind than associationism's mechanical combination, and turned to chemistry for an explanatory principle, much as Locke had turned to Newtonian physics a century-and-a-half earlier. He argued that the mind plays an active role in acquiring and assimilating sensory data, not merely through passive association, but also through a *creative synthesis*. In Mill's words:

> When many impressions or ideas are operating in the mind together, there sometimes takes place a process of a similar kind to chemical combination; . . . those ideas sometimes melt and coalesce into one another, and appear not several ideas but one. . . . The Complex Idea, formed by the blending together of several simpler ones, should . . . be said to *result from,* or be *generated by,* the simple ideas not to *consist of* them.[25]

Though Mill's view is a marked advance on associationism, it fails to incorporate the Kantian realization that the mind already possesses inborn structures that help in this synthetic process. It is in the combination of many of the ideas, which have already been presented in this book, that some approximation to Jung's archetypal position begins to emerge. Assume, like Spinoza, that there is a single inter-connected reality, an *unus mundus,* and that matter and psyche are actually merely two different aspects of that single reality. Assume, like Kant, that the human mind contains inherent structures that are part of that underlying reality. Sensory data is experienced relationally, then categorized and integrated using those inherent structures of the mind; i.e., archetypes. Then assume, like Mill, that this categorization and integration is an active process, from which new ideas emerge. Finally, from biology add the picture of an organic process which evolves across immense periods of time. That set of assumptions begins to approximate the starting point for Jung's psychology. As we will see later, mathematician

---

[25]Quotation in Edwin G. Boring, *A History of Experimental Psychology,* 2nd ed (New York: Appleton-Century-Crofts, 1950), p. 230. Mill's emphasis in all cases.

Kurt Gödel arrived at roughly the same conclusions. But that worldview remained for the 20th century to discover.

Imaginary Numbers

Mathematics, no less than philosophy, began to confront the problems inherent in the earlier pragmatic position. Initially the problems appeared in strange new discoveries in algebra and geometry. It wouldn't be until the second half of the 19th and beginning of the 20th century that these problems would push their way into the very foundations of mathematics.

A problem arose in algebra when mathematicians dealt with *square roots*. The square of a number is just the number multiplied by itself. For example, the square of 2 is 4 (i.e., 2×2). The square of 10 is 100. The square root is merely the inverse process. The square root of 4 is 2 (because $2 \times 2 = 4$). I'll use the standard mathematical notation $\sqrt{4} = 2$ for short. Similarly, the $\sqrt{100} = 10$ (since 10 squared is 100).

Actually I've cheated a little bit. The $\sqrt{4}$ is not only equal to 2 (that is, $+2$), but also -2 as well, since $-2 \times -2 = 4$. Similarly the square root of 100 is both $+10$ and -10. Another way to express this is to say that any positive number has both a positive and a negative square root. Looking at it from the other side, the square of both positive and negative numbers is always a positive number.

So far, so good. But then mathematicians encountered a problem—sometimes their calculations led to the square root of a negative number. What could the $\sqrt{-1}$ possibly mean? How could any number be multiplied by itself and get a negative number? That was the riddle that confronted mathematicians. They couldn't simply ignore the question as meaningless, since they kept solving equations and coming up with numbers like the $\sqrt{-1}$.

Italian mathematician Cardan was the first mathematician (in the 16th century) who was brave enough to actually express these strange numbers in symbols. He showed that a certain equation could be solved if 40 could be factored into $5 + \sqrt{-15}$ and $5 -$

CARDAN

√−15.[26] However, Cardan was quick to point out that this was just ideal doodling on his part since there couldn't be any such numbers—they were just *imaginary*. But the idea had been planted. Imaginary or not, they were useful. Not long afterward, mathematicians began using the symbol *i* to represent √−1. They freely used numbers like (5 + 15*i*) and (5 − 15*i*) in their equations. Still it bothered them that these numbers were only imaginary, that they had no physical meaning. The problem was that they were restricting themselves unnecessarily to supposed real numbers.

Finally, at the beginning of the 19th century, German mathematician Karl Friedrich Gauss[27] made an intuitive leap which connected Descartes' coordinates with imaginary numbers. Descartes had realized that positions on a graph could be represented by numbers. Gauss had the inverse realization: he saw that numbers such as (5 + 15*i*) and (5 − 15*i*)[28] could represent positions on a graph where the horizontal axis represented natural numbers, such as −2, −1, 0, +1, +2, etc., and the vertical axis

KARL FRIEDRICH GAUSS

---

[26] $(5+\sqrt{-15})\times(5-\sqrt{-15})=5\times5+5\times\sqrt{-15}-5\times\sqrt{-15}-\sqrt{-15}\times\sqrt{-15}=25-(-15)=25+15=40$
[27] Commonly considered the greatest mathematician of all time.
[28] Now called *complex numbers*.

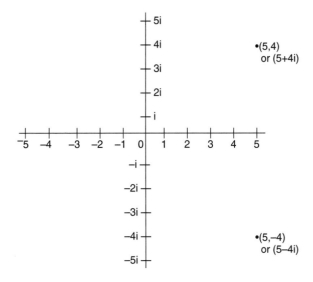

FIGURE 4.1.   GAUSS' USE OF THE PLANE TO REPRESENT IMAGINARY NUMBERS.

represented imaginary numbers, such as $-2i$, $-i$, 0, $+i$, $+2i$, etc. Therefore, any complex number could be represented by a point on the graph. For example, $5 + 4i$ would be the position $(5, 4)$; i.e., a point 5 units to the right of the origin and 4 units up. In turn, $5 - 4i$ would be $(5, -4)$; i.e., a point located five units to the right of the origin and 4 units down. (See figure 4.1.)

Gauss was a genius of the same order as Leonardo da Vinci: so far ahead of his colleagues that it is unlikely that many of his discoveries would have been made for decades or even centuries. A famous story about Gauss at 10 years old may give some idea of his ability. One day in school, the teacher wanted a little personal time in order to take care of paperwork, so he told students to add a series of 100 numbers, such as $897 + 900 + 903 + \ldots + 1{,}191 + 1{,}194$. This is a type of series that, while it will keep a class of grade school students busy, can be summed with a single equation by a mathematician.[29]

---

[29]We don't know the actual series Gauss' fellow students were given, but the one I've given is similar. In case you want to try it yourself, the answer is 104,500.

The teacher had barely stated the problem before Gauss had written the answer on his slate and turned it face down on the teacher's desk to show he was finished (as was the custom in German classrooms of the day). Gauss sat at his desk doing nothing for the rest of the class, while the other students slaved away at the problem. The teacher was less than thrilled at his impertinence and determined he would find a suitable punishment for young Gauss. However, at the end of the class, when he began checking the answers, he found that Gauss had written a single number which was the correct answer—the only correct answer in the class. The teacher went on to become Gauss' champion at the beginning of his remarkable mathematical career.[30]

Given Gauss' extreme genius, one might have thought that his discovery of the geometric representation for imaginary numbers was unique. After all, mathematicians had been struggling with the concept of imaginary numbers for many centuries, explicitly since the 16th century. Even though Descartes had provided the clue with his discovery of analytic geometry early in the 17th century, no mathematician had seen the implications in the nearly two hundred years since.

Despite this background of futility, in 1797, both the great Gauss[31] and an unknown Norwegian surveyor named Horst Wessel simultaneously discovered this radical new interpretation. Both discoveries went unnoticed and in 1806 a Parisian bookkeeper, Robert Argand, became the third to independently discover the geometric interpretation of complex numbers. Clearly this was more than a coincidence. The idea must have been in the air, just as the idea of the calculus was in the air when Newton and Leibniz simultaneously discovered it, and evolution by natural selection was in the air when both Darwin and Alfred Russel Wallace simultaneously discovered it. This seems to be a characteristic pattern in the history of the formation of a new symbol out of the unconscious. It starts with denial; then partial acceptance, but no understanding; then partial understanding; then full understanding only when an

---

[30]Eric Temple Bell, *Men of Mathematics*, pp. 221–222.
[31]Then only 20 years old and defending his doctoral dissertation.

explicit symbol system comes into existence. We will see a further example in the next section in our discussion of the development of non-Euclidean geometry.[32]

By transferring imaginary numbers into geometric coordinates, Gauss, Wessel, and Argand were taking a further step at uniting the algebraic and geometric views of reality, much as Descartes had when he discovered analytic geometry. Though they were not aware of it, all were attempting to discover a unitary reality which underlay the seeming parallelism of mind and matter. Algebra can be seen as dealing with products of the mind—numbers, and geometry, with points and lines, which ultimately are expressions of physical reality. But what if it is discovered that there is no necessary connection between geometry and physical reality? The problem would then deepen.

NON-EUCLIDEAN GEOMETRY

[In] the rise of non-Euclidean geometry . . . we find a startling case of simultaneity of discovery, for similar notions occurred, during the first third of the 19th century, to three men, one German, one Hungarian, and one Russian.[33]

Until the 19th century, it seemed self-evident to mathematicians that any formal axiomatic system was inherently consistent and complete; Euclidian geometry was a practical example of just such a formal system. Euclid developed geometry from ten axioms, which all seemed self-evident to mathematicians. For example, if L is a line, then there exists a point not on L. One can readily draw a line on a paper and a point at some other place on the paper as an illustration.

However, the famous fifth axiom, commonly called the *parallel axiom*, was not so self-evident. It said that for a given line L and a given point P not on line L, there existed one and only one line

---

[32]In this case the geometrical symbol of the Cartesian plane to represent complex numbers.
[33]Carl B. Boyer, *A History of Mathematics*, p. 585.

containing P that is parallel to L. This seemed to be so much less self-evident than all the other axioms that generations of mathematicians attempted to make it a theorem rather than an axiom and derive it from the other nine axioms. But to no avail; the only way to eliminate it was to give some other tenth axiom, equally non-self-evident, and derive the parallel axiom from it.

NIKOLAI IVANOVIC LOBACHEVSKY

In approximately 1830, mathematician Janos Bolyai [1802–1860] and Nikolai Lobachevsky [1793–1856] independently took another approach: they assumed the opposite of the fifth axiom—that more than one line could be drawn through the given point parallel to the given line. They hoped to derive a contradiction and thus prove the fifth axiom to be true. Instead they developed a strange geometry that was fully as consistent as Euclid's. Once again we have an example, as with the concept of evolution in biology, and imaginary numbers in mathematics, of a new concept emerging out of the air, and finding expression by different people.

> Non-Euclidean geometry continued for several decades to be a fringe aspect of mathematics until it was thoroughly integrated through the remarkably general views of G. F. B. Riemann.[34]

A quarter-century later in 1854, a third mathematician, Georg Riemann [1826–1866], independently developed still another non-Euclidian geometry by assuming that no line could be drawn through a given point parallel to a given line. This is the geometry

---

[34]Carl B. Boyer, *A History of Mathematics*, p. 588.

of the surface of a sphere, if a line is defined to be a great circle of the sphere. On such a surface, there is indeed no such thing as a parallel line since any two great circles have exactly two points in common. This was the geometry that Einstein later drew on in his conception of general relativity. Astronomer and physicist Sir Arthur Eddington remarked that "a geometer like Riemann might almost have foreseen the more important features of the actual world."[35]

BERNHARD RIEMANN

Mathematicians were understandably surprised to find that new axioms produced new geometries rather than contradictions. However, that led to a deeply disturbing realization. As long as Euclid's geometry could be assumed to be a self-evident picture of the world, one could turn to the world to show that no proposition could be both true and false. Once that was no longer possible, where could one turn for proof? Mathematicians began to grasp the fact that perhaps mathematics dealt with formal mathematical systems which had no necessary connection with physical reality.

This position was a great increase in abstract thought, though it was to lead to a further increase in the separation of mind and matter, an increased alienation from reality. The missing element was the archetypal concept: that there was a single reality that underlay both mind and matter, composed of archetypes which found their expression in both mind and matter through symbol formation. But it was still too early for such a concept to emerge; instead in the late 19th century, reductionism held sway, and finally reached its apotheosis in the *fin de siecle* period between the 19th and 20th centuries. Since this is when psychology finally emerged as a separate science, that's where we now turn our attention.

---

[35] Quotation in Eric Temple Bell, *Men of Mathematics*, p. 484.

CHAPTER 5

FOUNDERS OF EXPERIMENTAL PSYCHOLOGY

It is interesting to note that, in both philosophy and science, interest in psychology developed late and was at first incidental. Philosophy, setting out to account for the universe at large, began as cosmology, and only when it became involved in the problems of epistemology did it address itself seriously and directly to psychological material. Science, too, started as an attempt to explain the world at large, beginning with physics and astronomy. And physical science, like philosophy, first became seriously attentive to psychology when it met in science the counterpart of the problem of epistemology—the necessity of considering the observing organism in order to give a complete account of the observed universe.[1]

PSYCHOLOGY EMERGES AS A SCIENCE

The story of psychology as a separate field begins in the second half of the 19th century with the experimental research of Fechner, Helmholtz, and Wundt in Germany, and the clinical research of Charcot, Janet, and Bernheim in France. Most of current academic and experimental psychology can be traced back to the three Germans, most psychotherapy to the three Frenchmen.

As we trace first the founding of experimental psychology in this chapter, then clinical psychology in the next chapter, it is

---

[1] Quotation in Edna Heidbreder, *Seven Psychologies* (New York: Appleton-Century-Crofts, 1933), p. 76.

important to remember that these were going on simultaneously. And, as we will see, a similar split was occurring in mathematics at much the same time.[2] Since Kant's attempt at reconciliation of the mind–body problem had gone unheeded by science, increasingly fields split into opposites to deal with one or another aspect of the problem. While it may have been too early to acknowledge Kant's argument that it is the human mind that structures the physical reality we perceive, still the issue shifted from philosophy proper to the psychology of the human mind. There the natural split was between clinicians and experimentalists. The clinical psychologists, who developed out of a medical model, were most interested in results. The experimental psychologists, who developed out of an experimental scientific model, were most interested in those aspects of the mind which could be examined using experimental techniques. Clearly something was lost between the two areas.

In contrast, both Freud and Jung were unusual in that they had been experimental psychologists as well as practicing physicians. For example, Jung did pioneering work in word association and work with galvanic skin response that anticipated biofeedback research. Jung was also well-read in philosophy and well aware of the philosophical roots that underlay both clinical and experimental psychology. That allowed Jung to put both sides in perspective, and pick and choose from both camps, though he was always first and foremost a healer. Our discussion of experimental psychology's three pioneers will begin with Fechner, who was the only one of the three who shared Jung's broad erudition.

GUSTAV FECHNER AND WEBER'S LAW

. . . on the morning of October 22, 1850—he carefully notes the date—he came upon an idea that satisfied both the scientific and humanistic demands of his nature. It occurred to him that there might be an observable, even

---

[2]See chapter 7.

measurable relationship between the stimulus and the sensation and therefore between the physical and the mental worlds. . . .[3]

Gustav Fechner [1801–1887] was an interesting study in contrasts, and his work reflects those contrasts. Throughout his life he was pulled between the twin poles of mind and matter, in his case expressed by his interest in both metaphysics and science. His early work was first in physiology, then in physics. He experienced a crisis in mid-life, where he became ill and withdrew from the world. His earlier work had no meaning for him unless he could find some way of reconciling the science he practiced with the spiritual world in which he believed. After a dozen years as a reclusive invalid, he suddenly recovered.

> The primary result of [the crisis] was a deepening of Fechner's religious consciousness and his interest in the problem of the soul. . . . His philosophical solution of the spiritual problem lay in his affirmation of the identity of mind and matter and in his assurance that the entire universe can be regarded as readily from the point of view of its consciousness.[4]

Here is the first statement of the position Jung (and to a lesser extent Gödel) was later to express. However Fechner, with his emphasis on experimental science, took a much different route than either Jung or Gödel in his attempts to justify his position. Fechner felt that if the mind and body were two manifestations of a single consciousness, then there should be physical constants that reflected the connection between the two. In effect he was looking for the archetypes of order of the universe. As we will see later, Jung and Gödel both felt that number was the primary archetype of order that underlay both mind and matter.

---

[3] Edna Heidbreder, *Seven Psychologies*, p. 81.
[4] Quotation in Edwin G. Boring, *A History of Experimental Psychology* (New York: Appleton-Century-Crofts, 1950), p. 278.

As has already been discussed, Kant said that there were psychic constants which he called inherent structures or categories. Jung called them initially *primordial images*[5] and later *archetypes*.[6] Of course, long before either, Plato proposed the existence of idealized patterns of which the objects of the material world were but pale copies. The key addition of Kant was the explicit recognition that these eternal patterns existed in the human mind, and that it was the human mind that formed the meeting ground for the material and the spiritual.

ERNST HEINRICH WEBER

But Fechner, the experimental scientist, wanted to find some way to actually quantify physical relationships between the mental and physical realms. Fechner found just such quantification in the work of Ernst Heinrich Weber [1795–1878]. Weber conducted a series of experiments in which he tried to discover the threshold of sensory awareness. He had a subject hold a weight, then a second weight which was slightly heavier. He kept increasing the difference between the weights until the subject could detect a difference. He found that:

. . . the smallest perceptible difference between two weights can be stated as a ratio between the weights, a ratio that is independent of the magnitudes of the weights.[7]

Not only that, but the ratio was constant for all subjects, and moreover, the results were similar in his experiments with visual and auditory response. That may sound commonplace. After all, it merely says

---

[5] After Jacob Burckhardt. See C. G. Jung, *Collected Works, Vol. 7: Two Essays on Analytical Psychology* (Princeton: Princeton University Press, 1966), ¶ 101.

[6] From the Greek, meaning *prime imprinter*. For first use, see C. G. Jung, *Collected Works, Vol. 8: The Structure and Dynamics of the Psyche* (Princeton: Princeton University Press, 1960), ¶ 270.

[7] Quotation in Edwin G. Boring, *A History of Experimental Psychology*, p. 113.

that the heavier the weight, the larger the difference between it and the second weight before any difference can be detected. In other words, the sensory world is experienced through relationship, not absolute difference. However, remember that the laws of mental association see the mind as nothing more than a *tabula rasa* on which is recorded an endless chain of associations to sensory experiences. Our experience of the world should then be absolute, not relational.

The fact that sensory experience is relational should have been exciting enough to open up whole new directions for research. For example, does this relational ordering of sensory experience occur in the mind or at the level of the sensors themselves (more recent research seems to show the latter to be the case)? If our sensory experience is relational, do we have hierarchies of relationship proceeding from the sensory to the psychological? Do such relational perceptions occur in all species? Is there some lowest level of animal development at which they cease to occur? Do different species order reality in markedly different ways? Within humans alone, how does pathology affect this ordering, and at what levels? The questions are endless.

To Fechner, Weber's experiments were a revelation, and he called the results Weber's Law. Actually, it might better be called Fechner's Law since Weber never saw the full significance of his discoveries, nor did he develop the general form of the law. As Fechner stated Weber's Law, sensation (which Fechner felt to be a purely mental process) varied with the natural logarithm of the stimulus (which Fechner felt was purely physical). Another way of expressing Weber's Law is that response varies arithmetically as stimulus varies geometrically. Fechner spent the next decade extending that research, to which he gave the name *psychophysics*.[8]

---

[8]A hundred years later, S. S. Stevens vastly extended Weber's and Fechner's research on psychophysics. As with most pioneering results, Weber's initial guess was overly crude. Stevens showed that the ratio between sensation and stimulus was a *power function*, not merely a logarithmic function; i.e., the sensation equaled some constant that varied with the particular kind of sensation being measured, times the measurement of the stimulus to some power (often fractional). Though this modified Weber's Law, it further proved that the relationship between sensation and stimulus is relational, not direct. See S. S. Stevens, "Problems and Methods of Psychophysics," *Psychological Bulletin* (55, 1958), pp. 177–196, and S. S. Stevens, *Handbook of Experimental Psychology* (New York: Wiley, 1951).

In the course of that research, he developed many of the techniques of experimental psychology. He felt satisfied that he had accomplished his goal: to quantify the relationship between mind and body. Few experimental scientists since then have agreed with his self-assessment. William James, for example, stated:

> . . . in the humble opinion of the present writer, the proper psychological outcome [of Fechner's research] is just *nothing*.[9]

Despite James' negative opinion of Fechner's work, Fechner's belief in quantifiable results created experimental psychology, and his methods are still in use today. It is disappointing that Fechner's vision of a unity (which Fechner thought to be consciousness) underlying mind and matter has been almost totally ignored. This situation has recurred many times since. We will briefly describe one such example in the following section.

GESTALT PSYCHOLOGY VS. ASSOCIATIONISM

Much of the power of scientific experimentation lies in the ability to separate the observer and the observed, then limit the parameters under consideration. This is an incredibly powerful method, but an essentially artificial one. It is never truly possible to eliminate extraneous factors. Good scientists recognize this and design their experiments accordingly. Unfortunately, when the object under observation is a human being, there is a tendency to view a human subject as an object like other objects regardless of the humanism of the scientist. Again the best scientists avoid this trap, but it is a trap nevertheless.[10]

---

[9] William James, *The Principles of Psychology*, Vol. I: 1890 (New York: Dover, reprint, 1950), p. 534. James' emphasis.

[10] This problem has been exacerbated in recent years by the spate of research that built upon the research techniques of Stanley Milgram, in which the subject was deliberately deceived. For more on this, see "The Shadow Hidden Within the Light of Science" in my *Beginner's Guide to Jungian Psychology* (York Beach, ME: Nicolas-Hays, 1992).

Over and beyond this danger, lie the dangers inherent in the materialist position itself, the dangers of dismissing the psyche as an epiphenomenon. As has been shown earlier, this is a point of view that existed from experimental psychology's beginnings, and which was implicit in philosophy at least back to Locke, with his origination of associationism. If the human mind is only a jumble of associations of units of sensory experience, then why not ignore the inner experience and concentrate on the sensory stimulus itself and the physiological response to the stimulus? We have already discussed Weber's law and its implication that the human mind perceives relationships, not simple sensory units, and that this relational perception appears to be inborn. Early in the 20th century, Gestalt psychologists experimentally confirmed this hypothesis.

In a series of classic, independently conducted experiments by Gestalt psychologist Wolfgang Kohler [1887–1967], and neuropsychologist Karl Lashley [1890–1958], chickens were taught to distinguish two different shades of gray; let's call them Gray and Dark-Gray. If the chickens correctly identified Dark-Gray, they received a reward of food. With the chickens trained to pick Dark-Gray, the psychologists brought in a still darker gray, which we'll call Gray-Black. They exposed the chickens to Dark-Gray and Gray-Black.

Now, if associationism was correct, the chickens should once more have picked Dark-Gray, because they had supposedly made a straightforward association of Dark-Gray with a reward of food. In fact, a small percentage of chickens did just that. But the overwhelming majority of chickens picked Gray-Black, the darker shade. In other words, most chickens had associated a relationship, "darker," with getting a reward.[11]

It is important to stress that the chickens were not exposed to a series of situations in which they had to pick the darker shade of gray. They were only trained with the one pair of grays, yet most learned from that one situation to pick the darker shade. In these experiments, stimuli did not lead immediately to response; "be-

---

[11]Wolfgang Kohler, *Gestalt Psychology* (New York: Mentor Books/New American Library, 1947), p. 118.

tween the stimulus and the response, there occurs the process of organization."[12] Thus, even at the sensory level, experience is structured relationally. These experiments were extended to apes (thus much closer to humans), and to the perception of size (where the relationship of smaller to larger proved more primary than the actual size of an object).

These, and many similar experiments, show that not only humans, but animals also organize sensory perception. The question of how much organization goes on at various levels between the original sensory perception and the eventual complex organization in the psyche is an open question. In order to get a better picture of that complex organization, subjective information supplied by the subject should be as important to the scientist as the objective observation of behavior from without. Both are equally significant sources of data.

However, despite these incontrovertible results, behavioral psychology remains the most accepted psychology in America today (both by experimental and clinical psychologists). And behavioral psychology has no interest in subjective data, since it assumes no intervening organization between stimulus and response!

Hermann von Helmholtz and the Law of Conservation of Energy

By placing the resources of the physiological laboratories at the disposal of students of psychology, [Helmholtz] had made the development of an experimental psychology all but inevitable.[13]

Psychology was for him an exact science, dependent upon the use of mathematics . . . and upon experiment.[14]

---

[12] Wolfgang Kohler, *Gestalt Psychology*, p. 119.
[13] Edna Heidbreder, *Seven Psychologies*, p. 91.
[14] Quotation in Edwin G. Boring, *A History of Experimental Psychology*, p. 303.

The second of the trio of great German experimental psychologists was Hermann von Helmholtz [1821–1894]. Helmholtz was far and away the greatest of the three as a natural scientist, but the least interesting as a precursor of modern psychology. Though he did outstanding physiological research on vision and hearing, and measured the speed of the nerve impulse, probably his greatest impact on psychology was from his work as a physicist! Today, physicists, who work with the deepest levels of matter, and depth psychologists,

HERMANN VON HELMHOLTZ

who work with the deepest levels of psyche, are increasingly turning to each other's discipline for answers. But Helmholtz was a representative of his time, a thorough materialist who scoffed at psychic processes.

Interestingly, he did not dismiss energy as an occult concept, even though in many ways it is the least materialistic concept of all. Helmholtz was the first to formulate the Law of Conservation of Energy, which states that the sum total of energy is constant. As modified by Einstein to include transformations between matter and energy, it remains one of the two primary assumptions of physical science.[15] The Law of Conservation of Energy was a liberating concept for scientists of many different fields, including psychology. It meant that transformation was possible without occult explanations. Without such a law, any dynamic science is impossible. Both Freud and Jung were to draw on this law as a cornerstone of their thought. In fact, it was their difference on the nature of *psychic energy*, or *libido*, that caused their split.

---

[15]The other is the Law of Entropy: which proposes that organization always decreases. However, the work of Nobel prize winning chemist Ilya Prigogine has revealed that within *open systems* (i.e., virtually any real-life environment), organization can increase without upsetting entropy, by exporting disorder to the surrounding environment.

This word *energy* has become so commonplace that energy is thought of as a thing, a material object. We talk glibly of electrical energy or atomic energy. But energy is not a thing; it is only the possibility for transformation. Energy is the concept of an intermediate undefined state between two defined states. Though it is frequently useful to think of energy as a thing and discuss electrical energy or magnetic energy, one mustn't forget that this is only a heuristic aid. For example, Freud's concept of libido or psychic energy was enormously useful, but only a device. From his writings, it appears that Freud viewed libido as limited to sexual energy, which casts some doubt on the extent to which he understood this more general concept of energy. From his writings, it appears certain that Jung did.[16]

WILHELM WUNDT'S INTROSPECTIONISM

> Wundt is the senior psychologist in the history of psychology. He is the first man who without reservation is properly called a psychologist.[17]

Wilhelm Wundt [1832–1900], the last of the trio, is frequently called the founder of psychology. It might be more accurate to split the title of founder of experimental psychology among Wundt, Helmholtz, and Fechner, and reserve the title of founder of clinical psychology for Freud. Wundt founded a psychological laboratory in Leipzig in 1879; it was his work, and the work of his pupils in his laboratory, that led to the wide-spread development of experimental psychology.

Wundt was an encyclopedist rather than an originator. He brought together, classified, and published the many psychological facts that had already been discovered, and continued this process throughout his life. He called his method of research *introspectionism*; it is now a relic of the time, accepted neither by the behavior-

---

[16]See "On Psychic Energy" in C. G. Jung, *Collected Works,* Vol. 8, ¶ 1–130.
[17]Edwin G. Boring, *A History of Experimental Psychology,* p. 316.

ists and other experimental psychologists, nor any of the varied clinical disciplines. While the name introspectionism might bring to mind deep, and perhaps fuzzy, thoughts, that was hardly Wundt's territory. Rather he studied the simple reactions that behavioral psychology has mapped so well, but did it by experiments with trained human subjects who made simple discriminations. This seemed a reasonable extension of Weber's Law. Unfortunately, since he felt there was no place in experimental psychology for animal, child, abnormal, or applied psychology, his field of study was somewhat limited in scope. It was this narrowness that led to the counter-development of behavioral psychology.

Though Wundt's vision was narrow, his impact was great. The time was ripe for a quantitative, experimental psychology, and Leipzig became the gathering place for all the bright, young future experimental psychologists of the 1880's and 1890's. An Englishman, Edward Tichener, became an enthusiastic convert and brought Wundt's psychology to Cornell University. Largely through Tichener's autocratic presence, experimental psychology became the major psychological force in America at the end of the 19th century. While, like Wundt, Tichener's own views are largely forgotten, experimental psychology still dominates American academic psychology.

LIMITING THE PSYCHE TO CONSCIOUSNESS

Experimental psychology patterned itself after the physical sciences. It wanted to avoid anything that could be termed mystical or even philosophical at any cost. Eventually that attitude would lead to behavioral psychology which limited psychology to physical behavior, thus taking the psyche totally out of psychology. At the time of experimental psychology's founding, it was still the order of the day to point to consciousness as the distinguishing attribute of a human being, so the time was not yet ripe for the full reductionism of behavioral psychology. However, the idea that there might be psychic processes that were not conscious was abhorrent to Wundt and his followers.

In "On the Nature of the Psyche," Jung quotes "a representative of the Wundt school" as saying that once the idea of an unconscious is accepted, "one finds oneself at the mercy of all manner of hypotheses concerning this unconscious life, hypotheses which cannot be controlled by any observation." Wundt himself tried to get around the issue by near sophistry, insisting that there were no unconscious elements to the psyche, just "more dimly conscious ones."[18] Jung had little patience with such attitudes, which were out to protect theory at the expense of facts. Unlike some later psychologists and biologists, who could accept instinctual behavior yet deny unconscious psychic processes, Wundt realized that his rejection of the unconscious also implied a rejection of instinctual behavior. Jung quotes Wundt on this subject:

> If the new-born animal really had an idea beforehand of all the actions it purposes [sic] to do, what a wealth of anticipated life-experiences would lie stored in the human and animal instincts, and how incomprehensible it would seem that not man alone, but animals too, acquire most things only through experience and practice![19]

As Edna Heidbreder noted in the quotation that opened this chapter, psychology came into existence late in the 19th century because of "the necessity of considering the observing organism in order to give a complete account of the observed universe." In other words, because science could no longer ignore the problems presented by Kant a hundred years earlier. Yet so deadly was the fear of mind, that it was impossible to examine the possibility that the human mind contained cognitive invariants (i.e., archetypes), which structured our sensory perception and organization, and to some extent predetermined our behavior.

Of course, Fechner stood outside this orthodoxy. Fechner felt that "the idea of a psychophysical threshold is of the utmost impor-

---

[18]C. G. Jung, *Collected Works*, Vol. 8, ¶ 349–351, for all quotes.
[19]C. G. Jung, *Collected Works*, Vol. 8, ¶ 352.

tance because it gives a firm foundation to that of the unconscious generally."[20] Unfortunately, Fechner's experimental techniques were adopted while his ideas were ignored. Experimental psychology was a new discipline and its members patterned themselves on stern, no-nonsense physicists like Helmholtz, not those they regarded as dreamy romantics. Experimental science requires just such discipline in order to be effective, but it is unfortunate that the *Zeitgeist* had little room for any non-physical phenomena like the psyche.

If early experimental psychologists had to deal with the psyche at all, they wanted it reduced to consciousness, and consciousness reduced to tiny little elements that could be experimentally introspected, as Wundt taught. Perhaps that was a sensible beginning approach to a complex area; however, in time, it grew too limiting. Experiments with a strange borderline phenomenon currently known as hypnotism, could have had a critical impact on both experimental and clinical psychology. However, as we will see, only clinical psychologists, hungry for tools to deal with the mentally ill, availed themselves of this new tool.

---

[20]Quotation in C. G. Jung, *Collected Works,* Vol. 8, ¶ 354, n. 18.

CHAPTER 6

⌒⌒

FOUNDERS OF CLINICAL PSYCHOLOGY

Write in order the words magnetism, mesmerism, hypnotism, hysteria, suggestion, *translate them into proper names, writing Van Helmont, Mesmer, Braid, Charcot, Bernheim, and you have the outline of (clinical) psychology . . . before Freud.*[1]

HEAVEN ABOVE, HEAVEN BELOW

Experimental psychology can trace its origins to the Renaissance rediscovery of the power of the conscious mind. In contrast, clinical psychology originated in the study of unconscious processes. This could have occurred through the study of dreams or myths, but in fact hypnotism was the first bridge to the unconscious mind.

This book has already shown that an unbroken train of thought can be traced from its beginning in the Renaissance to its culmination in experimental psychology. A second train of thought also began in the Renaissance and eventually led to clinical psychology. This line began with a mysterious figure of the high Renaissance, 16th-century physician Philippus Aureolus Bombast von Hohenheim, more commonly known as Theophrastus Paracelsus [1490–1541]. Paracelsus was both renowned and reviled, the most famous physician of the 16th century and one of its

---

1Edwin G. Boring, *A History of Experimental Psychology* (New York: Appleton-Century-Crofts, 1950), p. 694. Boring's emphasis.

PARACELSUS

most prolific authors. Both his fame for his incredible skill as a physician, and the angry dismissal of his work by many of his colleagues, were products of his vision of man and the universe.

The Renaissance rediscovered the power of careful observation. That observation could be turned outward toward the macro-world or inward toward the micro-world. 1543, for example, saw the publication of both Andreas Vesalius' *Concerning the Structure of the Human Body* (which established modern human anatomy) and Copernicus' *Concerning the Revolution of the Heavenly Bodies* (which established modern astronomy). Paracelsus, like Jung four centuries later, was interested less in one or the other of the two worlds than in the necessary connections between the macro- and micro-worlds.

Jung said "there can be no doubt that Paracelsus was influenced by the Hermetic idea of 'heaven above, heaven below.' "[2] The alchemical dictum "heaven above, heaven below" implied that reality was an interrelated whole, each of whose parts reflected the totality. This concept has already been mentioned in the discussion of Fechner's theories. In Paracelsus' words:

> . . . in every human being, there is a special heaven, whole and unbroken; . . . for heaven is man and man is heaven, and all men are one heaven, and heaven is only one man.[3]

---

[2] C. G. Jung, "Paracelsus the Physician," in *Collected Works, Vol. 15: The Spirit in Man, Art, and Literature* (Princeton: Princeton University Press, 1942), ¶ 31.

[3] Quotation in C. G. Jung, "Paracelsus the Physician," ¶ 31.

ANDREAS VESALIUS

Interestingly, Paracelsus felt that love was the connection between the seemingly separate worlds inhabited by each human being.

> First of all it is very necessary to tell of the compassion that must be innate in a physician.
>
> Where there is no love, there is no art.
>
> The practice of this art lies in the heart: if your heart is false, the physician within you will be false.[4]

The idea that love, or eros, is the supreme principle of relationship will resurface in the 20th century, first with Eros reduced to sexuality by Freud. Later Jung would restore Eros to his full dignity in his exploration of the connections between the conscious mind and the outer world on one side, and the unconscious mind and the inner world on the other. However, first we have to follow the twisting path that led from Paracelsus to Freud and Jung.

Animal Magnetism, Mesmerism, and Hypnotism

Paracelsus, with his desire to find the connections between the micro-world of the human, and the macro-world of the universe, was interested in astrology and alchemy, and the effects of magnetism.

> Paracelsus established the doctrine that magnets, like the stars, influence human bodies, and Van Helmont [a century later] inaugurated the doctrine of animal magnetism.[5]

Van Helmont taught:

> that a magnetic fluid radiates from all men and may be guided by their wills to influence the minds and bodies of others.[6]

---

[4] All Parcelsus quotations in C. G. Jung, "Paracelsus the Physician," ¶ 42.
[5] Edwin G. Boring, *A History of Experimental Psychology*, pp. 695–696.
[6] Edwin G. Boring, *A History of Experimental Psychology*, p. 116.

Franz Anton Mesmer [1734–1815], late in the 18th century, caught the imagination of all Europe with his startling cures using animal magnetism. The scientific community refused to accept such a concept and either denied Mesmer as a fraud, or attributed his success to some personal power that Mesmer alone possessed.

It was only in the first half of the 19th century that James Braid [1795–1860] was able to present the phenomenon of hypnotism in a form acceptable to the scientific community. Thus hypnotism

FRANZ ANTON MESMER

came to be marginally accepted three hundred years after Paracelsus revealed it to the Western World, two hundred years after Von Helmot popularized the term animal magnetism, fully fifty years after Mesmer demonstrated its efficacy to all of Europe. When a concept does not readily fit into the framework of science, the scientific community denies the concept if it can, ignores it if it cannot. There is a sense in which this is appropriate; a general world model which can be usefully applied to many cases is more useful than a collection of exceptions that have only partial application. But it is always the great discoverers who sense when an exception is important and when a new model, which includes the exception, needs to be developed. Our own time is filled with such exceptions, all begging to be included in some wider explanation of reality.

Before Braid, hypnosis had to exist on the fringe of scientific respectability. It was an interesting curiosity, but hardly something with which respectable doctors and scientists would dirty their hands. Braid's limited initial assumption that hypnosis was simply a physiological phenomenon made the study of hypnosis acceptable to the scientific community. Prior to Braid, scientists theorized that animal magnetism resided in the *mesmerist*. The key shift in Braid's presentation, which made it acceptable to science, was to shift the responsibility from the physician to the patient. In Braid's early views, patients were mesmerized because they fixated on something until they paralyzed themselves.

> Later he came to recognize more clearly the importance of the factor of suggestion in inducing the phenomena, and his emphasis shifted even more from the physiological to the psychological aspect of the state.[7]

It is interesting to speculate what would have happened if Braid had initially presented suggestion as the cause of hypnosis. Would this have been dismissed as occultism in the same way that animal magnetism was dismissed? Was it only because Braid first presented a physiological explanation that hypnotism acquired any validity whatsoever?

Currently, most of the academic experimental research on hypnotism is performed by behavioral scientists, and it is once again common to dismiss hypnotism. They largely ignore the vast body of clinical hypnotic case studies as irrelevant. J. P. Sutcliffe, for example, dismissed the late Milton Erickson [1901–1980][8] as credulous. Sutcliffe argues that all of hypnotism can be explained as either (1) simulation of a hypnotic state by the patient; or (2) delusion on the part of the patient.[9] The central problem for clinical psychologists is that if hypnotic trance is accepted as a separate and distinct state of consciousness, the door is open for a general concept of *altered states of consciousness*.[10] And altered states of conscious-

---

[7] Edwin G. Boring, *A History of Experimental Psychology*, p. 128.

[8] A hypnotherapist of legendary ability, who was considered by many the world's greatest medical hypnotherapist.

[9] Ernest R. Hilgard, *The Experience of Hypnosis* (New York: Harvest/Harcourt Brace, 1965), pp. 14–20.

[10] As experimental psychologist and parapsychologist Charles Tart first termed it. See Charles T. Tart, ed., *Altered States of Consciousness* (New York: Anchor Books, 1969). Also see Charles T. Tart, *States of Consciousness* (El Cerrito, CA: Psychological Processes, 1975).

ness, of course, imply the existence of an organized unconscious. And that is anathema. Once again, experimental and clinical psychology proceed in very different directions.[11]

The Value of Subjective Experience in Psychology

The recognition that subjective experience was worthy of consideration was of central importance to those physicians who founded clinical psychology. Their job was not disinterested research into the nature of human psychology; their job was curing desperately ill fellow human beings. Clinical psychologists had no hope of helping their patients without acknowledging the importance of the patients' subjective experiences. Though far too frequently, they would try to discount the subjective experience as mere ravings, still they were far more likely than an experimental psychologist to at least be interested in the experience.

Thus the lines were initially drawn between experimental and clinical psychology. Interestingly, today to some extent those walls are coming down to the mutual benefit of both sides. Behaviorists have moved into clinical psychology and many have broadened their stance to include subjective responses, and even more importantly, the need for humanism to temper scientific objectivity. Clinical psychologists have learned the power of the scientific method, have realized that it does not have to be dehumanizing in the right hands. As an example, the new scientific theory of chaos and complexity offers a possibility of a scientific paradigm that can be equally acceptable to experimental and clinical psychologists. Still, there is a long way to go, and a deep breach remains between the two approaches.

---

[11]See Robert A. Baker, *They Call it Hypnosis* (Buffalo, NY: Prometheus Books, 1990). Baker provides a careful summary of all sides on this issue, though he totally denies the existence of a trance state. Also see Andre M. Weitzenhoffer, *The Practice of Hypnotism*, 2 vols. (New York: John Wiley & Sons, 1989) for an extended treatment of how hypnotism is actually used by both clinical and experimental psychologists. Weitzenhoffer, like most practicing hypnotherapists, does accept the existence of altered states of consciousness.

JEAN MARTIN CHARCOT

Jean Martin Charcot [1825–1893] was appointed at the Saltpêtrière clinic in France in 1862. Shortly after his appointment, he established a neurological clinic there, soon to be the most famous clinic in Europe. He specialized in patients who would now be classified as *neurotic*.[12] The majority of the patients at that time were women, and therefore their condition was dubbed *hysteria* (from the Greek for uterus: *hystera*). Psychologists are now quite aware that men are as prone to *neurosis* as women, but until very recently have simply been more reluctant than women to discuss their emotional problems.[13]

JEAN MARTIN CHARCOT

In any case, Charcot treated these patients with the new tool of hypnosis, with some success. He ignored Braid's later theory, that hypnosis was caused by suggestion, and preferred to consider both hysteria and hypnosis as physiological conditions of women.

> The similarity between the symptoms of hypnosis and hysteria led Charcot to think that hypnotizability is characteristic of hysteria and in a sense a symptom of it. That was a mistake.[14]

---

[12] Terms like neurotic unfortunately indicate that we still haven't come very far in labeling those suffering from emotional pain as somehow inferior to the rest of us.

[13] For example, in *Under Saturn's Shadow: The Wounding and Healing of Men* (Toronto: Inner City Books, 1994), p. 7, Jungian analyst James Hollis says that "twelve years ago, the ratio of women to men analysands in my practice was nine to one. Currently I see more men by a ratio of six to four. I believe this shift is replicated in the offices of other therapists."

[14] Edwin G. Boring, *A History of Experimental Psychology*, p. 698.

Charcot was in the ideal position to discover what Freud was later to term the *unconscious*. By unconscious, Freud meant literally that portion of our thoughts, feelings, and memories of which we have no conscious awareness. Charcot was treating hysteric patients in whom unconscious material was constantly coming to the surface of their minds. He was using hypnosis, which cut past any conscious prohibitions and gave him the opportunity to explore deep unconscious material. Unfortunately, because he regarded hypnosis as merely another evidence of hysteria, and because he considered hysteria to be a physiological complaint of women, he never took advantage of his opportunity.

PIERRE JANET

Pierre Janet [1859–1947] and Freud both studied under Charcot at his neurological clinic, though Freud only briefly. Janet was not only Charcot's student, but his successor as head of the clinic. Janet had several advantages over Charcot in furthering the study of the unconscious mind. First, he had Charcot's work on which to build. Second and more important, Janet was a much broader thinker than Charcot, with a background not only in medicine but also in academic psychology and philosophy. He became interested in hypnosis, not as a symptom of hysteria, and not only as an individual phenomenon, but as one of a number of processes that seemed to bypass conscious control. His life's work was, to use the title of his great youthful work, *L'Autotisme Psychologique* (the psychology of automatic response).[15]

> In 1892 Janet's main argument about hysteria was that it is a splitting of the personality, caused by a concentration of consciousness on one system of ideas and its retraction from others.[16]

---

[15]Pierre Janet, *L'Autotisme Psychologique* (Paris, 1889).
[16]Edwin G. Boring, *A History of Experimental Psychology*, p. 700.

Most practicing clinical psychologists would attest to the accuracy of Janet's description of this state; neurosis is indeed often characterized by a withdrawal of energy from normal areas and over-concentration in neurotic areas. For example, in a sexually repressed time, such as the Victorian era when Freud and Janet saw hysteric patients, neurosis centered around sexuality. In the present time, where there is an excess of sexual freedom and far too little outer stability, neurosis most normally centers on problems of self-definition.[17]

Much of Jung's work centered on accurate descriptions of exactly how such shifts of energy occurred. He realized that the area in which neurosis chooses to operate is a product of the culture and the time; thus, the over-concentration of attention is a symptom, not a cause. Charcot used hypnosis to release unconscious processes, but interpreted their cause as physiological. Janet realized that hypnosis provided an example of a phenomenon involving not merely physiological processes, but also unconscious psychological processes, and that there were a number of such unconscious processes.

However, it was still left to Freud to discover the unconscious mind, though even Freud never fully realized the scope of the unconscious, due to his mistaken belief that repressed sexuality was universal, not a product of a particular cultural. Jung, able to build on each of his great predecessors, was able to go further in his explorations, and would surely have echoed the words of Newton: "If I have seen further than other men, it is only because I have stood on the shoulders of giants."[18]

[17] Rollo May, *Love and Will* (New York: Laurel/Dell, 1969), pp. 38–39.
[18] W. W. Rouse Ball, *A Short Account of the History of Mathematics*, 1908 (New York: Dover Publications, reprint, 1960), p. 349.

CHAPTER 7

CANTOR'S SET THEORY OF TRANSFINITE NUMBERS

*Both in his time and in the years since, Cantor's name has sig-
nified both controversy and schism. Ultimately, transfinite set
theory has served to divide mathematicians into distant camps
determined largely by their irreconcilable views of the nature of
mathematics in general and of the status of the infinite in particular.*[1]

A RIFT IN MATHEMATICS

Late in the 19th century, while psychology was just beginning to
emerge as a separate field, mathematics was struggling to remake itself. Analytic geometry and calculus had virtually created mathematics as a modern field in the 17th century. Over the next two
hundred years, mathematicians fully explored the implications of
these new ideas, and now found themselves gripped by a new desire for rigor. They began to examine closely, almost philosophi-
cally, the nature of number itself.

The initial result of their examination was a powerful new
mathematical theory: the theory of sets. Set theory was to change
modern mathematics to much the same extent that Kant's concepts changed modern philosophy two hundred years earlier.
Though the product of many mathematicians, it reached its fullest
development in the theory of transfinite numbers, developed by

---

[1]Joseph Warren Dauben, *Georg Cantor: His Mathematics and Philosophy of the Infinite* (Princeton: Princeton University Press, 1979), p. 1.

GEORG CANTOR

the greatest mathematician of this period: Georg Cantor. Cantor—like Gödel after him—held a deeply spiritual belief that numbers were God's building blocks. In Cantor's hands, set theory was to reveal hidden mysteries: the nature of the infinite.

However, paradoxes appeared in Cantor's theory, paradoxes that threatened all of mathematics. Mathematicians began to split into opposing camps, based less on purely mathematical considerations, than on their philosophical model of reality, in much the same manner that the paradoxes of Hume and Berkeley had split philosophy a century-and-a-half earlier.

One group—the *constructivists*—took a similar stance to that of the pragmatists in philosophy, basically "a pox on your house." They argued that if infinity created paradoxes, then mathematics must restrict itself to the finite; i.e., to constructive proofs that involve only a finite number of steps. Unfortunately, any such mathematics is so restricted as to hardly qualify under the term mathematics. The two most significant new approaches were those of: (1) the *formalists*, and (2) the *logicians*. The former, under the leadership of David Hilbert in Germany and Giuseppe Peano in Italy, hoped to preserve most of Cantor's theory by presenting mathematics as a fully developed formal axiomatic system on the lines of geometry. The latter approach, which reached its apotheosis in the *Principia Mathematica* of Bertrand Russell and Alfred North Whitehead, hoped to reduce mathematics to symbolic logic.[2] In

---

[2] See A. N. Whitehead and Bertrand Russell, *Principia Mathematica* (Cambridge: Cambridge University Press, 1910, 1912, 1913).

1931, Kurt Gödel was to prove that both approaches were impossible. He was able to do so because he understood that mathematics is more than logic, more than a formal axiomatic system; mathematics deals with meaning: archetypal meaning.

This chapter will present the development of set theory, culminating in Cantor's theory of transfinite numbers. After shifting our ground to Sigmund Freud in the following chapter, we will continue with the false starts of the formalists and the logicians. Gödel's ideas will be presented in parallel with Jung's throughout the remainder of the book.

WEIERSTRASS' ATTEMPT TO DEFINE INFINITY IN FINITE TERMS

It is essentially a merit of the scientific activity of Weierstrass that there exists at present in analysis full agreement and certainty concerning the course of such types of reasoning which are based on the concept of irrational number and of limit in general.[3]

If mathematics only dealt with finite numbers, there would have been no need for set theory. As we pointed out earlier,[4] in the 18th century mathematicians began to question the blithe attitude both Newton and Leibniz took toward the strange, infinitely small quantities on which their calculus was based. Earlier we provided an understandable, non-mathematical description of a limit. By

KARL WEIERSTRASS

---

[3] Quotation by mathematician David Hilbert in Dirk J. Struik, *A Concise History of Mathematics* (New York: Dover, 1987), p. 161.
[4] See chapter 4.

the mid-19th century, mathematicians were ready to tighten that description. German mathematician Karl Weierstrass [1815–1907] developed the first key concept: though infinity could not by its very nature be delimited, at any point, it could be described in finite terms.

We need a little more mathematical detail so we can see what Weierstrass came up with (but don't worry, not too much). You will recall our earlier description of how limits work in calculus. In brief, we said that we could cover a shape with rectangles, then let the number of rectangles get larger and larger, while the rectangles themselves got narrower and narrower. Each time, we would sum the areas of the rectangles to get an approximation of the area inside the irregular shape. As the number of rectangles grew, the approximation would get closer and closer to a limit, which would be the actual area.

Weierstrass asked what do we really mean when we say that the sum approaches a limit? Simply that the sum of the rectangles can be made to differ from the limit by as small a quantity as we desire. More explicitly, if any desired difference is named, it is possible to pick a sufficient number of rectangles that the difference between their areas and the limit will be less than that quantity. For example, say the limit is calculated to be 25 square inches using calculus. Then pick some very tiny number for the difference: say one thousandth of a square inch. Weierstrass says that we can find a large enough number of rectangles that their sum will be within one thousandth of a square inch of 25 square inches. We'll say, just as an example, that it takes 250 rectangles to do this. If we decide to pick a still smaller difference, say one millionth of a square inch, perhaps it might take 5,000 rectangles. But no matter how small the difference desired, it is possible to come up with a sufficient number of rectangles so that the sum of their areas differs from the limit by less than that difference.

Now, of course, Weierstrass stated this in a rigorous mathematical form,[5] but that is of no particular significance to our dis-

---

[5] The term "Weierstrassian rigor" became synonymous with mathematical rigor in his time. See Dirk J. Struik, *A Concise History of Mathematics*, p. 160.

cussion. What is important is that he was able to rigorously define limits without ever mentioning infinity.

Weierstrass used an extension of the same technique to discuss irrational numbers. As early as the sixth century B.C., Pythagoras had discovered that $\sqrt{2}$ (i.e., the square root of 2) could not be expressed as the ratio of two counting numbers (i.e., 1, 2, 3, . . .). Over time, mathematicians had come to realize that there were a huge number of such numbers, which they called irrational—not a ratio—in contrast to so-called *rational* numbers like ½, or 23/47. Though this use of irrational originally had no pejorative meaning, it was also true that the term became singularly appropriate because of the degree of unease it caused mathematicians. We have already encountered a similar example, when we saw that mathematicians were so resistant to numbers like $\sqrt{-1}$ that they felt compelled to call them *imaginary* in order to express their displeasure.[6] We will encounter the same sort of resistance by mathematicians as we move on to Cantor's Theory of Transfinite Sets. And, it's fascinating that it was once again a comparison between rational and irrational numbers which caused their distaste.

Because irrational numbers could not be expressed as a simple ratio of integers, mathematicians were forced to use mathematically complex equations involving infinite series in order to calculate their value. This meant that they presented the same sort of problems involving infinity as calculus. Weierstrass got around this problem using a similar technique to the one that was so successful in dealing with limits. He defined an irrational number using a set containing a sequence of rational numbers that approached the actual value of the irrational number as a limit.

For example, the $\sqrt{2}$ which caused Pythagoras so much trouble, can be expressed in decimal notation as 1.414213 . . . (here our 3 little dots ". . ." have to do double duty, and mean not only that there is no end to the decimal expansion, but also that neither is there any definable pattern to it). Weierstrass would define the square root of 2 as the set (1.4, 1.41, 1.414, 1.4142, 1.41421, 1.414213, . . .). If we pick some tiny difference again, say $1/10^4$

---

[6]See chapter 4.

(i.e., one ten-thousandth), we know that the 4th member of the set (i.e., 1.4142) is less than $1/10^4$ from the actual value of the $\sqrt{2}$. Similarly for a desired difference less than $1/10^6$ (i.e., one millionth), we have only to move to the 6th member of the set.

Once again, as with limits in calculus, infinity is captured with only a finite set of numbers. It is important to stress that Weierstrass didn't say that this set approached the irrational number as a limit; he actually said that the set was the irrational number. Though this might seem an insignificant difference, he was shifting to a new frame of reference: set theory.

Since Weierstrass (and many other mathematicians from that time to the present) found sets so useful, we need to define just what a set is. A set is merely a collection of things of the same kind; e.g., the set of books about logic is composed of all the books about logic; the set of proofs for the existence of God is composed of all such proofs. Each item of the given kind is called a member of the set. It's important to grasp that the set is not the same as the members—the set is the collection, the assemblage, not the things assembled. In Weierstrass' case, he was considering sets of numbers; the concept of a set was so useful because it was not limited to numbers, but could include anything whatsoever.

Weierstrass' definition of the irrationals was important because it shifted the emphasis from an infinite series to a set where any irrational could be defined to any degree of precision with only a finite number of members. However, clever as this technique was, many mathematicians objected to it as a trick, since any set which defined an irrational number still had an infinite number of members, regardless of whether Weierstrass was able to limit his discussion to at most a finite number of the set's members. These mathematicians were never to be satisfied by any subsequent improvement on Weierstrass' technique. The shift to set theory, however, opened the door for most mathematicians, and prepared the way for still more clever attempts at describing the number line. Drawing on the concepts of set theory, both Georg Cantor and Richard Dedekind [1831–1916] developed new definitions of irrational numbers. Dedekind's technique, called the *Dedekind Cut*, has become traditional.

The Dedekind Cut

> Dedekind came to the conclusion that the essence of the
> continuity of a line segment is not due to a vague hang-
> togetherness, but to an exactly opposite property—the
> nature of the division of the segment into two parts by a
> point on the segment.[7]

Before we describe Dedekind's technique, we need to briefly discuss a term that will figure heavily throughout the rest of this book:
the *continuum*. The continuum is another name for the number line
(figure 7.1), hence a geometric concept involving space. Alternately, the continuum is the full set of all *real* numbers (i.e., both rational and irrational numbers), hence an arithmetic concept
involving numbers. Every spot on the number line corresponds to
either a rational or irrational number; going the other direction,
every rational or irrational number has its place on the number line.

We first met the continuum, extended in both horizontal and
vertical direction to describe a plane, in our discussion of René
Descartes' analytic geometry.[8] You will recall that Descartes discovered how to translate geometric positions and shapes into numeric
coordinates and algebraic equations. We met the continuum again
in the discussion of Gauss' geometric interpretation of imaginary
numbers.[9] Descartes had realized geometry could be reduced to
numbers; Gauss realized these special numbers could be reduced to
geometry. Obviously the continuum is the place where arithmetic
and geometry meet.

FIGURE 7.1. The Number Line or Continuum.

---

[7]Carl B. Boyer, *A History of Mathematics* (Princeton: Princeton University Press, 1969), p.
607.
[8]See chapter 2.
[9]See chapter 4.

We will look at the continuum, but restrict ourselves to the rationals. Remember, these are the numbers that represent fractions, that can be calculated by dividing one integer into another. Because the irrational numbers lie between the rationals, our line segment really has holes if we could look closely enough. However, since we can make fractions as small as we want, there are always more rationals; hence we could never find a microscope powerful enough to show us the holes.

Dedekind asked us to imagine a knife with an infinitely thin blade (i.e., it has no thickness at all) which cuts the continuum into two segments. Now every rational number to the left of the blade is clearly less than every rational number to the right of the blade. Dedekind said that there are three possibilities, and between them they describe all the rational and irrational numbers.

(1) There may be a biggest number in the leftmost segment; or

(2) There may be a smallest number in the rightmost segment; or

(3) There may be neither a biggest number in the leftmost segment; nor a smallest number in the rightmost segment.

In each of the first two cases, the Dedekind cut has exactly hit a rational number; hence Dedekind defines that particular rational number by the split of the continuum into two sets. In the latter case, the cut must have hit an irrational number. Dedekind defines every number—whether rational or irrational—by the two sets created by cutting the continuum in half with the Dedekind cut.

Now this may not be obvious. Take the rational cases first. If Dedekind's cut exactly hits a rational it has to end up in either the set to the left, or the set to the right (since the blade takes up no space at all). If it's in the left set, it has to be the biggest rational number there. Otherwise, it wouldn't have been to the right of the other numbers. Similarly if it's in the right set, it has to be the smallest rational number (since by definition it was to the left of all those numbers). Finally, if the cut landed on an irrational number, there is no end to how many rational numbers on each side get closer and closer to its value (remember that Weierstrass likewises used an infinite sequence of rational numbers to define each irrational number.)[10]

We can safely ignore Cantor's definition, which also used the concept of sets, as it is more difficult to easily describe, and since Dedekind's cut has become traditional. With these new more rigorous set theoretic definitions of number in place, it was a natural next step to begin to compare the set of rationals with the set of the irrationals in various ways, especially to see if one set was larger than the other. And that finally brings us to Cantor's theory of transfinite numbers.

CANTOR'S THEORY OF TRANSFINITE NUMBERS

In 1874, Georg Cantor [1845–1918] published his *Mengenlehre* (*Theory of Sets*), a systematic presentation of his theory of sets, in which he offered a new way of looking at infinity. As we have already discussed, from the 18th century on, mathematicians had become increasingly aware that there were problems involved in dealing with the infinite. Accordingly, they approached infinity with utmost caution, when they couldn't avoid it entirely. In 1831, mathematician Karl Friedrich Gauss[11] railed against infinity:

> I protest against the use of infinite magnitude as something completed, which is never permissible in mathematics. Infinity is merely a way of speaking, the true meaning being a limit which certain ratios approach indefinitely close, while others are permitted to increase without restriction.[12]

---

[10] Later Bertrand Russell realized that either of the two sets created by Dedekind's cut defines the other as well. Russell, therefore, suggested that the leftmost set alone would suffice to define all numbers. See Carl B. Boyer, *A History of Mathematics*, pp. 607–608 for this fact, as well as much of the above information on the Dedekind Cut. Also see Eric Temple Bell, *Men of Mathematics* (New York: Simon and Schuster, 1937/1965), pp. 519–522.

[11] Whose discovery of the geometric interpretation of imaginary numbers we discussed in chapter 4.

[12] Eric Temple Bell, *Men of Mathematics*, p. 556.

But Cantor's discoveries were over a half-century later, and much had been learned in that interim. He took the opposite tack from Gauss, arguing that:

> The uncritical rejection of the legitimate actual infinite is no lesser a violation of the nature of things . . . which must be taken as they are.[13]

It was with the "legitimate actual infinite" that Cantor was concerned, and he was convinced such infinite quantities were a part of things "as they are." For example, there is clearly no end to the integers; if a largest integer could be conceived, merely add one to it and it's no longer the largest. There is also clearly no end to the points on a line provided that a point is understood to be without dimension. On the surface, it seems that all one can safely assert is that there is an infinite number of positive integers, an infinite number of points on a line (and you will remember from our brief discussion of the continuum that the number of points on a line is equivalent to the real numbers; i.e., both the rational and irrational numbers). Cantor had the brilliance to question whether these infinities were the same size. Lest this sound like the medieval scholastic arguments about the number of angels who could stand on the head of a pin, the reader should be aware that Cantor found a way of quantifying infinity, and thus answering his own question.

> . . . whatever "number" as applied to infinite sets may mean, we certainly want it to have the property that the number of objects belonging to some class does not change if, leaving the objects the same, one changes in any way whatsoever their properties or mutual relations (e.g., their colors or their distribution in space).[14]

---

[13] Eric Temple Bell, *Men of Mathematics*, pp. 556–557.
[14] Kurt Gödel, "What is Cantor's Continuum Problem?" in Solomon Feferman (editor-in-chief), *Kurt Gödel, Collected Works, Volume II: Publications 1938–1974* (New York: Oxford University Press, 1990), p. 254.

Let's return to the concept of a set. What does it mean to say that two sets have the same number of members? For example, what does it mean to say that the set of fingers has the same number of members as the set of toes? If we think deeply about it, it merely means that we can pair off members of each of the two sets and have no members left over in either set. In our example, we could place each of our ten fingers on one of our ten toes.

Notice that it wouldn't matter what finger we match with what toe as long as we were careful not to pair any finger with two toes or any toe with two fingers. Further, we could define a *cardinal number*, in this case 10, which would characterize the number of members in each set. Having developed the cardinal number 10, it could then be used to describe the number of members of any set which can be paired off with the set of fingers. We would describe each as having the same *cardinality*. This provides an unequivocal way of defining numbers in terms of the size of sets (more exactly, by comparing sets to see if they are the same size).

This method of counting by pairing the members of one set with the members of another is commonly termed the *pigeon-hole* technique. Cantor found that the pigeon-hole technique produced surprising results with infinite sets. For example, he discovered that there were exactly as many even integers as there were both odd and even integers. He reasoned that for every integer i in the set of all integers, he could match i with the integer $2i$ in the set of even integers. For example, *1* in the set of all integers would be matched with *2* in the set of even integers, *2* with *4*, *3* with *6*, etc. No matter what integer you named in either set, this method uniquely defines the integer it corresponds to in the other set. Thus the pigeon-hole technique proved that the set of even integers is the same size as the set of all integers. Try it if it doesn't seem reasonable. At first it will seem obvious that there are more integers than even integers, since the odd integers are left out. But that isn't the point. If the two sets can be matched without any members of either set being left over, then they have the same cardinality. The problem isn't with the method, it's with infinity itself.

Cantor could use the same logic to show that the set of numbers evenly divisible by three is also just as big as the set of all integers. In fact the particular multiple made no difference; the set of numbers evenly divisible by a billion is still just as big as the set of all integers. Going in the other direction produced the same result. The integers are a sub-set of the rational numbers (remember: the fractions). For example, 2 can be expressed as 2/1 as a fraction; 3 as 3/1, etc. But think of all the other fractions: ½, 1/3, 357/962, etc. Surely there are more fractions than integers! Instead, Cantor used his pigeon-hole technique to prove that the set of rational numbers had exactly as many members as the set of integers.[15] This was a very surprising result indeed! In fact, Cantor proved that *any infinite sub-set of the set of rational numbers contains exactly the same number of members!* All have the same cardinality, which Cantor termed $\aleph_0$.[16] This number is commonly referred to as *countably infinite*, since all such sets can be paired off with the counting numbers 1, 2, 3, and so forth.

Cantor then asked if every infinite set was countably infinite; i.e., is every infinite set the same size as every other infinite set? The answer to that was even more surprisingly a resounding no; e.g., the infinity of real (i.e., both rational and irrational) numbers was found to be larger than the infinity of rational numbers. We have already mentioned several times that $\sqrt{2}$ was discovered to be an irrational number by Pythagoras. Another irrational number most people recognize is π (i.e., *pi*), since most of us were taught in school that the area of a circle is πr^2 (where *r* is the radius of the circle). On the surface, it would appear that surely there were just a few such strange numbers, and that most real numbers could be expressed as fractions. Appearances can be deceiving. In our discussion of the Dedekind cut, we have already had a hint there are a great many irrationals, since we could find them filling the holes between rational numbers on the number line. Cantor demonstrated just how many such holes there were.

---

[15] His matching technique will be omitted here in the interest of brevity.

[16] Aleph ($\aleph$) is the first letter of the Hebrew alphabet, so seemed a fitting choice to Cantor for the new type of number.

His proof is a clever application of the pigeon-hole technique which can be followed by non-mathematicians.[17] If it were true that the cardinality of the real numbers was the same as the cardinality of the rational numbers, we could pair up real numbers with integers (since both the rational numbers and the integers have cardinality $\aleph_0$, there wouldn't be any real numbers left over).

As we saw earlier in pairing up our fingers with our toes, it doesn't make any difference what pairing technique we use as long as it pairs every member of one set uniquely with a single member of the other set. For purposes of illustration only, let's assume that such a pairing technique has been developed for pairing the real numbers with the integers, and let's assume further that, within that pairing, the integer *1* corresponds to the real number *.20357 . . .* ; *2* corresponds to *.053489 . . .* ; *3* to *.8693217 . . .* , etc. I want to stress that any other pairing would be equally acceptable; we have just picked arbitrary numbers for our example.

Cantor was able to construct a real number which was not paired off with any integer. For example, we can construct a number which differs from the real number paired with the integer *1* in the first digit; from the real number paired with the integer *2* in the second digit; and so forth. Using our example above, this constructed number would contain anything other than a *2* in the first digit (*.20357 . . .*), anything other than a *5* in the second digit (*.053489 . . .*), anything other than a *9* in the third digit (*.8693217 . . .*), etc.

Because of how we constructed this number, it cannot be contained in the set which was originally paired off with the integers. If we insist that it is, all we have to do is ask which integer it pairs off with. Let's say it is assumed to pair off with the integer *529*. By the method of construction, we know that it differs from the number actually paired with *529* in the *529*th digit. Therefore, the real numbers cannot be paired off with the integers. And it is easy to see just how enormously large the reals are by considering this method of pairing.

---

[17]As with most highly original discoveries, Cantor's original proof was much more complex. Because this was such an important discovery, he continued to develop cleaner proofs. The proof we are describing is commonly called the *diagonal proof* and is one of the most famous proofs in mathematics.

For every number in the original paired set, our technique could have 9 possible alternatives that weren't in the set. So we could easily find $9 \times 9 \times 9$ . . . (continuing on a countably infinite number of times) additional numbers missing from the set. And there are many, many more missing numbers that just don't fit into our construction technique. The cardinality of the real numbers, which Cantor termed c for the continuum, is therefore greater that the cardinality of the integers. Sets of this size (or larger) are commonly referred to as *uncountably infinite*. The real numbers cannot be paired with the rational numbers because there are too many holes between the real numbers, holes filled with irrational numbers. Though we won't bother to prove it here, in fact there are so many irrational numbers that the real numbers can be paired with the irrational numbers. Hence there are uncountably many irrationals, and only countably many rationals.

At first all of this seems like some sort of a cheat, but upon deeper reflection it can be seen to be profound. First, it provides an unambiguous definition of size: two sets are the same size if their members can be paired off, using some easily understood pairing technique. This holds true both for finite and infinite sets. Second, the distinction between finite and infinite sets is also unambiguously defined: an infinite set is a set which can be put into a one-to-one relationship (this is a formal mathematical way of expressing the pigeon-hole technique) with a proper sub-set of itself (a subset is one in which some of the members of the full set are left out). Clearly that isn't true of any finite set—if we try to pair a finite set with any of its subsets, there are invariably members left over. However, when we come to infinite sets, this isn't true: as we have already seen, the rational numbers can be paired up with the integers, the even integers, etc. Each is, of course, a sub-set of the rationals. Similarly the real numbers can be paired up with the irrational numbers, which are again a sub-set, since the reals are composed of both rationals and irrationals.

Of course, the most provocative part of Cantor's set theory was his demonstration that not all infinite sets are of equal size: countably infinite sets such as the integers can not be matched with uncountably infinite sets such as the real numbers. But was that all? Did the integers and the real numbers take care of all of infinity?

In order to answer that question, Cantor provided still another concept: the *power set*.

Power Sets & the Continuum Hypothesis

For any set, Cantor defined its power set as the set of all the sub-sets of the original set. Key here is that the power set is one level higher than the original set: its members are themselves sets. For example, let's take the set of primary colors. We'll use brackets { } to define a set. So the set in question is {red, yellow, and blue}. The power set would consist of all the sub-sets of this set; first taken one at a time, then two at a time, finally three at a time.[18] So the power set would be: **{**{red}, {yellow}, {blue}, {red, yellow}, {red, blue}, {yellow, blue}, and {red, yellow, blue}**}**. (I've used bold brackets **{}** to indicate that the power set is a set, and normal brackets {} to indicate that its members are sets.)

Another way of looking at a power set is to consider it as composed of all the relationships between the original members of a set, all the ways they can be linked together in any combination. It is easy to see that as the original set gets bigger, the power set gets much, much bigger.[19] In our little example, the set of primary colors had three members, while the power set had eight (including the null set as the eighth). A set with four members would have a power set with sixteen members, and so forth. Cantor was able to demonstrate that the power set is always of a higher order of cardinality than the original set, *even if the set is infinite.* Thus the power set of the rational numbers has a cardinality bigger than $\aleph_0$, which Cantor termed $\aleph_1$. It in turn has a power set $\aleph_2$, and so on. So there is no biggest size for infinity, since we can always create a bigger infinity by taking the power set of the previous set.

---

[18]Actually even taken zero at a time. A special set called the *null set* was needed to complete set theory, just as zero is needed to complete the number line. In all of our discussions of the continuum and real numbers, we have implicitly included zero.

[19]The power set has 2^n members, where n is the size of the original set. Hence the notation 2^n is used to stand for the power set of any set of cardinality n (remember that cardinality is the same as size within Cantor's theory.

Cantor proposed that $\aleph_1 = c$; i.e., that the cardinality of the power set of the integers is the same size as the cardinality of the real numbers.[20] In other words, even though there is no end to infinity, Cantor proposed that all infinities are simply power sets of the integers. This seemingly innocuous proposal is called the *continuum hypothesis*, and is perhaps the most important unsolved problem in mathematics. It is critical because it asks the essential question that has occupied mathematicians and scientists since Pythagoras: is the whole world made up of the counting numbers, which can be seen as archetypes of the mind? Jung, with no mathematical sophistication at all, was to propose much the same thing in his late years. Though as sophisticated mathematically as Jung was psychologically, Kurt Gödel mulled over this same concept throughout his life.[21] For Cantor it was critical, because without it, his theory of transfinite numbers was incomplete. We will return to the continuum hypothesis and discuss it at some length later in this book, but now, before we leave Cantor, we need to address a more obvious paradox which soon appeared in his startling new view of reality, one which would later be found to be have implications far beyond set theory.

THE PARADOXES OF INFINITY

The results obtained by Cantor had already [toward 1900] so transformed thinking that these contradictions were called paradoxes—which sounds ever so much less disturbing.[22]

---

[20] Which, as you will recall, is the same as the number of points on a line.

[21] As we will see, together Gödel and mathematician Paul Cohen were able to prove that the continuum hypothesis was unprovable within formal set theory. Quite a discovery: an unprovable proposal! This was something that was implied by Gödel's Proof. However, both Gödel and Cohen firmly believed the opposite of Cantor and Jung: that the continuum hypothesis would eventually be proved false, within some more perfect set theory of the future.

[22] Quotation by Henri Lebesgue in Lucienne Félix, *The Modern Aspect of Mathematics* (New York: Basic Books, 1960), p. 49.

> It is not a little ironic in light of the subsequent history
> that the first mathematician to discover the antinomies of
> set theory was Cantor himself.[23]

We have already mentioned the first missing element in set theory: Cantor's inability to prove the continuum hypothesis. Cantor himself discovered another seeming paradox in his set theory. What if we consider the *set of all sets*. Since he felt that all sets could be clearly defined within his set theory, there seemed no logical inconsistency in defining such a set, which would contain all other sets as members. But what then of its power set; i.e., the set of all its subsets? By the definition of a power set, it had to be of larger cardinality than the set of all sets. But since the power set was a set, wasn't it by definition a member of the set of all sets? In that case, the power set had to be of equal or lesser cardinality than the set of all sets.

When Cantor discovered this, he regarded it not as a logical problem to be solved within set theory, but as a proof of the essentially mystical nature of the universe, of which set theory was a model. The set of all sets was an unfathomable concept, beyond human understanding in much the same way as the unpronounceable name of god in Judaism.

> . . . Although he [Cantor] does not seem to have consciously or immediately recognized the inconsistencies of set theory, he always emphasized the impossibility of a largest cardinal number, which he originally interpreted as meaning that the set of all cardinal numbers was an *incomprehensible one*. The set of all transfinite numbers, like the absolute itself, could be acknowledged, but it could never be completely understood . . . . He always regarded the absolutely infinite succession of transfinite numbers as a thoroughly appropriate symbol for the Absolute.[24]

---

[23]Joseph Warren Dauben, *Georg Cantor: His Mathematics and Philosophy of the Infinite*, p. 241.
[24]Joseph Warren Dauben, *Georg Cantor: His Mathematics and Philosophy of the Infinite*, p. 245.

This religious interpretation was unacceptable to other mathematicians, who split into opposing camps, some taking this as a sufficient reason to dismiss Cantor's theory out-of-hand, others attempting to find a logical way to plug what they regarded as small holes in a magnificent edifice. We will return to this issue later in this book, when we look at David Hilbert's and Giuseppe Peano's program of formally axiomatizing mathematics, and Bertrand Russell's attempt to reduce mathematics to logic.[25] For now, the reader will have to accept both that Cantor's theory of transfinite numbers still stands as mathematics' most brilliant edifice, and that the problems presented in set theory proved to be unsolvable. In fact, in proving them to be unsolvable, Kurt Gödel revolutionized mathematics, and beyond mathematics, potentially all of science.

---

[25]See chapter 9.

CHAPTER 8

SIGMUND FREUD

Freud's intimate knowledge of human nature made him both pessimistic and critical. He did not have a very high opinion of the bulk of mankind. He felt that the irrational forces in man's nature are so strong that the rational forces have little chance of success against them.[1]

[Freud] was the last great representative of rationalism, and his tragic fate was to end his life when this rationalism had been defeated . . .[2]

FREUD'S BACKGROUND

In our earlier discussion of Newton,[3] we saw that though he was one of the great innovators of all time, he was equally a representative of his times. The concepts that would lead Newton to his great theories of light and gravitation were in the air. Similarly, when Darwin developed his theory of evolution by natural selection, the concept of evolution was in the air, waiting to be expressed by the proper mind. We saw the same phenomenon in mathematics with the discoveries of non-Euclidean geometry and with imaginary numbers. When it is time for a new archetypal idea to emerge, it

---

[1]Calvin S. Hall, *A Primer of Freudian Psychology* (New York: Mentor/New American Library, 1954), p. 20.

[2]Erich Fromm, *Sigmund Freud's Mission* (New York: Harper Colophon/HarperCollins, 1959), p. 114.

[3]See chapter 2.

will find an outlet. At the beginning of the 20th century, the concept of the unconscious was in the air. In this case, it would be Viennese physician Sigmund Freud who would be the genius who captured the spirit of his time.

Sigmund Freud [1856–1939] began his long career as a scientist, not a physician—his specialty was the nervous system. It was only after fifteen years of work as a research scientist that he turned to clinical medicine in order to earn more money for his growing family. Though Freud always regarded himself as a scientist first and foremost, science is founded on careful observation and description, and Freud was more of an "explainer" than a "describer." The entire body of his work is characterized by a repeated pattern. Freud would first make careful observations, then develop a hypothesis to explain the observations. So far, this is precisely the scientific method. In part because of the difficulty of modeling the psyche, the hypotheses he developed were too often impossible to verify because they involved metaphysical models. There's nothing necessarily wrong with this either, since some of the most productive models are simply not open to scientific verification. However, it did prevent Freud from a chance at the scientific acceptance he wanted. Isolated from the mainstream of academia and science, he unfortunately soon hardened his hypotheses into immutable law.

It is ironic that Jung has often been accused of dealing in metaphysics, not facts. Actually, in contrast to Freud, Jung's preferred method was to describe what he actually found in the dreams and visions of his patients or himself. He then constructed limited models from these observations that were open to scientific investigation. As a rough example, his model of the archetypes of the collective unconscious—which are normally dismissed as unscientific—are open to a wide variety of scientific verification techniques.[4] In contrast, it is almost impossible to think of a way to scientifically prove whether the mind is actually structured into an

---

[4]As was pointed out in the introduction, there is a wide variety of scientific research which supports Jung's hypothesis. Unfortunately, the scientific community is largely unaware of, or hostile to, Jung's model. For more details, see Anthony Stevens, *Archetypes: a Natural History of the Self* (New York: Quill, 1982).

id, ego, and super-conscious.[5] Freud created theories, not models, and those theories still elude scientific examination.

However, Freud had no theories when he began his clinical work. He just wanted techniques that could help him deal with his patients' problems. Initially, under the guidance of Charcot and his colleagues, Freud used hypnosis.

> When Freud began the practice of medicine it was natural, in view of his scientific background, that he should specialize in the treatment of nervous disorders. . . . Freud spent a year in Paris (1885–1886) learning Charcot's method of treatment. However, Freud was not satisfied with hypnosis because he felt that the effects were only temporary and did not get at the seat of the trouble.[6]

Freud, by his own admission in letters to his friend Fliess, was not a very skilled hypnotist, and wanted a method that he could use with more success. Freud found that method when he began his cooperative work with an older colleague, Joseph Breuer. Breuer had already developed an alternative to hypnosis which interested Freud a great deal—the *cathartic* or *talking* cure. Breuer found that if hysteric patients were encouraged to talk about whatever came to mind, they felt relief and their symptoms decreased.

Freud experimented with patients and decided that Breuer's talking cure—or *free association*, as Freud came to call it—was preferable to hypnosis. He also began to turn to his patients' dreams as a source of unconscious material. It was when he combined the two and had the patients free-associate about their dreams, that Freud had the general method he was to use most frequently in the years to come. Using these new methods, Freud saw that, far from being meaningless anomalies, neurotic symptoms seemed to express an underlying dynamic. More and more, Freud came to believe

---

[5] Though I stress that it remains a serviceable metaphysical model nonetheless. Even crude adaptions like Transactional Analysis—with its translation of id, ego, and super-ego, into child, adult and parent—can serve effectively as a therapeutic model.
[6] Calvin S. Hall, *A Primer of Freudian Psychology*, p. 14.

that there was a whole system of unconscious thoughts, feelings, and memories that underlay conscious behavior.

Up to a point, Freud was a careful scientist. He methodically recorded the unconscious material that patients brought up in their dreams and free-associations. He subjected himself to the same careful examination.

> . . . in the 1890's, with characteristic thoroughness, Freud began an intensive self-analysis of his own unconscious sources . . . . By analyzing his dreams and saying to himself whatever came into his mind, he was able to see the workings of his own inner dynamics.[7]

It was a commonplace observation among the many therapists who worked at Charcot's clinic that the problems usually turned out to be sexual. Freud immediately sensed that this was a central concept and tried to convince Charcot and Breuer of its importance. Both were proper European gentlemen who were too embarrassed to deal with sexuality and, consequently, turned to other explanations. Though Freud was himself a thoroughly proper Victorian gentleman, equally embarrassed at addressing such a forbidden topic, he grew more and more convinced that sex was the key that opened the door to the unconscious mind. In actuality, psychologists since Freud have largely accepted that sex was only one such key, a key more characteristic of the culture and values of Victorian Europeans than of humanity in general.

Freud had a long creative life, and he continued to adapt and extend his theoretical system up to the end of his life. However, there were two key ideas that Freud formulated in the early years of his career that formed the core for all his later work, though both were to be extensively modified in later years. It is important to remember that his theories were to be revised only by Freud himself; he brooked no heresy from his followers.

The first was the idea that underlying our conscious thoughts lies a huge reservoir of unconscious thoughts, feelings, and memo-

---

[7]Calvin S. Hall, *A Primer of Freudian Psychology,* p. 15.

ries. His initial, justly famed exploration of the territory of the unconscious came in *The Interpretation of Dreams*, which he developed during the 1890's and first published in 1900.[8] The second concept was the primacy of the sexual instinct in human development. The initial statement of his sexual theories came in 1905 with the publication of *Three Essays on the Theory of Sexuality*.[9] Each concept is important enough to discuss individually.

THE INTERPRETATION OF DREAMS

In the opening chapter of *The Interpretation of Dreams*, Freud presented a history of "The Scientific Literature of Dream-Problems (up to 1900)."

> The peoples of classical antiquity . . . took it for granted that dreams were related to the world of supernatural beings . . . . It appeared to them that dreams must serve a special purpose in respect of the dreamer; that is, as a rule, they predicted the future.[10]

Freud moved on to Aristotle, with whose views he clearly felt more at home:

> In the two works of Aristotle in which there is a mention of dreams, they are already regarded as constituting a problem of psychology. We are told that the dream is not god-sent; . . . the dream is defined as the psychic activity of the sleeper.[11]

---

[8] In Dr. A. A. Brill, ed., *The Basic Writings of Sigmund Freud* (New York: Modern Library/Random House, 1938).

[9] Sigmund Freud, *Three Essays on the Theory of Sexuality*. Reprint of 4th edition of 1920. (New York: Basic Books/HarperCollins, 1962). In the next chapter, we will find that this *fin-de-siècle* period was also when mathematician David Hilbert proposed his goal of mathematical formalism, and the young Bertrand Russell decided that mathematics could be reduced to symbolic logic. All three goals—Freud's, Hilbert's and Russell's—proved to be premature attempts at synthesis.

[10] Dr. A. A. Brill, *The Basic Writings of Sigmund Freud*, p. 184.

[11] Dr. A. A. Brill, *The Basic Writings of Sigmund Freud*, p. 184.

Freud was thus clear from the outset that dreams told us only about the dreamer, and that he would have little patience with any theories of dream interpretation that seemed at all mystical or religious. In the body of the book, Freud then developed his own theory of dream interpretation, the theory that "every dream is the fulfillment of a concealed wish."[12] Calvin S. Hall summarized Freud's view as "we dream about what we fear."[13]

Freud felt that dreams revealed all the urges we repressed during waking consciousness. As civilized beings we can't allow ourselves to consciously acknowledge our primitive feelings of lust, hatred, greed, etc. During sleep, our ability to suppress such forbidden thoughts is weaker and they emerge into a shadowy consciousness. However, as a last protection, an internal *censor* twists the undesirable thoughts into symbols that hide their meaning from us.

It is true that, when people begin to record and study their dreams, the dreams exercise a fascination that far exceeds the manifest content of the dream. The elements of the dream seem to contain an energy of their own. This accords well with Freud's view, since the dream elements should be symbolic representations of our deepest desires. Dreamers often feel ambiguous toward the dream, just as they would if the dream was actually discussing "forbidden fruit." However, this ambiguous response is hardly universal; just as frequently, the response is unambiguously positive. Certain special dreams exercise such an intense fascination for the dreamer that they seem like messages from the gods, as the "ancients" and supposed "primitives" believed them to be.

The concept of the censor seems unlikely at best, and is little honored by modern dream workers. Dreams seem to speak a symbolic language of their own—not to conceal, but because they come from a part of the psyche that predates language. It is critical to realize that a symbol is not merely a sign, standing in one-to-one representation with something else. In Jung's words:

---

[12]Gerard Lauzun, *Sigmund Freud: The Man and his Theories* (Greenwich, CT: Fawcett, 1962), p. 48.
[13]Calvin S. Hall, *A Primer of Freudian Psychology,* p. 25.

> . . . a symbol always presupposes that the chosen expression is the best possible description or formulation of a relatively unknown fact, which is none the less known to exist or is postulated as existing.[14]

Freud viewed dream symbols as simple signs that could be reduced to a sexual interpretation. For the origination of this concept, Lauzun claimed priority for Freud's disciples Stekel and Rank, stating that:

> . . . it was under the influence of two other future dissenters, Stekel and Rank, that Freud wrote the chapters of *The Interpretation of Dreams* which deal with symbolism and compare dreams with poetry and myth; . . . the supposed symbolism in which anything long is a penis and anything hollow is a vagina.[15]

Regardless of priority, the reduction of all dream symbols to sexual images is a terrible impoverishment of the rich palette of dreams. It is only with very recent research in some quite disparate fields that we begin to realize why dreams speak in symbols. For example, linguist Noam Chomsky has developed a model of a *deep structure* which he asserts underlies all language; he argues that this deep structure is an inherent, inborn structure of the human mind.[16] Pioneer biologist/psychologist Jean Piaget carefully studied children's behavior and development. He argued that language develops out of motor actions.[17] A possible synthesis that seems to be emerging among many linguists and psychologists is that both are right: there is a deep structure that underlies language, and this deep structure is inborn, but it is evidenced first in motor actions and only gradu-

---

[14]C. G. Jung, *Collected Works, Vol. 6: Psychological Types* (Princeton: Princeton University Press, 1971), ¶ 814.

[15]Gerard Lauzun, *Sigmund Freud: The Man and his Theories*, p. 51.

[16]Richard L. Gregory, ed., *The Oxford Companion to the Mind* (New York: Oxford University Press, 1987), pp. 419–421.

[17]See Jean Piaget, *The Language and Thought of the Child* (New York: Meridian Book/World Publishing, 1955).

ally develops into a spoken language. In this respect, anthropologist Edward T. Hall, among others, has shown how large a part of language is non-verbal.[18]

Ethologists like Nobel prize-winning Konrad Lorenz revealed that all animals possess inborn symbolic responses which are triggered by specific cues in their environment, at different points in their development. When the correct situation occurs at the correct time, the animal will *imprint* their inner predisposition onto the actual event.[19]

For example, when Lorenz was studying the behavior of geese, one orphaned baby goose imprinted its inner model of a mother onto Lorenz. All that was necessary was for Lorenz to be the first creature that the baby goose saw when it woke into life. The baby goose, having decided that Lorenz was its mother, took to following Lorenz wherever he went, just as baby geese always follow their mother. Clearly, the inborn symbol that corresponded to mother wasn't an actual picture of a mother goose, because Lorenz could hardly qualify. Yet it did include many inborn characteristics of the relationship between mother and child, so that they did not have to be relearned with every generation of geese.[20]

Mircea Eliade's studies of primitive religious mythology offer still another source of information on such archetypal structures. Eliade has found that common symbols occur in the myths of cultures at similar stages of development. For example, the belief in a time when everything was perfect—such as the Garden of Eden episode in the Hebrew/Christian Bible—seems universal. Another example is the seemingly universal belief that there is a central axis that connects the human world with the world of the gods. Like the symbols in our dreams, these mythological symbols reappear in all cultures in all times with remarkable similarity. They are filtered through the particulars of a given culture just as the symbols in our dreams are filtered through our particular memories. Thus in Norse mythology, the central axis is pictured as a great tree, while the

---

[18] Edward T. Hall, *The Silent Language* (Greenwich, CT: Fawcett, 1959).

[19] Richard I. Evans, *Konrad Lorenz: The Man and his Ideas* (New York: Harcourt Brace, 1975).

[20] See Konrad Lorenz, *King Solomon's Ring* (New York: Crowell, 1952).

Judeo-Christian Bible speaks of it—in Jacob's great dream—as a ladder stretching up to heaven.[21]

The above examples from varied fields point once again to the likely existence of something similar to Plato's ideas or Kant's categories, which Jung was to carefully delineate as the archetypes of the collective unconscious. Chomsky's work points to a deep underlying structure that eventually shows itself as language. Piaget's work demonstrates that language exhibits itself first in motor actions, not words. Hall supports Piaget in showing the extensive amount of non-verbal language. Lorenz' work shows that all animals—including the human animal—possess similar inborn, instinctual, symbolic responses. Eliade's studies reveal that whole cultures express their deepest beliefs in symbolic terms which are, in large part, independent of the particular culture that expresses them.

Freud's realization that dreams spoke in a symbolic language was thus deeply important. However, his reduction of dreams to wish-fulfillment, and dream symbols to sexual signs, was an ill-chosen attempt to over-simplify their complexity. To quote Eliade on the need to include a place for religious symbolism in particular:

> . . . the *sacred* is an element of the *structure* of consciousness. . . . Religious symbols constitute a prereflective language. As it is a case of a special language, sui generis, it necessitates a proper hermeneutics.[22]

Three Essays on the Theory of Sexuality

In *Three Essays* Freud examined whether so-called sexual perversions were innate or developed. By perversions, Freud meant:

> . . . sexual activities which either (a) extend, in an anatomical sense, beyond the regions of the body that are

---

[21]See Mircea Eliade, *The Sacred and the Profane* (New York: Harvest/Harcourt Brace, 1959).
[22]Mircea Eliade, *No Souvenirs: Journal, 1957–1969* (San Francisco: HarperSanFrancisco, 1977), p. 313.

> designed for sexual union, or (b) linger over the inter-
> mediate relations to the sexual object which should nor-
> mally be traversed rapidly on the path towards the final
> sexual aim.[23]

He found that neurotics revealed all the sexual perversions in the
course of psychoanalysis. Since neurotics were "a numerous class of
people and one not far removed from the healthy," he felt that the
perversions were innate and that normal sexuality was developed.[24]
If perverse sexuality was innate, Freud theorized that it should be
found in infants, and that is exactly what he did find.

> There seems no doubt that germs of sexual impulses are
> already present in the newborn child and that these con-
> tinue to develop for a time, but are then overtaken by a
> progressive process of suppression. . . .The sexual life of
> children emerges in a form accessible to observation
> round about the third or fourth year of life.[25]

According to Freud, the child passes through three transitional
stages, usually by age five: the oral, the anal, and the phallic. Each
took its name from the erogenous zone stressed during that stage of
development. During the oral phase, sexuality expressed itself
through taking in with the mouth. Thumb-sucking is the example
most would think of, but every young child goes through a phase
where everything is put in the mouth during the course of a child's
ever-curious examination. In the anal stage, the child discovers and
glories in its first creation: its feces. The phallic stage marks the
child's discovery of its genitals—during this stage the child often
rubs itself in a masturbatory fashion.

Freud termed this tendency of sexuality to take on multiple
expressions and objects *polymorphous perverse* sexuality. After the

---

[23]James Strachey, ed., *Josef Breuer and Sigmund Freud: Studies in Hysteria*, reprint of 1955 edition (New York: Basic Books/HarperCollins, 1962), p. 16.
[24]James Strachey, *Josef Breuer and Sigmund Freud: Studies in Hysteria*, p. 97.
[25]James Strachey, *Josef Breuer and Sigmund Freud: Studies in Hysteria*, p. 42.

three transitional stages, a period of latency follows wherein the infant's polymorphous perverse sexuality is forced to adapt to the demands of society. Finally, in adolescence, the child's genitals once more become the main erogenous zone but this time a proper sexual object is found in a person of the opposite sex.

The adult personality is determined by the child's manner of dealing with these developmental stages. If the child fails to deal successfully with each of the states, adult sexuality will fail to find its full development in heterosexual genital sexuality. It is supposedly because of such psycho-sexual development problems that sexual perversions exist in adults. The perversions are not developed—instead, they are proof of an absence of proper development. The infant's sexuality is originally polymorphous perverse and remains that way in the adult if the child is not successful in dealing with one of the three early stages.

Freud was later to examine the psychological implications of the three psycho-sexual developmental stages at great length. He felt they were sufficient to explain all differences in personality. For example, psychologist Calvin S. Hall said, concerning the oral phase:

> Tactual stimulation of the lips and oral cavity by contact with and the incorporation of objects produces oral erotic (sexual) pleasure, and biting yields oral aggressive pleasure. . . . The mouth, therefore, has at least five main modes of functioning: (1) taking in, (2) holding on, (3) biting, (4) spitting out, and (5) closing. Each of these modes is a prototype or the original model for certain personality types. . . . The child, having learned to make a particular adjustment, uses the same adjustment when similar situations arise later in life. If taking things in through the mouth is pleasurable, as it is when the child is hungry, then taking in or incorporating knowledge or love or power when one feels empty may also be pleasurable.[26]

---

[26]Calvin S. Hall, *A Primer of Freudian Psychology,* pp. 103–104.

Freud thus came full-circle in his examination. He began by considering where sexual perversions originated, and found they were innate, that infants are polymorphous perverse. He traced the development stages that lead to adult sexuality, and found that the failure to successively deal with any stage left the adult with the original childish sexual perversion. More importantly, Freud now had a developmental scheme that could be used to reduce any adult problem to an infantile developmental problem. Any adult achievement, from art to religion, could also be reduced to a failure to develop a full adult sexuality.

The same strengths and weaknesses are seen here as in Freud's work on dream analysis. Freud's analysis in each case was incomparably brilliant, very like the sort of argument used in medieval scholastic philosophy. Unlike scholastic philosophers, Freud tried to be a descriptive scientist, describing what he had actually observed in patients before he made intellectual generalizations from his observations. But very unscientifically, Freud tended to see what he wanted to see. Very few others would be willing to accept so readily that all instinctive behavior is only a manifestation of sexual behavior—our behavior is too complex to reduce to a single explanatory principle like sexuality.

For example, a child turns to its mother's breast not merely for food and nourishment, and not merely for oral gratification, but also for love and tenderness. Experimental psychologist Harry F. Harlow's research with chimpanzees demonstrated that an infant chimp has as strong a need for nurturing as for food. In one experiment, two *mothers* were constructed for an orphaned chimp. Both mothers were roughly shaped like a mother chimp. One was a wire cage that provided milk; the other was warm and furry but gave no milk. Which would the baby chimp choose: the mother who provided food or the mother who provided something approximating warmth and nurturing? In actuality, the baby chimp would cling to the furry mother and only go to the wire mother long enough to get its hunger satisfied. Even a baby chimp already has a variety of needs, not least of which is the need for love.[27]

---

[27] Gene Bylinsky, "New Clues to the Causes of Violence," in *Annual Editions, Readings in Psychology '74/'75* (Guilford, CT: Dushkin Publishing Group, 1974), pp. 73–78.

Yet Freud was satisfied to see a child's thumb-sucking, for example, as a purely sexual satisfaction. Jung disagreed with Freud and said (in 1912, just at the point when he was beginning to split with Freud):

> . . . if we take the attitude that the striving for pleasure is something sexual, we might just as well say, paradoxically, that hunger is a sexual striving, since it seeks pleasure by satisfaction. But if we juggle with concepts like that, we should have to allow our opponents to apply the terminology of hunger to sexuality.[28]

It is interesting to compare Freud's stages of psycho-sexual development with other models of development. Piaget, for example, developed a model of childhood development, based on decades of research with children. His stages have fascinating similarities and differences from Freud's, and Piaget's are based on motor development, not sexual development. For example, the period from birth to about eighteen months is Freud's oral phase; from birth to 24 months is Piaget's sensory-motor stage. As we mentioned earlier, Freud sees it as a period when the child deals with aggression and acquisitiveness. Piaget presents it as a period when a toddler's basic motor actions are internalized so that the child can acquire inner *schemes of action*; i.e., plans for carrying out these motor actions. It adds to these schemes by assimilating new actions that fit into the scheme, or by modifying the scheme to accommodate the new actions. In *The Origin of Intelligence in the Child*, Piaget gives an example of how such schemes of action develop. He put a watch chain in a match box, then nearly closed the box. An older infant girl picked up the box, turned it over and tried to reach for the chain. When that didn't work, she poked inside with her finger and pulled out the chain. Later, outside the sight of the little girl, Piaget put the chain back in the box, then closed it again. This time he made the opening too small for the little girl's finger. She unsuccessfully

---

[28]C. G. Jung, "The Psychology of the Transference," in *Collected Works, Vol. 16: The Practice of Psychotherapy* (Princeton: Princeton University Press, 1966), ¶ 241.

tried to reach inside for the chain, using the technique which had worked so well before. When that didn't work:

> . . . she looks at the slit with great attention; then, several times in succession, she opens and shuts her mouth, at first slightly, then wider and wider! . . . Due to [her] inability to think out the situation in words or clear visual images she uses a simple motor indication, as signifier or symbol. . . . By opening her mouth [she] expresses, or even reflects her desire to enlarge the opening of the box.[29]

Immediately afterward, the little girl picks up the box, and instead of trying to reach inside for the chain, she uses her finger to widen the opening, then reaches inside for the chain! This is a wonderful example of Piaget's main theme that "thought is internalized action." Of course, it also fits well into Freud's oral phase of acquisitiveness, but why should we accept his argument that the whole stage of development be reduced to psycho-sexual development? Isn't Piaget's approach more likely to be on the right track than Freud's?

SUMMARY OF EARLY FREUDIAN IDEAS

Through his work with neurotic patients, Freud came to realize that an unconscious dynamic underlay their conscious actions. He tried to use hypnotism to tap that unconscious well, in the manner of Charcot, but found it an unsatisfactory method. Breuer's *talking cure*, which Freud came to call *free association*, gave Freud a tool to get beyond the conscious mind. Dreams were a rich source of unconscious material. Freud decided that dreams were wish fulfillment; their complexity was due to an inner *censor* who made a last attempt to prevent forbidden thought from coming into consciousness.

---

[29]Quotation from Piaget's *The Origin of Intelligence in the Child*, in Molly Brearley and Elizabeth Hitchfield, *A Guide to Reading Piaget* (New York: Schocken Books, 1969), pp. 143–144.

This unconscious material appeared overwhelmingly sexual to Freud. He found that his patients were invariably sexually disturbed; they exhibited all the sexual *perversions* in their desires. Freud theorized that this was because sexuality is originally *polymorphous perverse*—it will take any object. It is only by going through a proper sexual development before age 5, that proper adult sexuality develops. Freud felt that all human problems, and even all human achievements could be traced to problems in childhood sexual development.

Freud thus stood at the end of the long line of thought that we have traced from its beginnings in the Renaissance. That line began by glorying in human beings as impartial observers of physical reality. With Descartes, humanity became synonymous with its intellect—the great split between mind and body was now explicit. We developed an ever-greater ability to stand separate from the world around us, dissecting the world into ever smaller parts. Science grew from this ability, and science brought humankind a new power to dominate our world. We increasingly turned this power onto ourselves, separating our supposedly rational mind from our supposedly irrational body and emotions. Our body's needs and wisdom were increasingly hidden from consciousness, which viewed itself as a disembodied intellect.

As this separation grew over hundreds of years, hidden away from consciousness, a counterbalance also developed. This was a pull toward harmony, relationship, connectedness. Since the prevailing rationalism was unsympathetic to this viewpoint, it exhibited itself largely through fringe phenomena. One such phenomenon was hypnotism, which we have followed from Paracelsus to Freud. However, Freud himself stood firmly in the materialist camp, resisting any encroachments of "the black mud of occultism" (as Freud described it to Jung).[30]

> . . . reason, so Freud felt, is the only tool—or weapon—
> we have to make sense of life, to dispense with illusions

---

[30]C. G. Jung, *Memories, Dreams, Reflections* (New York: Vintage Books/Random House, 1965), p. 150.

(of which, in Freud's thought, religious tenets are only one), to become independent of fettering authorities, and thus to establish our own authority. . . .For him reason was confined to thought. Feelings and emotions were per se irrational, and hence inferior to thought.[31]

How ironic that Freud, an exemplary product of the rationalist tradition, should discover the unconscious mind. Freud was led to its discovery by rationalism itself—it explained so much. But because the mind and the body had long ago been split, and the body relegated to an inherently inferior position, Freud was confronted with a dilemma. On the one hand, he saw that our conscious lives are largely controlled by unconscious motivation. Yet for Freud this unconscious motivation was a primitive, instinctive, unreasoning force.

The picture was a gloomy one and one that Freud never resolved. At first, he hoped that the mere knowledge of the unconscious motivation would be enough to restore the rational mind's dominion over the primitive instincts. But he soon found that was an empty hope. He decided that the best we could do was understand this split inside ourselves, and hold to the side of rationality when faced with the void of the unconscious. Freud held to this pessimistic view of our possibilities, while he continued to develop his system of thought, hoping for some way out of this dilemma.

The way out lay in a synthesis of conscious and unconscious, of mind and body. It lay in relationship, not separation. It could be found not in 19th-century ideas, standing at the end of the rational tradition, but in 20th-century ideas, which had been only embryonic in the centuries before. But first we have to discuss how mathematics fell into much the same trap as Freud, due to an over reliance on supposedly rational thought.

---

[31]Erich Fromm, *Sigmund Freud's Mission*, pp. 2, 7.

CHAPTER 9

LOGIC'S TOWER OF BABEL

. . . Today we know that it is possible, logically speaking, to derive almost all of present-day mathematics from a single source, the Theory of Sets. It will suffice therefore to set forth the principles of one single formalized language, to indicate how one can write in this language the Theory of Sets, then to show how from this theory grow one by one the different branches of mathematics as our attention turns to them . . .[1]

MATHEMATICS' NEED FOR UNITY

Sparked by Cantor's transfinite set theory, a new mathematics developed at much the same time that psychology was itself emerging as a science. Both were undoubtedly attempts at scratching the same inner itch. The Renaissance ideal of humanity as observers had led to the split of mind and body so necessary to the objective, disinterested stance of science. Obviously such a split is intrinsically impossible, since mind and body are merely artificial separations of an inherently unified organism. Nor is it possible for a human being to exist except as part of a complex unity which includes all the supposed objects of observation. Eventually any study that goes deep enough finds itself staring at its own reflection.

---

[1] Quotation by Nicolas Bourbaki in Lucienne Félix, *The Modern Aspect of Mathematics* (New York: Basic Books, 1960), pp. 58–59. Nicolas Bourbaki is a fictional mathematician created by a group of French mathematicians in about 1930, to express their joint views about modern mathematics.

By the second half of the 19th century, this need to restore unity was the driving, though unacknowledged, force in all the arts and sciences. In particular, it was no longer possible for either philosophy or science to ignore the mind of the observer doing the observing. Similarly, mathematics was no longer able to ignore the unexamined, implicit assumptions out of which it had emerged. Cantor's careful attempt to describe the nature of number led to the first rigorous mathematical attempt to deal with infinity. That in turn revealed previously unimaginable paradoxes hidden at the core of infinity. Two major attempts were made to solve those paradoxes: (1) that of the formalists, led by David Hilbert, and (2) that of the logicians, led by Bertrand Russell.

In both cases they hoped to avoid the problems of infinity by reducing mathematics to finite axiomatic systems. Any mathematical system would consist solely of a finite number of definitions of relevant terms, a finite number of axioms, and a finite number of defined operations. The definitions, axioms, and operations were all to be totally empty of content! Mathematics was assumed to concern itself only with the formal manipulation of empty symbols. Perhaps from all that has already been discussed in this book it will be apparent that this was an impossible goal. Symbols are not empty and, in fact, it is precisely because symbols produce deep feeling responses that mathematics is able to develop.

> A symbolism not interpreted is only a game of signs; it is a language only if it takes on meaning and if one has the use of an interpretation of the symbols and of the symbolic game. . . . The problem of the role of intuition cannot be sidestepped.[2]

Though both the formalists and the logicians wanted to create such formal axiomatic systems, beyond that they diverged. The formalists were only interested in developing such axiomatic systems for mathematics. Russell wanted to develop a formal axiomatic system for a symbolic logic that included both traditional logic and mathematics under a single roof.

---

[2]Quotation by Jörgensen in Lucienne Félix, *The Modern Aspect of Mathematics*, pp. 58–59.

Mathematics and logic, historically speaking, have been entirely distinct studies. Mathematics has been connected with science, logic with Greek. But both have developed in modern times: logic has become more mathematical and mathematics has become more logical. The consequence is that it has now become wholly impossible to draw a line between the two; in fact, the two are one. They differ as boy and man: logic is the youth of mathematics and mathematics is the manhood of logic.[3]

Both formalists and logicians were themselves under the grip of a symbol, a symbol of unity. This desire for unity was clearly the *living symbol*[4] for mathematics in Hilbert's era. Nearly all of the great mathematicians were striving toward this formal unity of mathematics, either through a formal axiomatic system, or through the reduction of mathematics to symbolic logic. They were not able to stand outside their field and see that they were under a spell. And, though their efforts were foredoomed, the development of mathematical rigor was a necessary step in mathematics.

In this chapter we will largely discuss Russell's efforts, culminating in the *Principia Mathematica*. We'll return to Hilbert when we discuss the background for Gödel's ideas.[5] First we begin with *Peano's Postulates*,[6] which were to influence both Hilbert and Russell.

PEANO'S POSTULATES

Having reduced all traditional pure mathematics to the theory of natural numbers, the next step in logical analysis was to reduce this theory itself to the smallest set of

---

[3] Bertrand Russell, *Introduction to Mathematical Philosophy*, reprint of 2nd edition of 1920 (New York: Dover, 1933), p. 194.
[4] A term used by Jung to mean a symbol that still has deep meaning for a culture. This will be discussed at some length in chapter 15, in our discussion of Jung's concept of the Self.
[5] See chapter 12.
[6] Giuseppe Peano, *Arithmetices Principia Nova Methodo Esposita* (1889).

premisses and undefined terms from which it could be derived. This work was accomplished by Peano.[7]

The first important product of this new formalism was Peano's Postulates: five axioms from which the full arithmetic of the natural numbers or integers (i.e., 0, 1, 2, 3, . . .) can be derived. Giuseppe Peano [1858–1932] was an Italian mathematician and logician whose postulates have a simplicity and an elegance that strongly influenced his contemporaries in mathematical logic. Here is a summary of the five postulates, as we think of them today.

(1) Zero is a number.

(2) The successor of any number is a number.

(3) No two numbers have the same successor.

(4) Zero is not the successor of any number.

(5) If a set of numbers contains both zero and also the successor of every number in itself, then it contains all numbers.

With the exception of the last axiom, which is what mathematicians refer to as *mathematical induction*, the purpose of the axioms can be readily understood. For example, let's combine the first two. Since "zero is a number," we have at least one number (whatever a number is). Since "the successor of any number is a number," zero's successor is a number. We'll call it "one" as we normally do. Then "one" has a successor, which we'll call "two," and so forth. Clearly we can arrive at all the other positive numbers by taking successors one at a time.

Peano made sure that "no two numbers have the same successor," so he didn't end up in strange paradoxical number systems. After all, we wouldn't want to have "three" be the successor for both "one" and "two."

By saying that "zero is not the successor of any number," he created a first number. There is no number smaller than zero in his

---

[7]Bertrand Russell, *Introduction to Mathematical Philosophy*, p. 5.

system. (Note that once Peano developed zero and the positive integers, it was easy enough to extend this process to negative numbers, fractions, and so forth.)

The fifth axiom, which mathematicians call *induction*, is something different, reminiscent of the parallel axiom in geometry.[8] The scientific method is sometimes known as *induction*. It is more properly termed *incomplete induction*, in contrast with *mathematical induction*, or *complete induction*. A scientific theory is

GIUSEPPE PEANO

provisional; it is always possible that further experience might contradict the theory. In contrast with the incomplete induction of science, mathematical induction implies that something can be proved once and for all.

Mathematical induction says that if you want to prove some mathematical statement is true for all numbers, you only have to prove it is true in two cases. First, prove it's true for zero, since zero is the first number. Then prove that if it's true for any arbitrary number, then it's true for that number's successor as well. The trick here is that zero is a number, so it must then also be true for "one," then for "two," and on indefinitely for all numbers.

This is obviously a very powerful method of proof since it's quite a bit easier to prove an assertion is true in two circumstances than to prove it's true in any of an infinite number of circumstances (which is why natural science is provisional). But notice that induction involves infinite processes; i.e., there is no way to demonstrate the truth of induction in a finite number of steps. That is both the strength of mathematical induction and its Achilles' heel. For, as we will see later, infinite processes tend to involve us in self-refer-

---

[8] See chapter 4.

ential systems, and self-referential systems cannot always be reduced to logical analysis.

Just as calculus introduced the infinite concepts of infinitesimals and limits, then only later realized their potential problems, mathematical induction was used for hundreds of years before anyone realized that the method presented deep philosophical issues because of its implicit acceptance of infinite processes. By the mid-17th century, French mathematicians Pierre Fermat [1601–1665] and Blaise Pascal [1623–1662] had independently begun using versions of mathematical induction in their work. It was two hundred years, however, before August De Morgan [1806–1871] gave the process the explicit name of mathematical induction (in 1838). Another fifty years passed before Peano codified it fully and included it as the fifth and final postulate necessary for developing arithmetic.

Peano's Postulates were a stunning example of the possibilities of the new formalism. Using these five axioms, it was then at least theoretically possible to derive all the properties of arithmetic. Most colleges give a first-year mathematics course (for mathematics majors only), where the students derive the major properties of arithmetic using Peano's Postulates, or some similar system of axioms. Note that there is absolutely nothing contained in the five axioms that points to the nature of those properties. It is undoubtedly true that there are properties of the integers that have never yet been discovered. Peano's Postulates only provide the starting point: an elegant axiomatic method for producing arithmetic.[9]

In 1892, Peano announced a project "for a compendium of all the known theorems in mathematics to be stated and proved using [his] logic."[10] Perhaps it was too early, and his methods were still too little known, for only his fellow Italians picked up on his program.

---

[9]It should be mentioned that Peano's Postulates were equally influential for the system of mathematical notation in which they were presented as for the logic itself. The technical notation was to serve as the starting point for Bertrand Russell's development of his own extensive system of mathematical logic.

[10]Nicholas Griffin, ed., *The Selected Letters of Bertrand Russell, Vol 1: The Private Years (1884–1914)* (Boston: Houghton Mifflin, 1992), p. 204.

It was David Hilbert's similar program of 1900 which was to inspire mathematicians in general.[11]

BERTRAND RUSSELL DISCOVERS PEANO'S LOGIC

In 1854, the same year that Riemann published his strange new geometry,[12] George Boole [1815–1864] published his *Laws of Thought*, which presented a symbolic representational system for logical *syllogisms*.[13] These symbols could then be manipulated using a sort of algebra to determine the truth or falsity of complex logical relationships. This was a start at fulfilling Leibniz' goal of a "general method in which all truths of reason would be reduced to a

BERTRAND RUSSELL

kind of calculation."[14] Most contemporary philosophy students take a one or two semester course in which they learn Boole's method, and use it to determine the truth or falsity of progressively more complex logical statements. His system was a significant contribution toward the development of the computer; computer programmer/analysts still use "truth tables" based on Boole's system in summarizing all the possible logical paths a computer program has to consider.

---

[11]As we will see in chapter 12, when we discuss Gödel's response to Hilbert's program.

[12]See chapter 4.

[13]"From the Greek *syn* ("with" or "together") and *logizesthai* ("to reckon," "to conclude by reasoning"). A form of reasoning whereby, given two sentences or propositions, a third follows necessarily from them" (W. L. Reese, *Dictionary of Philosophy and Religion: Eastern and Western Thought* (Atlantic Highlands, NJ: Humanities Press, 1980), pp. 559–560). For example, if *A* implies *B*, and *B* implies *C*, then *A* implies *C*.

[14]See chapter 3.

Boole's system was to be combined with Peano's notation, then extended to almost unimaginable levels of complexity by philosopher and mathematician Bertrand Russell [1872–1970]. In the late days of the 19th century, Russell was a bright young man with a gift for describing difficult philosophical matters in elegant prose. He had already been studying mathematical philosophy for some years, and had achieved some notoriety for his work on geometry. But something was still lacking. When he attended the International Congress of Philosophy in Paris in 1900, he found what he had been looking for when he heard Peano speak.

Russell found Peano far and away the most impressive figure at the Congress, a man of unsurpassed logic and precision. He grew convinced that this must be due to the system of mathematical logic Peano had perfected. Within little more than a month following the Congress, Russell had devoured everything written by Peano and his Italian followers, and began first extending their technique, then using it to solve the problems with which he had been struggling.[15] It was an exhilarating time for Russell:

> . . . The time was one of intellectual intoxication. My sensations resembled those one has after climbing a mountain in a mist, when, on reaching the summit, the mist suddenly clears, and the country becomes visible for forty miles in every direction. . . . Intellectually the month of September 1900 was the highest point of my life.[16]

Peano was satisfied with the sufficiently difficult project of using his technique to "state and prove" all mathematical theorems. Russell had even more exalted ambitions for these new techniques than did Peano: he planned to extend Peano's logic beyond mathematics to philosophy—beginning with the philosophy of mathematics—then beyond that the sky was the limit. Russell thought that ultimately he could reduce all mathematics, all science and all philosophy to

---

[15] See Bertrand Russell, *The Autobiography of Bertrand Russell, the Early Years: 1872–World War I* (New York: Bantam Books, 1968), pp. 191–192.

[16] Bertrand Russell, *The Autobiography of Bertrand Russell: The Early Years*, p. 192.

this new symbolic logic. A grandiose plan indeed, and one which would never be achieved. Russell quickly convinced his older friend—philosopher/mathematician Alfred North Whitehead [1861–1947]—to join him in his effort. This project would occupy both men for the next ten years, and would eventually culminate in the three volumes and 4,500 pages of their *Principia Mathemetica*.

Within a year of Russell's initial intoxication with the possibilities of Peano's logic, he received three blows, each of which seemed to be telling him that there was more to life than logic, each of which he determinedly ignored. First, in February 1901, came the most profound mystical experience of his life. He was already in some emotional distress over a painful illness suffered by Whitehead's wife Evelyn, with whom Russell had an ambiguous relationship, composed about equally of admiration and sexual attraction.[17] In that mood, he heard a new translation of Euripedes' tragedy *Hippolytus*, read by its translator, his friend Gilbert Murray. This translation drew on the then new Nietzchean idea that underneath the calm, rational, structured *Appollonian* aspect that we present to the world, lies the wild, irrational, emotional *Dionysian* source of life. In other words, Murray was presenting one of the prefigurations of the *unconscious*.

> Suddenly the ground seemed to give way beneath me, and I found myself in quite another region. Within five minutes I went through some such reflections as the following: the loneliness of the human soul is unendurable; nothing can penetrate it except the highest intensity of the sort of love that religious teachers have preached; whatever does not spring from this motive is harmful, or at best useless. . . . At the end of those five minutes, I had become a completely different person. For a time, a sort of mystic illumination possessed me.[18]

---

[17]Though Russell probably exaggerated the extent of her illness (something he was wont to do); it is likely that her condition was in considerable part hypochondria. See Nicholas Griffin, *The Selected Letters of Bertrand Russell,* Vol. 1, pp. 215–218.

[18]Bertrand Russell, *The Autobiography of Bertrand Russell: The Early Years*, pp. 193–194.

Despite the intensity of this vision, which seemed clearly to be pushing Russell to acknowledge the importance of instinct and emotion, his logical project was too important for him to question. Eventually "*the mystic insight which I then imagined myself to possess* [my emphasis] has largely faded and the habit of analysis has reasserted itself."[19]

The second blow came three months later, when he discovered a deeply disturbing paradox inherent in his new logic. In effect, he had discovered that Cantor's paradox of the "set of all sets" was not restricted to infinite sets, but applied to all logic.[20] Again, rather than take this as a sign that his project was doomed to failure, Russell refused to take the hint.

> . . . At first, I supposed I should be able to overcome the contradiction quite easily, and that probably there was some trivial error in the reasoning. Gradually, however, it became clear that this was not the case.[21]

As he continued to work on the paradox to no avail, he confessed: "it seemed unworthy of a grown man to spend his time on such trivialities, but what was I to do?"[22]

Finally, the most devastating emotional blow hit. While bicycling one day, he suddenly realized that he was no longer in love with his first wife Alys. Initially he tried to talk himself out of this mood, and behave normally, but Alys could sense the difference. Within a short period of time, it was clear their marriage was at an end as an emotional partnership. Again Russell refused to confront the situation, and either seek a divorce or resurrect their marriage on a stronger foundation. He instead bottled up his feelings, and continued to live with Alys in a miserable state that satisfied neither for the next decade, the same period over which he struggled equally miserably with the *Principia Mathematica*.

[19]Bertrand Russell, *The Autobiography of Bertrand Russell: the Early Years*, p. 194.
[20]This will be discussed at some length later in this chapter.
[21]Bertrand Russell, *The Autobiography of Bertrand Russell: the Early Years*, p. 195.
[22]Bertrand Russell, *The Autobiography of Bertrand Russell: the Early Years*, p. 195.

Symbolic Logic Meets the Barber Paradox

The question "What is a number?" is one which has been often asked, but has only been correctly answered in our own time. The answer was given by Frege in 1884, in his *Grundlagen der Arithmetik.*[23]

Despite these wake-up calls from the unconscious, Russell continued on with his project. By 1902, he had been able to finish his first assault on the mountain: a book called *The Principles of Mathematics.*[24] Though he had been working on this book since 1898, it was Peano's logic that enabled Russell to finally finish it. Now that he was deeply committed to the goal of making logic supreme, he sat down and seriously studied a book he had had for several years, but had never previously been able to

GOTTLOB FREGE

understand: *Grundlagen der Arithmetik, Vol. 1 (The Foundation of Arithmetic)*, by German mathematician and logician Gottlob Frege [1848–1925], which covered much the same territory as Russell's *Principles of Mathematics*. Russell was amazed to find that Frege had anticipated many of Russell's own new ideas; in fact, in many cases Frege had gone beyond Russell in the rigor of his presentation. However, Frege had not yet come upon the paradox we mentioned as the second of Russell's blows, and with which Russell had since been struggling.

On June 16, 1902, Russell wrote to Frege praising his work, and closing with a description of the paradox. The second and con-

---

[23]Bertrand Russell, *Introduction to Mathematical Philosophy*, p. 11.
[24]Published the following year.

cluding volume of Frege's work was at the printer's when he received Russell's letter. Poor Frege was stunned to find his life's work destroyed by a single puzzle. However, he was too honest a man to deny the issue. He immediately replied to Russell that his "conundrum makes not only his Arithmetic, but all possible Arithmetics totter,"[25] then added a brief appendix to the book at the last minute, in which he said that:

> A scientist can hardly encounter anything more undesirable than to have the foundation collapse just as the work is finished. I was put in this position by a letter from Mr. Bertrand Russell.[26]

Russell appreciated the innate decency of Frege's act. As he told a friend in a letter many years later:

> As I think about acts of integrity and grace, I realize that there is nothing in my experience to compare with Frege's dedication to truth. His entire life's work was on the verge of completion. . . . His second volume was about to be published, and upon finding that his fundamental assumption was in error, he responded with intellectual pleasure clearly submerging any feelings of disappointment.[27]

How could a paradox be so powerful that it could destroy a life's work? Most of us regard a paradox as a type of puzzle to amuse or annoy, but hardly a cause for deep concern. The word paradox has many meanings: for example, "an assertion that seems false but actually is true," or that "seems true but actually is false." Or, "a line of reasoning that seems impeccable but which leads to a logical contradiction" (hence a fallacy). However, the word paradox will

---

[25] Nicholas Griffin, *The Selected Letters of Bertrand Russell,* Vol. 1, p. 245.

[26] Quotation from Martin Gardner, *Gotcha: Paradoxes to Puzzle and Delight* (San Francisco: W. H. Freeman, 1982), p. 16.

[27] Nicholas Griffin, *The Selected Letters of Bertrand Russell,* Vol. 1, p. 245.

be used in this book to mean a statement that, if assumed to be true, leads to the conclusion that the statement is false. If assumed to be false, it implies that it is true. Hence, "an assertion whose truth or falsity is undecidable."[28]

Russell coined a popular version of the paradox which had bedeviled Frege and called it *The Barber Paradox*. Consider a village where the barber shaves every male villager if and only if the villager does not shave himself. That's clear enough—some of the villagers shave themselves and some let the barber do the shaving, but everyone gets shaved. The paradox arises when we ask whether the barber (who incidentally is also a male; if not, the paradox obviously disappears) shaves himself. If we assume that he does, then, since the barber only shaves those who don't shave themselves, the barber cannot shave himself. Hence, if he does shave himself, he doesn't shave himself. If we assume that he doesn't shave himself, we get stuck in the circle again, since the barber shaves everyone who doesn't shave himself. Hence, if he doesn't shave himself, he necessarily does shave himself.

> By analyzing the paradoxes to which Cantor's set theory had led [Russell] freed them from all mathematical technicalities, thus bringing to light the amazing fact that our logical intuitions (i.e., intuitions concerning such notions as: truth, concept, being, class, etc.) are self-contradictory.[29]

The version of the paradox which Russell described to Frege concerned Cantor's theory of sets, which formed a central part of both Russell's and Frege's methods. You will recall that Cantor had discovered a paradox concerning the set of all sets.[30] Since it was necessarily the largest set imaginable, how could we reconcile the fact

[28]All quotations from Martin Gardner, *Gotcha: Paradoxes to Puzzle and Delight*, p. vii.
[29]Kurt Gödel, "Russell's Mathematical Logic," 1944, in Paul Benacerraf and Hilary Putnam, *Philosophy of Mathematics: Selected Readings* (Cambridge: Cambridge University Press, 1983), p. 452.
[30]See chapter 7.

that its power set had to be still larger, yet by definition must be included in the set of all sets? Russell discovered that there was a still more pervasive version of this paradox which extended to logic itself. Remember that "a set is a collection of things of the same kind," and that "the set is not the same as the members—the set is the collection, the assemblage, not the things assembled."[31] For that reason, most sets are not members of themselves. For example, the set of all even numbers is not an even number; the set of left-handed tennis players is not a left-handed tennis player. Let's refer to such sets as *normal*. But, contrary to expectations, there are sets which are members of themselves. For example, the set of all concepts which can be imagined is itself a concept which can be imagined. Therefore, it is a member of itself. We'll call such sets *abnormal*.

Russell mentally constructed a higher level set, the set of all normal sets. In other words, the members of this set were themselves sets, sets which did not contain themselves. The paradox arose, just as it did in the "Barber Paradox," when Russell asked whether this set was normal. If he assumed that it was normal, then since it was defined as containing all normal sets, it must contain itself. However, by the definition of normal set, a set which contains itself is not normal. Hence, if it's normal, then it's abnormal. Try assuming the opposite, that it's abnormal. Following a similar line of logic, you arrive at the conclusion that it must be normal. So, if it's normal, it's abnormal and, if it's abnormal, then it's normal.

In March of 1985, the public television science program "Nova" had an episode on the history of mathematics. In that episode they gave a superbly simple illustration of Russell's paradox. They asked the viewer to imagine that there was a central librarian for a state. She requested all the regional librarians to compile a directory volume which listed all the books in their particular library. When she received these directories, she found that some of the librarians had included their directory as one of the books in the library, and some had excluded it.

[31] From chapter 7.

She separated the directories into two different groups on that basis, then began to compile a master directory which listed all the directories in the second group; i.e., those directories which did not include themselves. However, when she had finished listing all the directories, she hit a snag. Should she list the master directory itself or not. And, of course, she was stuck just as Frege was stuck.

Self-Referential Systems

Why does such a paradox arise? The problem is because with both the "Barber Paradox" and in the paradox of the "set of all sets which do not contain themselves," we are dealing with *self-referential* systems. Self-referential systems are systems which refer to themselves. For example, consider the following sentence: "This sentence has five words." The sentence does, in fact, have five words, so the statement, though self-referential, is true. There is also no problem with false self-referential sentences, such as "This sentence has four words," which is false because it actually has five words. However, some self-referential statements present a more paradoxical situation: "This sentence is false." It's clearly self-referential, but is it true or false? When we try to decide, we find ourselves stuck in a vicious cycle. The truth or falsity of the statement is indeterminable.

As this simple example demonstrates, self-referential systems quickly become too complex for logic. The self-referential system par excellence is the mind. Since the mind is the only tool that we have for thinking about anything, that means that the mind is also the only tool which we can use to think about the nature of the mind. Jung was fond of emphasizing "the fundamental fact that in psychology the object of knowledge is at the same time the organ of knowledge, which is true of no other science."[32]

However, Jung was wrong in assuming that the problem is confined to psychology; if we think deeply enough about anything,

---

[32]C. G. Jung, *Collected Works, Vol. 10: Civilization in Transition* (Princeton: Princeton University Press, 1964), ¶ 1025.

we are led ineluctably to think about the process of thought. As an example which we have already discussed at some length, Kant ran up against the same issue in philosophy. Once the Renaissance ideal led men and women to separate themselves from nature in order to observe nature objectively, it was inevitable that they would eventually turn that observation upon themselves. Berkeley and Hume were merely the first in the Western World to demonstrate the nasty little paradoxes that appear when the mind thinks about itself.

Anthropologist Gregory Bateson stressed that all living creatures are complex feedback systems. A feedback system provides information to itself about its performance, which in turn is used to change that performance. That change leads to further feedback, thus forming a continuous loop. The information, which the system feeds back to itself so that it can better adapt to reality, is of a higher order of reality than the behavior that it comments on. Hence living creatures are complex self-referential systems.[33]

As physicist Werner Heisenberg [1901–1976] discovered, even confining our observation to non-living systems is not sufficient to protect us from the problem. At the subatomic level, our observation changes the object under observation, which is another way of saying that the subject, the object, and the act of observation are actually a single system—the split between subject and object is artificial. Thus, even in physical experiments, the subject is once again involved in a self-referential system.[34]

There is no necessary paradox in self-referential systems as long as the systems are finite. Mathematicians have been able to successfully prove the consistency and completeness of many finite mathematical systems. If the system is small enough and simple enough, they simply develop every implication of the system for every member of the system. Thus, if human beings can be viewed independently from the world around them, and if they are nothing more than the finite amount of "things" (such as pro-

---

[33]See Gregory Bateson, *Steps to an Ecology of Mind* (New York: Ballantine Books, 1972) and *Mind and Nature: A Necessary Unity* (New York: E. P. Dutton, 1979).
[34]Werner Heisenberg, *The Physical Principles of the Quantum Theory*, reprint of 1930 edition (New York: Dover Publications, 1949).

teins and nucleic acid, etc.) that make up their physical composition, there is a way out of the problem of self-referencing. The mind is then reducible to the brain, and the problem of the brain thinking about itself eventually winds down since it is at most a finite process.

That is still the most popular scientific position. The point of this book is that such a position seems increasingly untenable as we dig deeper into any of the systems that explore the universe, from philosophy to mathematics to physics to psychology; in fact, to any field at all. All fields of thought eventually involve themselves in infinite self-referential systems.[35] And the only way out of that dilemma lies in an archetypal hypothesis, such as developed by Jung and Gödel in their separate fields. But we are getting ahead of ourselves and need to get back to Russell's project.

PRINCIPIA MATHEMATICA: LOGIC'S TOWER OF BABEL

Though Russell was initially buoyed in reading Frege, by the discovery that he was not alone in his quest, Frege was no more able to solve Russell's paradox than Russell himself. Russell found himself in a strange position. Except for the paradox, his grandiose goal of subsuming all nature within logic seemed achievable. For example, in 1902, he was teaching a course at Cambridge where:

> . . . I began with 22 Pp's [i.e., primitive proposition, or axioms] of general logic . . . and I deduced from them all of pure mathematics, including Cantor[36] and geometry, without any new Pp's or primitive concepts. All this will appear in the book that I plan to publish with Whitehead. We could even deduce rational mechanics [i.e., Newtonian physics]. . . . [With some alternative defini-

---

[35] And if not literally infinite, of such a large size as to be forever beyond the ability to calculate. Allan Turing was the first to realize that there are such practical limits to what can be achievable by science.

[36] Cantor's transfinite set theory.

tions, we could do] the same for non-Newtonian mechanics.[37]

On the other hand, if he tried to resolve the paradox—and resolve it he must, or give up on his goal—the task became Herculean in size and scope. Russell struggled on, never dealing fully with any of his three calls from the unconscious. He suppressed his mystical experience, and tried to compensate by writing a never-completed book, aptly titled *Prisons*, which contained what might be thought of as a logician's religion: i.e., Russell accepted that humans have a need for the religious feeling, but he also acknowledged that there is no actual basis for religion. In other words, live a lie because it's a necessary lie. This was pretty pallid stuff that satisfied no one, including himself.

Russell seemed to be a man torn between his mind and his heart.[38] In 1903, his mood might be summed up in a letter he wrote to a female friend:

> But as for me, I have felt no emotions of any kind, except on rare occasions, for some time now; and this is a state of things most convenient for work, though very dull.[39]

His work consisted of an endless, mind-deadening struggle to somehow resolve the paradox. Russell confessed that, during 1903 and 1904, he used to sit all morning staring at a blank piece of paper, break for lunch, then stare again all afternoon. At day's end he sat with nothing more than when the day began.[40] Things began to improve slightly in 1905, when he discovered what has come to be called the *Theory of Descriptions*, then improved more in 1906, when he discovered the *Theory of Types*. However, these discoveries were stopgaps, not intellectual breakthroughs like his discovery of

---

[37]Nicholas Griffin, *The Selected Letters of Bertrand Russell,* Vol. 1, p. 227. Brackets mine.

[38]This state of affairs wasn't to be broken until 1911, when the *Principia* was completed, and he began a passionate affair with Lady Ottoline Morrell.

[39]Bertrand Russell, *The Autobiography of Bertrand Russell: The Early Years*, p. 225.

[40]Bertrand Russell, *The Autobiography of Bertrand Russell: The Early Years*, p. 200.

Peano in 1900. Though they enabled him to once more continue his project, even Russell recognized the limitation of his solution.

In effect he solved the paradox by defining it away. He began with classes, which were much the same as sets except that they were defined such that they could neither be members of themselves, nor have any actual existence. A class was defined to be on a higher order than its members. Classes of classes were on a higher order than classes, and so forth. Hence there could be no such thing as the set of sets which were not members of themselves, since by definition his classes did not include themselves. The problem wasn't in any way truly resolved; it was just pushed off to infinity.[41]

This solution of shoving the problem out of sight, like an ostrich sticking its head in the sand, was the same that some of Russell's philosophical allies called the *Vienna Circle*[42] used later in the 1920's in their creation of a philosophy known as *logical positivism*. Logical positivism insisted that since the ultimate questions about reality—metaphysical questions—were not open to either logical or experimental verification, they were not questions at all. Logical positivists confined all questions about the ultimate nature of reality to the dust heap of non-sense: literally not sensible, since they did not refer directly or indirectly to sensory perception. Their attitude was that if questions are too bothersome to fit into a theory, just define them away as non-questions.

However, Russell at least felt he had a way out, even if it wasn't the triumph he had hoped for.

> After this it only remained to write the book out. Whitehead's teaching work left him not enough leisure for this mechanical job. I worked at it from ten to twelve hours a day for about eight months in the year, from 1907 to 1910.[43]

---

[41]We will discuss this more in chapters 12 and 16, when we consider Gödel's insights, and his famous incompleteness proof.

[42]See chapter 16.

[43]Bertrand Russell, *The Autobiography of Bertrand Russell: The Early Years*, p. 201.

And what had they then accomplished? Well, the manuscript was so huge that they had to hire "an old four-wheeler"[44] to cart it off to the publisher. The publisher knew the audience for such a book was so tiny that they would be taking a loss on it. They were willing to absorb part of the loss, but not all. The Royal Society picked up another part, but ultimately Russell had to pay £100 for the privilege of having this product of ten years work published. And, having done that, he said later that he knew of only six people in the entire world who had read the whole book.[45] In fact, it is often said among mathematicians and logicians that no one except Russell and Whitehead has ever read all of the *Principia*, and even they may not have read all of each other's work. Though his life was to take many fascinating turns over another sixty years, he said that "my intellect never quite recovered from the strain."[46]

While it was presented as a joint work, it was clear that it was Russell's project from beginning to end. Whitehead's later work went in a direction opposite to Russell's; his philosophical position accords well with the viewpoints presented in this book, while Russell remained confident to his death that logic was sufficient to the solution of all of humanity's problems. Yet it seems clear now that the *Principia* not only didn't come close to accomplishing Russell's full goals, it is questionable whether it accomplished anything of substance. In Gödel's words:

> As to the question of how far mathematics can be built up on this basis [i.e., that of Russell and Whitehead in *Principia Mathematica*] . . . , it is clear that the theory of real numbers in its present form cannot be obtained . . . . The question whether (or to what extent) the theory of integers can be obtained . . . must be considered as un-solved at the present time. It is to be noted, however, that, even in case this question should have a positive an-

[44]Bertrand Russell, *The Autobiography of Bertrand Russell: The Early Years*, p. 201.
[45]Nicholas Griffin, *The Selected Letters of Bertrand Russell*, Vol. 1, p. 297.
[46]Bertrand Russell, *The Autobiography of Bertrand Russell: The Early Years*, p. 202.

swer, this would be of no value for the problem of whether arithmetic follows from logic.[47]

If Russell had been able to develop a consistent and complete arithmetic from the axioms of symbolic logic, then logic would indeed rule the universe. Logic would explain arithmetic, arithmetic would explain geometry and calculus, which would in turn explain physics and astronomy and the other sciences, and the sciences would explain the world. The universe would have been reduced to the manipulations of logical symbols. Like the builders of the biblical tower of Babel, Russell and Whitehead were attempting to construct an edifice beyond humankind's capability. Like the biblical tower, it also collapsed because of the limits of language. Kurt Gödel was to destroy what was left of Russell's dream much as Russell destroyed Frege's. As we will see, this was because Gödel's view of reality was broader than Russell's, as Jung's was more broad than Freud's.

---

[47]Kurt Gödel, "Russell's Mathematical Logic," in Benacerraf and Putnam, *Philosophy of Mathematics: Selected Readings*, p. 463.

CHAPTER 10

BACKGROUND FOR JUNG'S PSYCHOLOGY

My life is a story of the self-realization of the unconscious. Everything in the unconscious seeks outward manifestation, and the personality too desires to evolve out of its unconscious conditions and to experience itself as a whole.[1]

A LOVE OF NATURE

C. G. Jung [1875–1961] lived his whole life in Switzerland. His father was a minister in a rural region near Basel. Though Jung traveled widely to places as far separated as the American Southwest and East Africa, he remained at heart a Swiss, with his roots in the Swiss countryside.

> Jung loved animals and plants, not only when he was a child but all his life, and he could never see enough of the beauty of lakes, forests and mountains. Nature was for him of prime importance and striking descriptions of nature are scattered through all his works.[2]

---

[1] C. G. Jung, *Memories, Dreams, Reflections* (New York: Vintage Books/Random House, 1965), p. 3.
[2] Marie-Louise von Franz, *C. G. Jung: His Myth in Our Time* (New York: C. G. Jung Foundation for Analytical Psychology, 1975), p. 27. Also see Barbara Hanna, *Jung, His Life and Work: A Biographical Memoir* (New York: Capricorn Books/G. P. Putnam's Sons, 1976), pp. 11–18 for much about Jung's Swiss qualities.

C. G. JUNG

This earthy quality always remained an integral part of Jung. He was more interested in the reality he observed than in theoretical discussions that had no roots in the world.

> He remained faithful all his life to the conviction that the facts of nature are the basis of all knowledge; . . . for him nature is not only outside but also within.[3]

Jung was well-educated in literature and philosophy, in contrast to most of the early clinical and experimental psychologists, whose education was almost entirely scientific. He gloried:

> . . . in Goethe's *Faust*, which his mother brought to his attention when he was in the Gymnasium. "It poured into my soul like a miraculous balm." . . . For the rest of his life, and despite certain moral criticisms of the character of Faust, Jung kept his great admiration for Goethe and, indeed, loved him as one loves a kindred spirit.[4]

He was convinced that an accurate description of reality required both scientific precision and poetic understanding.

> [This made it] difficult to find a form in which to communicate his innermost convictions. . . . He tried to assume the scientific style of the contemporary psychological works, but he was never able entirely to give up poetic language.[5]

In an attempt to be scientific, his early experimental work was written in a turgid style that is reminiscent of scientific papers to this day. But his later work abounds in poetic passages that better capture the majesty of their subject. This combination has scared off many readers, just as a similar combination has made Hegel suspect

[3]Marie-Louise von Franz, *C. G. Jung: His Myth in Our Time*, pp. 32–33.
[4]Marie-Louise von Franz, *C. G. Jung: His Myth in Our Time*, pp. 34–35.
[5]Marie-Louise von Franz, *C. G. Jung: His Myth in Our Time*, p. 36.

as a philosopher, and C. P. Snow as a novelist. The latter has argued convincingly that our time needs people and thoughts that bridge the *two cultures* of science and the arts. C. G. Jung's work does just that.

GHOSTS AND SPIRITS

The farmers who lived in the region near Jung's childhood home accepted the reality of the earth that fed them; equally they accepted that there were other, unearthly aspects to reality. As a boy, Jung heard tales of ghosts and spirits, of poltergeists and possession. Unlike most intellectuals, he didn't dismiss these out-of-hand as superstition. If they were experienced as psychic realities, Jung wanted to know why, and he wanted to explore them. His first scientific paper was a study of a young female cousin who for a short time achieved local renown as a medium. What especially interested him was the contrast between his cousin's normal thoughts and speech, and some of the material she communicated while in a trance. This same contrast can be seen today between those who *channel* and the personalities they channel. As with Jung's cousin, most of the material tends to be either readily known to the person doing the channeling, or else so vague and overblown it has little meaning. But there is also occasional material that isn't so easily explained away.[6]

It was Jung's curiosity about phenomena such as this, phenomena which were readily dismissed by his colleagues, that led him to his greatest discoveries, and which has also prevented many from accepting Jung's ideas. He was never able to ignore experience just because it didn't fit his view of reality. In his spiritual autobiography, *Memories, Dreams, Reflections,* Jung spoke of his interest in psychic phenomena as a student, and the reaction of his fellow students.

---

[6]C. G. Jung, "On the Psychology and Pathology of So-Called Occult Phenomena," 1902, in *Collected Works, Vol. 1: Psychiatric Studies,* 2nd ed., Bollingen Series XX (Princeton: Princeton University Press, 1970), ¶ 37–155.

I read virtually the whole of the literature available to me at the time. Naturally I also spoke of these matters to my comrades, who to my great astonishment reacted with derision and disbelief or with anxious defensiveness. I wondered at the sureness with which they could assert that things like ghosts and table-turning were impossible and therefore fraudulent, and on the other hand at the evidently anxious nature of their defensiveness.[7]

In dealing with Jung's ideas, it is important to understand this stolid, earthy side to his personality. Jung always stressed that he considered himself a descriptive scientist. When Jung described concepts his colleagues regarded as mystical, such as his concept of the collective unconscious, Jung was describing something that he had personally experienced so many times that he could not justifiably ignore it. If Jung erred at all in spreading his ideas, it could be that, like Darwin, he collected evidence far beyond the point most would regard as necessary.

Though Jung was normally content to describe the reality he found, like all good scientists, he was a superb model-maker. Fortunately, Jung never confused his models with reality—his whole career was an attempt to develop ever better models to express the inexpressible. Since he was also modest enough to doubt that he was the first to develop similar ideas, he searched for earlier models which prefigured his own. In this book, we will discuss three such models: (1) the tripartite division of the psyche into consciousness, *personal unconscious*,[8] and *collective unconscious*; (2) the *archetypes of development*;[9] and (3) the *alchemical model*.[10] Let's begin with how Jung came to the concept of the unconscious.

---

[7] C. G. Jung, *Memories, Dreams, Reflections*, p. 99.

[8] See chapter 11.

[9] Term coined by the author, not Jung; see chapters 13, 14, and 15.

[10] Which presumed that, due to the psychological naivete of alchemists, alchemical operations were actually projections of inner developmental issues. See chapters 17 and 18.

Consciousness Emerging from the Unconscious

Because Jung felt that psychology was too young a science to develop a theoretical superstructure, he tried to content himself with describing what he encountered. However, as a clinical psychologist, he was also concerned with the practical problem of how to resolve these polarities as he encountered them in his patients. It was in his attempts to resolve their problems that Jung encountered a world that had been previously unknown to Western science. It was through his resolution to confine himself to description that he was able to produce such a detailed and accurate picture of the deepest levels of the human psyche. Finally, it was through Jung's immense erudition that he was able to relate what he encountered in the dreams and fantasies of his patients to the art, literature, philosophy, mythology, and religion of the world.

Jung found that his patients came into therapy because their conscious resources were inadequate to their problems. He felt that the emotional problems they presented reflected an attempt at a resolution from a new direction: the unconscious. Like Freud, Jung turned to the unconscious of his patients in an attempt to find a solution to their problems. Since Jung was a descriptive scientist rather than a theoretician, he found a much different world than Freud. Jung's 1935 lectures at the Tavistock clinic in London summarized his ideas at approximately the midpoint of his career. During these lectures, Jung commented that:

> [Freud] derives the unconscious from the conscious. . . .
> I would put it the reverse way: I would say the thing that
> comes first is obviously the unconscious; . . . in early
> childhood we are unconscious; the most important functions of an instinctive nature are unconscious, and consciousness is rather the product of the unconscious.[11]

This is one of the key distinctions between Jung's and Freud's views of the unconscious. Freud initially felt that the unconscious was

---

[11]C. G. Jung, *Analytic Psychology: Its Theory & Practice* (New York: Vintage Books, 1968), p. 8.

merely the repository for consciously repressed thoughts and feelings. Due to Jung's early research, Freud acknowledged that there were elements in the unconscious that seemed to be some sort of *race memory*. But since Freud had already developed his theory of the unconscious, he considered these race memories as little more than curiosities.

As a young doctor just beginning his life work, Jung was enormously impressed with Freud's ideas. Accordingly, Jung began his own exploration of the unconscious of his patients with the assumption that he would encounter only repressed products of consciousness. But the descriptive scientist won out as Jung continued his exploration. It was impossible to retain Freud's theories and deal adequately with the full contents of his patients' dreams. So he gradually discarded Freud's theories and just described what he found.

Jung recognized that, in dealing with the unconscious, we are encountering a world of which we know absolutely nothing, other than that it is not available to consciousness. "We often mean to convey something by the term, but as a matter of fact we simply convey that we do not know what the unconscious is.[12] The unconscious can only be viewed indirectly, through its by-products. This is the same world encountered by particle physicists, who are forced to deal with subatomic particles which can only be viewed indirectly, through their by-products. Particle-physicists record the interaction of subatomic particles in a bubble chamber. To anyone but a physicist, a picture of particle reactions in a bubble-chamber shows nothing but a bewildering jumble of lines—just so, the confusing, non-logical, seemingly incoherent scenes presented in our dreams. But both bubble-chambers and dreams can imply a great deal to those who observe, with openness and understanding, enough of either. Nineteenth century science still assumed it could directly observe nature; the 20th century has learned otherwise. The difference is profound.

Freed from the strait-jacket of Freudian dogma, Jung found a very strange world indeed, equally strange as and totally parallel to

[12]C. G. Jung, *Analytic Psychology: Its Theory & Practice*, pp. 6–7.

the world of particle physics. It was an undifferentiated world, seemingly free of the restrictions of time and space that define consciousness. "The area of the unconscious is enormous and always continuous, while the area of consciousness is a restricted field of momentary vision."[13]

CONFRONTATION WITH THE UNCONSCIOUS

When Jung published *Symbols of Transformation* in 1912,[14] he extended the symbolic interpretation of dreams far beyond the sexual interpretation Freud declared to be holy dogma for psychoanalysis. Jung examined the fantasies of a woman referred to as "Miss Frank Miller," which Theodore Flournoy had published in 1906. There is an oft-quoted cliché that Freudian patients have Freudian dreams and Jungian patients have Jungian dreams. Since Jung had no personal contact with Miss Miller, this book stands as a document to the lack of validity of the above cliché.

In it, Jung traced the "transformations and symbols of the libido" from tiny seeds in the early fantasies to full-blown development in the later fantasies. Just as the early dreams and fantasies of Miss Miller contain the seeds of later developments, Jung's earlier work contained the seeds of his later developments. In fact, more than two decades later, in *Psychology and Alchemy*,[15] Jung repeated this task with a series of four hundred dreams and visions of a patient with whom he had no personal contact.

Though Jung strove mightily to use Freud's interpretations wherever possible, he ranged far beyond sexual reductionism. He drew extensively on mythology to amplify images in Miss Miller's fantasies and show how her psyche was attempting to re-establish a

---

[13]C. G. Jung, *Analytic Psychology: Its Theory & Practice*, p. 8.

[14]Originally titled *Transformations and Symbols of the Libido*; extensively rewritten in the 2nd edition of 1952, which is published as *Collected Works, Vol. 5: Symbols of Transformation* (Princeton: Princeton University Press, 1967).

[15]Originally published in 1952, based on lectures given in 1935–1936, now published as C. G. Jung *Collected Works, Vol. 12: Psychology and Alchemy*, 2nd edition (Princeton: Princeton University Press, 1968).

psychic wholeness. Because Miss Miller was incapable of integrating the forces of the unconscious, and because her therapist also did not understand the process enough to help her integrate such forces, she eventually had a psychotic break. Jung carefully described how each element of the fantasies related to her on-going problems and showed the slow deterioration of the psyche due to the lack of conscious integration.[16]

Freud viewed Jung as his favorite son, and selected him to be his successor. However, the price Jung had to pay for this honor—uncritical acceptance of Freud's ideas—soon proved too high. Freud viewed Jung's new ideas as his expression of the Oedipal desire of a son to destroy his father.[17] Freud disinherited his "son" and "cast him forth into the wilderness."[18] With the publication of *Symbols of Transformation*, Jung was forced to resign all his positions in the psychoanalytic community, and became *persona non grata* to psychoanalysts everywhere. Excommunication would be a fair term for what Jung experienced.

Jung had deeply admired Freud and found his exclusion a painful isolation. Initially still under the sway of Freud's ideas, he reviewed his life—twice!—especially his childhood, hoping to find some explanation for what had happened, some reason to agree with Freud. But he found nothing and accepted that he was on his own. He realized that if he was right and Freud was wrong, then he would have to explore the unconscious forces within, no matter where they took him. During the period from 1913 to 1917, a so-called fallow period where he published little but in actuality laid the groundwork for most of his later publications, Jung did just that. Where before he had sometimes interposed Freudian theory

---

[16] I once had a patient in a similar situation, flooded with material from the unconscious in an attempt to restore psychic wholeness. She had already made one suicide attempt and was considering another. By helping her understand this strange material which bombarded her consciousness, the author reduced her fear. In under six months, she left therapy, totally transformed, not by therapy and not by conscious effort, but rather by her ability to integrate the material thrust upon her by the forces of the unconscious.

[17] And, of course, there was some truth in that evaluation. Jung would have been a difficult son for any father to keep in check.

[18] My biblical quotation, not Freud's.

between himself and the figures that appeared in his dreams, now he let himself sink deeply into dreams and visions, much like inducing a psychosis.[19] Some less complimentary biographers of Jung have, in fact, regarded this as a psychotic period.

Recently, psychiatrist John Nelson has written about the differences between psychosis and experiences like Jung's, experiences which philosopher Michael Washburn refers to as "regression in the service of transcendence." The differences between the two are as marked as the similarities. For example, schizophrenia usually first occurs in the teens or early 20s and takes a degenerative course, while an experience like Jung's most often occurs in mid-life (Jung was 38), is precipitated by an outer event (such as the break with Freud), and eventually is integrated into the person's life. Though both those experiencing the onset of schizophrenia and RIST suffer in the "sloughs of despond" (as John Bunyan already knew so well), those passing through this dark place on the way to a transcendence of their current ego state also have a wide variety of emotional experiences as their psyche tries to integrate this new material. In general, one might characterize the difference as that between one who has no strong ego developed and is swallowed up by what they are experiencing, and one who already has a strong ego which needs to be taken down a peg in order to be transcended.[20]

From 1913 to 1917, Jung lived in this symbolic world. He explored every dream and vision—no image was ignored from fear or laziness. In order to keep stability in his life during this period, Jung kept regular office hours with patients, and spent a normal amount of time with his wife and children. When the energy from the unconscious grew too overpowering, he would do yoga exercises, which helped to contain the energy. But the rest of the time, he allowed himself to journey into the strange and frightening land of the unconscious. Time and again, he found himself nearly over-

---

[19] See C. G. Jung, *Memories, Dreams, Reflections*, "Confrontation with the Unconscious," pp. 170–199.

[20] See Michael Washburn, *Transpersonal Psychology in Psychoanalytic Perspective* (New York: SUNY Press, 1994), pp. 254–256, and Michael Washburn, *The Ego and the Dynamic Ground* (New York: SUNY Press, 1995), pp. 171–202.

whelmed by the strange fantasies that invaded his thoughts. It was as if the nighttime world of dreams had invaded the day. This left him constantly in a state of anxiety, wondering when the next onset would begin. However, as he found himself surviving one inner battle after another, a sense of strength and purpose grew. He began to realize that this wasn't psychosis, but some task given him by a higher power.

As time passed, and he weathered the storms that raged within him, he slowly developed a psychic center where there was always calm, even during the storms. Finally, "the stream of fantasies ebbed away,"[21] and he could take stock of the world he'd explored. An unusually rich period of creativity followed.

If there was one thing Jung had learned during this trying period, it was the power of the images of the unconscious. During the worst of his inner battles, he discovered that whenever he could take the emotions that buffeted him and translate them into images, he felt calmer. This acceptance of the primacy of images was to be at the core of all his future psychology. Jung's split with Freud was caused by many differences, but primary was his disagreement with Freud's sexual reduction of dream images; e.g., a key is a penis, a cave is a vagina. In his work with patients, Jung had come to feel that dreams were far too complex for such easy translation. Now Jung had experienced the dream world firsthand, and knew not only intellectually, but emotionally, that a symbol was far more than a sign.

SYMBOLS, SIGNS AND ARCHETYPES

For Jung, a *symbol* needed to be clearly distinguished from a *sign*. A symbol was not something that stood in a concrete one-to-one relationship with something else. Nor was a symbol something purely abstract, such as "a printed or written sign used to represent an operation, element, quantity, quality, or relation, as in mathematics or music."[22] As long as a symbol was truly a symbol and not

---

[21]C. G. Jung, *Memories, Dreams, Reflections*, p. 206.
[22]*American Heritage Dictionary, 2nd College Edition* (Boston: Houghton Mifflin), p. 1230.

merely a sign, it was inexhaustible, an endless metaphor. A symbol was a living thing, not some dead abstraction which could be pinned down to the page.

> The symbol is alive only so long as it is pregnant with meaning.[23]

> Every psychic product, if it is the best possible expression at the moment for a fact as yet unknown or only relatively known, may be regarded as a symbol.[24]

A sign stands for something known; it is derivative, where symbols precede conscious understanding. Hence a symbol is reduced to a sign after the mystery it represented is fully understood. Consider the cross as a symbol. Jung commented that:

> . . . The way in which St. Paul and the earlier speculative mystics speak of the cross shows that for them it was still a living symbol which expressed the inexpressible in unsurpassable form.[25]

Though Jung never used the term *archetype* in this essay, there was a clear indication that he was discussing one of the two possible ways in which archetypes came into existence. In several contexts previously in this book, we have considered the other possibility; objects and events that have had meaning for a large number of people for a long period of time leave a record in the human psyche.

Though materialists would argue about where such a record is kept,[26] such a concept could be readily assimilated into science as we know it. But clearly it won't happen without a great deal of protest from the mainstream scientific community. When, in recent

---

[23]C. G. Jung, *Collected Works, Vol. 6: Psychological Types*, ¶ 816.

[24]C. G. Jung, *Collected Works, Vol. 6: Psychological Types*, ¶ 817.

[25]C. G. Jung, *Collected Works, Vol. 6: Psychological Types*, ¶ 816.

[26]Occult literature refers to such material as Akasic Traces; i.e., a trace in the ether; to indicate clearly that such a record is not contained in matter.

years, biologist Rupert Sheldrake postulated a similar process—*morphic resonance*—the scientific community reacted loudly and angrily.[27] This, despite the fact that Sheldrake had drawn extensively on existing behavioral research with rats—the meat-and-potatoes of experimental psychology—to argue for such morphic resonance.[28]

If it is hard to accept that oft-repeated events leave a trail in the psyche, it is clearly harder yet to accept that sometimes the archetype comes first and the objects or events that mirror it follow afterward. But how else to explain the creativity of the psyche?[29] When conscious methods are insufficient to resolve an issue, emotional energy is diverted into the unconscious. The longer the issue remains unresolved, the more the pressure builds. Eventually, something bursts forth into consciousness that is the "best possible expression at the moment for a fact as yet unknown"[30] (to use Jung's term).

If the problem that needs resolution is not confined to a single person, but rather engages most of humanity over a large period of time, then the emotional energy is correspondingly greater, as is the pressure, and as is the eventual symbol that emerges. Jung points out that a new living symbol must be both "the product of the most complex and differentiated minds of that age," yet also "must embrace what is common to a large group of men." This is quite a challenge and guarantees that a living symbol cannot possibly be something that can be appreciated by only the select few. Rather "the common factor must be something that is still so primitive that its ubiquity cannot be doubted."[31]

In our era—where living symbols are in short supply—people turn to dead symbols, like the cross or the flag, pretending that they still have energy. Those too honest to delude themselves in such a

---

[27] One comment in a reputable journal was "if ever there was a book fit for burning, it's this one."

[28] Rupert Sheldrake, *A New Science of Life: The Hypothesis of Formative Causation* (Los Angeles: J. P. Tarcher, 1981).

[29] Which will be addressed more directly in the next chapter.

[30] C. G. Jung, *Collected Works, Vol. 6: Psychological Types*, ¶ 817.

[31] All quotes from C. G. Jung, *Collected Works, Vol. 6: Psychological Types*, ¶ 820.

way frequently despair of any new meaning ever emerging. They fool themselves in turn with litanies of despair, such as existentialism or nihilism, as if the pronouncement that all was meaningless itself possessed some inherent meaning. Both groups deeply yearn for meaning and purpose in their lives. Over sixty years ago, Jung discussed the role of the individual in bringing a new archetypal symbol into existence.

> . . . Only the passionate yearning of a highly developed mind, for which the traditional symbol is no longer the unified expression of the rational and the irrational, of the highest and the lowest, can create a new symbol. . . . For this collaboration of opposing states to be possible at all, they must first face one another in the fullest conscious opposition. This necessarily entails a violent disunion with oneself, to the point where thesis and antithesis negate one another, while the ego is forced to acknowledge its absolute participation in both. If there is a subordination of one part, the symbol will be predominantly the product of the other part, and, to that extent, less a symbol than a symptom—a symptom of the suppressed antithesis. . . . Since life cannot tolerate a standstill, a damming up of vital energy results, and this would lead to an insupportable condition did not the tension of opposites produce a new, uniting function that transcends them. . . . I have called this process in its totality the *transcendent function.*[32]

Thus Jung explained exactly how the individual could help bring a new symbol into existence. It requires the "passionate yearning of a highly developed mind" as well as the acceptance of a "violent disunion with oneself." To the extent that a person avoids the tension by giving primacy to either the spiritual or the instinctual side of the problem, the emerging product is "less a symbol than a symptom." If one bears the tension, and does not yield to the pull

[32]C. G. Jung, *Collected Works, Vol. 6: Psychological Types,* ¶ 823–828.

of one side or the other, "the tension of opposites produces a new, uniting function that transcends them."

The late 20th century is a time when the tension has reached the breaking point. We have seen the twin poles of spirit and instinct pull people in first one direction, then in the other. Over the last 35 years, for example, the sexual revolution argued for the primacy of instinct, the "born again" movement the primacy of spirit; liberals argued for our social responsibility to others, conservatives for the need to take responsibility for oneself. Back and forth the pendulum has swung, carrying people in its wake. But neither side of the pendulum's swing can contain a final answer.

The power and mystery of the unconscious can easily overwhelm. Too often, when one discovers the power of the unconscious, one discounts one's own power and yields abjectly to the unconscious. Or, alternately, one arrogantly assumes that all these strange new things belong to oneself. In his own five-year struggle, Jung found of necessity that the ego had to be strong and vital in its turn. Only the equal and opposite pull of conscious and unconscious can produce a true synthesis.

CHAPTER 11

Jung's Model of the Psyche

One-fifth, or one-third, or perhaps even one-half of our human life is spent in an unconscious condition. Our early childhood is unconscious. Every night we sink into the unconscious, and only in phases between waking and sleeping have we a more or less clear consciousness. [1]

Conscious and Unconscious

Jung proposed that the totality of the human psyche (actual or potential) breaks down into three categories: (1) personal consciousness, (2) the personal unconscious, and (3) the collective unconscious. [2] Personal consciousness, of which modern men and women are so rightly proud, is a very transitory affair, consisting of whatever occupies our conscious awareness at a given moment of time. There is nothing which we retain permanently in consciousness, including our sense of identity or ego, which comes and goes. Consciousness is only a sliding frame which moves along, sometimes lit by awareness, sometimes not.

Everything passes into consciousness first by way of the unconscious. Even sense perceptions are first processed somewhere

---

[1] C. G. Jung, *Analytic Psychology: Its Theory & Practice* (New York: Vintage Books/Random House, 1968), p. 6.

[2] He was also much concerned throughout his life with the obvious fourth such element—collective consciousness—against which the individual must struggle during the individuation process; e.g., see C. G. Jung, *Collected Works, Vol. 8: The Structure and Dynamics of the Psyche* (Princeton: Princeton University Press, 1960), ¶ 423–424.

inside us, in a way of which we are largely unaware, and then pass into consciousness. Objects and events become conscious momentarily then pass out of consciousness again, as our awareness either shifts to something else, or turns itself off for awhile. Those things that were conscious are either recorded in some fashion or lost.

> . . . the *sum total of unconscious contents* falls into three groups: first, temporarily subliminal contents that can be reproduced voluntarily (memory); second, unconscious contents that cannot be reproduced voluntarily; third, contents that are not capable of becoming conscious at all. Group two can be inferred from the spontaneous irruption of subliminal contents into consciousness. Group three is hypothetical; it is a logical inference from the facts underlying group two.[3]

Jung was deliberately simplifying the extremely complex relationship between conscious and unconscious material in order to stress that consciousness is not the whole of the psyche. As examples of the first group, we can all recite the alphabet or the multiplication tables. Consider, however, the fact that a great deal of unconscious material can be accessed without ever passing into conscious awareness. For example, we don't have to be conscious of tying our shoes in order to correctly tie them, though we can make ourselves aware of how we tie them if necessary. We can even go through the process in our minds without actually touching shoes or shoelaces.[4] The relationship between conscious and unconscious is clearly complex.

Or consider the huge gray area that lies between Jung's first two categories, all that material which can be recovered into consciousness, but only with difficulty. We can all recall into consciousness events of emotional significance in our lives. The amount

---

[3]C. G. Jung, *Collected Works, Vol. 9ii: Aion, Researches into the Phenomenology of the Self* (Princeton: Princeton University Press, 1959), ¶ 4. Jung's emphasis.

[4]This complex relationship is, for example, why visualization is so effective in modern sports training.

of conscious recall of such events largely varies with the significance of the event; in his early work, Jung presented this in energetic terms. Emotion was psychic energy. Memories passed into consciousness when the energy level was high enough.[5]

There are many memories that are at the borderline of conscious recall for us. These might have been originally too insignificant to pay close attention to. We can try mental tricks of association in order to try and recall these hazy memories. If the tricks are clever enough, such as being put into a deep hypnotic trance, we can usually recall every detail of these borderline events. The energy model helps explain all this quite well.

Other memories are also not easily recoverable, not because they have too little emotional significance, but because they have too much. For example, if an event was too painful for us to accept, we may have recorded the memory fully, but erected psychic barriers to prevent our reexperiencing the pain. This could be a physical pain, such as a broken bone, or an emotional pain, such as an incident when we were deeply humiliated. These are what Freud means by "repressed" memories.

Another example would be an event that was too threatening to deal with. If, while crossing the street, we suddenly saw a car coming at us, we might block out the perception even before it caused us pain. Our conscious memory would end with the sight of the car coming at us. We might also have no conscious memory of an event that threatened our view of reality. For example, if someone had constructed a rigidly rationalist view of life, they might not see a ghost, if there was such a thing, even if it appeared before their eyes. The sight would be too threatening, in that their whole view of reality would be in jeopardy. So they wouldn't consciously see the ghost, nor would they be able to bring that memory into consciousness. However, it might be accessible by special techniques such as hypnosis.[6]

---

[5] C. G. Jung, *Collected Works, Vol. 8: The Structure and Dynamics of the Psyche*, ¶ 1–130.

[6] If anything, Jung understated the complexity of memory. Modern research on memory seems to indicate that it comes closer to being recreated each time than merely pulled out of the filing cabinet of memory. The literature in cognitive psychology on this subject is already vast, though final conclusions are still a long way off.

All of these memories are part of what Jung calls the personal unconscious. They constitute the totality of Freud's unconscious.[7] But Jung contended that there remained a much bigger entity than the personal unconscious, which he termed the collective unconscious.

COLLECTIVE UNCONSCIOUS

. . . there exists a second psychic system of a collective, universal, and impersonal nature which is identical in all individuals. This collective unconscious does not develop individually, but is inherited. It consists of pre-existent forms, the archetypes.[8]

The concept of biologically inherited instincts has risen and fallen in scientific acceptance several times in the past. In our time, the study of the relationship between learned and instinctual behavior has become the cornerstone of the new fields of ethology, best-known to the public through the popular works of Nobel prize winner Konrad Lorenz,[9] and sociobiology, whose best-known representative is its founder, biologist Edward O. Wilson.[10] There are also pioneering animal researchers like Jane Goodall, who, unsatisfied with the results previously obtained by observing animals in laboratory settings, have begun to observe animal behavior in its natural setting over long periods of time. This research has shown just how much behavior hitherto assumed to be exclusively human is also exhibited by animals. The clear implication is that much of human behavior seems to be affected by inherited genetic patterns.

---

[7] With the exception of the small place he allotted to vestigial race memories after Jung pointed out inescapably collective images in dreams.

[8] C. G. Jung, *Collected Works, Vol. 9i: The Archetypes and the Collective Unconscious* (Princeton: Princeton University Press, 1959), ¶ 90.

[9] See Konrad Lorenz, *King Solomon's Ring* (New York: Crowell, 1952); Richard I. Evans, *Konrad Lorenz: the Man and his Ideas* (Orlando: Harcourt Brace, 1975).

[10] See Edward O. Wilson, *The Diversity of Life* (Cambridge, MA: Belknap Press of Harvard University Press, 1992) for his most recent popular book. However, Wilson's viewpoint differs markedly from the archetypal hypothesis presented in this book.

Jung would have strongly supported all of this research. What he was the first to realize is that instinctual behavior implies equally archetypal cognitive patterns. Prior to Jung, instincts were vague amorphous concepts; he realized that they had to be highly specific if they were going to accomplish their goals. Yet they also had to be capable of adaption to the particular circumstances with which they were presented. Hence archetypes/instincts were necessarily form-less until actualized in someone's life.[11]

Jung worked at the Burgholzli Mental Clinic in Switzerland from 1900 to 1909. He developed a rapport with the schizophrenic patients there by the simple expedient of listening to them. It was common practice then, as now, to ignore their dissociative speech as meaningless ravings. In contrast, Jung paid close attention to the words and tried to sort out the associational string of thoughts which lay behind the seeming nonsense.

One of Jung's male schizophrenic patients had delusions of grandeur in which he considered himself God the Father and Christ united in one person. He liked Jung and evidently decided to initiate Jung into his religion, so that one day in 1906, he told Jung to look closely at the sun and he'd see something interesting. He told Jung if he looked closely he would see that the sun had a penis that hung down from it. When the penis swung from side to side, it created the winds. Jung had no idea what to make of this.

Four years later, after Jung had begun his deep studies of mythology, he came across a then-recently-published book by philologist Albrecht Dieterich, in which Dieterich translated a Mithraic ritual contained in a Greek papyrus. The ritual discussed the sun as a divinity and talked of a long tube coming down from the sun, which created the winds as it swung from side-to-side. Jung remembered his patient's strange vision. The patient's work-ing-class education and background had been far removed from such exotic topics as Mithraic rituals. He had been hospitalized since his early manhood, long before this particular manuscript was ever discovered and translated. As a patient, he had absolutely no way of acquiring this rare, scholarly book. Jung himself, at the time

---

[11] *Collected Works, Vol. 9i: The Archetypes and the Collective Unconscious,* ¶ 91–92.

of the original episode with the patient, had no detailed knowledge of mythology.

The most likely hypothesis Jung could propose was that the patient somehow tapped a collective memory. After all, the patient saw himself as a god, trying to initiate a new acolyte, Jung. The story of the sun's penis creating the wind was itself part of a ritual of initiation into the deeper mysteries of the Mithraic religion. To eliminate the possibility that—despite the centuries of separation—this was an incredible coincidence of fantasies rather than an archetype of the collective unconscious, Jung hunted for other historical appearances of this strange symbolism.

Jung found that there were medieval paintings which showed a long pipe extending down from the throne of god. A dove or the Christ-child descended down it to fertilize Mary. The dove was a common medieval symbol for the Holy Ghost, who is also commonly represented as a holy wind or spirit. Thus the same collective material was expressed by an artist, not a psychotic. Jung carefully checked the art in the local public art gallery in the town where the patient grew up, and found no such picture.[12]

This example was carefully chosen by Jung, out of thousands of examples of the collective unconscious that he gathered over the years, because of the seeming impossibility of any other explanation. Provided that we accept Jung's veracity, then either the patient somehow became aware of an ancient Mithraic ritual and incorporated it into his delusions, or he is drawing on some knowledge that he didn't acquire in his lifetime. The Mithraic ritual was an initiation into the cult of the sun god. Jung's patient also thought himself a god, and since he regarded Jung with patronizing affection, wanted to initiate Jung into the deeper mysteries. In turn, the me-

---

[12]In my own experience with psychotic patients, I have found that during psychotic episodes they frequently expressed collective material with no filtering through personal consciousness. They simply gave up the small grasp they had on an integrated personal consciousness and were overwhelmed by the collective material. That would explain why Jung's patient's collective fantasy was exactly as expressed in the ancient ritual. However, the same collective material, when experienced by a saint or an artist, should be expressed in a much more personal way because a stable personality will manage to integrate the collective material into the personal psyche rather than just being overwhelmed by it.

dieval artists, wanting to show how Mary was fertilized by God drew on the same inner sources. God as a wind is carried by a tube for the medieval artists just as with the schizophrenic patient and the Mithraic ritual.[13]

A Computer Model of the Mind

It is important to recognize that Jung's patient's fantasy of the sun's penis creating the winds was not only collective; it was also purposeful. The patient brought up that material because he wanted to initiate Jung into religious mysteries; thus he somehow tapped into collective material about religious initiation. Just as we are able to access personal memories that fit our needs, such as how to drive a car, what the answer to an exam question is, etc., we also seem able to access collective material when it is needed.

Jung realized that everything emerges into consciousness out of the unconscious. When we call up our memories of how to drive a car, it is not our consciousness that organizes those memories and makes them available; clearly, something in the unconscious is able to organize the memories that are necessary and make them available to our conscious mind. In the example of driving a car, the remembered behaviors may never even reemerge into consciousness; we may drive the car with no conscious awareness that we are doing so. This whole process is a mystery to which we have grown so accustomed that we have come to view it as commonplace.

---

[13]For details of the above case history, see C. G. Jung, *Collected Works, Vol. 8: The Structure and Dynamics of the Psyche*, ¶ 317–319. I have found numerous examples of collective material in dreams of my patients. In discussions with other therapists working with unconscious material, I found that many have also found such a preponderance of collective material that they no longer doubt its existence. It is difficult, however, to find an example as pure as Jung's because most of the unconscious material is mixed with personal memories. Furthermore, it's especially difficult in these days of widespread information to prove that dreamers could not have somehow come across the material in their reading or experience. Those who work with this collective material are convinced because they encounter it over and over, but their conviction isn't likely to sway scientists who assume that this is all nonsense.

Behavioral psychology, for example, views behavior as a simple response to stimulus. They use the model of a reflex-arc, assuming that a stimulus leads immediately to a response. This model ignores the essential creativity that takes place in everyday life because it places all behavior at the same level; behavioral psychology sees no need for hierarchies of behavior. Some examples that may show the complexity of the real-life situation follow.

For example, the part of our psyche that organizes and presents us with all the memories, psychic and muscular, needed to drive an auto, has to be on a higher level than the memories themselves. That is, there has to be something that organizes those memories; such an organizer is inherently at a different level of psychic organization than the memories it organizes. The unconscious is thus less a static repository of personal and collective material than an active organizational entity which serves and even anticipates the needs of consciousness.

As long as we don't get too enamored with the analogy, it is useful to draw a parallel between the way the human mind operates and the way that a computer operates. The same computer can run many different programs, just as a human can perform many different behaviors. Both the computer and the human mind store their programs in some sort of long-term memory until they are needed. The computer also needs a special program normally called an *operating system* (O/S) which operates at a higher level than any of the other programs. An O/S is like a foreman in a factory; it keeps things running smoothly. It knows which programs are running in the computer, which are waiting to run, and which have already run.

However, the O/S doesn't decide which programs need to be run, just as the foreman doesn't decided what products the factory should make. That is an executive decision; a human operator tells the computer which programs need to be run in what order of importance. The O/S then schedules the programs, locates them in its long-term memory, runs them when it has the time and resources to do so, prints the results, and stores the programs away again for later use.

Notice that there are at least three levels of operation at work here: (1) the executive level which decides which programs should be run; (2) a foreman level which keeps things running smoothly; and (3) a worker level which does the actual work we associate with the computer. By analogy, driving a car requires an executive decision on one level of the psyche, the organization and supervision of the necessary behaviors on a second level, and the actual behaviors on a third level. None of this is included in the stimulus-response model of the behavioral sciences. But even the computer model, which is more complex than the stimulus-response model, is woefully inadequate. It doesn't explain the extreme creativity of the unconscious.

CREATIVITY OF THE PSYCHE

In an interview later published in an audio cassette tape, anthropologist Gregory Bateson discussed the creativity of the learning process.[14] He told of friends conducting research into the learning patterns of dolphins, who wanted to find out how many new behaviors a dolphin could learn and remember in succession. They taught a dolphin these new behaviors in the time-honored behavioral-science way, by rewarding it with food; in this case, the new behavior was to be some new, fancy way of jumping out of the water.

The experimenters waited until the dolphin spontaneously performed some new action, and rewarded it. When it repeated the behavior, it was rewarded again. However, once the new behavior was well-learned, they no longer rewarded the dolphin until it performed a second new behavior. This was a little frustrating to the dolphin, but it finally did something new by chance and once more got a reward.

As the experiment continued, the dolphin grew increasingly frustrated; it swam around and around its pool in an agitated fashion. Suddenly, it performed each of the behaviors it had already created in rapid succession, then immediately did a dozen new

---

[14]Gregory Bateson, *Cybernetics and Mind* (North Hollywood, CA: Audio-Text Cassette #CBC972, n.d.).

jumps and turns one after another. The dolphin evidently deduced that each time it would have to demonstrate a new behavior in order to get a reward. Therefore, in order to cut the boring experiment short—and get all the rewards at once—it performed what it hoped would be enough new behaviors to satisfy the researchers for a good while. This creative response has no place in either the stimulus–response model or the computer model.

It could be argued that the dolphin's response was a product of conscious reasoning, but the dolphin's behavior better fits what contemporary author Colin Wilson has dubbed the *Eureka Effect*.[15] The phrase comes from the apocryphal tale about Archimedes, the greatest of the ancient Greek mathematicians. Archimedes had brooded for weeks over the question of how to determine the volume of irregular solids. While bathing, he noticed that his body raised the level of the water. He jumped from the bath and ran naked through the streets yelling "Eureka" (literally, "I found it!").

In that moment of insight, Archimedes realized that he could put an irregular solid into a container of water, measure the increase in the volume filled by the water and that would be the volume of the solid. Colin Wilson felt that this anecdote described the key elements of the creative solution to any problem: intense immersion (no pun intended) into all aspects of the problem, frustration when consciousness cannot resolve the issue, a moment of relaxation, then the burst into consciousness of an answer.

The most famous modern instance of the Eureka Effect is the famous ring-of-snakes dream of chemist Friedrich August von Kekule. Kekule had worked for months in an attempt to discover the structure of the last remaining major organic compound: benzine. Then, one afternoon, while sitting in his study, he relates,

> I turned my chair to the fire and dozed . . . . Again the atoms were gamboling before my eyes. This time the smaller groups kept modestly in the background. My mental eye, rendered more acute by repeated visions of

[15]Colin Wilson, *Inside the Outsider (I)* (North Hollywood, CA: Audio-Text Cassette #36049, n.d.).

this kind, could distinguish larger structures, of manifold conformation; long rows, sometimes more closely fitted together; all twining and twisting in snakelike motion. But look! What was that? One of the snakes had seized hold of its own tail, and the form whirled mockingly before my eyes. As if by a flash of lightning I awoke. . . . Let us learn to dream, gentlemen.[16]

Such "ring" patterns had never previously been discovered in organic chemistry. Seemingly, von Kekule's unconscious solved the problem for him, then presented the solution to his conscious mind in the form of a symbol which he could understand, that of a snake seizing its own tail.

The creativity of the unconscious can be clearly seen in hypnotic work. We have already discussed how hypnotism finally achieved scientific acceptance in the Western World in the 19th century, when James Braid advanced his theory that hypnosis was caused by suggestion.[17] That has remained the accepted wisdom among most hypnotists until recently. The late Milton Erickson, generally considered the greatest clinical hypnotist of our time, thought otherwise. In one of his most important papers, "Hypnotic Psychotherapy," originally written in 1948, Erickson said that:

Direct suggestion is based primarily, if unwittingly, upon the assumption that whatever develops in hypnosis derives from the suggestions given. It implies that the therapist has the miraculous power of effecting therapeutic changes in the patient, and disregards the fact that therapy results from an inner resynthesis of the patient's behavior achieved by the patient himself. . . . The therapist merely stimulates the patient into activity, often not knowing what that activity may be, and then guides the patient and exercises clinical judgment in determining

---

[16]Quotation in Arthur Koestler, *The Act of Creation* (New York: Dell, 1964), p. 118.
[17]See chapter 6.

the amount of work to achieve the desired results. How to guide and to judge constitute the therapist's problem, while the patient's task is that of learning through his own efforts to understand his experiential life in a new way.[18]

The examples above illustrate the creativity of the unconscious. They seem to imply that the unconscious is the breeding ground for the ideas and behaviors which only later become conscious. If so, then it becomes important to describe the dynamics of the relationship between consciousness and the unconscious.

---

[18] *The Collected Papers of Milton H. Erickson on Hypnosis, Vol. 4*, Ernest Lawrence Rossi, ed. (New York: Irvington Publishers, 1980), pp. 38–39. I have used such methods in clinical work with a variety of patients. The following case history shows how Ericksonian hypnosis taps the creativity of the unconscious to solve psychological problems.

The patient had recently made a nearly successful suicide attempt. Since then, many commonplace situations had become frustrating puzzles. She might hear the phone and have no idea what it was or what to do. Or she could be brushing her hair and then stare at the hairbrush, wondering what it was. Gradually, she was relearning the elements of her world and how to behave in that newly strange world. Meanwhile, she was vomiting dozens of times a day. She asked if something could be done to stop the vomiting.

A traditional hypnotist would put the patient into a hypnotic state, then suggest in many ways that she should stop vomiting. The hypnotist might guess from the patient's situation that she was filled with anxiety and concentrate on suggestions to relax her. I tried Ericksonian techniques. After inducing a hypnotic state, I asked the patient's unconscious if it would be willing to solve the problem. Finger signals were used to get the unconscious to show that it agreed to take on the task.

A week later the patient came back thrilled. The vomiting had continued for another day. On the following day, she went to get a soft drink from the refrigerator. Without noticing it, she instead reached in the pantry next to the refrigerator and pulled out a box of noodles. She glanced at the box in surprise and decided to cook the noodles. She ate them and didn't vomit afterwards. For the rest of the week, she found herself enjoying cooking full meals rather than just grabbing snacks whenever the mood hit her. And she never vomited again.

Later in the treatment of the same patient, she began having anxiety attacks. Again, rather than attempt to go directly after the problem, I asked the unconscious to solve it. The unconscious agreed to substitute new behavior which would serve the same purpose as was served by the anxiety attacks themselves. Later in the week, when she started becoming very anxious, the patient spontaneously decided to clean out her fish tank. This was something she had wanted to do for a long time. She cleaned the tank and went out and bought new fish. Not only did the purposeful action prevent the occurrence of the anxiety attack, the fish tank turned out to be a source of relaxation and tranquility. When she felt anxious, she watched the fish and grew calm. Her anxiety attacks quit entirely within weeks.

How Archetypes Emerge into Consciousness

As we have already seen in this chapter, neither the behavioral model nor the computer model do justice to the complexity of the human psyche. In an interesting recent book, Charles Hampden-Turner presented 60 different *Maps of the Mind*.[19] Few, if any, of the models he describes come close to capturing the dynamic creativity of the human psyche; this dynamic relationship of conscious and unconscious is particularly difficult to model. Jung pointed out that consciousness emerged from the unconscious rather than the other way around. His life-long goal was to try and describe the nature and organization of the psyche in which such a dynamic could operate. It was this attempt to develop a dynamic model of the psyche that made Jung's task so difficult.

Since the unconscious itself was beyond examination, Jung could only infer its structure from unconscious material which emerged into consciousness. That's why Jung was so careful in his observation, recording and describing his patients' dream material. And that's why he was so fascinated with myths, fairy tales, primitive art, and other material which he considered to contain unconscious material little changed by conscious artistic manipulation. In their primitive, untouched forms, all of these could help provide a picture of the organization and structure of the unconscious.

Jung initially referred to the *primordial images*,[20] and only later to the *archetypes*,[21] of the collective unconscious. It is understandable that he originally thought of the archetypes as primordial images, since it was the symbolic images that he encountered in the dreams of his patients. But over time he came to realize that the images were personal or cultural and that we could make no conclusions about the structure of the archetypes themselves:

> . . . an archetype in its quiescent, unprojected state has
> no exactly determinable form but is in itself an indefinite

---

[19]Charles Hampden-Turner, *Maps of the Mind* (New York: MacMillan, 1981).

[20]C. G. Jung, *Collected Works, Vol. 7: Two Essays on Analytical Psychology* (Princeton: Princeton University Press, 1966), ¶ 101.

[21]C. G. Jung, *Collected Works, Vol. 8: The Structure and Dynamics of the Psyche*, ¶ 270.

structure which can assume definite forms only in pro-jection.[22]

As an example, all animals beyond a certain level of complexity appear to have an archetype for Mother. They instinctively know a great deal about what to expect from a Mother. But remember how Konrad Lorenz found that a baby goose's concept of mother could stretch to accommodate itself to the very un-gooselike Lorenz.[23] The best way to express the situation seems to be that the archetype comes first, but the archetype is empty until the actual experience provides it with the content necessary for expression. Of course, in saying this, we are merely saying that the actual structure of archetypes in the unconscious is beyond human observation. This is much the same as physicist David Bohm's hypothesis that there is an *implicate order* from which the *explicate order* of the physical world we know emerges.[24]

> It is in my view a great mistake to suppose that the psyche of a new-born child is a *tabula rasa* in the sense that there is absolutely nothing in it. In so far as the child is born with a differentiated brain that is predetermined by heredity and therefore individualized, it meets sensory stimuli coming from without not with *any* aptitudes, but with *specific* ones, and this necessarily results in a particular, individual choice and pattern of apperception. These aptitudes can be shown to be inherited instincts and preformed patterns, the latter being the *a priori* and formal conditions of apperception that are based on instinct. . . . It is not . . . a question of in-herited *ideas* but of inherited *possibilities* of ideas.[25]

It is one thing to recognize that the psyche has both personal components and impersonal, collective components, and that the

---

[22]C. G. Jung, *Collected Works, Vol. 9i: The Archetypes and the Collective Unconscious*, ¶ 70.

[23]See chapter 8.

[24]David Bohm, *Wholeness and the Implicate Order* (London: Ark Paperbacks, 1980).

[25]C. G. Jung, *Collected Works, Vol. 9i: The Archetypes and the Collective Unconscious*, ¶ 66. Jung's emphasis in all cases.

consciousness develops out of the unconscious. It is quite another to articulate a process that adequately describes this complexity. As we saw in our discussion of Gustav Fechner,[26] sensory perception is relational. As we saw in the discussion of Lorenz' goose, even complex relationships like that between mother and child seem to be carried in the child ready to be activated at the proper time.

> There are as many archetypes as there are typical situations in life. Endless repetition has engraved these experiences into our psychic constitution, not in the form of images filled with content, but at first only as *forms without content*, representing merely the possibility of a certain type of perception and action. When a situation occurs which corresponds to a given archetype, that archetype becomes activated and a compulsiveness appears, which, like an instinctual drive, gains its way against all reason and will, or else produces a conflict of pathological dimensions, that is to say, a neurosis.[27]

Take as an example the simplest of animals, the one-celled paramecium. A paramecium doesn't have to know a great deal to survive. It eats whatever it recognizes as food; it runs from everything it recognizes might eat it. The paramecium's body does not have to learn how to swallow the food, or how to propel itself away from danger; nor does its mind (if the term can be used that loosely) have to learn what food is and what an enemy is. Both the body's and the mind's knowledge are already stored in the paramecium because generations of its ancestors have experienced both food and enemies. Those remembered patterns are archetypes.

COMPLEX AND ARCHETYPE

Let's examine how a human baby first encounters the world through the lens of archetypal experience. Some of that archetypal experience takes visual form, some muscular; the former could be called the archetypal image, the latter instinct. But both are merely parts of the archetype itself, which cannot be other than inferred from the archetypal image and the instinctual behavior. It is the complex relationship between the archetype and consciousness that fascinated Jung.

Consider, for example, a human baby seeking its Mother's breast for nourishment. Since the breast isn't always there when the baby is hungry, the baby begins to realize that the breast is not like its own hands and feet, there to serve its needs whenever called upon. A baby's recognition that its mother's breast is separate from itself is a beginning of consciousness, a consciousness of baby as a thing separate and distinct from the rest of the world. This consciousness is the ego, which emerges as the baby separates its concept of itself from its surroundings. And to help it in this separation are archetypal residues of the relationship between baby and Mother. As the baby experiences life, the archetype of Mother is given substance; the baby adds the knowledge of its particular Mother. But it's critical to realize that underneath that particular, personal experience is an archetype of Mother.[28]

The recognition that the human mind has an enormous, perhaps infinite, depth of experience on which it can call, and that there is a correspondingly enormous number of archetypes, makes a crucial difference in understanding how we learn complex behaviors. For example, the capacity to learn language appears to most contemporary linguists to be inborn. This explains how rapidly virtually all children learn language.

We have argued above that the human psyche contains archetypes and that there are two sides to the archetype: archetypal image and instinctual behavior. Since we experience the world relationally, the archetypes are activated in many, perhaps all, human situations. As we personally experience the world through the archetypes, the archetypes are given a particular, highly personal

---

[28]And an archetype of ego, but more of this later.

form. Eventually the world is almost entirely encountered through our personal memories; the archetypes lie deep within.

Jung had to discover this dynamic from the outside. In patients, he encountered first their personal memories. In early experiments in word association, he found that patients responded more slowly to certain words. He gradually discovered that all of those words had something to do with a particular subject; e.g., the patient's personal experience of mother. He called this grouping of memories around the experience of mother a *complex*, in this case a *mother complex*.

Since the patient's response was slower when the issue had to do with mother, Jung guessed that the patient had some emotional blockage concerning mother. That is, there was energy trapped in the unconscious around the concept of mother. Much of the analytic task became a process of stripping away the personal memories in order to find out what lay at the core of this complex. Freud found Jung's concept of a complex extremely useful and appropriated it for his own use; he theorized that at the core of a complex was a primal sexual memory that the patient had repressed. In practice, Jung found that usually there was no such single memory, or if there was, that the memory wasn't necessarily sexual. More importantly, the complex still had energy for the patient after all of the personal memories were brought into consciousness. At the core of the mother complex, Jung found not a personal memory of mother but a collective, archetypal memory of the complex relationship between child and mother.

Thus archetypes are activated when necessary, and accumulate personal memories around themselves to form complexes. We relate to things and people through these complexes. However, an additional element enters the picture to enormously broaden possibilities, and that element is consciousness: ego-consciousness.

ACTUAL AND POTENTIAL

Consciousness itself is as great a mystery as the unconscious. We think about it less because we experience it directly; i.e., we are conscious of this or that, and take this mysterious relationship for granted. At the core of consciousness is a sense of *I*, an *ego*. All consciousness is in relationship to the ego, which thus forms the center of consciousness. Our consciousness is inseparable from our sense of identity.

> The ego is a complex datum which is constituted first of all by a general awareness of your body, of your existence, and secondly by your memory data; you have a certain idea of having been, a long series of memories.[29]

A few pages earlier, we discussed the complex relationship between archetype and experience, using the mother archetype as an example. We said that, as the baby discovers that the mother's breast is separate and distinct from itself, an awareness of self (i.e., ego) begins to take form.

The emergence of an ego appears to be the first dynamic interaction of the conscious and unconscious. The ego forms the center of consciousness and takes form at the boundaries where it experiences itself as separate from its surroundings. Like any other complex, it accumulates personal experience which grows to surround the ego archetype. As the center of consciousness it relates both to the sensory world outside and to the unconscious world inside.

> . . . the ego [is] a complex of psychic facts. This complex has a great power of attraction, like a magnet; it attracts contents from the unconscious. . . . It also attracts impressions from outside, and when they enter into association with the ego they are conscious. If they do not, they are not conscious.[30]

Each of us forms our sense of identity, our ego, as much by defining what we aren't as by what we are. The baby who decides that his toes, though quite distant from his vision, are still part of his body, but the breast he suckles on is not, is forming a sense of identity. Much of what we could become is only a potential; that potential may or may not come to be actualized and, thus, be included in our ego. For example, we might have an inborn poten-

---

[29]C. G. Jung, *Analytic Psychology: Its Theory & Practice*, p. 10.
[30]C. G. Jung, *Analytic Psychology: Its Theory & Practice*, p. 10.

tial for musical ability, but circumstances may never allow us to express that potential in life.

What does it mean to say that someone has an inborn potential for musical ability? It's a commonplace to say that it's "in their genes"; i.e., that someone has a genetic predisposition for musical ability in much the same way that they have a genetic predisposition toward blue eyes and brown hair. Today we realize that genetic inheritance is a language coded with combinations of a mere four acids on paired helical chains of DNA and RNA. Microbiologists, using recombinant DNA techniques, have been able to change the DNA chains in viruses such that later generations of viruses have new properties, predetermined by the scientists. New plants are already being developed using these techniques; soon it will be new animals.

While the technology of such research is amazing, the critical fact is that DNA is a language of potentiality and scientific researchers are learning to read that language. It was initially thought to be a fairly straightforward language, but with more study, researchers have found that it is much more complex than they first imagined. For example, certain combinations were originally thought to have unique meanings; now scientists realize that the same DNA chain can have different meanings in different contexts. It was also once thought that DNA chains in a given organism were immutable; more recently, DNA chains with self-changing properties have been discovered. Undoubtedly, more research will reveal ever deeper mysteries in this exciting new field of science. However, it is likely to be a very long time before such research can ever say much about the question we have posed here; i.e., what does it mean to have an inborn potential for musical ability?

Different sciences normally deal not only with different fields of study, but also with different fields at different levels of organization. For example, chemistry exists as a separate science because physics cannot explain chemical interactions. Many scientists would argue that this is only because of the limitations of our present level of knowledge. Other scientists would assert that the organization of molecules, which is chemistry's domain, can never be reduced to an organization of atoms, which is the domain of physics. That is, when atoms reach a certain level of complexity those scientists would assert that something new comes into existence: molecules.

Correspondingly, when organic molecules reach a certain level of complexity, again something new comes into existence: cells. Once again a new field of science is necessary to deal with this level of organization: biology. Since humans are conscious, we can presuppose that, at a certain level of organization of specialized brain cells, something new comes into existence once more: consciousness. Again a new field is needed: psychology.

No one field can explain all phenomena—physicists and chemists and biologists and psychologists are all needed. As exciting as the biological research into inherited traits and predispositions is, research like Jung's is equally necessary if we are to sort out how the conscious and unconscious relate in the development of the individual human psyche.

Jung's studies indicated that some of the information which emerges into consciousness—such as his schizophrenic patient's vision of the sun's penis creating the winds—is collective. The exactness of detail of such collective memories is a far cry from a vague "inborn potential for musical ability," but both have to be included within any model that is to deal adequately with the human psyche. Instinctual behavior of even the simplest creatures is incredibly complex: the detailed, species-specific songs of birds; the intricate, species-specific webs of spiders, etc. There are seemingly very few limits on what can be passed on genetically. And, of course, humans are hardly limited to a repertoire of instinctual behavior; we have still a higher level of ability open to us: consciousness.[31]

Conscious and unconscious, personal and collective, this is the world to which Jung opened our eyes. Once we accept the concept of a collective unconscious, it provides a natural explanation for a wide variety of otherwise puzzling phenomena. That then leads us ineluctably to the need to carefully observe and describe the structure and dynamics of the collective unconscious. That brings us first to archetypes in general, then past that to the archetypes of development, which are critical to the individuation process of all of us.

---

[31]By this time, it seems to be indisputable that there are other conscious animals: dolphins, porpoises, whales, apes, chimps. Undoubtedly, as research mounts and our anthroprocentricism lessens, we will be willing to accept that perhaps consciousness is broadly shared among a wide variety of living creatures.

CHAPTER 12

BACKGROUND FOR GÖDEL'S PROOF

. . . when the drapery, which reveals its form more or less accurately, is torn away, there remains mathematics itself, which lives in human thought and is only symbolized by the signs of formalism.[1]

HERR WARUM

Kurt Gödel [1906–1978] and both his parents were born in what was then Brünn, Moravia, later Brno, Czechoslovakia. Unlike Jung's solid Swiss background, Gödel's was mixed. His parents were part of a large German-speaking community, and raised their children as part of that community, separated from the majority Czechs. His first sixteen years were spent in Brünn, the next sixteen in Vienna (where he became an Austrian citizen), and the remaining nearly 42 years in the United States (where he eventually became an American citizen).

Gödel's father was a prominent director of a textile factory, and his family lived in relative affluence. Even World War I—which was to change the region drastically—had little impact on the Gödel family. Kurt was a precocious boy known affectionately within his family by the pet name—*Herr Warum*[2]—for his insatiable curiosity. That quality was not to abate throughout his life.

---

[1]Lucienne Félix, *The Modern Aspect of Mathematics* (New York: Basic Books, 1960), p. 61.
[2]Mr. Why, a name that surely many another parent of bright children can sympathize with. *Kurt Gödel Collected Works, Vol. I, Publications 1929–1936*, Solomon Feferman, editor-in-chief (New York: Oxford University Press, 1986), p. 3.

KURT GÖDEL

During his university years in Vienna, Gödel came to spend a good deal of time with the *Vienna Circle*, a group of philosophers, logicians, and linguists who in the 1920s and 1930s developed a school of philosophy known as *logical positivism*. The goal of logical positivism was "to purify philosophy—sifting out its metaphysical elements, and reconstituting the discipline with logic as its [guiding principle]."[3] Logical positivism in part combined physicist Ernst Mach's empiricist philosophy with Bertrand Russell's logicist position. Logical positivism was most directly influenced, however, by the early ideas of a pupil of Russell's—Ludwig Wittgenstein—as published in Wittgenstein's *Tractatus Logico-philosophicus* in 1919.[4]

Though Gödel was excited by the ideas being considered by the Vienna Circle, he had already formed his philosophical views before he came to Vienna, and those views were directly opposed to those of logical positivism. Gödel had little faith in any attempt to reduce philosophy and mathematics to logic; he was convinced that the *mathematical objects* with which mathematicians concern themselves were every bit as real as the physical objects we encounter in everyday reality. These views were already central to Gödel's personal philosophy by the time he came to Vienna, and may have been formed as early as his teenage years, when he first read Kant.[5] Of interest for us and our discussion, Gödel evidently responded more to the archetypal hypothesis which underlay Kant's philosophy, than to the specific philosophical details which were dated by Gödel's time.

---

[3] W. L. Reese, *Dictionary of Philosophy and Religion* (Atlantic Highlands, NJ: Humanities Press, 1980), p. 314.

[4] By the time the Vienna Circle was developing logical positivism, Wittgenstein had already repudiated the ideas he had expressed in *Tractatus Logico-philosophicus*. Wittgenstein is another figure of almost unequaled intellect, who, like Jung and Gödel, refused to accept early fame, and instead went his own direction. He figures in our history only peripherally, since his thought went a different direction than Jung and Gödel.

[5] Solomon Feferman, "Kurt Gödel: Conviction and Caution," in S. G. Shanker, ed., *Gödel's Theorem in Focus* (London & New York: Routledge, 1988), pp. 100–101.

GÖDEL ENCOUNTERS HILBERT'S PROGRAM

Hilbert saw to the heart of the matter. . . . He sought to develop a method that would yield demonstrations of consistency as much beyond genuine logical doubt as the use of finite models for establishing the consistency of certain sets of postulates—by an analysis of a finite number of structural features of expressions in completely formalized calculi.[6]

DAVID HILBERT

Of more immediate interest for Gödel than the ideas of the Vienna Circle was a slim book by David Hilbert and Wilhelm Ackermann, called *Foundations of the Theory of Logic.*[7] When Hilbert defined his program in 1900, Cantor's set theory of transfinite numbers was both firmly entrenched in mathematics, yet under attack on all sides. Hilbert feared that not only Cantor's theory—but all mathematics—was in danger. Hilbert, however, was an optimist who hoped to preserve transfinite set theory by using a formal axiomatic method to develop the number system—including transfinite numbers—thus dealing with infinity through a finite number of definitions, rules, and operations. In contrast with Russell, Hilbert realizes that infinity could still stick its head in through the back door, since those finite definitions, rules, and operations could be used in an infinite number of ways to generate

---

[6] Ernest Nagel and James R. Newman, *Gödel's Proof* (New York: New York University Press, 1958), pp. 32–33. Nagel's and Newman's volume is the best general introduction to Gödel's Proof, and will be drawn on extensively in the pages to follow.

[7] David Hilbert and Wilhelm Ackermann, *Grundzüge der theoretischen Logik* (Berlin: Springer, 1928).

mathematical truths. Therefore, it was also necessary to find some way outside the system itself to demonstrate that the system was both *complete* and *consistent*.[8]

For example, by 1899 Hilbert had managed to develop a formal axiomatic system for geometry, which reduced geometry to arithmetic, thus completing the task René Descartes had begun two-hundred-fifty years earlier with his discovery of analytic geometry. Though Descartes had the great realization that marks all such revolutions in thought, it was much too early for him to realize that this equivalence needed to be formally demonstrated. Hilbert was able to do just that, demonstrating that if arithmetic was complete and consistent, so was geometry. Hence his program of 1900 to prove arithmetic also complete and consistent. The whole system was like a house of cards: if you pulled out one key card at the base—arithmetic—the house of cards would come tumbling down.

Almost three decades had passed since Hilbert first conceived his program and identified twenty-three significant problems mathematics needed to solve pursuant to that goal. Though his program had excited the interests of mathematicians worldwide, none of them were Gödel, and the major problems remained unresolved.

> . . . Cantor's doctrine, too, was attacked on all sides. So violent was this reaction that even the most ordinary and fruitful concepts and the simplest and most important deductive methods of mathematics were threatened and their employment was on the verge of being declared illicit.[9]

Russell and Whitehead had taken a different direction, with their goal of subsuming all mathematics and philosophy within logic. Their *Principia Mathematica* purported to provide a system in

---

[8]By complete, mathematicians mean that no true statements can be made within a system that cannot be derived from the axioms of the system. By consistent, mathematicians mean that if a statement can be derived from the axioms of a system, then its opposite cannot also be derived; i.e., a statement cannot both be true and false at the same time.

[9]David Hilbert, "On the Infinite," in Paul Benacerraf & Hilary Putnam, *Philosophy of Mathematics: Selected Readings* (Cambridge: Cambridge University Press, 1983), p. 190.

which all mathematics was included within logic. Hilbert, like Gödel was too much the mathematician to believe this either possible or desirable.

> . . . We find ourselves in agreement with the philosophers, notably with Kant. Kant taught—and it is an integral part of his doctrine—that mathematics treats a subject matter which is given independently of logic. Mathematics, therefore, can never be grounded solely on logic.[10]

Hilbert regarded *Principia Mathematica* as only one possible formal axiomatic system for mathematical logic, and assumed that any such system would have to be demonstrated to be sound using mathematics. In their *Foundations of the Theory of Logic*, Hilbert and Ackermann presented still another formal axiomatic system for mathematical logic. Since Hilbert saw logic as a sub-set of mathematics, rather than the other way around, he was able to address epistemological issues which Russell and Whitehead never thought to question. It wasn't possible for them to both argue for the universality of logic, and to question whether logically derived systems, like their own, were complete and consistent. As Bertrand Russell wrote in a letter much later:

> You note that we were indifferent to attempts to prove that our axioms could not lead to contradictions. In this Gödel showed that we had been mistaken. But I thought that it must be impossible to prove that any given set of axioms does *not* lead to a contradiction, and, for that reason, I had paid little attention to Hilbert's work.[11]

Hilbert himself had deep problems with his own position, though he didn't yet realize it. At one and the same time, he believed every

---

[10] David Hilbert, "On the Infinite," in Paul Benacerraf & Hilary Putnam, *Philosophy of Mathematics*, p. 192.

[11] From Bertrand Russell's letter to Leon Henkin of April 1, 1963, in John W. Dawson, Jr., "The Reception of Gödel's Incompleteness Theorem," in S. G. Shanker, *Gödel's Theorem in Focus*, p. 90.

bit as much as Gödel that mathematics was concerned with archetypal forms, yet he still hoped to reduce such potentially infinite forms to empty symbols, devoid of meaning. This combination of beliefs was, of course, impossible, as Gödel was to prove.

> As a further precondition for using logical deduction and carrying out logical operations, something must be given in conception, viz., *certain extralogical concrete objects which are intuited as directly experienced prior to all thinking.*[12]

> Still it is consistent with our finitary viewpoint to deny any meaning to logical symbols, just as we denied meaning to mathematical symbols, and to declare that the formulas of the logical calculus are ideal statements which mean nothing in themselves.[13]

As the major problems from 1900 remained unresolved, they found their way into this new volume, in some cases reformed within the axiomatic system presented there. It was here that Gödel first encountered Hilbert's program and the problems whose resolutions he hoped would put mathematics on a sound footing. It was perhaps also here that Gödel first came in contact with Russell's and Whitehead's *Principia Mathematica*, though this is less clear. Of Hilbert's problems, Gödel was to prove one,[14] disprove another,[15] and figure heavily in proving the undecidability of a third.[16] More importantly, Gödel's contributions would effectively bring an end to Hilbert's program.[17]

---

[12]My emphasis—note that Hilbert is explicitly accepting *archetypes*, though he doesn't seem to realize it. David Hilbert, "On the Infinite," in *Philosophy of Mathematics*, p. 192.

[13]Here Hilbert is trying to take back the archetypal meaning he just granted to symbols. David Hilbert, "On the Infinite," in *Philosophy of Mathematics*, p. 197.

[14]Which is commonly termed the "completeness problem." We will not deal with it in this book as its interest is largely mathematical except as it led Gödel to his incompleteness proof.

[15]The "consistency problem." In the course of proving this to be false, Gödel produced his famous incompleteness proof.

[16]Cantor's continuum hypothesis. Hilbert considered this important enough to identify as the first problem on his list. We dealt with this briefly in chapter 7 and will deal with its implications in depth in chapter 19.

[17]Though to this day there are still diehards who hope to get around Gödel's results and still achieve Hilbert's objectives.

In the remainder of this chapter, we will discuss Gödel's essential insight into what was wrong with both Hilbert's and Russell's separate approaches. We will deal with his famous incompleteness proof in chapter 16, then reserve further discussion of Cantor's continuum hypothesis to the final chapter of this book.

Gödel's Insight

As you will recall, Bertrand Russell was never able to fully resolve the problem presented by the paradox he himself had discovered: the paradox of the set of all sets that do not include themselves. He was only able to achieve a partial resolution in *Principia Mathematica* by the trick of defining a hierarchy of classes of elements, classes of classes, classes of classes of classes, ad infinitum. Even Russell regarded his solution as a sorry state of affairs.

David Hilbert realized that any formal logical system, such as that presented in *Principia Mathematica* was itself subject to epistemological considerations of completeness and consistency. Such issues were essentially *meta-mathematical*,[18] i.e., they transcended mathematics, and could only be resolved outside the system in question. Unless this was to lead to an infinite regress, the resolution itself had to be finite. For example, the statement that "arithmetic is consistent and complete" is a meta-mathematical statement. Hilbert recognized that this statement could not be resolved within arithmetic because it transcended arithmetic. Perhaps, however, it is overstating Hilbert's understanding of the issue to say he saw the meta-mathematical issues this clearly. If so, he would have realized the impossibility of his goal. Gödel was quite clear on all these issues. As he said at a later time:

---

[18]*Meta* means above, beyond, transcending, as in metaphysics, which is the field of philosophy which deals with ultimate questions, questions which transcend physical explanation. Similarly, meta-mathematical statements are statements about mathematics which transcend mathematics.

> . . . A complete epistemological description of a lan-
> guage A cannot be given in the same language A, because
> the concept of truth of sentences of A cannot be defined
> in A.[19]

Gödel's succinct summary above implicitly acknowledges that the paradoxes which caused Cantor, Frege and Russell so much grief can never be defined away. Cantor's theory of transfinite sets had been attacked because of the paradox of the "set of all sets."[20] The logicians like Frege hoped to avoid the issue by reducing mathematics to mathematical logic. Russell then destroyed Frege's hopes when he discovered the paradox of the "set of all sets which do not contain themselves" within mathematical logic.[21] Russell in turn attempted to create a new logical system which resolved the paradox by creating a hierarchical chain of classes, classes of classes, etc., trailing off into infinity. Gödel saw that any such system was itself subject to the same problem. Russell could never succeed at pushing the issue away because it would always be possible to pose questions about his system which could not be resolved within his system. In particular, you could ask, as Hilbert and the formalists did, whether it was complete and consistent.

However, Gödel saw deeper than Hilbert. The problem wasn't infinity, nor was there a need to reduce mathematics to finite processes. Speaking of this problem, Gödel complained in 1967, of the "blindness (or prejudice, or whatever you may call it) of logicians at the time, according to which non-finitary reasoning was not accepted as a meaningful part of meta-mathematics."[22] Nor did Gödel accept that proving arithmetic (or any other system) consistent automatically proved that every true statement could be determined within the system. The idea that there could be true statements that could neither be proved true

---

[19]Quotation by Gödel in Solomon Feferman, "Kurt Gödel: Conviction and Caution," in *Kurt Gödel: Collected Works*, Vol. 1, p. 105.

[20]See chapter 7.

[21]See chapter 9.

[22]Solomon Feferman, "Kurt Gödel: Conviction and Caution," in *Kurt Gödel: Collected Works*, Vol. 1, p. 102.

nor false within an axiomatic system never even occurred to either Russell or Hilbert.

> How indeed could one think of *expressing* meta-mathematics *in* the mathematical systems themselves, if the latter are considered to consist of meaningless symbols which acquire some substitute of meaning only *through* meta-mathematics.[23]

Gödel was able to come to this realization because it was embedded within his belief system. Much like Pythagoras and Plato, much like Kant, Gödel believed that mathematics dealt with eternal archetypal entities such as number and shape. Gödel's difference from his predecessors lay largely in the degree of sophistication with which he approached this understanding. After all, twenty-three centuries separated Gödel from Plato. Even Kant's realization was a century-and-a-half in the past. The concept of archetypes of a collective unconscious had slowly emerged over that period of time within the human psyche. It was finally beginning to appear in all fields, though except for Jung and, to a lesser extent Gödel, no one was yet able to step outside their own field and see that each field was saying similar things within their own language. In this book, we've emphasized Gödel and Jung because Gödel's mathematical expression of the archetypal hypothesis is the purest possible, and Jung's the most completely articulated, since he is describing the psyche within which the archetypal hypothesis found expression.

The fact that we have restricted ourselves to these two areas should not blind the reader to the underlying fact that, since the archetypal hypothesis was itself emerging as a symbolic expression within the human psyche, it inevitably had to emerge in parallel in all fields. For example, in art during the Middle ages, art was concerned less with outer reality than inner, spiritual truth. In the Renaissance artists shifted their gaze outwards to the world, and tried to accurately capture that reality. This inevitably led to increased abstraction,

---

[23]Quotation by Kurt Gödel, in Solomon Feferman, "Kurt Gödel: Conviction and Caution," p. 107.

such as the brilliant attempt to use perspective to fool the eye into believing it was seeing a three-dimensional reality on a two-dimensional canvas. Step-by-step painting evolved in parallel with the evolution we've described in psychology and mathematics.

Late in the 19th century, at much the same time that the theory of the unconscious was beginning to emerge in psychology and Cantor's transfinite set theory in mathematics, abstract art began to emerge. Artists were struggling with the paradoxical realization that the physical world as it actually was, and the world as they conceived it in their minds, were separate and distinct, yet somehow came together in the art they produced on the canvas. That led briefly to a fully abstract art in which art was valued in and of itself. Still later, artists tried to advance past that position to an essentially archetypal recognition that there were artistic values that transcended the separation of world, mind and picture. The fact that the issue still remains unresolved in art can be readily seen in the multiplicity of artistic styles that jostle for position in the current art world.

A similar history could be followed in music, in architecture, in literature, etc. Of course, in order for any such history to be meaningful to our discussion, it would need the same level of explicit parallels to be drawn as have been drawn in this book between the growth of psychology, and the growth of mathematics. But rest assured that those parallels would be there. With this background for Gödel's proof in place, it is now time to return to Jung and discuss his primary model of the individuation process.

CHAPTER 13

ⵥⵥⵥ

Archetypes of Development: Shadow

We do not like to look at the shadow-side of ourselves; therefore there are many people in our civilized society who have lost their shadow altogether; they have got rid of it. They are only two-dimensional; they have lost the third dimension, and with it they have usually lost the body.[1]

Childhood Development

Ego-consciousness seems largely to come into existence at boundaries. At first there is a lack of differentiation, e.g., once more our examples of baby and mother's breast. When we say, "I am this," we are equally saying, "I am not that," and vice-versa. Growth involves prohibition and limitations of many sorts imposed by our physical, familial, and societal environments. A child who is praised for certain behaviors and scolded for others will soon exhibit only the approved behaviors. At first, the child needs the praise and scolding from its parents in order to remember which are the good behaviors, which the bad. After a while, it no longer needs the parents' reminders; presumably it hears them internally.[2] Many a parent has secretly observed their child doing something naughty, and then saying to itself out loud: "bad girl [or boy]."

---

[1] C. G. Jung, *Analytic Psychology: Its Theory & Practice* (New York: Vintage Books/Random House, 1968), p. 23.
[2] This is what Freud terms the super-ego.

However, such an internal parent seems likely to be a transitional phase. After awhile, we *are* the person who exhibits such-and-such behaviors and doesn't exhibit other opposing behaviors. It's a more efficient state of mental organization to always behave in a certain way than to have to make a decision whenever the issue comes up. The memory that we ever behaved in such *bad* ways recedes from consciousness; we are no longer aware that we could ever behave any other way. However, if the person into which we develop deviates too far from our essential being,[3] a compensatory figure forms in the unconscious: the *shadow*. All those parts of our personal life which have been deemed unsuitable and denied collect around a single archetypal core. Everything we regard as bad, as "not us," accumulates around this center.

Vampires and Werewolves

Like Freud, Jung used his patients' dreams as a window into the world of their unconscious. Early in analysis, their dreams are frequently filled with strange, frightening shadow figures. While the shadow normally appears in dreams as a person of the same sex as the dreamer, early shadow figures are less explicitly defined and frequently non-human: animals, aliens from another planet, subhuman figures, vampires, werewolves. Gradually, as analysis progresses, shadow figures develop more human characteristics, frequently passing from animals and aliens to dark-skinned people: Blacks, Arabs, Indians, etc.[4]

> . . . the more remote a complex is from consciousness, the more unusual, bizarre, mana-filled, grandiose, or grotesque a symbol is apt to be.[5]

---

[3] Which Jung terms the Self. See chapter 15.

[4] In the dreams of Caucasians; Caucasians just as readily fill the shadow role for non-Caucasians. This tends to have no relationship to the person's degree of outer prejudice or lack of it. The psyche is merely searching for anyone with whom the dreamer has little or no familiarity.

[5] Julius C. Travis, "The Hierarchy of Symbols," in *The Shaman from Elko* (San Francisco: C. G. Jung Institute of San Francisco, 1978), p. 224.

As an analysis continues, shadow figures evolve past primitives to strangers, to casual acquaintances, to friends. The progression is from the unknown, feared, despised, to the known, respected, comfortable. The progression is also from a vague, ill-defined *otherness* to a precise, accurate portrait of the dreamer's particular shadow personality.

> . . . as the patient gains in strength, the symbol for the
> same complex changes its form, and the change will fol-
> low a design which is roughly and generally uniform.[6]

PROJECTION AND TRANSFERENCE

Freud was the first psychologist to discover the process of transference and projection; i.e., the patient's tendency to transfer or project inner conflicts onto the analyst. Freud's description was highly accurate as far as it went, and ran as follows: neurosis is a symptom of our inability to acknowledge and deal with an inner conflict. As long as the conflict remains unresolved, it occupies more and more of our attention. Since we are not able to consciously acknowledge the source of the conflict, we encounter the conflict wherever we turn. Since, during the period of therapy, the relationship with the analyst is likely to be our most important relationship, we project our inner conflict onto the therapist and experience the conflict with the therapist.[7]

When someone cannot admit that they have forbidden desires—such as sexual desires unconnected with love—they block any awareness of such desires from consciousness. In the unconscious, those illicit desires actively organize into a personified whole, which the dreamer might be willing to admit into consciousness, since the personification seems so clearly to be *other*. Perhaps the dreamer is willing to acknowledge that there are prim-

---

[6] Julius C. Travis, "The Hierarchy of Symbols," in *The Shaman from Elko*, p. 232.

[7] Though Jung saw projection and transference as much broader and more complex than Freud, the limited sense of projection described above is helpful in understanding shadow issues. For the Jungian view of projection and transference, see Marie-Louise von Franz, *Projection and Re-Collection in Jungian Psychology: Reflections of the Soul* (La Salle: Open Court, 1980).

itive people, like natives of the South Seas, who indulge in wild sexual orgies. That is an image that the dreamer's consciousness can accept because it is so far from the dreamer's self-image.

If the dreamer consciously engages with the dream-image, a struggle for resolution of the problem can begin. For example, the dreamer may start by wondering how the natives can be debased enough to indulge in indiscriminate sexuality. Gradually their self-awareness progresses, until they begin to realize that they themselves have such desires. It may be a long, tortuous path to arrive at an honest admission of those forbidden desires, but once a dialog between conscious and unconscious has begun, the problem has a chance to be resolved.

If, instead, the dream image is dismissed as having nothing to do with the dreamer, the need for resolution of this conflict will grow stronger; increasingly more emotional energy will be diverted to the shadow figure. When the energy level is high enough, the person can no longer hold it back and it bursts into consciousness. But since the patient still can't acknowledge that they are in any way like that wild, sexually-depraved native, they project it out onto someone it seems to fit. Jung says that "projections change the world into a replica of one's own unknown face."[8]

The fit doesn't have to be very close if the energy is strong enough. We might see anyone who disagrees with our sexual morality as a sexual pervert. Frequently the issue is projected or *transferred* onto the analyst. Freud felt the two twin poles of the therapy process were free-association to dream content, and resolution of the transference onto the psychoanalyst. In order to promote the latter process, Freud felt that psychoanalysts should reveal as little of themselves as possible to the patient. In that way, the analyst forms an ideal blank screen on which the patient can project their conflicts. Jung had less confidence in the value of the transference.

> . . . Anyone who thinks that he must *demand* a transfer-
> ence is forgetting that this is only one of the therapeutic

---

[8]C. G. Jung, *Collected Works, Vol. 9ii: Aion, Researches into the Phenomenology of the Self* (Princeton: Princeton University Press, 1959) ¶ 9.

factors, and that the very word *transference* is closely akin to *projection*—a phenomenon that cannot possibly be demanded. I personally am always glad when there is only a mild transference or when it is practically unnoticeable.[9]

The shadow figures produced in dreams by the unconscious exactly mirror the issue; therefore, to the extent possible, dreams are the ideal place to deal with shadow issues. If the shadow is instead projected onto someone in the outer world, the fit is less perfect; it's rare that we encounter someone who exactly fits our shadow. However, it is an unusual person who can work up the emotional energy to confront the shadow figures of dreams with the same intensity that they can deal with the shadow projections they encounter in the world. Therefore, integrating the personal contents of the shadow normally takes an interaction with the outer world as well as with the shadow figures in dreams.

INTEGRATING THE SHADOW

Jung did not develop the concept of the shadow theoretically. Jung had noticed that, in most patients, early dreams in an analysis were filled with shadow figures and that the problems which first emerged in analysis were those which have been characterized here as shadow problems. He watched the shadow figures evolve as the patient sorted out the personal from the collective. Jung's key realization was that, though the type and variety of these shadow figures and the concomitant conflicts were wide and varied,[10] the nature of the essential problem was the same for all patients: how to get patients to acknowledge that the shadow figures were part of their own psyche, that they had such thoughts and desires. The issue at this stage was not how to deal with the desires; the issue was merely to acknowledge that one had such desires. This requires great courage on the part of patients.

---

[9] C. G. Jung, *Collected Works, Vol. 7: Two Essays on Analytical Psychology* (Princeton: Princeton University Press, 1966), ¶ 8–9. Jung's emphasis in all cases.
[10] In no way limited to a sexual issue such as I've used as my example above.

Jung saw that there was a single collective entity underlying the multiplicity of shadow figures that appeared in dreams. This collective entity is the shadow, while the images with which the shadow clothes itself in dreams are personal to the dreamer. Though in the following quotation, Jung speaks of the personification of another archetype—the anima/animus—his argument applies equally to the personification of the shadow.

> I have often been accused of personifying the anima and animus as mythology does; . . . the personification is not an invention of mine, but is inherent in the nature of the phenomena. It would be unscientific to overlook the fact that the anima is a psychic, and therefore a personal, autonomous system. . . . The anima is nothing but a representation of the personal nature of the autonomous system in question. What the nature of this system is in a transcendental sense, that is, beyond the bounds of experience, we cannot know.[11]

It is critical in dealing with archetypes to understand that the archetype is not the image it wears any more than we are the clothes we wear. The archetypes are eternal principles that reside in the human psyche. As such, they are beyond any individual human's ability to *integrate* into the personality. When Jung speaks of *integrating* an archetype such as the shadow, he really means integrating the personal experiences and memories that have clustered around the archetype. The archetypes, as collective entities, cannot be integrated into individual consciousness without doing great harm to that individual consciousness. Personal experiences accumulate around the archetypes to flesh them out. As time passes, we encounter an archetype only through a penumbra of such personal experiences and images. Once we are able to differentiate the personal experiences which surround the archetypes from the collective experience of the archetype itself, and integrate the personal

---

[11]C. G. Jung, "Commentary on *The Secret of the Golden Flower*," in *Collected Works, Vol. 13: Alchemical Studies* (Princeton: Princeton University Press, 1967), ¶ 61.

into our consciousness, the archetype is reduced to the collective and once again is beyond our ability to integrate.

> . . . Though the *contents*[12] of anima and animus[13] can be integrated, they themselves cannot, since they are archetypes. As such, they are the foundation stones of the psychic structure, which in its totality exceeds the limits of consciousness, and therefore can never become the object of direct cognition. . . . Hence they remain autonomous despite the integration of their contents, and for this reason they should be borne constantly in mind.[14]

EXPANDED EGO

> . . . the more we become conscious of ourselves through self-knowledge, and act accordingly, the more the layer of the personal unconscious that is superimposed on the collective unconscious will be diminished.[15]

The shadow appears when the ego has accepted too limited a view of itself. The fact that the shadow appears at all is evidence of the fact that the human psyche seems to have some function that pushes the individual toward their potential. Now this might be viewed as nothing more than a homeostatic principle, like a thermostat. When the temperature in a room deviates too far from a reference temperature, the thermostat turns the heater or the air conditioner off or on to compensate. Even if that were all that was involved in this operation—and the human psyche is hardly that simple—it would imply at a minimum that there existed a reference point with which the ego could be compared. This reference

---

[12] Jung's emphasis.
[13] And the other archetypes as well.
[14] C. G. Jung, "Commentary on *The Secret of the Golden Flower*," in *Collected Works*, Vol. 13, ¶ 20.
[15] C. G. Jung, *Collected Works, Vol. 7: Two Essays on Analytical Psychology*, ¶ 178.

point is what Jung termed the *Self*.[16] If the ego deviates too far from the Self, compensatory mechanisms go into action and, in our initial example, the shadow appears.

Until the shadow is integrated into the personality, the world appears filled with opponents or adversaries who are actually products of the unconscious; afterward, people can be seen as individuals, even people who disagree with us. As we have already illustrated, shadow figures initially appear as feared or despised creatures. As we confront the shadow figures and regain the parts of the shadow that are actually part of our own personality, the shadow figures evolve, until they are represented by close friends or relatives. By regaining those previously denied character traits, the ego expands; its range of choices of possible behaviors expands. When confronted by situations which previously led immediately to a single behavior—much like the behaviorists' stimulus-response model—now we have a choice. Successful integration of the personal contents of the shadow enables us to accept that there are other parts to our personality. Until the shadow is acknowledged, we are like cardboard figures with no depth. Afterward, we have more faces than the one we present to the world.

Though the shadow—as an archetype which appears in all of us—is collective, the resolution of the problem that the shadow presents is accomplished by accepting parts of our unique personality that have previously been unnoticed or rejected. Thus most shadow issues are personal issues.

While an increase in choices means an expanded healthier existence, it also means an increase in moral dilemmas. At such a point, a new archetype enters the picture: the *anima/animus*.

---

[16]See chapter 15.

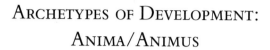

CHAPTER 14

ARCHETYPES OF DEVELOPMENT: ANIMA/ANIMUS

The autonomy of the collective unconscious expresses itself in the figures of the anima and animus. They personify those of its contents which, when withdrawn from projection, can be integrated into consciousness. To this extent, both figures represent functions[1] *which filter the contents of the collective unconscious through to the conscious mind.*[2]

CONNECTING FUNCTION
BETWEEN CONSCIOUS AND UNCONSCIOUS

Jung's studies of his patients' dreams and behavior convinced him that each of us, male or female, contains both masculine and feminine characteristics. Since neither sex normally accepts and uses the behaviors associated with the opposite sex, those behaviors remain unconscious. In the unconscious, they personify into contra-sexual figures, just as the unacknowledged same-sex side of our personality forms into the shadow. This female within the male Jung called the anima; the male within the female he termed the animus.

Where the shadow is largely the personified archetypal expression of our hidden personal character traits, the anima/animus lies farther away from our personal experience. At the most basic level, the anima/animus is the personified archetypal expression

---

[1] Jung's emphasis.
[2] C. G. Jung, *Collected Works, Vol. 9ii: Aion, Researches into the Phenomenology of the Self* (Princeton: Princeton University Press, 1959), ¶ 20.

of the relationship between conscious and unconscious. We have already discussed how archetypes from the unconscious accrete personal experiences to form complexes, and how the ego, as the center of consciousness, is the most important of such complexes.[3] The anima/animus forms the connection between the ego and the unconscious. As such, it is obviously a complex psychological function. However, it was Jung's discovery that this complex function is personified in the psyche by contra-sexual archetypal figures.

Jung felt that the connecting function between conscious and unconscious in a male was the soul. He used the Greek term for soul—*anima*—in order to differentiate from the Christian religious connotations associated with the word soul. Jung's anima was the connecting link between body and spirit that the Greeks, and most other ancient cultures, referred to in the tripartite separation of a human into body, soul, and spirit.

> . . . She is not an invention of the conscious, but a spontaneous product of the unconscious. Nor is she a substitute figure for the mother. On the contrary, there is every likelihood that the numinous qualities which make the mother-imago so dangerously powerful derive from the collective archetype of the anima, which is incarnated anew in every male child.[4]

Jung drew a major distinction between the anima and animus. While anima is Greek for soul, animus is Greek for mind or spirit.

> . . . I have called the projection-making factor in women the animus, which means mind or spirit.[5]

Thus Jung already differentiates between the male and female condition, and their concomitant paths toward individuation. A male's

---

[3] See chapter 11.
[4] C. G. Jung, *Collected Works, Vol. 9ii: Aion, Researches into the Phenomenology of the Self*, ¶ 14.
[5] C. G. Jung, *Collected Works, Vol. 9ii: Aion, Researches into the Phenomenology of the Self*, ¶ 14.

task in resolving the problem of the anima is to integrate his soul; a woman's in resolving the animus to integrate her spirit. Obviously, Jung felt that the normal course of development already forces a man to integrate his spirit, a woman her soul. Thus, the goal of each, in integrating the anima/animus, is the same as was the case with the shadow, the restoration of a missing wholeness.

Some of the particularity with which Jung defined the anima and animus now sounds sexist. Characteristics which Jung regarded as timeless can now be seen as in part culturally determined, rather than inherent in the formless archetype itself. Few women would any longer be comfortable with a characterization of men as rational creatures with developed minds, and women as irrational with developed feelings and intuitions. However, before dismissing Jung's concept of the anima/animus out of hand as sexist, two things should be remembered:

(1) Jung was arguing for the equal importance of what were regarded as masculine and feminine characteristics, in a time when this was an almost unheard of stance;

(2) In the archetypal history of the psyche, recent developments in the relationship between the sexes matter very little.

Much of what Jung describes as anima and animus characteristics are still meaningful for modern men and women. The most important factor is that the need to integrate the anima/animus is the next step toward wholeness in the psyche. As I have pointed out repeatedly, since the Renaissance there has been a great development of the mind, at the expense of the body and emotions. With the increase in humanity's role as an objective observer of physical reality, mind began to withdraw from its previous unconscious unity with nature. However, the split between mind and body was already well underway long before the Renaissance. Christianity stressed the need for subjugation of the body, with its sinful temptations, to the spirit which served God. Christianity, Buddhism, and Islam, the three great modern religions, each sounded this new theme in its own manner. In contrast, the idea that the body is inherently evil was not central to more ancient religions, such as Hinduism and Judaism.

In the Middle Ages, Christianity effectively brought an end to any speculative thought that went beyond the bounds of dogma. However, Christianity did cause an enormous increase in theological thought. Theology, during the Middle Ages, centered on the need for men and women to increase their spiritual connection with God at the expense of their physical connection with reality. The Renaissance further increased that separation of mind and body as the observing mind turned its power upon the physical world. We turned increasingly to the physical world for proof rather than to religious dogma. As we relied less and less upon the authority of religion, we also believed less in the spiritual experiences that underlie religion. The period since the Renaissance has seen the further separation of mind from spirit, splitting the tripartite division of body-soul-spirit still further into body-soul-spirit-mind. Unfortunately, during this development, the role of the soul, with its emphasis on feeling, valuing, and relating, has been largely ignored.

While I feel the above to be a fair summary of the history of the psyche since the Renaissance, from the masculine viewpoint, a question remains as to what that same history would look like from the feminine side. Obviously, as revisionist histories are written which point out the hidden role of women,[6] much could be added to the above. Jung himself felt that a major transition was taking place in the human psyche in our time. This transition involved an attempt to restore a psychological wholeness which had been absent since human beings developed an ego. This new conscious wholeness would include an integration of the feminine principle. Incomplete attempts at wholeness, such as the Christian trinity, needed the addition of the feminine to become true symbols of wholeness. Such a recognition was a great attempt at bridging the gap between masculine and feminine, at a time when few yet recognized the importance of such a reconciliation.

---

[6]And blacks and other minorities.

Masculine/Feminine Syzygy

Men and women have always been both fascinated and mystified by the opposite sex. Of course, in large part this was because of the physical pull of sexuality, but there is so much more than just sex that draws men and women together. Jung stressed that the syzygy between masculine and feminine is an archetypal fact of the human psyche.

> We encounter the anima historically above all in the divine syzygies, the male-female pairs of deities. These reach down, on the one side, into the obscurities of primitive mythology, and up, on the other, into the philosophical speculations of Gnosticism and of classical Chinese philosophy, where the cosmogonic pair of concepts are designated yang (masculine) and yin (feminine). We can safely assert that these syzygies are as universal as the existence of man and woman.[7]

In our time, a fascination with the characteristics of the opposite sex has nearly become an obsession. The woman's movement has fought for women's rights to try on the hitherto masculine robes of power and achievement. In compensation, the more progressive men began to try on the feminine garb of sensitivity and vulnerability. Less progressive men have reacted against the women's movement, and formed a men's movement in opposition. At the more experimental fringes of society, attempts at androgyny have become commonplace. At one point, androgynous figures pushed their way increasingly into popular culture. Though there has been a counterswing away from all such experimentation among the general population, there is no turning back the clock, even for those conservatives and religious fundamentalists who would like to do so. Women are now an accepted part of the work force, even if they still only earn about two-thirds what a male earns for doing the

---

[7] C. G. Jung, *Collected Works, Vol. 9i: The Archetypes and the Collective Unconscious* (Princeton: Princeton University Press, 1969), ¶ 120.

same level of work. Women own independent businesses, run corporations, serve in the congress, the senate, as governors, and cabinet members. Though again, in all cases, they still do so in numbers disproportionately smaller than men due to residual prejudice. Still it is important to remember that, until very recently, all of these changes in status were unimaginable. Certainly they were still unimaginable when Jung described the characteristics of the anima and animus.

This attempt to discover and develop the contra-sexual elements within our personality has created a confusing time for most of us. Jung recognized this difficulty seventy years ago in his studies of the anima/animus. Shadow issues required courage to resolve, the courage to face the dark side of our psyche. But the actual personality traits which the shadow possesses are known quantities. After we give up our protests, we recognize the face in the mirror. At base, all men share the same physical and emotional experience. However, even the most modern man or woman does not know fully what it is like to be the opposite sex.

CULTURAL OR BIOLOGICAL?

The psychological worlds inhabited by men and women have been separate in nearly every culture and time. In almost every culture throughout history, women's roles have centered around the home and family, men's roles around the world outside the home. In the first throes of the sexual revolution, it was commonplace to profess that the only differences between men and women were cultural. Researchers in many fields began, for the first time, to study male/female differences. The study of the nature and origin of such differences has become a broad one that includes psychologists, sociologists, anthropologists, biologists, sociobiologists, ethologists, historians and practitioners in other sub-fields too numerous to name. They have found that:

(1) The differences between men and women are varied and deep; and yet

(2) The differences between the average members of the opposite sex are less than the differences between widely
varying members of the same sex.

This pairing of results goes a long way toward describing exactly
what the situation is in integrating the anima/animus. Though we
all have available within us the characteristics we associate with the
opposite sex, both our personal and archetypal experience of the
opposite sex is largely one of differences, not similarities.

> No man is so entirely masculine that he has nothing fem-
> inine in him. . . . The repression of feminine traits and
> inclinations naturally causes these contra-sexual demands
> to accumulate in the unconscious.[8]

At the biological level, it is easy to see why men contain undeveloped feminine characteristics and vice-versa. A male is merely a female with a missing X-chromosome. The male sex organs develop
as an add-on to the natural simplicity of the female sex organs.
Without sufficient amounts of the male sex hormone, testosterone,
at key points in development, the male would develop into the female. Both sexes have characteristic chemical and hormonal bal-
ances that vary within characteristic cyclic patterns. This biological
picture of developed differences coupled with undeveloped similarities seems to be repeated in the psyches of men and women.

MOODS AND OPINIONS

The anima/animus is further from consciousness than the shadow.
While the shadow as archetype is collective and impersonal, its
contents are largely personal. The anima/animus, as the bridge between conscious and unconscious, is much less personal. Because of
that distance from personal awareness, anima/animus issues are

---

[8]C. G. Jung, *Collected Works, Vol. 7: Two Essays on Analytical Psychology* (Princeton: Princeton
University Press, 1966), ¶ 297.

more complex to resolve. Throughout the ages, men and women have learned how to relate to each other without ever learning what the other's experience is like. The relationship between men and women is like a dance where each responds to the other's movements. Similarly, dealing with the contra-sexual elements within is also like a dance, where each shifts in response to the other. What seems to be archetypally contained within all of us is the experience of the opposite sex in myriad different situations.

Dealing with anima/animus issues brings more of those archetypal experiences into consciousness where we can integrate the experiences into our personal lives. When a man integrates the contents of the shadow, he integrates hitherto unadmitted masculine personality traits. In contrast, when a man integrates the contents of the anima, he integrates the broadened possibilities of relating to the feminine. If a man is the stereotypical macho, dominating, unemotional type, he learns the experience of being responsive instead of dominating, caring instead of unemotional. But he learns these characteristics within the framework of being a male relating to a woman. He doesn't become a woman.

> . . . We can see how it is possible to break up the personifications, since by making them conscious we convert them into bridges to the unconscious. . . . They cannot be integrated into consciousness while their contents remain unknown. The purpose of the dialectical process is to bring these contents into the light; and only when this task has been completed, and the conscious mind has become sufficiently familiar with the unconscious processes reflected in the anima, will the anima be felt simply as a function.[9]

Because Jung's concern with the anima and animus was in large part to help his patients, he wrote a great deal about the characteristics that the anima and animus exhibit when they "confront the conscious mind in personified form."[10] Jung provided one short

---

[9]C. G. Jung, *Collected Works, Vol. 7: Two Essays on Analytical Psychology*, ¶ 210.
[10]C. G. Jung, *Collected Works, Vol. 9ii: Aion, Researches into the Phenomenology of the Self*, ¶ 20.

summary of their characteristics which is especially useful in this discussion.

> If I were to attempt to put in a nutshell the difference between man and woman in this respect, i.e., what it is that characterized the animus as opposed to the anima, I could only say this: as the anima produces moods, so the animus produces opinions.[11]

What is a *mood*; how does a mood differ from a feeling, for example? Moods are collective, feelings are personal. Depression and manic elation are both examples of moods. Both are collective, independent of consciousness. In contrast, a feeling is a relationship between a conscious ego and another thing or person. We say "I like you," or "I hate that." Without the conscious sense of identity, there is no feeling. A mood envelops the ego, swallows it. Depressed people have little or no sense of identity—they become the depression. Moods can be seen as unconscious collective substitutes for conscious feelings. Thus, to the extent that men can learn to accept their feelings and relate to people and things through those feelings, there is no need for the anima to project collective moods onto the outer world.

Opinions are analogous. We have strong, unyielding opinions on those issues we haven't really thought about. The strength of the opinion lies in its collective unconscious nature. A woman, in the grip of her animus, cannot consciously examine the opinions she expresses, any more than a man, in the grip of the anima, can feel the mood he's possessed by. Therefore, when the man is relating to a woman through the anima, and the woman to the man through her animus, we get a combination of the worst qualities of each.

> . . . when animus and anima meet, the anima draws his sword of power and the anima ejects her poison of illusion and seduction.[12]

---

[11] C. G. Jung, *Collected Works, Vol. 7: Two Essays on Analytical Psychology*, ¶ 331.
[12] C. G. Jung, *Collected Works, Vol. 9ii: Aion, Researches into the Phenomenology of the Self*, ¶ 15.

Again it is important to realize that Jung assumed that the characteristics of women and men in his time were universal. In our time, the characteristics he attributes to the anima and animus still largely fit, but it is becoming more frequent that they can no longer be sorted out so cleanly. It comes closer to say that both men and women possess traits we associate with masculinity or femininity. To the extent that either predominates in the person's conscious personality, the other will form in the unconscious in compensation.

Jung was continually trying to find ways to deal with the full complexity of the archetypes. In his early writings he used the Greek words Logos and Eros, instead of thought and feelings as used in this book. But, in time, he rejected these terms as unsatisfactory, largely because they were too removed from the actual experiences of the archetypes.

> . . . I do not, however, wish this argument to give the impression that these compensatory relationships were arrived at by deduction. On the contrary, long and varied experience was needed in order to grasp the nature of anima and animus empirically. Whatever we have to say about these archetypes, therefore, is either directly verifiable or at least rendered probable by the facts.[13]

As we will see later,[14] Jung eventually turned to alchemy as a source of symbols better able to picture the inner processes of the psyche. A famous alchemical picture in a 14th century text portrays the process of development of the masculine psyche as a tree sprouting from the genital area of a man who has been wounded by an arrow in his side.[15] In a 16th century alchemical text, a woman's developmental path is shown as a tree sprouting from the crown of the head of a fully erect, physically powerful woman.[16]

---

[13]C. G. Jung, *Collected Works, Vol. 9ii: Aion, Researches into the Phenomenology of the Self*, ¶ 14.
[14]See chapters 17 and 18.
[15]See C. G. Jung, *Collected Works, Vol. 12: Psychology and Alchemy* (Princeton: Princeton University Press, 1968), ¶ 357, fig. 131.
[16]Johannes Fabricius, *Alchemy: The Medieval Alchemists and their Royal Art* (Copenhagen: Rosenkilde and Bagger, 1976), p. 133.

The alchemical pictures portray the differences in the two journeys. The man has to be wounded, forced to turn in upon himself. The woman has to stand strong and erect. Obviously, both are stances unnatural to the sexes as we knew them until recently.[17] The tree representing a man's process of individuation is shown growing from his sex organs, as a symbol of his instincts, the source both of his deepest sensations and feelings, and of his creativity. The tree representing the woman's process of individuation grows from the top of her head, the source of logical thought and spiritual enlightenment. Both paths of individuation are pictured as trees to symbolize the organic quality of the growth that has to take place. Clearly, the symbolic pictures describe more than can be captured by merely saying that the anima represents a man's feelings, the animus a woman's thinking. Yet still they are culturally limited portraits of the traits of men and women.

Regardless of the oversimplification involved in the statement, the integration of the personal contents of the anima is marked for most men by an increased ability to recognize and accept their emotions. Men who have integrated the anima feel a sense of rootedness and meaning which is not natural for most men; they are able to relate equally to both the outer and inner worlds through their ability to make subtle discriminations of feeling. For most women, integrating the personal contents of the animus enables them to make sharp, analytic distinctions. They are able to act in both the inner and outer world with the swiftness of thought. Freed from the need for outward projection, the anima/animus can return to its psychological function of bridging the gap between conscious and unconscious.

> All these traits, as familiar as they are unsavoury, are simply and solely due to the extraversion of the animus. The animus does not belong to the function of conscious relationship; his function is rather to facilitate relations with the unconscious. . . . The animus, as an associative

---

[17] Though again we have to remember that there have been outstanding men and women in all times who didn't fit such sexual stereotypes.

function, should be directed inwards, where it could associate the contents of the unconscious.[18]

It is well to remember that the integration of the anima/animus, even more than the integration of the shadow, is a life-long process to which we return over and over during the process of individuation. However, there are deeper levels yet to the psyche. Jung recognized that there was still a further level of the individuation process, where the archetype of the Wise Old Man or the Chtonic Mother are activated. This is the third of our archetypes of development: the Self.

> The shadow can be realized only through a relation to a partner, and anima and animus only through a relation to a partner of the opposite sex, because only in such a relation do their projections become operative. The recognition of the anima gives rise, in a man, to triad, one third of which is transcendent: the masculine subject, the opposing feminine subject, and the transcendent anima. With a woman the situation is reversed. The missing fourth element that would make the triad a quaternity is, in a man, the archetype of the Wise Old Man . . . and, in a woman, the Chtonic Mother. These four constitute a half immanent and half transcendent quaternity.[19]

---

[18] C. G. Jung, *Collected Works, Vol. 7: Two Essays on Analytical Psychology*, ¶ 208–209. Obviously, what Jung says of the animus is equally true of the anima.

[19] C. G. Jung, *Collected Works, Vol. 9ii: Aion, Researches into the Phenomenology of the Self*, ¶ 42.

CHAPTER 15

ARCHETYPES OF DEVELOPMENT: SELF

. . . the more numerous and the more significant the uncon-scious contents which are assimilated to the ego, the closer the approximation of the ego to the Self, even though this approx-imation must be a never-ending process.[1]

THE PARADOX OF THE SELF

Jung found that beyond the anima/animus archetype was an arche-type of transcendence and wholeness he called the Self. By capital-izing Self, he meant to imply an entity that is both personal and transcendent. Today, many psychological paradigms talk of a Higher Self, a God within, etc.; these closely match Jung's concept of the Self. However, few of these modern paradigms as yet capture the complexity Jung found in the Self. The Self is the paradox from which all paradox originated.

Its representations in dreams reflect this paradox. Sometimes, it appears in god-like form to fit our human expectations; but sometimes it appears as an animal, much like the gods who ap-peared in animal form to our ancestors. Sometimes the Self appears as a natural force, as when God appeared to Moses as a burning bush. Or an abstract design whose very structure captures its more-than-human character. Usually the Self can be identified beneath its masks by the incredibly powerful impact it has on the dreamer. But

---

[1]C. G. Jung, *Collected Works, Vol. 9ii: Aion, Researches into the Phenomenology of the Self* (Prince-ton: Princeton University Press, 1959), ¶ 23.

sometimes, like Zeus walking on Earth in disguise, the Self appears as a commonplace figure one hardly notices at the time.

The Self cannot be limited by human expectations. More than either the shadow or the anima/animus, the Self is beyond restrictions of space or time. Jung found that at the deepest levels of the unconscious, there are seemingly no longer any such limits: dreams can roam over times hundreds or even thousands of years in the past; dreams can show events years in the future. The Self transcends all limits of personal morality, yet its values are beyond denial. The Self can be the dreamer's deepest personality, the process of development, and the goal of the process, all wrapped up in one entity.

NEED FOR WHOLENESS, NOT PERFECTION

Jung's studies of dreams and mythology convinced him that three-part divisions of reality, such as body–soul–spirit or the Christian trinity, were incomplete attempts to model the wholeness of reality. At times of stress, when a patient badly needs to restore psychological wholeness, dreams abound with four-part, bipolar arrangements. Jung later discovered, in his studies of oriental religious symbolism, a counterpoint to the symmetric figures that appeared in his patients' dreams; these were the beautiful symmetric patterns called *mandalas*, the most satisfying of which are normally four-sided. These were exactly the sort of patterns Jung's patients spontaneously produced in their dreams and visions. Art therapist Rhoda Kellog's studies of preschool art seem to confirm that such mandalas are archetypal, not learned:

> The mandala or circle image seems to be the predominant one in young children who are first learning how to draw. Initially, a two-year old with pencil or crayon just scribbled, but soon he seems to be attracted by the intersection of lines and begins to make crosses. Then the cross is enclosed by a circle and we have the basic pattern of a mandala. As the child attempts to do human

figures, they first emerge as circles, contrary to all visual experience.[2]

If Jung is correct in his interpretation that the Christian trinity and the ancients' model of body-soul-spirit are failed attempts at a mandala, then the period of human history since the Renaissance can be seen as an attempt to evolve a new picture of wholeness. This wholeness would reflect a balance of four parts of the human being: body, soul, mind, and spirit.

Regardless of our philosophical and religious beliefs, all of us know intuitively what is signified by each of these four terms. We know what it means to have body experiences that have nothing to do with emotion. We know when emotional experiences have touched us to our soul. We can separate purely mental experience from spiritual experience. And we have all had experiences in which all these parts seem to be participating equally in a harmonious whole. In his work with the psyche Jung encountered physical, emotional, intellectual, and spiritual problems; all are part of our common lot as human beings, and none should be excluded from any psychology that purports to deal with the whole person.

Humanity's unique task is to find a harmonious balance between the four divisions. Modern men and women have learned far too well how to use the mind to hold the body, soul, and spirit in check. Families teach children how to control instinctual needs. Society further demands that individuals be willing and able to subsume their individual needs within society's needs. The mind's ability to control the instinctual and spiritual needs was a necessary step in the evolution of consciousness, but one that has gone too far. In dealing with shadow issues, we are effectively reversing that process, recognizing that the body, soul, and spirit have needs that must be acknowledged, not repressed. Consider the body as an example; the body operates as a whole, not as a collection of separate parts. Before the over-development of the mind at the expense of the body, men and women were normally more in tune with their bodies than we are now. The ancient Greeks, whom we admire so

---

[2]Edward F. Edinger, *Ego and Archetype* (Baltimore, MD: Penguin Books, 1972), p. 8.

much for the products of their minds, assumed that the body and mind formed a whole with each influencing the other. In contrast, modern men and women have subjugated body to mind; the body's needs frequently go unnoticed, unless it produces something dramatic, like an illness, to call attention to itself.

The body's primary need is for harmony in all its parts. It won't tolerate a one-sided development which works, for example, to the benefit of a kidney at the expense of the other organs with which it connects. Since most of us are no longer able to listen to the body, we presume that its needs are limited to the simple gross needs that are the only ones that still penetrate into our consciousness: the need for food, water, sleep, or sex. In actuality, each of the individual parts of our four-part division of body-soul-mind-spirit seem to contain the other three. We have grown incredibly adroit at containing the body, emotions, and spirit within intellectual paradigms. There is nothing inherently wrong with such a containment; it is a powerful tool which was unavailable to our ancestors. But the body also contains the mind, soul, and spirit; the soul contains the body, mind, and spirit, etc. When we subjugate our physical, emotional, and spiritual needs to our intellect for too long a period, they protest at the imbalance.

The goal of the Christian era has been perfection: further, higher, more! Such perfection always subjects the whole to one of its parts. Jung discovered that our proper goal should be wholeness. As we saw in our discussion of the shadow, this need for wholeness seems to be an inherent function of the human psyche; when there is too large an imbalance between the ego and the Self, the shadow appears as the first step toward rejoining us with Self.

Wholeness can only be achieved if each of the four parts can harmoniously contain and honor the other three. Millions of years of evolution have enabled our bodies to record and adjust for every sensation, thought, or feeling. No matter how overly cerebral we become, our body still breathes, circulates blood, digests food, etc. If the mind is hard at work, the body sends more oxygen and food to the brain. If we are in emotional pain, the body manufactures tranquilizing chemicals to reduce the pain. In moments of spiritual transcendence, the body controls breathing and other autonomic functions in order to produce a feeling of oneness. In other words, the integration of mind, soul, and spirit into the body is a wonderful gift of our evolutionary heritage; we all possess it without further effort.

The integration of the contents of the shadow into the conscious personality can be seen as the final step in the integration of body, soul, and spirit within the mind. An integrated whole demands both control and harmony. The archetype of the shadow is originally activated because the ego has accepted a limited definition of itself, at the expense of undeveloped possibilities or denied desires, frequently those of the body. Jung said that "the body is very often the personification of this shadow of the ego. Sometimes it forms the skeleton in the cupboard, and everybody naturally wants to get rid of such a thing."[3] Once the personal characteristics represented by the shadow personality are accepted as part of the whole personality, mind is once more willing to acknowledge the needs of the body, soul, and spirit.

Of course, such an integration doesn't happen once and for all. We spend a lifetime recovering the personal traits that the shadow has accumulated. None of us is ever so whole that they don't deny healthy parts of their personality out of laziness or fear or myriad other reasons. Rhoda Kellog's previously reported research on children's art shows that the need for wholeness seems inborn. We have already seen in our discussion of the shadow that it appears when the ego deviates too far from the Self. In the above presentation, the author has tried to present the integration of the shadow using the model of body-soul-mind-spirit. The Self might be seen as the limit of that process, in which body, soul, mind, and spirit form an integrated whole. Jung was continually looking for models which could help illustrate the process of individuation. It is important to realize that the process of individuation is an observably psychological process; the models are attempts to picture that process without doing too much damage by over-simplification.

---

[3] C. G. Jung, *Analytic Psychology: Its Theory & Practice* (New York: Vintage Books/Random House, 1968), p. 23.

TRANSCENDENT FUNCTION

> There is nothing mysterious or metaphysical about the term *transcendent function*. It means a psychological function comparable in its way to a mathematical function of the same name, which is a function of real and imaginary numbers. The psychological *transcendent function* arises from the union of conscious and unconscious contents.[4]

Throughout this book, we have stressed that a symbol is not merely a sign; that a symbol is an attempt to express something as yet not understood. We saw how, in times like our own, there is a desperate attempt to synthesize a new *living symbol* that can once more satisfy our mutual need for meaning. Such a synthesis can only occur if the tension between opposites—such as instinct and spirituality—is accepted and lived with, despite the discomfort. If either instinct or spirituality is given precedence, no synthesis occurs. When only one side of the polarity is honored, a symptom, not a symbol, emerges.

The mystery, of course, is how such a living symbol does emerge. As Jung has carefully pointed out, such a symbol cannot be a product of consciousness alone; it can only be produced by the opposition of conscious and unconscious, and within that opposition, it is the unconscious which gives birth to it. That seems to necessitate the existence of a function in the unconscious whose purpose is to restore wholeness in the organism, whether the organism is a person or a civilization. If there isn't such a function, how is it that creative solutions originate, how is it that new living symbols emerge to capture a person or even all the people of an epoch?

It is easy to see how such a function serves a causal, compensatory purpose. The organism is a whole of which consciousness is only a part. When consciousness becomes too one-sided for the or-

---

[4]C. G. Jung, *Collected Works, Vol. 8: The Structure and Dynamics of the Psyche* (Princeton: Princeton University Press, 1960), ¶ 131. As we saw in chapter 4, mathematicians originally resisted the mathematical concept of transcendent functions (more commonly known as "imaginary numbers") much the same as psychologists have resisted its psychological namesake.

ganism's good health, some function is necessary to balance the one-sidedness and restore health. At this level, the function is little more than a complex version of a thermostat, cooling things down when they get too hot, heating them up when too cold. As Jung said, "The self could be characterized as a kind of compensation of the conflict between inside and outside."[5]

But this function also seems to serve a teleological purpose. In *Symbols of Transformation*, and later in *Psychology and Alchemy*, Jung described how later developments were prefigures in early fantasy images. The resolution of Jung's personal crisis, which began with his excommunication by Freud, not only restored him to psychic health, but also produced a change of viewpoint which provided Jung with the material he developed more fully over the rest of his life. If Jung had remained with Freud, and taken the path expected of him, it is unlikely we would now find it necessary to write about him and his discoveries.[6]

The wholeness which emerges from the unconscious is not a return to the way things were before the crisis; nor is it contained in either side of the earlier, supposed dichotomy. We, as 20th-century men and women, have seen all our vaunted institutions crumble around us. Neither side of the many argumentative polarities has the final answer. Must art be abstract or must it mirror physical reality? Must music be harmonic or must it be atonal? Is light a wave or a particle? Is the purpose of religion to help the individual soul find spiritual awakening or should religion speak to the rights of all individuals? Must the American government protect people from the greed of business, or should it protect the rights of businesses, since the success of business is necessary to the success of the economy?

Clearly none of these questions can be adequately answered as stated. They presume a dichotomy that we have to be able to transcend. And, of course, as long as we are locked into the polarized

---

[5] C. G. Jung, *Collected Works, Vol. 7: Two Essays on Analytical Psychology* (Princeton: Princeton University Press, 1966), ¶ 239.

[6] Or remember the author's patient, who felt in such psychic danger that she had to attempt suicide. She was not merely restored to health, but transformed into a new, far more creative woman than ever before. The psychic danger was a call to transcend her current self-image. See chapter 10.

form of such questions, it is impossible to find any such transcendent solution. All the questions indicate is that we are no longer comfortable with the current choices available to us. Somehow we must find new ways of viewing reality that transcend these seemingly irreconcilable opposites.

That need for transcendence, which Jung termed the *transcendent function*[7] is also the Self. And, since the ultimate goal of this process is prefigured in the original images, that goal is also the Self. Thus the Self is both process and goal. This is quite a paradox and paradoxes are usually not welcome, but this paradox is not the result of metaphysical speculation but a simple description of how symbolic resolutions emerge.[8]

ABRAHAM MASLOW AND SELF-ACTUALIZATION

Jung was wise enough to recognize that such a function did exist in the human psyche, and to describe the symbolic forms it took and the way in which it manifested itself. In more recent times, psychologist Abraham Maslow pointed out that we all seem to have a *hierarchy of needs*, progressing from the need for such physical necessities as food and water to the ultimate need for *self-actualization*; i.e., the need to become all that one can be.

Maslow identified men[9] that others considered to be self-actualized, then asked for descriptions of these men. Culling from these lists, he listed fourteen qualities these men seemed to exhibit: wholeness, perfection, completion, justice, aliveness, richness, simplicity, beauty, goodness, uniqueness, effortlessness, playfulness, truth, and self-sufficiency. Surprisingly, these same terms were used over and over in describing such men, an indication that there was a commonality that transcended their individual differences.

---

[7] C. G. Jung, *Collected Works, Vol. 8: The Structure and Dynamics of the Psyche*, ¶ 131–193.

[8] We have encountered a similar inherent paradox in our history of mathematics. The paradox of the set of all sets found in Cantor's transfinite set theory appeared again when Russell and the logicians shifted the field from mathematics to logic. As we will see, Gödel proved that the paradox is indelibly embedded within any logical system.

[9] Even as recently as Maslow, such studies were limited to men.

Maslow found that normal people exhibited these same qualities in their best moments, moments that he termed *peak-experiences*. This convinced Maslow that these values were indeed transcendent values. When self-actualized people were questioned as to the values they considered to be ultimate, one or another of the above values seemed to emerge. However, when they were closely questioned as to what that value meant to them, it quickly emerged that it contained all the other values as well. That is, truth was whole, perfect, complete, just, alive, rich, simple, beautiful, good, unique, effortless, playful, and self-sufficient. At this highest level, Maslow found all values seemed to merge into a single value that could not be described directly.[10]

Self and Mystical Experience

Jung had earlier discovered much the same as Maslow in his explorations of the Self. The pathways to the Self vary, but not infinitely; they definitely fall into categories much like Maslow's categories.[11] Yet all pathways, which are the Self, seem to lead to the same goal, which is also the Self. At that goal, all values seem to merge into a value that transcends description.

This has been the experience of mystics and saints throughout all history when they try to describe the mystical moment; that is, the moment of *peak-experience*. Many have attempted to describe their essentially indescribable experience. Most have described it in terms of their particular religious or spiritual value-system; i.e., in terms of an experience of Jesus or Buddha, etc. Yet to the extent that they truly had a transcendent experience, they all fall back on words that are much like Maslow's.

When I have questioned schizophrenics about their experiences, they frequently describe the same sort of experience as the mystics or Maslow's self-actualizers; however, when the schizo-

---

[10]Abraham Maslow, *Toward a Psychology of Being* (New York: Van Nostrand Reinhold, 1968).
[11]Though Maslow's attempt to enumerate exactly what such categories are does seem a little over-reaching.

phrenics tried to integrate the experience into their lives, they failed and the peak-experience becomes a *nadir-experience.*[12]

Finally, though this enumeration is properly endless, the same words are used over-and-over in the description of *trips* on LSD, mescaline, peyote, psilocybin, and other hallucinogenic drugs. The ubiquity of the descriptions of the experience points to an archetypal content. But since the primary quality of this experience is the transcendence of all other experiences and values, this archetype seems to transcend all other archetypes. That is, in fact, exactly what Jung found of the Self. In an effort to separate the personal experience of the Self, which was channeled through each person's unique qualities and experience, in his later writings, Jung termed the ground from which the Self emerged the *unus mundus.*[13]

EASTERN SPIRITUAL TRADITIONS

Many people of our time, no longer finding any meaning in traditional Western symbols, are turning to Eastern symbols, and therein lies a danger. Eastern spiritual traditions have long examined the interplay of conscious and unconscious mind. Jung read widely in such traditions, but was forced sadly to reject them as offering guidelines for Westerners to use. Jung felt that Western tradition had developed the individual ego at the expense of the collective ego. Therefore, Westerners had first to deal with the shadow that formed in the unconscious in opposition to the ego.

Jung saw that Easterners had the opposite problem. Their tradition had developed a collective ego at the expense of the individual ego. Therefore, Eastern spiritual paths start from their place of strength, the collective ego, and further dissolve the individual ego. This slowly forms a compensatory individual ego within the unconscious which only appears fully developed at the end of the spiritual journey.

---

[12]A term coined by Maslow to contrast with peak-experience.
[13]The unitary world: I have already mentioned this in chapter 4 in the discussion of Spinoza, and will have more to say in chapter 18.

Hindu, Buddhist, and Sufi masters who have emerged from this training tend to be strong individualists who couple wisdom with personal idiosyncracies in an appealing whole. Jung realized that when Westerners try to dissolve their personal ego before they have resolved shadow issues, shadow issues grow to godlike proportions. Therefore, Jung felt that the Eastern paths were dangerous for Westerners, that a Western path must be found.

PASCAL, LAO TZU, AND HOLOGRAMS

Blaise Pascal, a renowned 17th-century philosopher and mathematician, said that God (or the universe, for he considered the two synonymous) is an infinite sphere whose center is everywhere and whose circumference is nowhere. Lao Tzu said the same thing two thousand years earlier. They, and Jung, were attempting to express the fact that everyday people in exceptional moments understand that they contain the entire universe. Since every person is capable of that same experience, the universe has as many centers as it has people. Maslow and Jung both said that exceptional people continually live a close approximation to that exceptional experience.

Jung described our lives as the *circumambulatio* of the Self[14]; that is, as a spiral journey around this inner center. For Jung, life was not a straight-line progress toward some distant goal. Rather, it was a journey to find a center within ourselves which we could approach infinitely closely, but never fully reach. For Jung, the Self was transcendent, but each of us experiences the Self through the filter of our unique existence. The Self is our individual window into a single transcendent world.

Karl Pribram, one of the world's most respected neurophysiologists, has argued that the human brain contains the entire universe. Pribram has come to the conclusion that the universe is a hologram and individual human minds are each part of the holo-

---

[14] C. G. Jung *Collected Works, Vol. 12: Psychology and Alchemy* (Princeton: Princeton University Press, 1968), ¶ 186, 188, and elsewhere throughout this volume and the rest of the collected works.

gram.[15] A hologram has the unique quality that each of its parts can reproduce the whole. If the part is small enough, like a single human mind in comparison to the universe, the reproduction can be fuzzy and indistinct. As more and more parts are added, the clarity increases; however, at each stage the whole is represented. This is a contemporary way to say, as Pascal and Lao Tzu said, that the universe is an infinite sphere whose center is everywhere and whose circumference is nowhere.

There is clearly no final way to describe or to delimit the Self. Jung's greatness lay in recognizing that it was not a metaphysical concept, but an objective fact of psychic existence. Because of the necessary complexity in approaching any of the three key archetypes of development; Jung searched for another description of this process which could better capture some of the complexity of this objective psychic experience. He found this further description in an unexpected place, the forgotten field of alchemy. But first it is finally time to discuss Gödel's famous incompleteness proof.

---

[15] Karl Pribram, "The Brain," in Alberto Villoldo and Ken Dychtwald, eds., *Millennium: Glimpses into the 21st Century* (Los Angeles: J. P. Tarcher, 1981). Also see Ernest Lawrence Rossi, "As Above, So Below: the Holographic Mind," *Psychological Perspectives, Fall 1980* (Los Angeles: C. G. Jung Institute, 1980).

CHAPTER 16

GÖDEL'S PROOF

Kurt Gödel's achievement in modern logic . . . is a landmark which will remain visible far in space and time.[1]

MAPPING ARITHMETIC AND LOGICAL SIGNS ONTO NUMBERS

Gödel discovered how to carefully map meta-mathematical statements about arithmetic onto arithmetic. Then the truth or falsity of the meta-mathematical statements could be established by determining the truth or falsity of mathematical equations. In effect, a system could be made to talk about itself. This insight by Gödel is one of the great discoveries in mathematical history, perhaps the single greatest. In many ways, it is more important to the future of science than any of the better-known achievements of 20th-century science, such as relativity and quantum mechanics in physics, or the discovery of the structure of DNA in biology.

> To what extent is a dialectic suitable to that which it intends to grasp and express? And to what extent is a formalism equivalent to the dialectic whose structure it claims to show? These questions bring us to the fundamental problem of knowledge, to the problem of the agreement of the thought with the object of the thought, to the problem of the simultaneous and con-

---

[1] Famed mathematician John von Neumann, in John W. Dawson, Jr., "The Reception of Gödel's Incompleteness Theorem," in S. G. Shanker, *Gödel's Theorem in Focus* (London & New York: Routledge, 1988), p. 74.

joined equivalence and non-equivalence of the sign and of the thing indicated.[2]

The key to Gödel's proof lay in the development of a method of mapping the elementary signs of arithmetic and logic onto arithmetic. When we discussed Peano's Postulates, we saw that arithmetic could be developed using only a few elementary signs:

(1) "0" (zero); and

(2) "s" (successor).

In addition, symbolic logic required a few additional elementary signs:

(3) "∼" (not);

(4) "∨" (or);

(5) "⊃" (if . . . then . . . ; e.g., *if* all domestic animals have four legs, and a cow is a domestic animal, *then* cows have four legs);

(6) "∃" (there exists; as in *there exists* x, such that such-and-such is true);

(7) "=" (equals); and a few punctuation marks:

(8) "," (comma);

(9) "(" (left parenthesis); and

(10) ")" (right parenthesis).

He also added signs for variables:[3] *numerical* variables,[4] *sentential* variables,[5] and *predicate* variables.[6] Gödel was thus able to map all

---

[2] Quotation by Ferdinand Gonseth in Lucienne Félix, *The Modern Aspect of Mathematics* (New York: Basic Books, 1960), pp. 58–59.

[3] Signs that stand for quantities which *vary* depending on what is substituted for them.

[4] $x, y, z, \ldots$, which stand for numbers or numerical expressions. Gödel assigned these the prime numbers greater than 10: 11 to x, 13 to y, and 17 to z, . . .

[5] $p, q, r, \ldots$, which stand for mathematical *sentences*; i.e., equations, or logically separate parts of equations; e.g., $2 = 1 + 1$, or $p \supset q$. Gödel assigned these the square of the prime numbers greater than 10; i.e., $p = 11^2$, $q = 13^2$, $r = 17^2$, . . .

[6] P, Q, R, which stand for relationships that can be defined as the mathematics is developed from the signs already defined; e.g., for the *square root* of a number, the relationship *less than*, etc. Gödel assigned these the cube of the prime numbers greater than 10; i.e., $P = 11^3$, $Q = 13^3$, $R = 17^3$, . . .

the elementary signs of arithmetic and logic onto a relatively few whole numbers. On the surface this seems little different from what Boole, Frege, Peano, Hilbert, Russell and Whitehead had done in mapping logic and arithmetic onto elementary signs. However, there is a tremendous advance in Gödel's decision to further map the signs onto the numbers which they purported to discuss.

As you will recall, Russell had tried to avoid his own paradox by constructing his system of classes, classes of classes, etc. He never thought to examine the internal integrity of the system he constructed. Hilbert had already proved geometry was consistent if arithmetic was complete and consistent. He constructed a system similar to Russell's, which purported to be sufficient to develop all of arithmetic. Hilbert hoped further to find a finite meta-mathematical way of proving the consistency and completeness of such a system. In both cases, they found it necessary to shift the emphasis away from the area under discussion: Russell with his endless levels of classes, Hilbert with his dream of a finite proof outside the system.

Gödel turned their method upside-down and mapped the signs of logic and arithmetic back onto arithmetic itself. In other words, he created the *ouroboros*, the snake that swallows its own tail. Jung was fascinated by this ancient symbol, which he felt symbolized the primary unity that lies beneath all diversity. Gödel's Proof seems to demonstrate that it is just that. However, as we'll see later, Gödel gave the snake a few twists before he let it swallow its tail.

Having dealt with the elementary signs of arithmetic and logic, Gödel then had to find some way to convert arithmetic formulas into numbers. If we think about it, an arithmetic formula is nothing but a sequence of elementary signs; so all Gödel had to do was devise a method that assigned a unique number—now normally termed a Gödel number—to each unique sequence of signs. Thus, if a formula was given, a Gödel number could be calculated; if a Gödel number was given, it could be translated back into the formula. Although the mapping technique was clever, the achievement was not in the technique, but in the recognition that some such technique could be developed.

In the discussion which follows, formulas will be expressed in words. Normally, formulas would be nothing but a sequence of mathematical signs. Words have been substituted for signs in an attempt to simplify the understandably difficult task of presenting mathematics for non-mathematical readers. Consider the formula: $(\exists x) (x = sy)$; i.e., "there exists a number x, such that x is the successor to a number y." The parentheses are used as punctuation to make clear where logical statements end. Each elementary sign of this formula has already had a Gödel number assigned to it above; e.g., left parenthesis = 9; there exists = 6; x = 11; right parenthesis = 10; equals = 7; successor = 2; y = 12. Thus the sequence of ten signs that make up the formula corresponds to a sequence of ten Gödel numbers: 9, 6, 11, 10, 9, 11, 7, 2, 12, 10.

Gödel defined the Gödel number of the formula by taking the first ten prime numbers,[7] raising each to the power of the Gödel number for the elementary sign in its position, and multiplying them together. The first ten prime numbers are 2, 3, 5, 7, 11, 13, 17, 19, 23, and 29. Therefore, the Gödel number for our simple formula is

$$2^9 \times 3^6 \times 5^{11} \times 7^{10} \times 11^9 \times 13^{11} \times 17^7 \times 19^2 \times 23^{12} \times 29^{10}.$$

This is a very big number, but Gödel wasn't concerned with its size. What interested Gödel was the fact that this number could be converted back into a unique sequence of signs. A basic mathematical proof demonstrates that any number can be expressed as the product of prime numbers in one and only one way. The reader will have to take this on faith as the proof strays too far from our concern here.

The details above demonstrate the cleverness of Gödel's method of mapping, but are not in and of themselves significant. The point is that since formulas were nothing more than sequences of elementary signs, and elementary signs already had Gödel numbers, formulas could also be converted into Gödel numbers. The next step Gödel took was similar. Just as formulas were sequences of signs, proofs (or demonstrations; the words are used interchangeably in mathematics) are sequences of formulas. If a proof involved a sequence of 10 formulas, Gödel converted it into a Gödel number by taking the product of the first 10 prime numbers in order, each raised to the power of the Gödel number of the corresponding formula.

---

[7] A prime number has no divisors except 1 and itself.

It is far beyond the capabilities of even the largest current computers to break such numbers down into their prime factors (though mathematicians have recently been making great inroads into the problem of factoring on a computer). But again, that's not the point. The Gödel number of a proof, large as it was, could still *theoretically* be converted to a unique sequence of Gödel numbers of formulas, each of which could be converted to a unique sequence of Gödel numbers of signs, each of which could be converted to its appropriate sign. Thus, the entire proof could lie hidden in a single Gödel number.

THE AMAZING CODE

If this sounds impossible to the reader, consider the similar scheme described by Martin Gardner.[8] A scientist from another galaxy visits our planet. When he decides that it's time to return home, his host suggests that he take a set of the Encyclopedia Britannica back with him, since it provides an excellent summary of the knowledge of our planet. The alien scientist says that sounds like a good idea, but the weight is prohibitive. Instead, he takes out a metal rod and, measuring carefully, he inscribes a single line on it. He says that the mark records the entire Encyclopedia Britannica.

His host is astounded and asks him to explain. The scientist says that he examined the encyclopedia and found that it contained less than a thousand different letters and symbols. Therefore, he converted each letter and symbol to a three digit number, adding zeros on the left as necessary. Thus the entire encyclopedia could be expressed as an enormous string of three digit numbers. For example, the word CAT would equal 003001020 (assuming that A = 001, B = 002, etc.).

By putting a decimal point in front of the number, the alien scientist converted it to a decimal fraction. Then he carefully measured the rod and made a mark which split it into two parts, A and

---

[8] Martin Gardner, "The Amazing Code," in *Gotcha: Paradoxes to Puzzle and Delight* (San Francisco: W. H. Freeman, 1982), p. 48.

B, where A/B equaled the decimal fraction. Therefore, when he returned to his galaxy, he could remeasure the two parts of the rod, convert their ratio into a decimal, and convert the decimal number back into the information contained in the Encyclopedia Britannica.

Gödel's numbers aren't as big as this number, but the method is similar. In each case, non-numeric statements are mapped onto numbers. The only reason that the alien scientist's method won't work is because there is no measuring technique in the universe capable of such refinement. However, both his method and Gödel's are theoretically possible, though Gödel's is more elegantly designed.

MAPPING META-MATHEMATICS ONTO MATHEMATICS

With all arithmetic signs, formulas, and proofs mapped onto integers, Gödel was able to move on toward the goal of this process: mapping meta-mathematical statements onto simple arithmetic statements. And, of course, these formulas could in turn be converted into Gödel numbers. Gödel came to the culmination of his magnificent proof by considering a very special case where the Gödel number of the formula was itself contained in the formula. This would involve him in a deliberately chosen self-referential system. Gödel was very careful in the choice of the meta-mathematical statement in question. He wanted to prove that there was at least one arithmetic formula whose truth or falsity could not be demonstrated using the elementary signs of arithmetic, provided one assumed arithmetic to be consistent. If there was at least one such formula, then the goal of the formalists was impossible.

Earlier we saw how Cantor proved that the infinity of real numbers was bigger than the infinity of integers by showing that, no matter what matching scheme was chosen, there was at least one real number that could not be matched with an integer.[9] Gödel went about his proof in much the same way.

---

[9]See chapter 6.

A formal expression of this meta-mathematical statement was "for every x, where x is the Gödel number of a proof, x is not the Gödel number of a proof for the formula whose Gödel number is z." Let's describe it more colloquially as "there is a formula which cannot be demonstrated" (and that formula has Gödel number z). Gödel had to devise a formula such that the formula would itself be the representation of this meta-mathematical statement within arithmetic. In other words, the formula would represent a statement that the formula itself could not be proved.

We can see that the formula in question must be a strange one. In order for a statement about a formula to map onto the formula, the formula must map onto a variable within itself. In effect, it has to contain itself as a variable. Therefore, the meta-mathematical statement that there is a formula which cannot be proved can be mapped onto the formula itself. The formula can in turn be mapped onto a variable within itself, and the variable is the Gödel number of the formula.

Let's recall the image of the *ouroboros*, the snake that swallows its own tail. Instead of a snake, imagine a good-sized length of ribbon. If we connect one end of the ribbon to the other, making a ring, we can color the top side of the ribbon one color, say red, and the bottom side another color, say blue. Take another length of ribbon and give it a twist before you connect the two ends into a ring. Such a construction is called a Möbius strip.[10] If you try and color the top side red now, you'll find that there doesn't seem to be a top and bottom any more. In fact, you will have colored the whole ribbon red when you return to your starting point. Stage magicians use a variant on this called *The Afghan Bands* as a startling effect. Rather than coloring the ring of ribbon, they cut it in half along its length. Instead of two rings of equal size, they end up with a single ring twice as big.

You could think of a simple version of the *ouroboros* with no twist as corresponding to the simplest paradox. One side would say: "the statement on the other side is true." The other side would say:

---

[10]Named after its discoverer: 19th-century German mathematician August Ferdinand Möbius.

"the statement on the other side is false." That's an endless loop. However, the Möbius strip corresponds to a more complex paradox, such as: "the statement that 'the statement is false' is false." The untwisted paradox merely forms a chain which asserts, then contradicts, then contradicts the contradiction, and so forth. The twisted paradox forms an assertion that it itself is false. In other words, it is self-referential.

The mathematics of Gödel's actual construction is beyond the scope of this book, but, in effect, Gödel constructed an arithmetic formula which asserted that it was itself not demonstrable. The meta-mathematical statement that mapped onto this formula stated that the formula was not demonstrable. In other words, he constructed not an untwisted paradox, not a twisted paradox, but a paradox with two twists. To correspond to our examples above, the twice-twisted paradox would assert that "the statement that 'the statement that [the statement is false] is false' is false."

It was thus a three-step process. There was a meta-mathematical statement that said: some formula is not demonstrable. The representation of that meta-mathematical statement was the formula that could not be demonstrated. It couldn't be demonstrated because the formula in turn asserted that its opposite was true. Quite perplexing!

Why all that work to make such a strange embedded statement? Gödel was convinced that attempts to reduce mathematical truth to consistency were futile. The truth of any system can necessarily only be determined outside that system. When you try to fit something bigger into something smaller, something has to be left out. Remember how Bertrand Russell tried to avoid the paradox of the *set of all sets which do not contain themselves* by creating his *theory of classes*, in which he had first classes, then classes of classes, etc. Each time he created bigger entities, thus avoiding the problem infinitely. Gödel did the reverse; in effect, he mapped classes of classes onto classes, classes onto their own elements. Recall what mathematicians mean by the word consistent: simply that you cannot prove both the truth and the falsity of a given formula. By constructing the twice-twisted paradox, Gödel could map it onto an arithmetic formula that was still twisted.

. . . if a formula as well as its contradictory can both be derived from a set of axioms, the axioms are not consistent. Accordingly, if the axioms are consistent, neither the formula nor its contradictory is demonstrable. In short, if the axioms are consistent, the formula is undecidable—neither the formula nor its contradictory can be formally deduced from the axioms.

Very well. Yet there is a surprise coming. For although the formula is undecidable if the axioms are consistent, it can nevertheless be shown by meta-mathematical reasoning to be true. . . . In the first place, on the assumption that arithmetic is consistent, we have already established the meta-mathematical statement.[11] It must be accepted, then, that this meta-mathematical statement is true. Secondly, the statement is represented within arithmetic by that very formula itself. Third, we recall that meta-mathematical statements have been mapped upon the arithmetical formalism in such a way that true mathematical statements[12] always corresponds to true arithmetical formulas . . . Accordingly, the formula in question must be true.[13]

What does that mean? Well, we've already seen that if arithmetic is consistent, then there is a formula which is undecidable; that is, it's truth or falsity cannot be determined. Now it's gotten worse. Mathematicians say that an axiomatic system is complete if all true statements within that system can be derived from the axioms. But Gödel's upstart of a formula has now been proved to be true, and it cannot be derived from the axioms: i.e., if it were, its opposite could also be derived. That means that there is a true arithmetic formula which cannot be derived from the rules of arithmetic, and, therefore, arithmetic is incomplete.

---

[11] Gödel's assertion that "the formula is not demonstrable."

[12] And Gödel's statement is now proved to be true.

[13] Ernest Nagel and James R. Newman, "Gödel's Proof," in James R. Newman, ed., *The World of Mathematics* (New York: Simon and Schuster, 1956), pp. 1692–1693.

This is quite a lot for the reader to absorb. Please realize that it was equally strange to mathematicians when they were first confronted with it. New ways of viewing reality are always strange and puzzling. However, recall the Barber Paradox, which asked if the barber, who shaved everyone who didn't shave themselves, shaved himself. We saw that there was no way to answer that question; any answer implied its own opposite. Gödel's formula did much the same thing.

A close analogy to the paradoxical formula in Gödel's Proof is the Liar Paradox attributed to the sixth century Greek poet Epimenides. "Epimenides is reputed to have said 'all Cretans are liars.' Considering that he was a Cretan, did Epimenides speak truly?"[14] Gödel created a formula that said that it was itself a lie. Clearly such a formula could not be demonstrated within arithmetic, since no matter which way you turned it, it turned itself upside-down once again.

The reason Gödel's proof is taken so seriously, while paradoxes like the Liar Paradox are dismissed as plays on words, is because of the mathematical rigor of the development of the paradox. While Gödel's method of mapping was new to mathematicians, it was totally sound. His method couldn't be discarded without discarding all of logic and mathematics. Yet if his proof was accepted, then the attempt to reduce mathematics (and by extension any other such system) to logic was inherently flawed and incomplete.

> That completeness' price is inconsistency, for logistic systems rich enough to contain recursive arithmetic, including all set theories worth their name formalized as such systems, is a result which was doubly unexpected: first, for its content; second, for the fact that it could be proved according to standards of rigor which were the highest known, higher even than those customarily used in mathematical proofs.[15]

---

[14] Martin Gardner, *Gotcha: Paradoxes to Puzzle and Delight*, p. 4.

[15] A. A. Fraenkel and Y. Bar-Hillel, *Foundations of Set Theory* (Amsterdam: North-Holland Publishing Company, 1958), p. 304.

SIGNIFICANCE OF GÖDEL'S PROOF

Some mathematicians were quick to see the implications of Gödel's proof, including John von Neumann and Alfred Tarski. Von Neumann and Tarski, along with J. Barkley Rosser and Gödel, himself, all extended the original proof, to show that any logical system which contains recursive number theory, including elementary arithmetic and calculus, is essentially undecidable.

The vast majority of mathematicians of the time, however, simply remained unaware of Gödel's incompleteness theorem. Even among the formalists and logicians who were most concerned with the issues Gödel was addressing, there was general confusion as to exactly what Gödel had or had not proved. They examined every aspect of the proof, trying to find some way of evading its consequences, but to no avail. When it became clear that Gödel's proof wasn't going to be toppled, they then behaved like their counterparts in philosophy, the logical positivists. The formalists said, all right, we'll accept that there is no ultimate proof of consistency and completeness. Therefore, mathematics is the field that develops all the conclusions that *can* be consistently derived from a rigorously defined, finite set of axioms. In other words, if problems get too big for us, let's pretend that they aren't there; the ostrich technique once more.

> It seems likely that many working mathematicians either remained only vaguely aware of them [i.e., Gödel's conclusions] or else regarded them as having little or no relevance to their own endeavors.[16]

Many years later, Bertrand Russell wrote of his own puzzled reaction to Gödel's incompleteness proof.

> I realized, of course, that Gödel's work is of fundamental importance, but I was puzzled by it. It made me glad that

---

[16]John W. Dawson, Jr., "The Reception of Gödel's Incompleteness Theorem," in Shanker, *Gödel's Theorem in Focus*, pp. 87–88.

I was no longer working at mathematical logic. If a given set of axioms leads to a contradiction, it is clear that at least one of the axioms must be false.[17]

When Gödel heard of Russell's reaction he commented with some sympathy that "Russell evidently misinterprets my result; however, he does so in a very interesting manner."[18] Gödel had put an end to the dreams of Russell and Hilbert, and all others who wanted to remove the mysteries from the world.

Modern mathematics is essentially a field where mathematicians agree among themselves on formal methods to deal with intuitive concepts. The core of the field is all intuition—it comes from some non-logical source within us. Like most of us, mathematicians are more comfortable dealing with hard facts than fuzzy concepts like intuition. Until the appearance of the formalists and the logicians in mathematics, the vast majority of mathematicians were unconscious Platonists; i.e., they took it for granted that mathematical truth was of necessity physical truth as well. However, I stress that they did this unconsciously. When formal methods appeared, most mathematicians assumed they could have their cake and eat it, too: both Platonic mathematical truth and formal axiomatic verification. Mathematician Andrzej Mostowski expressed the problem that confronted them this way:

> . . . until we succeed to build a formal system coinciding with the intuitive mathematics, there is no immediate connection between the problem of completeness of any proposed formal system and the problem of existence of essentially unsolvable mathematical problems.[19]

---

[17] From Bertrand Russell's letter to Leon Henkin of April 1, 1963, in John W. Dawson, Jr., "The Reception of Gödel's Incompleteness Theorem" S G. Shanker, ed., *Gödel's Theorem in Focus* (London & New York: Routledge, 1988), p. 90.

[18] Gödel's response to seeing Russell's above remarks, in a July 2, 1973 letter to Abraham Robinson, in John W. Dawson, Jr., "The Reception of Gödel's Incompleteness Theorem," p. 91.

[19] Andrzej Mostowski, *Sentences Undecidable in Formalized Arithmetic: An Exposition of the Theory of Kurt Gödel* (Amsterdam: North Holland Publishing Company, 1952), p. 3. Unfortunately, translations of mathematical texts are frequently like translations of Japanese and Korean instruction manuals.

Russell and Whitehead, who were first philosophers and only secondarily mathematicians, were conscious of the issues at stake, but
too intoxicated with the triumphs of symbolic logic to question the
limits of logical systems. In contrast, Gödel, who was first a mathematician and only secondarily a philosopher, always remained
conscious of the philosophical underpinnings of mathematics. This
led him to closely examine the relationship between logic and experience, the finite and the infinite, etc. In this examination, he
never varied in his belief that mathematical intuitions were every
bit as real as sensory perceptions.

> Despite their remoteness from sense experience, we do
> have something like a perception also of the objects of set
> theory, as is seen from the fact that the axioms force
> themselves upon us as being true. I don't see any reason
> why we should have less confidence in this kind of per-
> ception, i.e., in mathematical intuition, than in sense
> perception. . . . They, too, may represent an aspect of ob-
> jective reality.[20]

Contemporary mathematician René Thom clearly expresses a similar Gödelian belief that mathematics deals with archetypal values:

> . . . everything considered, mathematicians should have
> the courage of their most profound convictions and thus
> affirm that mathematical forms indeed have an existence
> that is independent of the mind considering them.[21]

All science is based on logic and mathematics. Gödel's Proof
implies that all science is inherently flawed and incomplete to the
extent that it is limited to a logic or a mathematics devoid of intuition. However, the issue is even more pervasive than that. Though
Gödel's Proof addresses the foundations of all science, it is still only

---

[20] Philip J. Davis and Reuben Hersh, *The Mathematical Experience* (Boston: Houghton Mifflin, 1981), p. 319.
[21] Philip J. Davis and Reuben Hersh, *The Mathematical Experience*, p. 319.

a partial formulation of the limits of the problem. The larger issue is the recognition that the world is a unity.

When, in the Renaissance, we began to consciously separate ourselves from that unity in order to observe the world which lay outside, we were creating an artificial distinction. We were playing a game, though we didn't realize it at the time. As an example of the game, look down at your hands and pretend that they belong to someone else. By doing so, you can learn a great deal about your hands that you wouldn't be aware of as long as you remained unconscious of their separate existence and merely used them as a part of your total body. But it is still just a game; your hands remain connected to your arms, which are in turn connected to the trunk of your body. Your body remains a single, unbroken entity despite the fact that you can observe parts of it separately.

The rewards for playing such a game are obvious; they lie about us in mankind's intellectual and physical achievements. Clearly it was important for us to learn this game and learn to play it well. But eventually it ceased to be a game; the snake swallowed its tail again. As our observations of reality became more detailed, we found ourselves looking into a microscope and seeing ourselves looking back. Gödel's Proof is the 20th century's greatest intellectual expression of this truth, but the truth transcends even Gödel.

I have attempted to trace the development within mathematics of the chain of events that led from the base of arithmetic and geometry upward, seemingly ineluctably, toward Gödel's Proof. By the time we climb to that peak, the air is cold and thin around us, and human issues seem small and remote. The world is thus demonstrated to be a necessary unity by mathematics, mankind's most abstract and powerful tool.

It is at the human level, however, that such conclusions will have to be integrated into our lives. Logic's greatest achievement points to its own inadequacy to deal with the full extent of reality. It is consciousness that has shown us that we are each unique individuals, not merely parts of a unified whole. It is consciousness that has then led us back to realizing that we are also inseparable parts of a unified reality. It is consciousness that will have to integrate those two seemingly irreconcilable facts into a new unity.

CHAPTER 17

ALCHEMY AS A MODEL OF PSYCHOLOGICAL DEVELOPMENT

I had to find evidence for the historical prefiguration of my inner experiences. That is to say, I had to ask myself, "Where have my particular premises already occurred in history?" If I had not succeeded in finding such evidence, I would never have been able to substantiate my ideas.[1]

JUNG'S REDISCOVERY OF ALCHEMY

Having discovered the collective unconscious, Jung patiently recorded what he found there. He found a number of archetypes which he discussed throughout the years. The archetypes of development[2] were of a different order, since they corresponded to psychological stages of development. Jung was never satisfied with this single model for the stages of development, feeling that it captured only part of the mystery.

For example, in order to resolve the problems presented by the shadow, a joining of two previously opposed parts of the personality has to occur. What is the nature of the union and what steps need to be followed to create it? Because the archetypes of development were centered around personified unconscious figures, they had an unusual richness that captured the character of the problems involved at each stage. Any one such personified

---

[1] C. G. Jung, *Memories, Dreams, Reflections* (New York: Vintage Books/Random House, 1965), p. 200.
[2] The shadow, anima/animus, and self; see chapters 13, 14, and 15.

THE STAGES OF THE ALCHEMICAL JOURNEY.

model, however, can only go so far in revealing structure. As Jung never tired of pointing out, the archetypes of the collective unconscious are empty of content until they pass through an individual life. The personification of the archetypes of development is one model the psyche has taken in presenting the individuation process to consciousness; Jung was convinced that there were others. Just as there are major benefits in relating to the stages of individuation through personification, there are other benefits in viewing those stages in a more abstract representation. The key, of course, is finding the ways in which the psyche itself has chosen to present the archetypes which represent the individuation process.

The unconscious is similar to the world quantum physicists like Werner Heisenberg found inside the atom. Heisenberg said that one can observe either the momentum or the position of a subatomic particle, but not both.[3] Similarly, if Jung froze the process of psychological development, he was able to discover the archetypes that were operative at each stage; these were the shadow, anima/animus and Self. By way of analogy only, those would correspond to the position of the subatomic particle. Jung also wanted to find out more about the process, the momentum. But for that he needed a different model.

From 1918 to 1926, he studied the early Christian Gnostics, who he felt were struggling with similar inner issues. And clearly in their struggle, they had encountered the collective unconscious, since their beliefs were presented largely through symbolic images: creation myths, symbolic presentations of the relationship between man and God, etc. Unfortunately, Jung could only explore Gnostic thought through the writings of the early Christian scholars who were their opponents. And, over and beyond the difficulties in dealing with the Gnostic material at second-hand, was the inherent difficulty that they were struggling with issues almost two thousand years in the past. The Gnostics might have been his spiritual ancestors, but eventually Jung came to accept that they were just too far

---

[3] Werner Heisenberg, *The Physical Principles of the Quantum Theory* (New York: Dover, 1949), pp. 48–52.

removed from him in time to have been able to grasp the psychological significance of the material they presented.[4]

He needed to find some historical prefiguration of his ideas
that was intermediate in time between the Gnostics and himself.
He was to find this in alchemy. As so many times in his life, Jung
was led to this discovery through his dreams. For several years, he
had a continuing dream in which he would discover some previously unknown part of his house. Sometimes this had to do with
his parents, but more often there was an added guest wing which
served as a museum of ancient history. Over the course of numerous dreams, he explored this museum, finally coming to an old library. When he opened one of the books, he found that it was filled
with wonderful symbolic pictures. He was so thrilled that when he
woke, he found that his "heart was palpitating with excitement."

Now just before he had this final dream in the cycle, Jung had
found a quotation he needed to check and thought it might have
something to do with Byzantine alchemy. So he ordered some
books on alchemy from an antiquarian bookdealer. Several weeks
later, when the books arrived he found a 16th-century parchment
filled with symbolic pictures much like those in his dream. With
that discovery he began a new process of exploration which was to
continue for the rest of his life. In *Man and His Symbols*, Jung dis-
cusses this series of recurring dreams which led up to his discovery
of alchemy.

> As the rediscovery of the principles of alchemy came to
> be an important part of my work as a pioneer of psy-
> chology, the motif of the recurring dream can easily be
> understood. The house, of course, was a symbol of my
> personality and its conscious field of interests; and the
> unknown annex represented the anticipation of a new
> field of interest and research of which my conscious
> mind was at that time unaware. From that moment, 30
> years ago, I never had the dream again.[5]

---

[4] See C. G. Jung, *Memories, Dreams, Reflections*, pp. 200–201.
[5] C. G. Jung, *Man and his Symbols* (Garden City, NY: Windfall Books, Doubleday, 1964), p. 54.

A Short History of Alchemy

Alchemy has generally been presented as a foolish, superstitious predecessor to chemistry. Most of us know little or nothing of the actual practice of alchemy. Perhaps we visualize solitary men working with beakers and flasks—that portrait would be partially accurate. We might be aware that the goal of alchemy was the production of the *philosopher's stone*, but we have little idea what that might be. We might also vaguely remember that alchemists attempted—and sometimes claimed to have succeeded in—the transmutation of lead into gold.

This gives us a picture of the alchemist as either a greedy fool or a charlatan. Though alchemists included both fools and charlatans among their number, as has every other calling, most alchemists were neither. They were likely to be intelligent, religious, inquisitive, and necessarily solitary. In order to understand how alchemy could possibly offer anything of substance for depth psychology, we have to understand a little of the history of alchemy.

Alchemy and Christianity came into existence in the Western world at roughly the same time. Alchemy developed into a separate field during the first through the third century A.D. However, its roots can be traced to 330 B.C., when Alexander the Great conquered Egypt, founded the city of Alexandria, and created the greatest library of the ancient world. The library, which housed nearly half a million manuscripts, brought scholars from all over the world. Even though a great part of the library burned during Caesar's conquest of Alexandria in 80 B.C., it remained a haven for scholars.[6] During this period, commerce, warfare and Christianity all served to mix cultures that had hitherto gone their separate ways. John Stillman, in his history of alchemy and early chemistry, said of these times that:

> Greek philosophy, Egyptian arts, Chaldean and Persian mysticism met and gave rise to strange combinations not

---

[6] John Maxson Stillman, *The Story of Alchemy and Early Chemistry*, 1924 (New York: Dover, reprint 1960), p. 137.

always conducive to improvement upon the relative clarity of the Greek foundation.[7]

Obviously, Stillman shared the view of alchemy as a naive pre-science that I mentioned earlier. His views are typical of the histories of alchemy written from the viewpoint of Western science. In contrast, Jungian analyst Marie-Louise von Franz[8] sees alchemy as an advance which combined Greek theory with Egyptian experimentation.

> The Greek philosophers who, as you all know, initiated rational thought regarding the problems of nature, of matter, space and time, etc., made practically no or very few experiments. Their theories are bolstered by certain observations but it never really occurred to them to actually experiment. On the other hand, in Egypt there was a highly developed chemical-magical technique, but in general the Egyptians gave it no thought, either philosophical or theoretical. It was simply the handing down by certain priestly orders of practical recipes, plus some magic religious representation but I should say without theoretical reflection. When the two trends of Greek and Egyptian civilization came together they united in a very fruitful marriage, of which alchemy was their child.[9]

The first great alchemists were also Gnostic Christians. Christianity was largely the religion of the simpler, less-educated members of society. The Gnostics tended to be more intellectual; they viewed Christianity as the newest and greatest of the *mystery religions*, in which deep truths were hidden beneath the innocent words preached to the masses. Gnostics wanted a personal experience of God, not merely a collective religion interpreted for them by

---

[7]John Maxson Stillman, *The Story of Alchemy and Early Chemistry*, p. 137.

[8]To whom the author is indebted for much of this history of alchemy.

[9]Marie-Louise von Franz, *Alchemical Active Imagination* (Irving, TX: Spring Publications, 1979), p. 1.

ALCHEMICAL MINING.

priests. Because of this need for personal experience, they developed a complex symbolic system to describe the relationship between God, humanity, and the world.[10] Of course, as Jung said, "it seems highly unlikely that they had a psychological conception of [their symbolic images]."[11]

The alchemists were trying to discover the deepest secrets of the universe. That meant searching for the building blocks of both matter and psyche, for they saw no clear distinction between the two. For them, there was only a relationship between the experimenter and his experiment. An alchemical operation had to be conducted at a propitious time because they believed that the micro

---

[10]Since Jung's time, much more material has come to light on the wide variety of views lumped under the title of Gnostic. Christianity was just beginning to solidify into the form it would hold for so many centuries, while those with divergent views were united more by their opposition to the ruling ideas than any unity of beliefs. That being said, there is still much to say for the view of Gnostics as ancient precursors of modern men and women on a spiritual quest.

[11]C. G. Jung, *Memories, Dreams, Reflections*, p. 201.

world of their experiments was connected with the macro world of the cosmos. They had to meditate deeply on both their own inner nature and the inner nature of the matter upon which they were experimenting. It is easy to see why this seemed to Jung a prefiguration of modern depth psychology, in which psychologists must observe not only their patients' psyches, but their own as well, since the two are inextricably connected in the process of therapy.

After the third century A.D., the alchemical tradition spread[12] to the Moslem world. There existed in Islam, as in Christianity, a split between the outer-oriented religion of the masses, and a more inner-oriented, mystical religion followed by the intellectuals. The latter eagerly adopted alchemy as one more avenue into the greater mysteries. Alchemy reached its peak in the Islamic world during the tenth century. As the Moslem world became the center of intellectual achievement, it attracted European Christian scholars. In Spain, the mystery teachings spread to the Jewish mystics; the Cabala was the product.

Whether directly from the Moslems, or by way of the Spanish Jews, alchemy spread again in the West at roughly the time of the Renaissance. It reached its peak in the 15th and 16th centuries, and still existed in some form during the 17th and 18th centuries. Goethe, for example, was still familiar with the alchemical writings and drew on them in *Faust*, much as other authors drew on the Bible or Shakespeare. By Jung's time, however, alchemy was largely unknown to the educated reader, and the alchemical allusions in Goethe meant nothing to Jung when he read *Faust* with such fascination in his youth. However, it may have been this early reading that unconsciously led Jung to alchemy in the latter part of his life.

Bringing Order out of Chaos

Jung had to discover Gnostic thinking largely through the writings of their opponents in the organized Church. Therefore, he wasn't aware of Gnostic alchemical writing until after he had the dream

---

[12]Along with mathematics and other deep mysteries.

we've quoted and began his alchemical research. What he found would have daunted most scholars. Alchemical writings were a mixture of philosophy, religion, mysticism, scientific theory, and "cookbook" recipes for experiments. Both the early texts, written in Greek, and the later Latin texts were impossible to translate literally.

> . . . sulphur is called theion and theion means also the divine. Then a material called arsenikon is often mentioned. Arsenikon simply means male, and in contrast to theion, which really means sulphur, you cannot define in old treatises what is meant by arsenikon; it might be anything.[13]

Jung had to go through the texts and list the words and their possible meaning in that text. He made concordances in which he listed all the references to a given word in any alchemical text in an attempt to bring some order to its usage. This was the method used by the alchemists themselves.

> Even the alchemists had said: "One book opens the other. Read many books and compare them throughout and then you get the meaning. By reading one book alone you cannot get it, you cannot otherwise decipher it."[14]

Because of the translation problem, the alchemists frequently differed among themselves over the meaning of a word. This increasingly led them to ascribe deeper meanings to words than might originally have been intended.

> They themselves got mixed up by not being able to consult with their colleagues, because they were all lonely experimenters. Therefore, they spoke about an esoteric

---

[13] Marie-Louise von Franz, *Alchemical Active Imagination*, p. 9.
[14] Marie-Louise von Franz, *Alchemical Active Imagination*, p. 17.

and exoteric language, and thus got into a completely
Babylonian confusion of languages.[15]

Jung gradually began to make some sense out of the confusion. He
saw that matter and psyche were not differentiated for the alchemists, that they could talk simultaneously of physical and psychic operations. Because of this lack of differentiation, he saw
further that their unconscious issues were projected out onto matter, in much the same way as we project qualities of the shadow,
anima/animus, or Self onto the people around us.

If the projection of unconscious, and even archetypal, material
onto matter seems strange, consider science itself. The existence of
any spiritual reality has been consciously denied by modern scientists. However, the need for spiritual values seems to remain intact in
the unconscious, where it is projected out onto matter. For example, the quest of a modern physicist for the ultimate building blocks
of matter is hardly a disinterested scientific study. Similarly, the biologist's search for the language of life in DNA and RNA generates a
zeal that is more spiritual than intellectual. The emphatic insistence
of scientists that everything can ultimately be reduced to physical
properties is surely a projection. There is no objective need for such
an emphasis. When a new theory threatens this essentially religious
viewpoint,[16] its author is considered a heretic who should be ex-
communicated from the scientific community.

Because alchemists were solitary men engaged in a quest
which involved both outer and inner exploration, their writings inevitably documented the progressive stages of this quest. Once Jung
could make sense of their strange manner of writing, he was able to
trace the paths of inner development represented symbolically by
the alchemical operations. The later alchemists were themselves
aware of the dual nature of their studies, which makes their material less psychologically useful. The early alchemists, however, were
blithely unaware, which makes their symbolic material correspondingly more useful.

---

[15]Marie-Louise von Franz, *Alchemical Active Imagination*, p. 10.
[16]Such as Rupert Sheldrake's theory of morphogenetic fields.

Jung recorded his discoveries in this field in his later writings. These are collected in *Psychology and Alchemy*, *Alchemical Studies*, *Aion*, "The Psychology of the Transference," and in his magnum opus *Mysterium Coniunctionis*.[17] A discussion of the latter volume in the next chapter will conclude our examination of Jung's alchemical studies.

---

[17]C. G. Jung *Collected Works, Vol. 12: Psychology and Alchemy* (Princeton: Princeton University Press, 1968); *Collected Works, Vol. 13: Alchemical Studies* (Princeton: Princeton University Press, 1967); *Collected Works, Vol. 9ii: Aion: Researches into the Phenomenology of the Self* (Princeton: Princeton University Press, 1959); "The Psychology of the Transference" in *Collected Works*, Vol. 16: *The Practice of Psychotherapy* (Princeton: Princeton University Press, 1966); *Collected Works, Vol. 14: Mysterium Coniunctionis* (Princeton: Princeton University Press, 1963). The title means the mysterious or miraculous union.

CHAPTER 18

MYSTERIOUS UNION

Mysterium Coniunctionis is really the summa *of Jungian psychology, and I think it is safe to say that if you can achieve a really living and working relationship to this book, you then achieve simultaneously a living, working relationship to the autonomous psyche.*[1]

MYSTERIUM CONIUNCTIONIS

Mysterium Coniunctionis represented Jung's second great attempt to express the process of psychological development through the archetypes of the unconscious. His first was through the archetypes of development: the shadow, anima/animus, and the Self.[2] In *Mysterium Coniunctionis* he approached psychological development from a different direction. Rather than concentrating on the archetypes that represented each stage of psychological development, he centered instead on the psychic unions that formed as one stage gave way to the next. With the completion of *Mysterium Coniunctionis*, Jung felt that he had said all that he had to say on alchemy. From its completion in Jung's 80th year to the end of his life, he turned to more personal writings: his spiritual autobiography *Memories, Dreams, Reflections*; *Man and his Symbols*, which introduced the wider reading public to Jung; his correspondence with many of the other great thinkers of his time.

---

[1] Edward Edinger, *The Mysterium Lectures*, Joan Dexter Blackmer, transcriber and editor (Toronto: Inner City Books, 1995).
[2] See chapters 13, 14, and 15.

Jung's pre-alchemical work has been described thoroughly for the intelligent lay public by many later writers. In fact, many readers have only encountered Jung through his translators. Unfortunately, the ideas in Jung's works on alchemy, especially the ideas in *Mysterium Coniunctionis*, have not yet been presented to a wider public. Marie-Louise von Franz[3] and Edward Edinger,[4] among others, have made noble attempts to spread Jung's late alchemical thoughts to a wider audience, but it's difficult to find a way to present such complex material. There seems to be no way to make Jung's concepts simple, any more than there is a way to make Gödel's ideas simple. Both are attempts to describe the ultimate nature of the universe and, therefore, lie beyond facile presentation. What follows is merely a tiny taste of the riches contained in Jung's great final work.

CONJUNCTION OF OPPOSITES

Mysterium Coniunctionis began at the point where most of Jung's writings ended. Time and again, throughout his writings, Jung described how the unconscious compensated for an overly narrow consciousness. This compensation produced a polarity, an opposition demanding resolution. The polarity between conscious and unconscious led in turn to a psychic attempt at mediation. Jung described in great detail the nature of the conflict at various stages of psychic development. However, in *Mysterium Coniunctionis,* Jung went straight to the end-point of that process, the conjunction of opposites.

Deep conflicts cannot be resolved by compromise, by splitting the issue down the middle. Instead, our attempts at mediation form

---

[3] See Marie-Louise von Franz, *Alchemical Active Imagination*; and "An Introduction to the Symbolism of Alchemy" (Unpublished lecture notes, 1959).

[4] See Edward Edinger, *Anatomy of the Psyche* (La Salle, IL: Open Court, 1985), which is a compilation of articles on the alchemical operations published in *Quadrant* from 1978–1982. Also see Edward Edinger, *The Mysterium Lectures.* The latter records lectures Edinger gave on *Mysterium Coniunctionis* in 1985–1986 to a sophisticated audience of Jungian analysts-in-training.

a new opposition. Thus, the conjunction of opposites becomes a *quaternio*; i.e., a four-way opposition, not merely a polarity. Such a strange opposition naturally led the alchemists, as it later led Zen Buddhist masters, to the use of paradox as a way to express the inexpressible.

As we have discussed in the chapters on the archetypes of development, Jung had discovered that the human psyche inevitably personified psychic conflicts. In *Mysterium Coniunctionis*, Jung spent nearly 300 pages on his description of three such personifications of inner polarities which he had discovered in alchemical literature: (1) the Sun and the Moon, more often presented in alchemy as Sulphur and Salt; (2) King and Queen; and (3) Adam and Eve.

Alchemists usually personified the mediating figure which formed between these opposites as Mercurius, or Hermes Trismegistos, a legendary figure who was the Greek god Hermes made man, much as Jesus is considered to be God made man. Thus Mercurius represented perfectly the struggle between matter and spirit

HERMES TRISMEGISTOS

which we have come to consider our unique problem. The god Hermes was the messenger of the gods, thus admirably suited to moving easily between the world of gods and the human world; that is, the world of the unconscious archetypes and the world of consciousness.

He was a protean god who could be either a benefactor or a dread enemy. As the god of thieves, he could assist us in recovering psychic treasure from the unconscious. As the god of borders, he could teach how to live on the border between polarities. Able to contain oppositions within himself, Mercurius formed the second polarity that combined with any of the other primary polarities to create a psychic quaternio.

Though this sounds far removed from psychology, it is tremendously useful to the psychologist willing to put up with the difficulty of the material. Twentieth century men and women have reached an impasse. Rationality, taken to its logical extreme, has produced paradoxical conclusions in mathematics, physics, art, music, literature, and philosophy. We children of the 20th century have all struggled to find some way to give meaning to disinterested fact, some way to rationally validate that in which we believe. None of us can any longer be indifferent to this problem. However, in earlier times, most were still able to remain blissfully unaware of the conflict. It was left to the lonely few who pushed into the depths of the psyche to be caught in this modern trap.

The Gnostic Christians knew of the conflict; they wanted to experience their divine nature directly, not through the intercession of an organized body of religious beliefs. That inevitably led them to experience the problem of the opposition between spirit and flesh. They attempted to reconcile the two, not merely to subjugate flesh to spirit as the organized Church proposed. Thus they struggled unsuccessfully with the issue. Any knowledge of the nature of their struggle and their attempts at reconciliation are therefore enormously useful to us.[5]

However, the Gnostic Christians fought their inner battles nearly two millennia ago; the alchemists are much closer to us in time and

---

[5] Again I stress that the Gnostics were hardly a heterogenous group.

COMBAT BETWEEN THE FIXED AND THE VOLATILE.

spirit. Coming into full flower with the Renaissance,[6] alchemy struggled with the opposition between meaning and truth, between separation and harmony, in much the same way as we are now struggling. Because the alchemists were largely unconscious of the true nature of their inner conflict, at least during the early centuries of alchemy, this conflict found symbolic representation in their alchemical experiments. Thus, by studying the records of these experiments, we can see our own struggle cleansed of the obfuscation of an over-developed rationality. If the alchemists talked of the opposition between Sun and Moon, King and Queen, Adam and Eve, it was because each of these polarities had some unique symbolic message to express about the nature of the inner conflict and its possible resolution.

---

[6]It is no coincidence that alchemy began to flourish at much the same time the history recorded in this book began. Alchemy unconsciously prefigured all the issues we have dealt with in this book.

We stand at the end of the Christian era, an era wherein humanity has expanded upwards and outwards in an unprecedented fashion. But this incredible progress has created a polarity, an opposition in which we feel lonely and separated, cut off from our instinctual roots. Jung pointed out that we in the modern world need to once more seek inside ourselves for archetypal solutions that bridge the seeming opposites: good and bad, sin and salvation, instinct and spirituality. Because the alchemists were seeking the philosopher's stone which would heal all ills, unite all opposites, bridge all chasms, inevitably they touched just those archetypal roots we need to find ourselves.[7]

PERSONIFICATION OF OPPOSITES

For example, in the opposition between Sun (or Sulphur) and Moon (or Salt), the alchemists said much less about the Sun than they did about the Moon. It was as if the nature of the day, or consciousness, was clear to everyone, but the nature of the night, or the unconscious, needed clarification. In the opposition between King and Queen, the emphasis in the alchemical literature was on the King, and how a dying King could be regenerated into a new vital King. In the opposition between Adam and Eve, there was an explicit separation of the *Old Adam* and the *New Adam*. The *Old Adam*, the first man, was frequently represented as an enormous man as big as a mountain. The *New Adam*, however, was frequently seen as a wheel or a wheel with three legs. Thus the *New Adam* was an attempt at capturing a wholeness which transcended human personification.

Wherever possible, in bringing together this material, Jung tried to describe not only the alchemical symbols but their probable psychological meaning. In an earlier book, *Psychology and Alchemy*, Jung traced the process of psychological development through the symbols of a single man's dreams.[8] There he showed

---

[7] See C. G. Jung, *Collected Works, Vol. 14: Mysterium Coniunctionis* (Princeton: Princeton University Press, 1963), ¶ 674.

[8] Though not identified in the text, the man was famed quantum physicist Wolfgang Pauli, who later collaborated with Jung on an attempt to develop a view of reality which encompassed both the physical world and the world of the psyche.

how a modern man's dream symbols were pre-figured in alchemy. In *Mysterium Coniunctionis*, Jung once again traced the process of psychological development through the symbols of alchemy. But here Jung was dealing with the deepest oppositions in the human psyche, conflicts that have not yet been resolved by humanity. The alchemical texts are, therefore, while invaluable guides to the nature of the inner struggle at different points of development, are necessarily incomplete in their ultimate resolution of the inner conflict. If the issues had been totally resolved by the alchemists, we would not be struggling with them today.

NATURE OF CONJUNCTION

The discussion of the personification of opposites, which we have mentioned so briefly above, occupies the first four-hundred-and-fifty pages of *Mysterium Coniunctionis*. In the last and greatest part of *Mysterium Coniunctionis*, Jung discussed the three stages of the alchemical conjunction as models of the stages of psychological development. In approximately one hundred pages, Jung summarized all that he knew about the psyche. In this part, more than in any other of his works,[9] Jung brought these mysteries down to a very human level.

Jung began by summarizing the conclusions he'd reached in the earlier parts of the book. He described the conjunction of opposites as the central idea of alchemy. He reiterated that alchemists were not merely speaking of chemical experiments when they discussed combinations of various elements. Instead, they were projecting archetypes from the unconscious onto the matter of their experiments. Because these projections were archetypal, they were *numinous*;[10] that is, they had an awe-inspiring effect on the alchemists. Since inevitably the human psyche personifies its con-

---

[9] With the possible exception of C. G. Jung, *Collected Works, Vol. 7: Two Essays on Analytical Psychology* (Princeton: Princeton University Press, 1966).

[10] A word coined by the theologian Rudolph Otto, from the Latin *numen*, meaning creative energy or genius. See Rudolph Otto, *The Idea of the Holy* (London: Oxford University Press, paperback reprint, 1958).

flicts, the alchemists personified the material substances they dealt with. However, because they were trying to capture archetypal forces, there was no single way to personify these forces, and their projections took diverse forms.

ALCHEMICAL CREATION MYTH

The alchemists grounded their beliefs in a *creation myth*;[11] they said that in the beginning there existed a primal quaternio of the four elements: Fire, Air, Water, and Earth. Fire acted upon Air to create Sulphur, Air upon Water to create Mercury, Water upon Earth to create Salt. Since there was nothing left for Earth to act upon, only three principles were created. Then the Sulphur and Mercury combined to create Male, Salt and Mercury to create Female. In each case, Mercury (i.e., Mercurius) was the mediating element. The goal of the alchemical process was then to join Male and Female into a new union that combined all the opposites from which they were created.

Jung pointed out that, viewed as a projection of psychological issues, this myth described how consciousness might have emerged from the unconscious state. The four elements stood for the basic building blocks of consciousness. For example, the Greeks had a theory of human personality based on relative amounts of the four *humors*, each of which corresponded to one of the four elements. Jung had already discovered that when order is beginning to form in the psyche, ordered geometric patterns appear: mandalas.[12] As we have discussed earlier in this chapter, as consciousness confronts an issue, a polarity forms. An attempt to reconcile the polarity forms a further polarity, creating a four-sided breakdown: the

---

[11] In this, they resembled the Gnostics, who also had a detailed symbolic creation myth. For much more on the significance of creation myths in a wide variety of cultures, see Mircea Eliade, *Gods, Goddesses, and Myths of Creation* (New York: Harper & Row, paperback edition, 1974).

[12] See chapter 15.

quaternio. The quaternio is a natural symbol of an intermediate form of wholeness, either as consciousness is just forming, or just beginning to break down.

Interestingly, the alchemical creation myth goes beyond this point, and shows the four elements combining to form the three key alchemical substances: salt, sulphur and mercury. Clearly this corresponds to a progressive development of consciousness, which is much less in danger of falling apart into the chaos of unconsciousness. Of the three, mercury—or Mercurius, as it was personified—was special. It alone was able to join with either of the other two elements, thus reducing the original quaternio into a polarity of masculine and feminine. That split stood for the current state of affairs to the alchemists. Their task was to combine the masculine and the feminine, both in nature and within themselves, to form the magical unity of the philosopher's stone—quite a remarkable mythology to describe first how primitive consciousness arises, then how it progressively becomes more unified, with the goal of a new conscious unity.[13]

THREE UNIONS

Though the alchemists began with the idea of a single union between male and female, they found the issue was more complex in practice. Eventually three successive unions emerged: (1) the *Unio Mentalis*, or mental union; (2) the union of the mind with the body; and (3) the union of the mind and body with the *unus mundus*, or unitary reality. Over the same period of time that the concept of a single union developed into three successive unions, a deeper understanding of the underlying psychological principles also formed. The great 16th-century alchemical writer, Gerard Dorn, commented that:

---

[13] See C. G. Jung, *Collected Works, Vol. 14: Mysterium Coniunctionis*, ¶ 657.

We conclude that meditative philosophy consists in the overcoming of the body by mental union. This first union does not as yet make the wise man, but only the mental disciple of wisdom. The second union of the mind with the body shows forth the wise man, hoping for and expecting that blessed third union with the first unity.[14]

Quite obviously, the final union was less understood; it was difficult for the alchemists to separate themselves from the process in which they were engaged sufficiently to understand this final union. But all their writings discussed this *mysterium coniunctionis* in terms of a total unity of opposites in which all polarities vanished. Jung understood this to be a reunion of the individual with the *unus mundus*, the ultimate ground of reality.

In more purely psychological terms, Jung described the adept's[15] alchemical journey as beginning in unconsciousness, the original *unus mundus*. Consciousness forced the dissolution of this original unity and left the adept in conflict, trying to reconcile elements previously united in the unconscious. A new union could only be formed when an original union has been destroyed and the individual elements carefully separated and purified.

Unio Mentalis

Each union must be preceded by a conscious separation of elements from some original unconscious unity, followed by a now conscious reunion of selected elements. Before the mind could be one within itself, it must withdraw from its original unconscious union with the body and emotions. The mental union occurred when the adept was able to accept the unconscious, discarded parts of his per-

---

[14] C. G. Jung, *Collected Works, Vol. 14: Mysterium Coniunctionis*, ¶ 663.
[15] I.e., the alchemist.

CULMINATION OF THE *UNIO MENTALIS* RELEASES THE ANIMA.

sonality. Once this was accomplished, the mind was one and could control the body.[16]

Though this is the same stage Jung earlier characterized as the shadow stage,[17] the alchemical description explained much that was usually overlooked in discussing shadow issues. Issues are undifferentiated in the unconscious; it is only consciousness that separates. Therefore, as long as the shadow remains unconscious, it is necessarily merged with the urges of the body. This was clear in the alchemical symbolism, but rarely mentioned in discussions of the shadow archetype. Once the shadow was successfully integrated into consciousness, one could consciously acknowledge previously forbidden desires, but still choose not to act out those desires in re-

---

[16] See C. G. Jung, *Collected Works, Vol. 14: Mysterium Coniunctionis*, ¶ 670–672.
[17] C. G. Jung, *Collected Works, Vol. 14: Mysterium Coniunctionis*, ¶ 707.

ality. Thus conscious fantasy could prevent unconscious forces from overpowering consciousness.[18]

The *unio mentalis* is, however, only the first of the three stages of the conjunction. Though it brings an increase in self-knowledge, that knowledge has to be acted upon for true change to take place in the individual. The unity within the mind must be further united with the physical reality of the body.[19]

UNION OF MIND AND BODY

The second step on the way to the production of this substance[20] was the reunion of the spirit with the body. For this procedure there were many symbols. One of the most important was the *chymical marriage*, which took place in the retort. . . . Already in the fourteenth century it began to dawn on them that the lapis was more than a chemical compound . . . . For in the individual was hidden that "substance of celestial nature known to very few."[21]

In their attempts to achieve this second union, alchemists rediscovered the technique that remains the core of all the mystery religions, all the mystical schools. That technique is what Jung termed *active imagination*; most of us are more familiar with it as meditation.

---

[18]I once used this technique to work with a patient who sexually molested young boys. He was also receiving behavioral treatment under a court order. The behavioral treatment consisted of aversion therapy to make him lose sexual desire for young boys. The patient was growing more and more angry and frustrated under such treatment. I allowed him to fantasize without criticism. These fantasies revealed that his desire for young boys was because he himself had never developed emotionally past that age, due to many issues that are outside the scope of this discussion. Once the patient was free to acknowledge his desires, it became possible for him to honor them without acting them out. With the knowledge that he had the ability to control whether or not he acted on his desires, he gained a great deal of self-confidence. At that point, his desires began to slowly mature into the need for an adult sexual relationship.

[19]See C. G. Jung, *Collected Works, Vol. 14: Mysterium Coniunctionis,* ¶ 664.

[20]The "lapis" or Philosopher's Stone, which could heal all ills.

[21]C. G. Jung, *Collected Works, Vol. 14: Mysterium Coniunctionis,* ¶ 677.

UNION OF MIND AND BODY.

Until recently, every school of spiritual development considered meditation a mystery open only to the chosen few. Now we live in a time when all the mysteries are available in the local bookstore (or perhaps even the supermarket) for the slight cost of a paperback book.

But it's important to realize that the alchemists considered meditation as the second stage of the conjunction, not the first. First came the *unio mentalis*, the stage of self-knowledge. We have already discussed how Jung felt that Eastern spiritual techniques were inappropriate for Westerners because these techniques ignored the shadow.[22] Without a separation of the shadow, with its largely personal garb, from the deeper, more exclusively collective parts of the unconscious, shadow issues can achieve monumental stature. When we are forced to self-knowledge, we gain a place of solidity on which to stand and confront the strange symbols of the collective unconscious.

---

[22]See chapter 15.

Meditation provides a method for by-passing consciousness in an attempt to directly obtain unconscious material. Jung's technique of active imagination should at times be considered as a safer alternative to other meditative techniques which can produce violent reactions from the unconscious. For example, in many oriental techniques of meditation the meditator is instructed to ignore the visions and fantasies produced by the unconscious. The concept is that those are just empty fantasies thrown up by ego-consciousness; the acolyte should not be confused by these but should strive for direct union with God, Atman, etc.[23] Ignoring the unconscious in this way is potentially dangerous without the self-knowledge gained by struggling with the shadow.

At this point, many begin to realize just how painful consciousness can be. There is a great temptation to pretend that this is all nonsense and to retreat back to an unconscious state. However, this is no longer an option. It is not only dangerous to continue the process at this stage; it can be even more dangerous to try and retreat back to a previously unconscious state. Though it is true that a person could have taken their life down some other path in which they never arrived at this point, there is no going back. Jung was so emphatic in stressing this that he even said that it could lead to actual physical death: "the unconscious has a thousand ways of snuffing out a meaningless existence with surprising swiftness."[24]

Most meditative techniques regard the fantasy material that arises at this point as extraneous to the goal, and recommend various techniques for either resisting it, or accepting it as it arises, then returning to the meditative process. Again this is fine, as long as there is nothing dangerous in the unconscious which has to be dealt with by consciousness. But if there is, ignorance is less likely to be bliss than deadly. In contrast, rather than ignoring the fantasy material produced by the unconscious, both Jung and the alchemists recommended actively engaging with the fantasies.

Jung's technique of active imagination was to extend the fantasy or dream into consciousness and let it evolve there, without

---

[23] The Self in Jung's terms.
[24] C. G. Jung, *Collected Works, Vol. 14: Mysterium Coniunctionis*, ¶ 675.

any attempt to consciously manipulate the fantasy. The proper role for consciousness in this process is purely as an observer. One could begin with anything from the unconscious: a lingering memory of a dream, a fantasy that arises spontaneously into consciousness, a seemingly irrational mood that troubles us. All these are products of the unconscious that are close enough to the border of consciousness to demand attention. All that is necessary is to turn our full attention to the fantasy (for example), and let it emerge.[25]

This can be as difficult a process as meditation, since we will want to do anything except remain passive observers. In fact, it has been my own observation that active imagination is as likely to be misused as meditation. In the early stages, it is difficult to remain with the fantasy without thinking about something else, and without attempting to consciously manipulate the story. These are the same sort of problems meditators encounter in the early stages.

If this process proceeds as it should, at some point our role as passive observer leads us to the realization that the fantasy concerns us. We become emotionally involved because we know that it deals with issues that matter in our lives. A purely aesthetic issue becomes a moral issue, and we are forced to confront painful issues within ourselves.[26]

Unfortunately, there are other less wholesome directions that the process can take. Inevitably if we stay with the fantasy long enough, collective images emerge from the unconscious. These archetypal images have more than human energy, which can damage the personality unless strict precautions are taken. When we take responsibility for the fantasies, inevitably we become emotionally involved. And usually the emotions that come up are difficult ones, like sadness and fear. It is easier to run away from such emotions and instead let the collective energy overwhelm us. All too often the fan-

---

[25] C. G. Jung, *Collected Works, Vol. 14: Mysterium Coniunctionis*, ¶ 749.
[26] C. G. Jung, *Collected Works, Vol. 14: Mysterium Coniunctionis*, ¶ 753. Note that there are other dangers inherent in active imagination as well. Where traditional meditative techniques tend to undervalue the products of the unconscious, all too often there is a tendency for those using active imagination to overvalue anything produced by the unconscious. As with all steps in the process of individuation, it is the ability to hold a tension between consciousness and the unconscious that leads to ultimate success.

tasy becomes grandiose, and the people engaging with it become inflated. Rather than seeing the archetypal story as reflecting personal issues for which they must accept responsibility, they "swallow" the collective energy and begin to think what a remarkable person they are. Or they are themselves "swallowed" by the energy, and fall into a depression.

Because Jungian psychology has not addressed this issue, it is rare to see anyone who successfully resolves the second coniunctio. A combination of meditation and active imagination, such as the techniques developed by those dealing with ceremonial magic, would be very helpful. In general, this means carefully evolving some protective structures within the psyche before one dives too deeply into the unconscious.

Union with Unus Mundus

The third and final stage of the alchemical process was the union of the individual with the *unus mundus*. The distinction we draw between the inner world of the mind and the outer physical world is, in this view, illusory; both are merely manifestations of the *unus mundus*. The seeming incompatibility of the two worlds is due to our sensory limitations. The union with the *unus mundus* is thus the stage in which we transcend such dualistic limitations. As Jung pointed out, this is the stage so often discussed in mystical literature.

> We could compare this only with the ineffable mystery of the *unio mystica*, or *tao*, or the content of *samadhi*, or the experience of *satori* in Zen, which would bring us to the realm of the ineffable and of extreme subjectivity where all the criteria of reason fail. Remarkably enough this experience is an empirical one in so far as there are unanimous testimonies from the East and the West alike, both from the present and from the distant past.[27]

---

[27] C. G. Jung, *Collected Works, Vol. 14: Mysterium Coniunctionis*, ¶ 771.

Perhaps the best-known Western compilation of descriptions of this experience is Bucke's *Cosmic Consciousness*, first published in 1901.[28] In more recent times, several scientifically-trained individuals who have gone through the process have tried to record their experience. In 1973, Franklin Merrell-Wolff gave a step-by-step account of his experience, which had occurred thirty-seven years earlier, in a book called *Pathways Through to Space*.[29] He tried to bring all the concepts together in a philosophic whole in a companion volume: *The Philosophy of Consciousness Without an Object*.[30] In 1972, John C. Lilly, M.D. gave his account of a similar, though perhaps less psychologically complete experience, in *The Center of the Cyclone: an Autobiography of Inner Space*.[31] But as rich as both accounts are, they are still conscious attempts at providing rational explanations for their experience.[32] The alchemical descriptions have the advantage that they come straight from the unconscious, unclouded by conscious rationalizations.

> . . . if a union is to take place between opposites . . . it will happen in a third thing, which represents not a compromise but something new.[33]

> . . . we come to the conclusion that its most conspicuous quality, namely, *its unity and uniqueness* . . . presupposes a *dissociated consciousness*.[34] For no one who is one himself needs oneness as a medicine—nor, we might add, does anyone who is unconscious of his dissociation, for a *conscious* situation of distress is needed in order to activate the archetype of unity.[35]

---

[28] Richard Maurice Bucke, M.D., *Cosmic Consciousness* (New York: E. P. Dutton, 1923).

[29] Franklin Merrell-Wolff, *Pathways Through to Space: A Personal Report of Transformation in Consciousness* (New York: Warner Books, 1973).

[30] Franklin Merrell-Wolff, *The Philosophy of Consciousness Without an Object* (New York: Julian Press, 1973).

[31] John C. Lilly, *The Center of the Cyclone: An Autobiography of Inner Space* (New York: Bantam Books, 1972).

[32] Merrell-Wolff, more than Lilly, attempts to describe without pre-judging.

[33] C. G. Jung, *Collected Works, Vol. 14: Mysterium Coniunctionis*, ¶ 765.

[34] Jung's emphasis.

[35] C. G. Jung, *Collected Works, Vol. 14: Mysterium Coniunctionis*, ¶ 772.

If this begins to sound familiar to the reader, it should. I previously quoted Jung on the production of a new *living symbol:*[36]

> . . . For this collaboration of opposing states to be possible at all, they must first face one another in the fullest conscious opposition. This necessarily entails a *violent disunion with oneself*, to the point where thesis and antithesis negate one another, while *the ego is forced to acknowledge its absolute participation in both.*[37]

This quotation was from *Psychological Types*, first published in 1921, eight years before Jung encountered his friend Richard Wilhelm's translation of the Chinese alchemical text, *The Secret of the Golden Flower*. *Mysterium Coniunctionis* itself wasn't to be published until the mid-fifties.[38] Jung was able to anticipate the information he would gain from the alchemists years later because he went through the same experience as the alchemists in his confrontation with the unconscious! He knew the necessity for a "violent disunion with oneself" because he had experienced just that. He knew that "the ego is forced to acknowledge its absolute participation in both"[39] because he had been forced to do just that. Clearly, the alchemists, though writing hundreds of years in the past, had something to say of worth to modern men and women.[40]

At this point, just as we are discussing the deepest mysteries of the human psyche, we must leave because we have passed beyond issues which the alchemists were able to solve. In *Mysterium Coniunctionis*, Jung drew on the work of the alchemists to present a symbolic description of the journey we have to take at this critical point in our history. For the alchemists, this attempt was largely un-

---

[36] See chapter 10.

[37] C. G. Jung, *Collected Works, Vol. 6: Psychological Types* (Princeton: Princeton University Press, 1971), ¶ 824. My emphasis in both cases.

[38] It was originally published in two volumes: Vol. 1 in 1955 and Vol. 2 in 1956.

[39] Matter and spirit, or empirical and transcendental.

[40] For a modern model which is consistent with the alchemical model presented by Jung, see Michael Washburn's two books: *Transpersonal Psychology in Psychoanalytic Perspective* (Albany, NY: SUNY Press, 1994) and *The Ego and the Dynamic Ground: A Transpersonal Theory of Human Development*, 2nd ed. (Albany, NY: SUNY Press, 1995).

conscious and limited to the lonely few. For us, this must be a journey taken by all if we are to reach some new level of human consciousness.

Mysterium Coniunctionis was the culmination of Jung's work, and cannot be briefly summarized, as has been attempted in these pages, without sacrificing most of its richness. Much of its value lies in the incredible detail in which it described the elements of the alchemical process. Innumerable practical psychological problems are explicated by the symbols of alchemy. Even at five-hundred-and-fifty pages of text, Jung was largely limited to summarizing the alchemical material, with an occasional explication of its psychological significance. A full hermeneutic study of *Mysterium Coniunctionis*[41] still lies ahead for future scholars. If it were ever done, it would be an invaluable aid to both clinical and theoretical psychologists. Jung has drawn the blueprint from which an imposing edifice can be built.

---

[41]As well as *Aion* and the shorter alchemical works. Again for the serious reader I would recommend they read Edward Edinger's *The Mysterium Lectures*, which provides a welcome guide to *Mysterium Coniunctionis*. Jung would surely have approved of Edinger's concentration on the alchemical images.

CHAPTER 19

NUMBER AS ARCHETYPE

. . . The sequence of natural numbers turns out to be unexpectedly more than a mere stringing together of identical units: it contains the whole of mathematics and everything yet to be discovered in this field.[1]

It has turned out that (under the assumption that modern mathematics is consistent) the solution of certain arithmetical problems requires the use of assumptions essentially transcending arithmetic; i.e., the domain of the kind of elementary indisputable evidence that may be most fittingly compared with sense perception.[2]

FROM THE RENAISSANCE IDEAL TO JUNG AND GÖDEL

We've come a long way in our history of the archetypes. With the dawn of the Renaissance, we awoke from our long slumber and looked out again at the world around us. For a long while that was intoxicating enough. But as we've seen, inevitably we came at some point to observe the mind doing the observing. That involved us in nasty little questions about the relationship between the world outside and the world inside our minds. In

---

[1] C. G. Jung, "Synchronicity: an Acausal Connecting Principle," 1955, in *Collected Works of C. G. Jung, Vol. 8: The Structure and Dynamics of the Psyche* (Princeton: Princeton University Press, 1969), ¶ 870.

[2] Kurt Gödel, "Russell's Mathematical Logic," in Paul Benacerraf and Hilary Putnam *Philosophy of Mathematics: Selected Readings* (Cambridge: Cambridge University Press, 1983), p. 449.

the late 17th century, flushed with Newton's success in seemingly subsuming everything in heaven and earth within his laws, Locke developed an explicitly rationalist/materialist description of the mind. By the 18th century, Berkeley and Hume poked holes big enough to drive a freight train through in Locke's model. There was no longer the possibility of ignoring the issue. Kant took a huge step toward resolution of the problem with his theory that the human mind contains categories which organize our perceptions of the world. Though the categories he picked were more the product of his time and culture than true cognitive invariants, he had seen the essential point: all perception is psychological. Though Kant's realization should have led immediately to the development of psychology, it was too early to affect anyone except other philosophers. The rest of the world went on apace, hardly noticing the difference.

We've seen how mathematics followed a similar path. When it came out of its slumber early in the 17th century, the first product was analytic geometry, which demonstrated the equivalence of geometry and arithmetic.[3] That soon led to the discovery of calculus by Newton and Leibniz. Calculus enabled scientists to quantify both their observations and their theories to an extent hitherto inconceivable. Make no mistake about it, calculus is the most significant tool science has ever developed. But calculus depended on infinite processes, a fact that at the time was only dimly appreciated. Just as Locke's attempt to present a materialist picture of the mind led to the problems presented by Berkeley and Hume, the development of calculus should have led ineluctably to the problems of infinity. The problem of infinite limits in calculus, however, was well hidden in the foundations of mathematics, so for two hundred years there was no mathematical Berkeley or Hume to clearly define the problem.[4] And with no clearly defined problem, there was no mathematical Kant to resolve the problem. Instead, Euler was

---

[3] At least in a practical way, if not with formal precision.

[4] In fact, Berkeley was one of the few to point to the deeper problems of calculus. But mathematicians were hardly going to worry about the objections of a philosopher. They had work to do developing the implications of the calculus.

the chief representative of the era, and Euler was more concerned with building a great edifice based on mathematics, than with examining its foundations.

Though still consciously unresolved, the issue continued to evolve in the unconscious. By the second half of the 19th century, psychology finally emerged from the unconscious, wearing the twin faces of experimental and clinical psychology. It took someone like Freud, who bridged both camps, to discover the unconscious. It took someone like Jung, who bridged not only both camps, but also science and philosophy, to discover the collective unconscious.

At the same time that psychology began to emerge out of philosophy, Cantor's discovery of transfinite set theory defined a new mathematics. For the first time, all of mathematics was (at least potentially) brought under a single umbrella, much as Newton had done for physics two centuries earlier. With mathematics' foundations now fully in view, the previously hidden problems could no longer be ignored. Paradoxes appeared in mathematics, much as they had appeared in philosophy, and they wouldn't go away. Russell tried to shift the ground to logic, but the paradoxes still wouldn't go away. Hilbert tried to shift to finite meta-mathematical solutions, but the paradoxes lay hidden there as well. Eventually Gödel was able to prove that the paradoxes would never go away, because the core of mathematics is number, and every number is a true symbol.

FREUD AND RUSSELL

The work of both Sigmund Freud in psychology and Bertrand Russell in mathematics were examples of premature attempts at synthesis. Neither was able to take the necessary next step toward the archetypal hypothesis. After much intellectual struggle, each had an intellectual epiphany which too quickly hardened into dogma.[5]

---

[5] In Freud's case, his psycho-sexual theory, as it evolved out of the Oedipus complex. In Russell's case, his conviction that the entire world could be reduced to symbolic logic.

Neither was willing to modify their initial positions despite strong evidence to the contrary.[6]

It is interesting to speculate what would have happened in each case if they had been more flexible. In contrast with Jung and Gödel, both of whom were introverts uncomfortable with the attention of the wider world, Freud and Russell were both extroverts, with almost unequaled ability to communicate their concepts to a wider world. If Freud had been willing to give up some of his authority, and to fully accept the concept of the collective unconscious, it might have allowed him to work hand-in-hand with Jung in developing a true archetypal psychology. Given how significant an impact Freud has had on the world, it is easy to imagine that the archetypal concepts might be as widely known as psychoanalytic concepts.

If Russell had been willing to accept that his desire for the supremacy of logic was inherently flawed, he might very well have come to Gödel's proof of the necessary incompleteness of all logical systems decades before Gödel.[7] Given his status in both the philosophical and mathematical worlds, it is quite likely that the proof might have immediately driven both fields in new directions. Perhaps philosophy would have once more become a significant factor in intellectual life; perhaps mathematics might have rallied around this new position and advanced in areas such as cybernetics earlier and further than it did. For example, just imagine if the develop-

---

[6] Freud, when confronted with a new set of ideas by his young successor Jung, was unwilling to give up his patriarchal authority stance, or to open the floodgates to the "black mud of occultism." Russell chose to ignore the three blows he received from the unconscious: (1) his mystical insight that feeling and intuition were primary; (2) the paradox of the set of all sets; and (3) his loss of love for his first wife Alys.

[7] As we have seen in our discussion of Russell, he was never comfortable with the demands that his feelings and intuition placed upon him, and retreated into a world where logic ruled. Interestingly, in social issues such as his fights for women's rights and for pacifism, Russell had the courage of his convictions, even to the point of being jailed as a pacifist during the First World War. Eventually he even broke from his passionless first marriage and conducted a long-term affair with Lady Ottoline Morrell. He received the Nobel Prize in literature in 1950 for his philosophic writings, and lived nearly a hundred years. However, he was never able to confront the inadequacy of his attempt to reduce mathematics to logic. Though he began his philosophical life as a Kantian, he gradually divorced himself further and further from feeling and intuition, until eventually he came to believe in the omnipotence of logic.

ment of computers had started in the 1920s instead of the 1940s. In addition to his scientific writing, Russell was also probably the greatest intellectual popularizer of all time. He would have been in an ideal position to communicate these strange new ideas to the broader public, much as Einstein's concept of relativity became known almost universally. It is even possible that Russell—a charismatic figure who personified the intellectual—might have filled Einstein's position in the public eye decades before Einstein.

On the other hand, it is perhaps more likely that it was not yet time for the archetypal hypothesis to emerge in either field. Time after time, we have seen how ideas gestate over a long period of time, then emerge whole, seemingly out of nowhere. But, of course, they do not really appear out of nowhere; they develop out of sight in the unconscious, only to emerge in the consciousness of a small number of supremely gifted individuals whose minds are flexible enough to stretch and include strange new concepts.

JUNG AND GÖDEL

Jung and Gödel were clearly such men. Jung was a virtual contemporary of Russell, both a generation younger than Freud.[8] Jung's excitement at discovering Freud, then meeting him in 1906 was comparable to Russell's excitement at discovering Peano in 1900. When in the grip of such excitement, there is always a tendency to swallow the new ideas whole, then puff up like a bullfrog. Russell did just that. Jung had much the same reaction after Freud anointed him his successor, making a hitherto unknown young psychologist the second most important psychoanalyst in the world. In contrast to Russell, though, Jung never swallowed the pill whole. Though Jung did not fully break with Freud until 1913, almost from the beginning of their association he saw Freud's limits and began to develop his own ideas on the sly.

Gödel, born in 1906, was a generation younger than Jung and Russell. Like Jung and Russell, as a young man he was prodigiously

---

[8] Freud born in 1856, Russell in 1872, Jung in 1875.

bright, yet not quite sure in what direction he should go with his abilities. In his case, it was Hilbert's program for mathematics that excited his interest, as Russell had been excited by Peano's logic, and Jung by Freud's psychoanalytic psychology. Gödel first began to be taken seriously during his college years, when he attended meetings of the *Vienna Circle*. This was a group of philosophers, logicians and linguists who were evolving what would come to be known as *logical positivism*.[9] Gödel could very well have taken a place at the forefront of this movement, but sensing the limitations of their position, chose to go his own way instead.

Jung developed most of his ideas in isolation from the psychoanalytic community after his expulsion from the movement in 1913. By 1930, virtually all of the main lines of his psychology were in place, except his alchemical model, which would develop slowly over the rest of his life. Gödel developed his incompleteness proof in 1930, and published it in 1931. Over the next few years, he developed some important extensions of this work, then struggled with Cantor's continuum hypothesis for over a decade, with his most important proof in this area in 1940.[10] From the 1940s until his death in 1978, Gödel spent as much or more time on philosophical speculations,[11] most of which are still unpublished at this point in time. Where their ideas were to overlap was in their separate yet similar speculation on the nature of number. We'll begin with Jung, since it was so unlikely that he would ever have come to such a point.

JUNG AND THE NATURE OF NUMBER

I felt a downright fear of the mathematics class. The teacher pretended that algebra was a perfectly natural affair, to be taken for granted, whereas I didn't even know

---

[9] See chapter 12.

[10] Which was to be complemented by a proof by mathematician Paul Cohen in 1963. This will all be discussed later in this chapter.

[11] Including continued thought on the continuum hypothesis.

what numbers really were. They were not flowers, not animals, not fossils; they were nothing that could be imagined, mere quantities that resulted from counting. To my confusion these quantities were now represented by letters, which signified sounds, so that it became possible to hear them so to speak.[12]

It is fascinating that, though Jung struggled with mathematics as a boy, and never became comfortable with it as a man, his study of archetypes eventually brought him back to the primacy of number. Throughout his career Jung took a scientific approach to the material he encountered in dreams, myths, fairy tales, art, science, etc. He observed patiently, described what he had observed carefully, then tried to construct models that fit the observed facts. But all great scientists—and Jung was certainly a great scientist—have an additional ability: a nose for what is significant in the mass of data. This ability to sniff out something important that others might overlook was at work even in his late days.

Through his study of his patients' "number" dreams, Jung came to believe that the smaller *natural numbers*[13] are symbols in much the same sense that the people and events of our dreams are symbols of personified collective character traits and behavioral situations. The integers seemed to correspond to progressive stages of development within the psyche. In brief, one corresponds to a stage of non-differentiation; two—polarity or opposition; three—

---

[12] C. G. Jung, *Memories, Dreams, Reflections* (New York: Vintage Books/Random House, 1955), p. 27. Jung's problem was not so much that he had no mathematical ability as that he saw too deeply into what mathematics actually is. I had a similar experience in the 2nd grade, when a homework assignment introduced the concept of zero. There were a number of problems where zero was added or subtracted from various numbers. The answer was, of course, always the same number. Most of the other children in the class just regarded this as still another rule to be memorized and experienced no more difficulty than with any other such incomprehensible rule. But I sat alone in my room that night, staring at the problems, in tears at their seeming senselessness. How could I add something to a number and the number remained unchanged? And then an understanding burst forth, and I had the first mystical experience of my life. The immensity of the concept of nothingness overwhelmed me. The realization that mathematicians were brilliant enough to be able to capture that immensity in a symbol awed me. I determined on the spot to be a mathematician.
[13] For example, the *integers:* 1, 2, 3, . . .

movement toward resolution, as expressed in the Christian trinity; four—stability, wholeness, as in a quaternity, or a mandala, which is most commonly four-sided.[14]

As so many times before in his career, Jung went beyond this limited model, and took a brilliant leap toward generalization of these discoveries: he speculated that number itself—as expressed most basically in the small integers—was *the most primitive archetype of order.*

> There is something peculiar, one might even say mysterious, about numbers. . . . [If] a group of objects is deprived of every single one of its properties or characteristics, there still remains, at the end, its *number*, which seems to indicate that number is something irreducible, . . . [something which] helps more than anything else to bring order into the chaos of appearances. . . . It may well be the most primitive element of order in the human mind. . . . We [can] define number psychologically as *an archetype of order* which has become conscious.[15]

Since the natural numbers were each true symbols of order, the implication was that the development of mathematics reflected the progressive development of order within the psyche. Even more than that, Jung felt that number might be the primary archetype of order of the *unus mundus* itself; i.e., the most basic building blocks of either psyche or matter are the integers.[16] The question is, of course, whether or not Jung was right. Let's begin by examining to what extent the natural numbers are archetypal.

---

[14] Jung's colleague Marie-Louise von Franz has extended this work in her *Number and Time* (Evanston: Northwestern University Press, 1974).

[15] C. G. Jung, "Synchronicity: an Acausal Connecting Principle," in *C. G. Jung Collected Works, Vol. 8: The Structure and Dynamics of the Psyche* (Princeton: Princeton University Press, 1960), ¶ 870.

[16] Marie-Louise von Franz, *Number and Time*, p. 13.

INTEGERS

God made the integers, all the rest is the work of man.[17]

Number is a very ancient archetype that seems to predate humanity itself. In *Number and the Language of Science*, mathematician Tobias Dantzig mentions a number of examples of animals and even insects who seem to possess a number sense. In one striking example, he tells the story of a crow who had built its nest in the watchtower on a squire's estate. The squire was determined to shoot the crow, but the crow was too canny; whenever the squire or his men would enter the tower, the crow would fly away until the coast was clear.

The squire tried sending two men into the barn. One stayed hidden in the tower and one came out again. However, the crow was too smart and wouldn't return until the second man also came out. The experiment was tried on successive days—unsuccessfully—until finally five men went in and only four came out. This time the crow evidently thought that all the men had come out, and returned to the watchtower. The squire was finally rid of the crow.[18]

The story seems to demonstrate that a crow (or at least the crow in the story) has a sense of "one," "two," "three," and "many." When five men went in and four came out, the crow saw "many" go in and "many" come out and thought that it was safe to return. Interestingly, early 20th-century anthropologists found that the numeric systems of some African, South American, Oceanic and Australian cultures had the same limitations. For example, the Australian Aborigines—who we now realize have a very sophisticated culture—only had numbers for "one" through "six," and "many."

Though crows are very intelligent birds, no one would argue that human beings and crows are of comparable intelligence. It is more likely that the archetypal quality of the smaller numbers is so ancient that it predates humanity itself, and is carried in the her-

---

[17]Quotation by Leopold Kronecker in E. T. Bell, *Men of Mathematics* (New York: Simon and Schuster, 1937/1965), p. xv.

[18]Tobias Dantzig, *Number and the Language of Science* (New York: MacMillan, 1954), p. 3.

itage of creatures even as primitive as insects. Because human beings are capable of *counting* ("one, two, three, . . ."), we imagine
that is how numbers were arrived at. But when crows can recognize "one," "two," "three," and "many," few of us would argue they
arrived at these numeric relationships by counting per se. Instead
there must be a pattern recognition, a "primordial image" (to use
Jung's earlier formulation of "symbol") that corresponds to the
smaller integers. In other words, we have an innate sense of what
"one" and "two" and "three" mean.[19]

> Now if we conceive numbers as having been discovered,
> and not merely invented as an instrument for counting,
> then on account of their mythological nature they be-
> long to the realm of *godlike* human and animal figures
> and are just as archetypal as they.[20]

As civilization developed, there was a need for ever larger numbers;
e.g., for financial transactions, for measurement of property, etc. This
need puts a strain on any system of separate and distinct symbols.
Even among great mathematicians, it is the rare genius for whom
virtually all numbers come to possess true symbolic stature. One
such was the famed 20th-century Indian mathematician Ramanujan. Once while sick, Ramanujan was visited by his friend and colleague, G. H. Hardy. On the way over, Hardy noticed that the
number of his cab was 1729. When he arrived at Ramanujan's
sickbed, he mentioned it as "rather a dull number." "No, Hardy,"
said Ramanujan. "It is a very interesting number. It is the smallest
number expressible as the sum of two cubes in two different ways."[21]

---

[19] In fact, the Australian Aborigines actually limit themselves to "one" and "two," then use
composites of "one" and "two" to make up numbers up to "six." For example, "three" is
"two" and "one," "four" is "two" and "two," "five" is "two" and "two" and "one," "six" is
"two" and "two" and "two." They count in pairs, so that they wouldn't be likely to notice if
two pins were removed from a heap of seven pins, but would instantly recognize if only one
pin had been removed. See Tobias Dantzig, *Number and the Language of Science*, p. 14.

[20] C. G. Jung, *Collected Works, Vol. 10: Civilization in Transition* (Princeton: Princeton University Press, 1969), ¶ 776. Jung's emphasis.

[21] 1729 equals both $12^3 + 1^3$, and 10^3 and 9^3. Anecdote from Robert Kanigel, *The Man Who
Knew Infinity* (New York: Charles Scribner's Sons, 1991), p. 312.

For most of us, however, this archetypal pattern recognition is unlikely to extend past the smaller counting numbers. Since, at this stage, the recognition of number is the recognition of a primordial image or pattern, there is as yet little if any distinction between arithmetic and geometry. As soon as arithmetic and geometry split and go different directions, it becomes much less clear that Jung is necessarily right in his guess that all mathematics emerges from the smaller counting numbers.[22] Geometry by its very nature deals with continuous lines and figures and planes, while arithmetic develops out of ever grander extensions of the discrete counting numbers. At the time when Jung was developing these ideas, he was corresponding with physicist Wolfgang Pauli. Pauli, inspired by Jung, was searching for a neutral language which could underlie both the physical and psychological worlds.[23] Pauli recognized that the issue came to a head when the development of arithmetic reached the point where it was forced to deal with infinite quantities.

> If, therefore, a more general concept of archetype is used today, then it should be understood in such a way that included within it is the *mathematical primal intuition* which expresses itself, among other ways, in arithmetic, in the idea of the infinite series of integers, and in geometry, in the idea of the continuum.[24]

At this point, Jung's speculation becomes identical with Cantor's continuum hypothesis; i.e., are there any infinities that lie between the infinity of the integers and the infinity of the geometric continuum?

---

[22] And, as we saw in chapter 1, the split between arithmetic and geometry is quite ancient.

[23] See Wolfgang Pauli, "The Influence of Archetypal Ideas on the Scientific Theories of Kepler," in C. G. Jung and Wolfgang Pauli, *The Interpretation of Nature and the Psyche* (New York: Pantheon Books, 1955). Also see Charles R. Card, "The Archetypal View of Jung and Pauli," *Psychological Perspectives* #24 & #25 (Los Angeles: C. G. Jung Institute, 1991).

[24] Quotation by Wolfgang Pauli, in Charles R. Card, "The Archetypal Hypothesis of Wolfgang Pauli and C. G. Jung: Origins, Development, and Implications," in K. V. Laurikainen and C. Montonen, eds., *Symposia on the Foundations of Modern Physics, 1992* (Singapore: World Scientific Publishing Co., 1993), p. 382.

Cantor's Continuum Hypothesis

Cantor's continuum hypothesis is simply the question: How many points are there on a straight line in Euclidean space? An equivalent question is: How many different sets of integers do there exist? This question, of course, could arise only after the concept of *number* had been extended to infinite sets.[25]

In our mathematical history we have seen time and again how, though arithmetic and geometry inhabit separate realms, it is inordinately productive when either turns to the other for a new way of thinking about a problem. Descartes vastly increased the power of geometry with his discovery of analytic geometry, which allowed mathematicians to use algebra to solve geometric problems. Going in the opposite direction, Gauss was able to solve the problem presented by imaginary numbers by realizing that they could be viewed as positions on the geometric plane. Back and forth goes the cross-fertilization between the two fields. This is because at their extremes—dealing with the discrete counting numbers and the geometric continuum respectively—arithmetic and geometry seem like very different fields. There is, however, a great fuzzy area where they overlap, since reality itself is more fuzzy than not. Similarly, though at their extremes mind and matter seem totally distinct, the boundaries between the two are fuzzy. There is little black-and-white in the real world.

The continuum hypothesis marks the point where the boundaries of arithmetic and geometry are very hazy indeed. There is no dispute that the power set of the countable numbers[26] is the same size as the continuum. But the continuum hypothesis says that there are no infinities that lie between the two. Clearly, starting with the small natural numbers, we build up ineluctably to the

---

[25] Kurt Gödel, "What is Cantor's Continuum Problem?" in *Collected Works* (New York: Oxford University Press, 1986), p. 754.

[26] Remember this is all the combinations of the natural numbers, taken one-at-a-time, two-at-a-time, on and on.

countable infinity of all integers.[27] But taking all the combinations of those numbers is a very different thing than merely accumulating. On the human level, we certainly understand how much more complex it is to deal with relationships than with things. We can think of countable infinity as the limit of what we encounter in dealing with the things of the world. The uncountable infinity of the continuum is the limit of what we encounter dealing with the relationships in the world. The higher infinities beyond the continuum are all power sets of the continuum, hence relationships between relationships, etc. Though Cantor remained convinced that the continuum hypothesis was true, from the beginning others were less sure.

> . . . As early as 1905 René Baire . . . suggested that Cantor's continuum hypothesis assumed the identifiability of two concepts that were intrinsically different and of non-comparable orders of magnitude. . . . The two ideas were inherently antithetical: the nature of the continuum, regarded as the collection of all infinite sequences of integers was something totally different.[28]

As always, Gödel had a different take on the issue from the other mathematicians of his time. Since he had already proved that any system at least as rich as arithmetic contains undecidable mathematical truths, he guessed that the continuum hypothesis might be just such an undecidable proposition.[29]

> . . . there are (assuming the consistency of the axioms) *a priori* three possibilities for Cantor's conjecture: It may be demonstrable, disprovable, or undecidable. The third alternative . . . is the most likely. To seek a proof for it is, at present, perhaps the most promising way of attacking

---

[27] Which, remember, is the same size as all fractions or rational numbers.

[28] Joseph Warren Dauben, *Georg Cantor: His Mathematics and Philosophy of the Infinite* (Princeton: Princeton University Press, 1979), p. 269.

[29] Though as we will see later, Gödel ultimately hoped to prove the continuum hypothesis to be false within a broader mathematics.

the problem. One result along these lines has been obtained already, namely that Cantor's conjecture is not dis-
provable from the axioms of set theory, provided that
these axioms are consistent.[30]

The "result along these lines" which Gödel mentions above was
his own proof in 1940 that if a modified set theory which does
not include the continuum hypothesis[31] is consistent, then it will
remain consistent if the continuum hypothesis is added as an additional axiom. However, this was only half of what was needed
to prove that the continuum hypothesis was undecidable within
set theory. In order to prove the other half, Gödel needed to
show that if a modified set theory which does not include the
continuum hypothesis is consistent, then it will still be consistent
if the continuum hypothesis is assumed to be false. Though Gödel
made some progress toward a solution, he was never able to prove
it, as it was simply too complex to be resolved with the mathematical tools available at the time. Finally, in 1963, mathematician
Paul Cohen was able to prove the second half of the problem,
thus showing that within set theory, the continuum hypothesis
was undecidable. Gödel was the first to applaud Cohen's achievement.

Consider how important this joint proof of Gödel and
Cohen was. Gödel's incompleteness proof had demonstrated that
every logical system contains essentially undecidable propositions.
Skeptical mathematicians had scoffed that mathematics could
safely ignore this result, since the only such undecidable propositions must be strange beasts like the self-referential statement
Gödel constructed to prove his theorem.[32] Now Gödel and
Cohen had shown that the continuum hypothesis, which was one
of the most important unsolved problems in mathematics, was
undecidable within set theory. And, since by this time mathemat-

---

[30] Kurt Gödel, "What is Cantor's Continuum Problem?" pp. 259–260.
[31] Or the axiom of choice, which Gödel proved to be equivalent to the continuum hypothesis.
[32] In 1977, Paris and Harrington discovered a "numerically simple and interesting proposition, not depending on a numerical coding of notions from logic, which is undecidable." See
Kurt Gödel's Collected Works, Vol 1, p. 140.

ics and set theory were inseparable for most mathematicians, this was a haunting proof.

Though this should have been some ultimate vindication for Gödel, he wasn't satisfied; even before Cohen had demonstrated his half of the proof, Gödel had already conjectured that even if the continuum hypothesis was undecidable within set theory as then constituted, within some extended set theory it would eventually be resolved one way or the other.

> It is to be noted, however, that on the basis of the point of view here adopted, a proof of the undecidability of Cantor's conjecture from the accepted axioms of set theory . . . would by no means solve the problem. For if the meanings of the primitive terms of set theory . . . are accepted as sound, it follows that set-theoretical concepts and theorems describe some well-determined reality, in which Cantor's conjecture must be either true or false. Hence its undecidability from the axioms being assumed today can only mean that these axioms do not contain a complete description of that reality.[33]

Like most of Gödel's statements, a great deal is expressed in a short space. Like Cantor and Hilbert, Gödel was confident that set theory was an important positive step for mathematics. In fact, he believed that it necessarily describes a "well-determined reality," perhaps the mathematical reality which underlies the reality in which we actually exist—perhaps Jung's *unus mundus*?; in any case, some "well-determined reality." And Gödel is confident that the continuum hypothesis must be either true or false within that particular reality. Since he and Paul Cohen together proved that the continuum hypothesis is neither true nor false, but undecidable within set theory as it is currently constituted, then Gödel can only assume that is because the current set of axioms is insufficient to fully define that reality; i.e., that there are further axioms yet to be discovered.

---

[33]Kurt Gödel, "What is Cantor's Continuum Problem?", p. 260.

There might exist axioms so abundant in their verifiable consequences, shedding so much light upon a whole field, and yielding such powerful methods for solving problems (and even solving them constructively, as far as that is possible) that, no matter whether they are intrinsically necessary, they would have to be accepted at least in the same sense as any well-established physical theory.[34]

Whereas Gödel's incompleteness proof seemed to some to ring the death knell for the development of mathematics, Gödel clearly has faith that mathematics is inexhaustible. He *knows* that set theory is the right direction for mathematics, and he *knows* that within an extended set theory, the continuum hypothesis is resolvable, and finally he *knows* that any axioms powerful enough to enable the continuum hypothesis to be resolved will necessarily be powerful enough to lead mathematics in wonderful new directions.

So far, Gödel's faith has not been justified. Almost fifty years have passed since he wrote those words in 1947, and no extension of set theory has yet been discovered in which the continuum hypothesis can be resolved. Perhaps it is truly an undecidable proposition, or perhaps mathematics is waiting for another Cantor, another Gödel. While we wait, it is intriguing to know that both Gödel and Paul Cohen feel that eventually the continuum hypothesis will be resolved, and when it is, it will prove to be false!

You will recall that Cantor used the symbol $\aleph_0$ for countable infinity—i.e., the infinity of natural numbers, and $2^{\aleph_0}$ for the power set of $\aleph_0$—hence the infinity of the continuum. The continuum hypothesis says, in mathematical terms, that $2^{\aleph_0} = \aleph_1$. This says that the continuum is the very next transfinite number after the infinity of the integers. Gödel points out just how far this is from being proved.

---

[34] Kurt Gödel, "What is Cantor's continuum problem?" p. 261. Note that this is almost exactly what Jung meant when he discussed psychological truth. In such cases, reference to physical reality for determining truth or falsity is beside the point.

But, although Cantor's set theory now has had a development of more than seventy years and the problem evidently is of great importance for it, *nothing has been proved so far about the question what the power of the continuum is*. . . . Not even an upper bound, however large, can be assigned for the power of the continuum.[35]

In other words, there might be one other infinity in between, or a million, or a countably infinite number, or even an uncountably infinite number of infinities in between the integers and the continuum. Cohen believes that there probably is no limit on the number of such infinities.

. . . Although Cantor would have found the prediction upsetting, [mathematician Paul] Cohen suggested the likelihood that the continuum hypothesis was obviously false. . . . Cohen conjectured, in fact, that $2^{\aleph_0}$ might well turn out to be larger than any transfinite aleph. . . . In Cohen's view, the continuum was clearly an incredibly rich set one produced by a bold new axiom which could never be approached by any piecemeal process of construction.[36]

That is where things rest at this point. Jung guessed that the natural numbers were the primary archetypes of order in the psychoid world of the *unus mundus*, and that all mathematics develops out of the natural numbers. Cantor would have agreed with him 100 percent. But I wonder if even Jung would have agreed with himself, had he lived longer. For, after all, isn't the attempt to reduce the world to the archetypes of the small natural numbers much the same as the attempt of Russell and Whitehead to reduce mathematics to logic, the attempt of physicists to reduce the physical world to first atoms, then subatomic particles, then most recently to quarks? Isn't it more likely that the world is richer than we can ever hope to comprehend?

---

[35]Kurt Gödel, "What is Cantor's continuum problem?" p. 256.
[36]Joseph Warren Dauben, *Georg Cantor: His Mathematics and Philosophy of the Infinite* (Princeton: Princeton University Press, 1979), p. 269.

After all, we are still very early in our understanding of the archetypal nature of reality. Plato's argument was that everything we see, hear, or touch in the world about us is merely a shadow of an ideal object existing in an ideal world. Though this is clearly an early attempt at describing the archetypal nature of reality, it lacks so much. Plato's ideal world lies, like the early views of God and heaven, totally separate from us and our experience.

With the shift of emphasis in the Renaissance back to careful observation of the world, we started down a long path that would inevitably lead us to observe ourselves observing. But this realization is only very recent. Jung's whole psychology developed out of an attempt to deal with the problems presented by the fact that the world outside is somehow contained within our minds, while at the same time, we and our minds are obviously contained within the world. His depth psychology explored the world within, especially as it found expression in the dreams, myths, fairy tales, and other unconscious expressions of human beings. At each level of the psyche, he discovered structure and order. As he went deeper and deeper, it is only natural that eventually he arrived at a level where that structure and order had little or no human qualities attached to it. That was the level of number as archetype.

Science proceeded in the opposite direction, by exploring the outer world at ever greater depth. Mathematics played a pivotal role in that process, since all science depends on quantification, and as science itself becomes more abstract, it requires ever more subtle mathematical tools. Though the scientific method is a tool that can be turned on any phenomenon whatsoever, without mathematics there is no science.

Gödel's incompleteness proof demonstrated once and for all that mathematics is bigger than logic. And so is science; and so are all human endeavors. But, if logic is insufficient, perhaps mathematics, as it develops out of the simple archetypal counting numbers, is enough. Jung thought that there was a unitary reality—the *unus mundus*—that underlay both psyche and matter, and speculated that the primary archetypes of this unitary reality were the simple counting numbers. In this case, each number is, itself, a true symbol: undefinable and inexhaustible—a much less reductionistic stance than the hope that all reality can be reduced to logic. But even so, doesn't it seem unlikely that we will ever find any lowest level to reality? Is it really so surprising that the continuum hypothesis proves intractable?

The world is a place of magic and wonder. Sometimes in our childish arrogance we overlook that wonder and think our little toys are greater than the world. But then we grow older and wiser, and once more our sense of wonder is restored. Jung and Gödel have, each in their own way, tried to open our eyes to the magic around us, and within us. The archetypal hypothesis is a starting point to explore that wonder, not an end point to circumscribe its possibilities.

BIBLIOGRAPHY

Abraham, Frederick David, Ralph H. Abraham, and Christopher D. Shaw. *A Visual Introduction to Dynamical Systems Theory for Psychology*. Santa Cruz: Aerial Press, 1990.
>   First book on applications of non-linear dynamics to psychology. Contains quotation from Leibniz used in this book.

Aiken, Henry D., ed. *The Age of Ideology: The 19th Century Philosophers*. New York: Mentor Books/Houghton Mifflin, 1956.
>   Section on Immanuel Kant especially useful.

Asimov, Isaac, and Jason A. Shulman, eds. *Isaac Asimov's Book of Science and Nature Quotations*. New York: Weidenfeld & Nicholson, 1988.
>   Wonderful collection of quotations relevant to science.

Baker, Robert A. *They Call it Hypnosis*. Buffalo, NY: Prometheus Books, 1990.
>   Though Baker totally denies the existence of hypnosis as a separate and distinct state of consciousness, he presents a fair and balanced history of the varied views on hypnosis.

Ball, W. W. Rouse. *A Short Account of the History of Mathematics*. Reprint of 4th edition of 1908. New York: Dover Publications, 1960.
>   Chatty, enjoyable short history of mathematics, especially strong on early mathematics.

Bateson, Gregory. *Cybernetics and Mind*. N. Hollywood, CA: Audio-Text Cassette #CBC972, n.d.
>   Lecture contains anecdote about creativity of dolphins.

———. *Mind and Nature: A Necessary Unity*. New York: E. P. Dutton, 1979.
>   Bateson's last book. A deeply moving attempt by a great thinker to discover ultimate truth.

———. *Steps to an Ecology of Mind*. New York: Ballantine Books, 1972.
>   Bateson's classic book that uses information theory to show how the human mind operates on successive meta-levels.

Bell, Eric Temple. *Development of Mathematics*. New York: McGraw-Hill, 1940.
>   Excellent companion to *Men of Mathematics*.

———. *Men of Mathematics*. New York: Simon and Schuster, 1937/1965.
>   Reads like a detective novel as Bell traces mathematics' history through its greatest mathematicians. Unfortunately, stops short of Gödel.

Benacerraf, Paul & Hilary Putnam, eds. *Philosophy of Mathematics: Selected Readings*. Cambridge: Cambridge University Press, 1983.

> Includes Kurt Gödel's "Russell's Mathematical Logic," David Hilbert's "On The Infinite," as well as many other essays on the philosophical implications of modern mathematics.

Berlin, Sir Isaiah, ed. *The Age of Enlightenment: The 18th Century Philosophers*. New York: Mentor Books/Houghton Mifflin, 1956.

> Berlin's introduction provides clear history of how Locke's, Berkeley's, and Hume's ideas led to Kant's great synthesis. Sections on Hume, Berkeley, and Locke were drawn on for this book.

Bohm, David. *Wholeness and the Implicate Order*. London: Ark Paperbacks, 1980.

> Quantum physicist on the nature of reality. Accords well with Jung, as well as Pribram and Sheldrake among other seminal thinkers in contemporary science.

Boring, Edwin G. *A History of Experimental Psychology*, 2nd ed. New York: Appleton-Century-Crofts, 1950.

> Despite its age, considered the classic of its field. An especially valuable history used extensively in researching the history of experimental psychology for this book. Boring belies his name.

Boyer, Carl B. *A History of Mathematics*. Princeton: Princeton University Press, 1968.

> Though it lacks Bell's exciting presentation, Boyer's volume is often a more reliable history.

Brearley, Molly and Elizabeth Hitchfield. *A Guide to Reading Piaget*. New York: Schocken Books, 1969.

> It's often difficult to find the main threads of Piaget's ideas while reading his own books. This is the best single volume introduction to Piaget I've found.

Brill, Dr. A. A., ed. *The Basic Writings of Sigmund Freud*. New York: Modern Library/Random House, 1938.

> *The Interpretation of Dreams* was used in this book.

Bronowski, Jacob. *The Common Sense of Science*. New York: Modern Library/Random House, 1953.

> Bronowski is so confident in the scientific approach that he can be infuriating.

Bucke, Richard Maurice, M.D. *Cosmic Consciousness*. New York: E. P. Dutton, 1923.

> Classic study of people who seem to have attained a "cosmic consciousness."

Bylinsky, Gene. "New Clues to the Causes of Violence." In *Annual Editions, Readings in Psychology '74/'75*. Guilford, CT: Dushkin Publishing Group, 1974.

> Discusses Harry F. Harlow's experiments with substitute mothers for baby chimpanzees.

Card, Charles R. "The Archetypal Hypothesis of Wolfgang Pauli and C. G. Jung: Origins, Development, and Implications." In *Symposia on the Foundations of Modern Physics, 1992*, K. V. Laurikainen and C. Montonen, eds. Singapore: World Scientific Publishing Co., 1993.

> Further material by Card on Jung and Pauli's joint attempt to discover the characteristics of the *unus mundus* which underlies both the psyche and the world.

————. "The Archetypal View of Jung and Pauli." In *Psychological Perspectives* #24 & #25. Los Angeles: C. G. Jung Institute, 1991.
> Clearest statement anywhere of Jung's archetypal hypothesis in the broad sense intended by Jung and Pauli.

Dantzig, Tobias. *Number and the Language of Science*. New York: MacMillan, 1954.
> A classic volume on number and its application in science. Anecdotes about number sense in animals were used in this volume.

Dauben, Joseph Warren. *Georg Cantor: His Mathematics and Philosophy of the Infinite*. Princeton: Princeton University Press, 1979.
> The standard biography of mathematician Georg Cantor. A masterpiece at describing how Cantor's transfinite set theory developed.

Davis, Philip J. and Reuben Hersh. *The Mathematical Experience*. Boston: Houghton Mifflin, 1981.
> Contains fascinating quotes from Gödel and René Thom about the archetypal nature of mathematical thought.

Descartes, René. *Descartes: Philosophical Writings*. New York: Modern Library, 1958.
> Selections from Descartes' most important philosophical writing, including *Discourse on Method* and *Meditations on First Philosophy*, among others.

De Santillana, Giorgio, ed. *The Age of Adventure: The Renaissance Philosophers*. New York: Mentor Books/Houghton Mifflin, 1956.
> Introduction and sections on Da Vinci, Michelangelo, and Copernicus used in this book.

Edinger, Edward F. *Anatomy of the Psyche*. La Salle, IL: Open Court, 1985.
> Study of Jung's alchemical model of the psyche. Organized around the alchemical operations of *calcinatio, solutio, coagulatio, sublimatio, mortificatio, separatio,* and *coniunctio.* Material was previously published in Jungian journal *Quadrant.*

————. *Ego and Archetype*. New York: Penguin Books, 1972.
> Explores relationship between individual ego and collective unconscious. One of the best books on Jungian psychology ever written by anyone but Jung himself.

————. *The Mysterium Lectures*. Joan Dexter Blackmer, transcriber and ed. Toronto: Inner City Books, 1995.
> Records Edinger's lectures on Jung's *Mysterium Coniunctionis*, given at the Jung Institute of Los Angeles in 1985–1986.

Eliade, Mircea. *Gods, Goddesses, and Myths of Creation*. New York: HarperCollins, 1974.
> Contains material on a wide variety of creation myths.

————. *No Souvenirs: Journal, 1957–1969*. San Francisco: HarperSanFrancisco, 1977.
> In these journals, the reader is privileged to watch Eliade's key ideas emerge across time.

————. *The Sacred and the Profane*. New York: Harvest/Harcourt Brace, 1959.
> Eliade's thoughts on the history of religion correspond closely to Jung's.

Erickson, Milton H. *The Collected Papers of Milton H. Erickson on Hypnosis,* 4 vols. Ernest L. Rossi, ed. New York: Irvington Publishers, 1980.
Especially interesting material on the induction of trance. Case studies complement experimental work on perception. Articles on general history of hypnosis parallel material from Boring quoted in this book. "Hypnotic Psychotherapy" paper is perhaps Erickson's key early essay on the nature of hypnosis as a therapeutic tool.

Evans, Richard I. *Konrad Lorenz: The Man and his Ideas.* New York: Harcourt Brace, 1975.
As with all the books in this series, a superb combination of a dialog with the subject, a summary of his central ideas, and key selections.

Fabricius, Johannes. *Alchemy: The Medieval Alchemists and their Royal Art.* Copenhagen: Rosenkilde and Bagger, 1976.
A monumental attempt to present actual alchemical writings and describe their psychological significance.

Félix, Lucienne. *The Modern Aspect of Mathematics.* New York: Basic Books, 1960.
An unusual and wonderful book, which manages to discuss most of the important issues in modern mathematics while keeping actual mathematics to a minimum.

Fraenkel, A. A. and Y. Bar-Hillel. *Foundations of Set Theory.* Amsterdam: North-Holland Publishing Company, 1958.
More than most math texts moves in and out between Gödel's Proof and its philosophical implications.

Fremantle, Anne, ed. *The Age of Belief: The Medieval Philosophers.* Boston: Mentor Books/Houghton Mifflin, 1954.
Summary of scholastic philosophy.

Freud, Sigmund. *Three Essays on the Theory of Sexuality.* Reprint of 4th ed. of 1920. New York: Basic Books/HarperCollins, 1962.
Arguably Freud's greatest book. Discussed in some detail in this book.

Fromm, Erich. *Sigmund Freud's Mission.* New York: Harper Colophon/HarperCollins, 1959.
Excellent description of Freud's personality and *idées fixes.*

Gamow, George. *The Great Physicists from Galileo to Einstein.* New York: Dover, 1961.
As with all of Gamow's books, a delightful, lucid cover of its subject matter.

Gardner, Martin. *Gotcha: Paradoxes to Puzzle and Delight.* San Francisco: W. H. Freeman, 1982.
As always with Gardner, both playful and serious. Many of these paradoxes are relevant to the issue of self-referential systems.

Gödel, Kurt. *Kurt Gödel: Collected Works, Vol. I, Publications 1929–1936.* Solomon Feferman, editor-in-chief. New York: Oxford University Press, 1986.
All of Gödel's early works, including the incompleteness theorem. Also contains biographical material on Gödel.

———. *Kurt Gödel: Collected Works, Vol. II: Publications 1938–1974.* Solomon Feferman, editor-in-chief. New York: Oxford University Press, 1990.
Includes Gödel's "What is Cantor's Continuum Problem?"

Gregory, Richard L., ed. *The Oxford Companion to the Mind*. New York: Oxford University Press, 1987.
> Material on Noam Chomsky (which Chomsky himself wrote) referred to in this book.

Hall, Calvin S. *A Primer of Freudian Psychology*. New York: Mentor Books, New American Library, 1954.
> Very good short summary of Freudian psychology, much better than his companion volume on Jung's psychology.

———. *Psychology: An Introductory Textbook*. Cleveland: Howard Allen, 1960.
> Contains material on Freud not in the *Primer*.

Hall, Edward T. *The Silent Language*. Greenwich, CT: Fawcett Publications, 1959.
> Is language inborn or learned? The answer is key to the conception of the human mind.

Hampden-Turner, Charles. *Maps of the Mind*. New York: MacMillan, 1981.
> Compendium of models of the human mind.

Hampshire, Stuart, ed. *The Age of Reason: The 17th Century Philosophers*. Boston: Mentor Books/Houghton Mifflin, 1956.
> Section on Leibniz especially useful.

Hannah, Barbara. *Jung, his Life and Work: A Biographical Memoir*. New York: Capricorn Books/G. P. Putnam's Sons, 1976.
> A wonderful complement to *Memories, Dreams, Reflections*, and von Franz' *C. G. Jung: his Myth in our Time*.

Heidbreder, Edna. *Seven Psychologies*. New York: Appleton-Century-Crofts, 1933.
> The battle between behavioral psychology and gestalt psychology is presented especially well.

Heisenberg, Werner. *The Physical Principles of the Quantum Theory*. Reprint of 1930 edition. New York: Dover Publications, 1949.
> Based on lectures delivered at the University of Chicago. Covers not only his own contributions but those of his fellow physicists.

Hilbert, David and Wilhelm Ackermann. *Grundzüge der theoretischen Logik*. Berlin: Springer, 1928.
> The book which inspired Gödel to prove the completeness of all consistent logical systems, then later the necessary incompleteness or inconsistency of all formal logical systems.

Hilgard, Ernest R. *The Experience of Hypnosis*. New York: Harvest Book/Harcourt Brace, 1965.
> Excellent representation of the currently prevailing academic position on hypnosis, which is in sharp contrast to the view of those actually working with hypnosis in therapy.

Hollis, James. *Under Saturn's Shadow: The Wounding and Healing of Men*. Toronto: Inner City Books, 1994.
> A Jungian analyst's compassionate account of men's psychological issues.

James, William. *The Principles of Psychology*, 2 vols. (1890). New York: Dover Publication, 1950.
> Classic work. Especially useful on implications of physiological psychology.

Janet, Pierre. *L'Autotisme Psychologique*. Paris, 1889.

> Janet's pioneering work on the psychology of automatic processes in the unconscious.

―――. *Analytic Psychology: Its Theory & Practice*. New York: Vintage Books, Random House, 1968.

> Commonly referred to as the "The Tavistock Lectures." A series of five lectures given at the Tavistock Clinic in London in 1935. Excellent presentation of Jung's thought at mid-career. Also can be found in a slightly different translation in C. G. Jung, *Collected Works, Vol. 18: The Symbolic Life*, 2nd printing with corrections, Bollingen Series XX. Princeton: Princeton University Press, 1980.

Jung, C. G. *The Collected Works of C. G. Jung, Vol. 1: Psychiatric Studies*, 2nd ed. Bollingen Series XX, G. Adler & R. F. Hull, eds. Princeton: Princeton University Press, 1970.

> Includes "On the Psychology and Pathology of So-Called Occult Phenomena," which discusses trance phenomena with a young country girl who achieved brief local fame as a medium.

―――. *The Collected Works of C. G. Jung, Vol. 5: Symbols of Transformation*, 2nd edition of 1952. Bollingen Series XX, G. Adler & R. F. Hull, eds. Princeton: Princeton University Press, 1967.

> Jung's break-through work, which led to his split with Freud.

―――. *The Collected Works of C. G. Jung, Vol. 6: Psychological Types*. Bollingen Series XX, G. Adler & R. F. Hull, eds. Princeton: Princeton University Press, 1971.

> The first book written after Jung's confrontation with the unconscious. A knowledge of psychological types is the first step toward an understanding of the individuation process. Contains invaluable section of key definitions at the end, including "symbol."

―――. *The Collected Works of C. G. Jung, Vol. 7: Two Essays on Analytical Psychology*. Bollingen Series XX, G. Adler & R. F. Hull, eds. Princeton: Princeton University Press, 1966.

> Seminal essays on the nature of Shadow, Anima/Animus, and Self. Because Jung describes how the experience of each archetype at various stages, is particularly useful for someone actually struggling through such issues in their life, as well as for practical clinical work.

―――. *The Collected Works of C. G. Jung, Vol. 8: The Structure and Dynamics of the Psyche*. Bollingen Series XX, G. Adler & R. F. Hull, eds. Princeton: Princeton University Press, 1960.

> Contains three key essays: "On Psychic Energy," "The Transcendent Function," and "Synchronicity: An Acausal Connecting Principle."

―――. *The Collected Works of C. G. Jung, Vol. 9i: The Archetypes and the Collective Unconscious*. Bollingen Series XX, G. Adler & R. F. Hull, eds. Princeton: Princeton University Press, 1969.

> The largest collection in the Collected Works of Jung's ideas on archetypes in general and on specific archetypes. Sections on Mother archetype and Child archetype especially useful for clinical work.

―――. *The Collected Works of C. G. Jung, Vol. 9ii: Aion, Researches into the Phenomenology of the Self*. Bollingen Series XX, G. Adler & R. F. Hull, eds. Princeton: Princeton University Press, 1959.

> One of the most complex books in the Collected Works. Explains a great deal about the dynamic relationship between the ego and the Self.

———. *The Collected Works of C. G. Jung, Vol. 10: Civilization in Transition.* Bollingen Series XX, G. Adler & R. F. Hull, eds. Princeton: Princeton University Press, 1964.

> Contains a wide variety of articles and essays.

———. *The Collected Works of C. G. Jung, Vol. 12: Psychology and Alchemy,* 2nd ed. Bollingen Series XX, G. Adler & R. F. Hull, eds. Princeton: Princeton University Press, 1968.

> Traces the evolution of individual and archetypal images in dreams of a single patient. Extremely useful in clinical work, as it describes and explains representative dream images at various stages of analytic process.

———. *The Collected Works of C. G. Jung, Vol. 13: Alchemical Studies.* Bollingen Series XX, G. Adler & R. F. Hull, eds. Princeton: Princeton University Press, 1967.

> Contains many key papers on alchemy not included in *Psychology and Alchemy*, or *Mysterium Coniunctionis*, including Jung's commentary on "The Secret of the Golden Flower," and "The Philosophical Tree," among others.

———. *The Collected Works of C. G. Jung, Vol. 14: Mysterium Coniunctionis.* Bollingen Series XX, G. Adler & R. F. Hull, eds. Princeton: Princeton University Press, 1963.

> The culmination of Jung's studies in alchemy. One of the greatest books in Jungian psychology.

———. *The Collected Works of C. G. Jung, Vol. 15: The Spirit in Man, Art, and Literature.* Bollingen Series XX, G. Adler & R. F. Hull, eds. Princeton: Princeton University Press, 1966.

> Includes "Paracelsus the Physician," which discusses how Paracelsus saw physical and psychic, micro and macro worlds as connected.

———. *The Collected Works of C. G. Jung, Vol. 16: the Practice of Psychotherapy.* Bollingen Series XX, G. Adler & R. F. Hull, eds. Princeton: Princeton University Press, 1966.

> Includes "The Psychology of the Transference," which uses alchemical symbolism of marriage of king and queen to examine nature of all relationships, whether between patient and analyst, man and woman, or ego and Self.

———. *Letters,* 2 vols. Bollingen Series No. 95. G. Adler & A. Jaffe, eds. Princeton: Princeton University Press, 1975.

> Like many others, Jung in his letters often comes across more directly as a human being than in his published works.

———. *Man and his Symbols.* Garden City, NY: Windfall Books, Doubleday, 1964.

> A readable coffee-table book. Excellent book to introduce the new reader to Jungian psychology.

———. *Memories, Dreams, Reflections.* New York: Vintage Books, Random House, 1965.

> A unique document: an auto-biography of Jung's spiritual progress. Probably the best book to introduce someone to the spirit of Jungian psychology. Invaluable for clinical work because it discusses Jung's personal experiences at various stages of psychic development.

Jung, C. G. & Wolfgang Pauli. *The Interpretation of Nature and the Psyche.* New York: Pantheon Books, 1955.
> Includes two essays: Pauli's "The Influence of Archetypal Ideas on the Scientific Theories of Kepler," and Jung's "Synchronicity: an Acausal Connecting Principle." The latter was later republished with some editorial changes in *The Collected Works of C. G. Jung, Vol. 8.*

Kanigel, Robert. *The Man Who Knew Infinity.* New York: Charles Scribner's Sons, 1991.
> Engrossing history of Indian mathematical prodigy Ramanujan.

Koestler, Arthur. *The Act of Creation.* New York: Dell, 1964.
> The most exhaustive attempt at delimiting creativity, which offers many insights, especially how creativity occurs at the juxtaposition of multiple, seemingly unconnected viewpoints.

Kohler, Wolfgang. *Gestalt Psychology.* New York: Mentor Books/New American Library, 1947.
> The classic presentation of gestalt psychology. Contains description of experiment with perception of chickens referred to in this book.

Kroneberger, Louis. *Alexander Pope: Selected Works.* New York: The Modern Library, 1951.
> No one ever recorded the attitudes of the 18th century better than poet Alexander Pope.

Kuhn, Thomas S. *The Structure of Scientific Revolutions.* Chicago: University of Chicago Press, 1970.
> A classic volume which shows difference between practice of "normal" science and development of scientific revolutions.

Laurikainen, K. V. & C. Montonen, eds. *Symposis on the Foundations of Modern Physics,* 1992. Singapore: World Scientific Publishing Co., 1993.
> Fascinating material by physicists who are beginning to explore the extent to which modern physics implies an archetypal hypothesis.

Lauzun, Gerard. *Sigmund Freud: The Man and His Theories.* New York: Fawcett Publications, 1962.
> Describes much of what went on "behind the scenes" between Freud and his followers.

Lilly, John C. *The Center of the Cyclone: An Autobiography of Inner Space.* New York: Bantam Books, 1972.
> A record of dolphin researcher John Lilly's personal experiments with altered states of consciousness. The best of several such volumes of Lilly's.

Lorenz, Konrad. *King Solomon's Ring.* New York: Crowell, 1952.
> Delightful book. Contains the story and drawings of Lorenz' baby goose who "imprinted" the Mother archetype onto Lorenz.

Maslow, Abraham H. *Toward a Psychology of Being.* New York: Van Nostrand Reinhold, 1968.
> Maslow's most significant book. It records most of his key ideas about self-actualization.

May, Rollo. *Love and Will.* New York: Dell, 1969.
> Discusses how types of clinical problems varied in different eras; how Freud's emphasis on sexual problems was sign of his time rather than inherent.

Merrell-Wolff, Franklin. *Pathways Through to Space: A Personal Report of Transformation in Consciousness.* New York: Warner Books, 1973.
> Probably the best account in Western literature of the mystical experience.

————. *The Philosophy of Consciousness without an Object.* New York: Julian Press, 1973.
> Companion volume to the above. Tries to place his experiences into spiritual and philosophical framework.

Moonitz, David. Private communication. 1994.
> Discussed concept of infinitesimals in calculus.

Mostowski, Andrzej. *Sentences Undecidable in Formalized Arithmetic: An Exposition of the Theory of Kurt Gödel.* Amsterdam: North Holland Publishing Company, 1952.
> For mathematicians only; carefully constructed proofs of Gödel's Theory.

Nagel, Ernest and James R. Newman. "Gödel's Proof." In James R. Newman, ed., *The World of Mathematics.* New York: Simon and Schuster, 1956.
> Nagel's and Newman's first attempt at explaining Gödel's Proof to a broad audience, which was later adapted and expanded for their book of the same title.

————. *Gödel's Proof.* New York: New York University Press, 1958.
> A true gem of presenting complex mathematical material for a general (though necessarily sophisticated) public. I am indebted to Nagel's and Newman's book for a great deal, over and beyond the direct material on Gödel's Proof.

Otto, Rudolph. *The Idea of the Holy.* London: Oxford University Press, 1958.
> In which Otto first coined the term *numinous,* a singularly apt term for the awe experienced in confronting the divine.

Piaget, Jean. *The Language and Thought of the Child.* New York: Meridian Book/World Publishing, 1955.
> Though Piaget is not a Jungian, his work can be seen as corroborating many of Jung's ideas on developmental psychology.

Pribram, Karl. "The Brain." In Alberto Villoldo and Ken Dychtwald, eds., *Millennium: Glimpses into the 21st Century.* Los Angeles: J. P. Tarcher, 1981.
> Neuro-physiologist Karl Pribram on the holographic nature of the brain.

Reese, W. L. *Dictionary of Philosophy and Religion: Eastern and Western Thought.* Atlantic Highlands, NJ: Humanities Press, 1980.
> Mammoth one-volume encyclopedia of philosophy. Entry on Kant especially useful.

Richter, Jean Paul. *The Notebooks of Leonardo Da Vinci.* 2 vols. New York: Dover, 1970.
> Contains Da Vinci's actual notes and drawings. Many quotes capture the Renaissance ideal.

Robertson, Robin. *Beginner's Guide to Jungian Psychology.* York Beach, ME: Nicolas-Hays, 1992.
> Contains more detailed description than the present volume of key elements of Jungian psychology, centering around the path of individuation.

Robinson, Abraham. *Non-Standard Analysis.* Amsterdam: North-Holland Publishing Company, 1966.
> First rigorous, self-consistent use of the concept of infinitesimals.

Rossi, Ernest Lawrence. "As Above, So Below: the Holographic Mind." *Psychological Perspectives, Fall 1980.* Los Angeles: C. G. Jung Institute, 1980.
> Describes Pribram's theory of the holographic mind and relates it to Jung's ideas and ideas of mystics.

Russell, Bertrand. *The Autobiography of Bertrand Russell: The Early Years: 1872–World War 1*. New York: Bantam Books, 1968.

> Approximately two-thirds letters to and from Russell, framed with autobiographical material in Russell's pellucid prose. All the events leading up to *Principia Mathematica* are recorded in this volume.

————. *Introduction to Mathematical Philosophy*. Reprint of 2nd edition of 1920. New York: Dover Publications, 1933.

> In this book written for the general educated public, Russell describes his own view of what constitutes mathematical philosophy. Basically Russell believes that mathematics can be reduced to logic, though mathematics is a more convenient tool to use in practice. He essentially summarizes in non-mathematical terms: modern set theory, and the theory he and Whitehead developed in *Principia Mathematica*.

————. *The Selected Letters of Bertrand Russell, Vol 1: The Private Years (1884–1914)*. Nicholas Griffin, ed. Boston: Houghton Mifflin, 1992.

> Used for much biographical material on Russell and the events that led up to *Principia Mathematica*.

————. *Our Knowledge of the External World*. New York: Mentor Books, 1956.

> A wonderfully lucid defense of Russell's belief in a scientific philosophy he calls "logical atomism." This incorporates the ideas he and Whitehead developed in *Principia Mathematica*, together with Wittgenstein's early ideas (which he later repudiated).

————. *Wisdom of the West*. New York: Premier Books/Fawcett World Library, 1959.

> My favorite one-volume history of philosophy.

Schultz, Duane P. *A History of Modern Psychology*. New York: Academic Press, 1969.

> Written from the materialist/rationalist position. Contrasts with Boring and Heidbreder, whose presentation is less limited by theory.

Shanker, S. G., ed. *Gödel's Theorem in Focus*. London & New York: Routledge, 1988.

> Necessary companion volume to Gödel's collected works, which places his incompleteness theorem in historical, mathematical, and philosophical context. Contains several articles quoted in this book.

Sheldrake, Rupert. *A New Science of Life: The Hypothesis of Formative Causation*. Los Angeles: J. P. Tarcher, 1981.

> Uses data from behavioral psychology to support concept of morphogenetic fields, which closely correspond to Jung's archetypes.

Smith, David Eugene. *A Source Book in Mathematics*. Reprint of 1929 edition. New York: Dover, 1959.

> Wonderful selection from seminal mathematical papers and books. Among others, includes both Newton and Leibniz on the calculus, and Berkeley's "Analyst," in which he picks philosophical holes in the underlying theory of calculus.

Stevens, Anthony. *Archetypes: A Natural History of the Self*. New York: Quill, 1982.

> A masterful compilation of the scientific support for Jung's concept of archetypes.

Stevens, S. S. *Handbook of Experimental Psychology*. New York: Wiley, 1951.

> This and the following reference include material on Stevens' now classic experimental work on psychophysics, which extended Weber's and Fechner's work and

showed that the relationship between sensation and stimulus was a power law relationship, not a logarithmic relationship.

————. "Problems and Methods of Psychophysics." *Psychological Bulletin,* 55, 1958.

See above entry.

Stillman, John Maxson. *The Story of Alchemy and Early Chemistry*. Reprint of 1924 edition. New York: Dover, 1960.

Materialist history of alchemy, which views alchemy as trivial predecessor of chemistry.

Strachey, James, ed. *Josef Breuer and Sigmund Freud: Studies in Hysteria.* Reprint of 1955 edition. New York: Basic Books/HarperCollins, 1962.

The classic early works written with Breuer, especially "Anna O."

Struik, Dirk J. *A Concise History of Mathematics*. 4th rev. ed. Reprint of 1948 edition. New York: Dover, 1987.

A wonderfully succinct volume, capturing the entire history of mathematics in little over 200 pages of lucid prose.

Tart, Charles T., ed. *Altered States of Consciousness*. New York: Anchor Books/Doubleday, 1969.

The classic book which originated the phrase "altered states of consciousness."

————. *States of Consciousness*. El Cerrito, CA: Psychological Processes, Inc., 1975.

Best single work on altered states of consciousness.

Travis, Julius C. "The Hierarchy of Symbols." In *The Shaman from Elko*. San Francisco: C. G. Jung Institute of San Francisco, 1978.

Unusual article tracing the order in which symbols appear in dreams over the course of an analysis.

von Franz, Marie-Louise. *Alchemical Active Imagination*. University of Dallas, Irving, TX: Spring Publications, 1979.

Valuable material on history of alchemy.

————. "An Introduction to the Symbolism of Alchemy." Unpublished lecture notes, 1959.

Lecture notes on very early alchemical texts.

————. *C. G. Jung: His Myth in Our Time*. New York: C. G. Jung Foundation for Analytical Psychology, 1975.

Ideal companion work to Jung's own *Memories, Dreams, Reflections*. No one knew Jung and his work better than von Franz. This is written as a biography both of his life and psychic development.

————. *Number and Time*. Evanston: Northwestern University Press, 1974.

Extends Jung's late idea that number was the primary archetype. Conclusions reached in chapter 19 of current volume disagree with von Franz' position that quaternity is primary archetype of order.

————. *Projection and Re-Collection in Jungian Psychology: Reflections of the Soul*. La Salle: Open Court, 1980.

Best single volume on extended concept of transference and projection, as developed in Jungian psychology.

Washburn, Michael. *The Ego and the Dynamic Ground: A Transpersonal Theory of Human Development*, 2nd ed. Albany, NY: SUNY Press, 1995.

———. *Transpersonal Psychology in Psychoanalytic Perspective*. Albany, NY: SUNY Press, 1994.

> In these two books, Washburn puts together a comprehensive theory of human development reconciling the traditional Freudian psychoanalytic developmental theory with a Jungian transpersonal developmental theory.

Weitzenhoffer, Andre M. *The Practice of Hypnotism*. 2 vols. New York: John Wiley & Sons, 1989.

> An excellent collection of induction techniques and applications for hypnosis in clinical practice.

Whitehead, Alfred North. *An Introduction to Mathematics*. Reprint of 1911 edition. New York: Galaxy Book/Oxford University Press, 1958.

> Wonderful summary of mathematics as Whitehead viewed it just after he and Russell had completed *Principia Mathematica*.

———. *Science and the Modern World*. Reprint of 1925 edition. New York: Mentor Books/New American Library, 1948.

> One of the most provocative books ever written on science and its relationship to the world. The chapter on mathematics is drawn on in this book.

Whitehead, Alfred North & Bertrand Russell. *Principia Mathematica*. 3 vols. Cambridge, U.K.: Cambridge University Press, vol. 1, 1910; vol. 2, 1912; vol. 3, 1913.

> Perhaps the single most important failure in scientific history. Though Whitehead's name is listed first, Russell is the principal force in the project. He was attempting to reduce arithmetic to logic, as the first step toward subsuming all mathematics, then all science, within logic. Despite a decade of grueling effort, Russell was never able to resolve a key paradox that undercut the entire project. Gödel later proved the impossibility of the whole undertaking.

Wilson, Colin. *Inside the Outsider (I)*. N. Hollywood, CA: Audio-Text Cassette #36049, n.d.

> How can men and women break through from the mundane world into the suprapersonal world? Discussion of "Eureka" experience of creativity.

Wilson, Edward O. *The Diversity of Life*. Cambridge, MA: Belknap Press/Harvard University Press, 1992.

> An enthralling book for the general public on the ecological viewpoint, by sociobiology's founder, Edward O. Wilson.

INDEX

Robin Robertson is a psychologist, magician, mathematician and writer. His most recent books include *Beginner's Guide to Jungian Psychology*, *Beginner's Guide to Revelation*, and (as editor) *Chaos Theory in Psychology and the Life Sciences*.